THE

CUTTHROAT

———⬥———

TITLES BY CLIVE CUSSLER

DIRK PITT® ADVENTURES

Odessa Sea (with Dirk Cussler)
Havana Storm (with Dirk Cussler)
Poseidon's Arrow (with Dirk Cussler)
Crescent Dawn (with Dirk Cussler)
Arctic Drift (with Dirk Cussler)
Treasure of Khan (with Dirk Cussler)
Black Wind (with Dirk Cussler)
Trojan Odyssey
Valhalla Rising
Atlantis Found
Flood Tide
Shock Wave
Inca Gold
Sahara
Dragon
Treasure
Cyclops
Deep Six
Pacific Vortex!
Night Probe!
Vixen 03
Raise the Titanic!
Iceberg
The Mediterranean Caper

SAM AND REMI FARGO ADVENTURES

Pirate (with Robin Burcell)
The Solomon Curse (with Russell Blake)
The Eye of Heaven (with Russell Blake)
The Mayan Secrets (with Thomas Perry)
The Tombs (with Thomas Perry)
The Kingdom (with Grant Blackwood)
Lost Empire (with Grant Blackwood)
Spartan Gold (with Grant Blackwood)

ISAAC BELL ADVENTURES

The Cutthroat (with Justin Scott)
The Gangster (with Justin Scott)
The Assassin (with Justin Scott)
The Bootlegger (with Justin Scott)
The Striker (with Justin Scott)
The Thief (with Justin Scott)
The Race (with Justin Scott)
The Spy (with Justin Scott)
The Wrecker (with Justin Scott)
The Chase

KURT AUSTIN ADVENTURES
Novels from The NUMA ® Files

Nighthawk (with Graham Brown)

The Pharaoh's Secret (with Graham Brown)

Ghost Ship (with Graham Brown)

Zero Hour (with Graham Brown)

The Storm (with Graham Brown)

Devil's Gate (with Graham Brown)

Medusa (with Paul Kemprecos)

The Navigator (with Paul Kemprecos)

Polar Shift (with Paul Kemprecos)

Lost City (with Paul Kemprecos)

White Death (with Paul Kemprecos)

Fire Ice (with Paul Kemprecos)

Blue Gold (with Paul Kemprecos)

Serpent (with Paul Kemprecos)

OREGON® FILES

The Emperor's Revenge (with Boyd Morrison)

Piranha (with Boyd Morrison)

Mirage (with Jack Du Brul)

The Jungle (with Jack Du Brul)

The Silent Sea (with Jack Du Brul)

Corsair (with Jack Du Brul)

Plague Ship (with Jack Du Brul)

Skeleton Coast (with Jack Du Brul)

Dark Watch (with Jack Du Brul)

Sacred Stone (with Craig Dirgo)

Golden Buddha (with Craig Dirgo)

NONFICTION

Built for Adventure: The Classic Automobiles of Clive Cussler and Dirk Pitt

Built to Thrill: More Classic Automobiles from Clive Cussler and Dirk Pitt

The Sea Hunters (with Craig Dirgo)

The Sea Hunters II (with Craig Dirgo)

Clive Cussler and Dirk Pitt Revealed (with Craig Dirgo)

THE
CUTTHROAT

AN ISAAC BELL ADVENTURE

❖

CLIVE CUSSLER
AND JUSTIN SCOTT

G. P. PUTNAM'S SONS · NEW YORK

PUTNAM

G. P. PUTNAM'S SONS
Publishers Since 1838
An imprint of Penguin Random House LLC
375 Hudson Street
New York, New York 10014

Copyright © 2017 by Sandecker, RLLLP
Penguin supports copyright. Copyright fuels creativity, encourages
diverse voices, promotes free speech, and creates a vibrant culture. Thank
you for buying an authorized edition of this book and for complying with
copyright laws by not reproducing, scanning, or distributing any part of
it in any form without permission. You are supporting writers and
allowing Penguin to continue to publish books for every reader.

Library of Congress Cataloging-in-Publication Data
Names: Cussler, Clive, author. | Scott, Justin, author.
Title: The cutthroat / Clive Cussler and Justin Scott.
Description: New York : G.P. Putnam's Sons, 2017. |
Series: An Isaac Bell Adventure ; 10
Identifiers: LCCN 2017002791 (print) | LCCN 2017003022 (ebook) |
ISBN 9780399575600 (hardback) | ISBN 9780399575617 (EBook) |
ISBN 9780735215702 (international edition)
Subjects: LCSH: Bell, Isaac (Fictitious character)—Fiction. |
Private investigators—Fiction. | Serial murders—Fiction. |
BISAC: FICTION / Action & Adventure. | FICTION / Suspense. |
FICTION / Historical. | GSAFD: Suspense fiction.
Classification: LCC PS3553.U75 C88 2017 (print) |
LCC PS3553.U75 (ebook) | DDC 813/.54—dc23
LC record available at https://lccn.loc.gov/2017002791

Printed in the United States of America
1 3 5 7 9 10 8 6 4 2

BOOK DESIGN BY LUCIA BERNARD

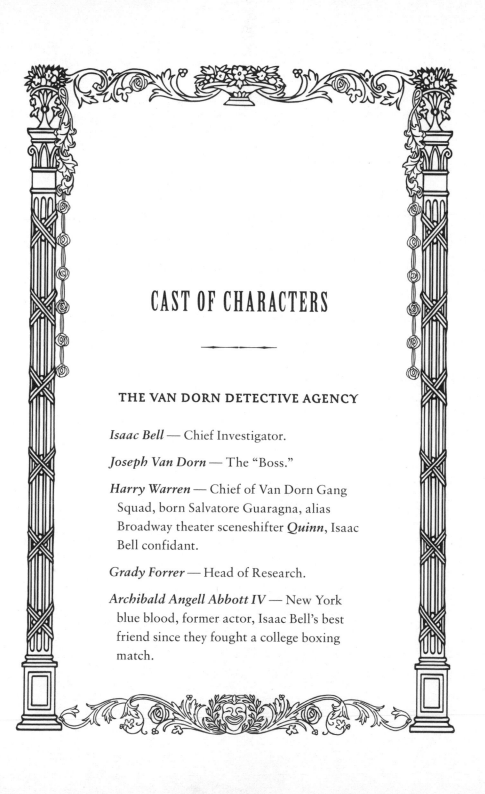

CAST OF CHARACTERS

THE VAN DORN DETECTIVE AGENCY

Isaac Bell — Chief Investigator.

Joseph Van Dorn — The "Boss."

Harry Warren — Chief of Van Dorn Gang Squad, born Salvatore Guaragna, alias Broadway theater sceneshifter *Quinn*, Isaac Bell confidant.

Grady Forrer — Head of Research.

Archibald Angell Abbott IV — New York blue blood, former actor, Isaac Bell's best friend since they fought a college boxing match.

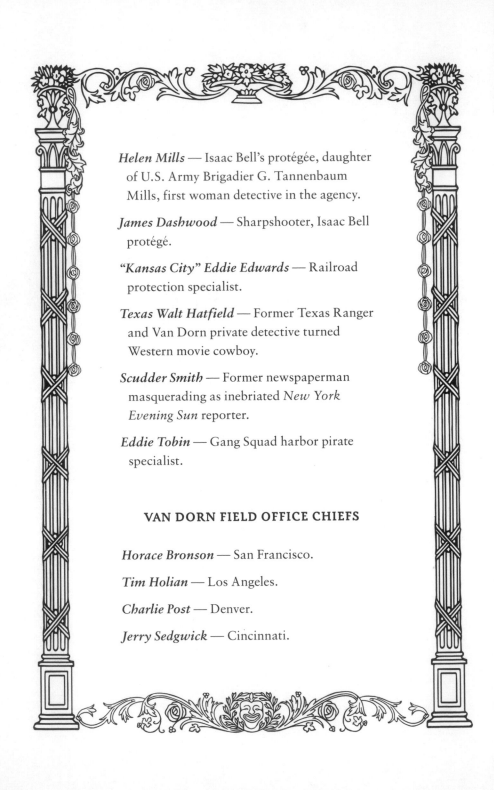

Helen Mills — Isaac Bell's protégée, daughter of U.S. Army Brigadier G. Tannenbaum Mills, first woman detective in the agency.

James Dashwood — Sharpshooter, Isaac Bell protégé.

"Kansas City" Eddie Edwards — Railroad protection specialist.

Texas Walt Hatfield — Former Texas Ranger and Van Dorn private detective turned Western movie cowboy.

Scudder Smith — Former newspaperman masquerading as inebriated *New York Evening Sun* reporter.

Eddie Tobin — Gang Squad harbor pirate specialist.

VAN DORN FIELD OFFICE CHIEFS

Horace Bronson — San Francisco.

Tim Holian — Los Angeles.

Charlie Post — Denver.

Jerry Sedgwick — Cincinnati.

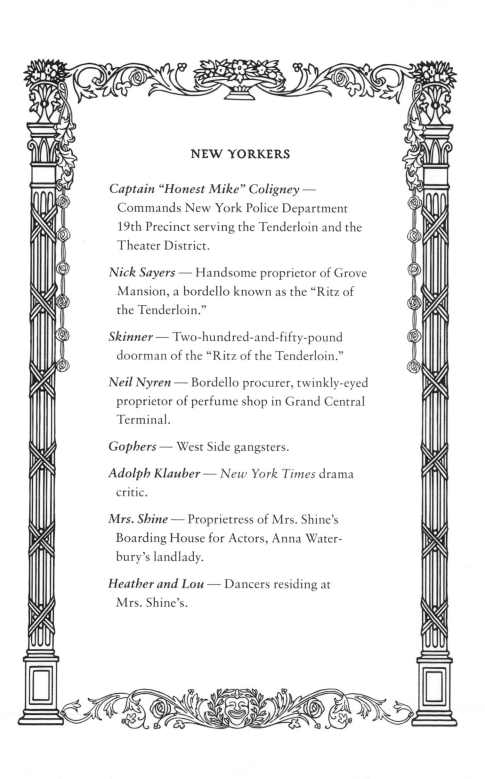

NEW YORKERS

Captain "Honest Mike" Coligney — Commands New York Police Department 19th Precinct serving the Tenderloin and the Theater District.

Nick Sayers — Handsome proprietor of Grove Mansion, a bordello known as the "Ritz of the Tenderloin."

Skinner — Two-hundred-and-fifty-pound doorman of the "Ritz of the Tenderloin."

Neil Nyren — Bordello procurer, twinkly-eyed proprietor of perfume shop in Grand Central Terminal.

Gophers — West Side gangsters.

Adolph Klauber — *New York Times* drama critic.

Mrs. Shine — Proprietress of Mrs. Shine's Boarding House for Actors, Anna Waterbury's landlady.

Heather and Lou — Dancers residing at Mrs. Shine's.

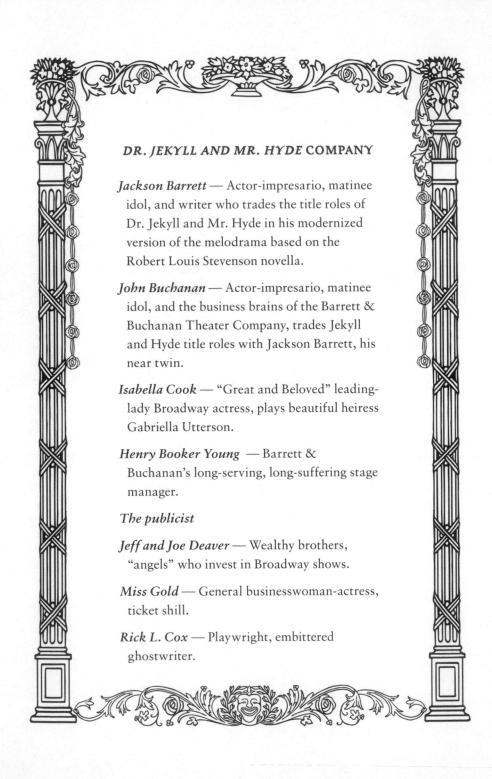

DR. JEKYLL AND MR. HYDE COMPANY

Jackson Barrett — Actor-impresario, matinee idol, and writer who trades the title roles of Dr. Jekyll and Mr. Hyde in his modernized version of the melodrama based on the Robert Louis Stevenson novella.

John Buchanan — Actor-impresario, matinee idol, and the business brains of the Barrett & Buchanan Theater Company, trades Jekyll and Hyde title roles with Jackson Barrett, his near twin.

Isabella Cook — "Great and Beloved" leading-lady Broadway actress, plays beautiful heiress Gabriella Utterson.

Henry Booker Young — Barrett & Buchanan's long-serving, long-suffering stage manager.

The publicist

Jeff and Joe Deaver — Wealthy brothers, "angels" who invest in Broadway shows.

Miss Gold — General businesswoman-actress, ticket shill.

Rick L. Cox — Playwright, embittered ghostwriter.

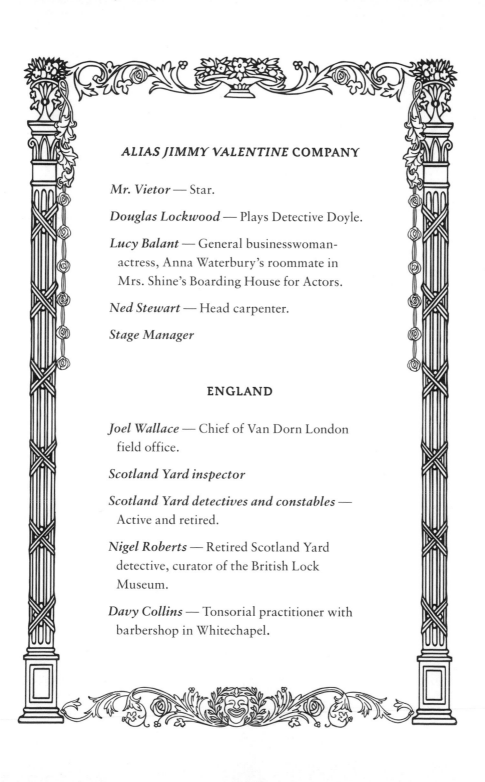

ALIAS JIMMY VALENTINE COMPANY

Mr. Vietor — Star.

Douglas Lockwood — Plays Detective Doyle.

Lucy Balant — General businesswoman-actress, Anna Waterbury's roommate in Mrs. Shine's Boarding House for Actors.

Ned Stewart — Head carpenter.

Stage Manager

ENGLAND

Joel Wallace — Chief of Van Dorn London field office.

Scotland Yard inspector

Scotland Yard detectives and constables — Active and retired.

Nigel Roberts — Retired Scotland Yard detective, curator of the British Lock Museum.

Davy Collins — Tonsorial practitioner with barbershop in Whitechapel.

Wayne Barlowe — London newspaper illustrator and artist.

London Emily — Manchester laudanum addict, crucial witness.

Lord Strone — British Military Intelligence, Secret Service Bureau.

Abbington-Westlake — British Admiralty, Naval Intelligence, Foreign Division.

Reginald — Espionage shadow.

James Mapes — Actor, Garrick Club member.

Granger — Cruel critic.

Dolly — West End chorus girl, Detective Joel Wallace's new friend.

Dolly's mother — Former dancer in *Tra-la-la Tosca*.

MOVIE MAKERS

Marion Morgan Bell — Isaac Bell's bride of one year, his beloved confidante, well-known filmmaker.

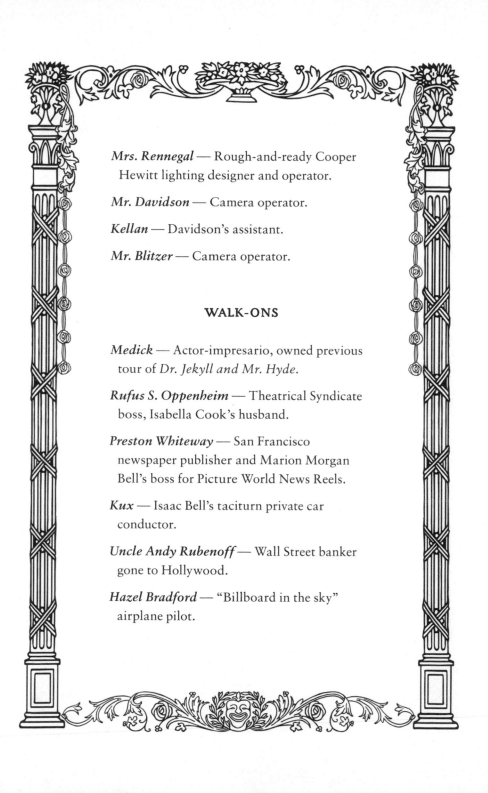

Mrs. Rennegal — Rough-and-ready Cooper Hewitt lighting designer and operator.

Mr. Davidson — Camera operator.

Kellan — Davidson's assistant.

Mr. Blitzer — Camera operator.

WALK-ONS

Medick — Actor-impresario, owned previous tour of *Dr. Jekyll and Mr. Hyde*.

Rufus S. Oppenheim — Theatrical Syndicate boss, Isabella Cook's husband.

Preston Whiteway — San Francisco newspaper publisher and Marion Morgan Bell's boss for Picture World News Reels.

Kux — Isaac Bell's taciturn private car conductor.

Uncle Andy Rubenoff — Wall Street banker gone to Hollywood.

Hazel Bradford — "Billboard in the sky" airplane pilot.

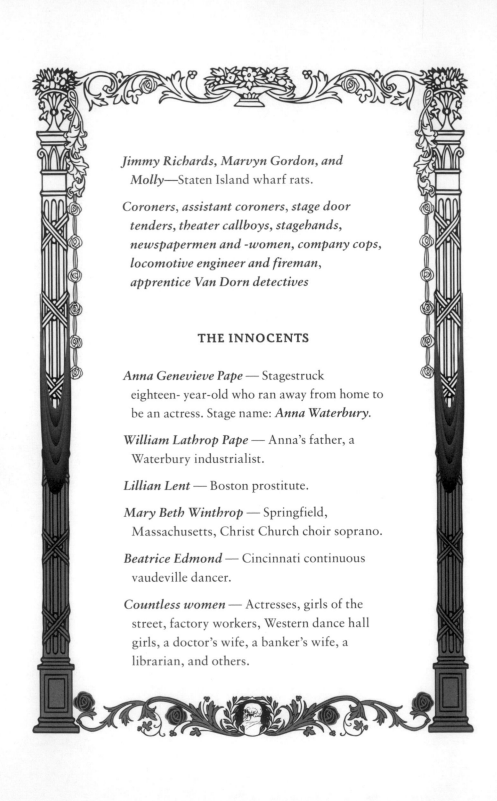

Jimmy Richards, Marvyn Gordon, and Molly—Staten Island wharf rats.

Coroners, assistant coroners, stage door tenders, theater callboys, stagehands, newspapermen and -women, company cops, locomotive engineer and fireman, apprentice Van Dorn detectives

THE INNOCENTS

Anna Genevieve Pape — Stagestruck eighteen- year-old who ran away from home to be an actress. Stage name: *Anna Waterbury*.

William Lathrop Pape — Anna's father, a Waterbury industrialist.

Lillian Lent — Boston prostitute.

Mary Beth Winthrop — Springfield, Massachusetts, Christ Church choir soprano.

Beatrice Edmond — Cincinnati continuous vaudeville dancer.

Countless women — Actresses, girls of the street, factory workers, Western dance hall girls, a doctor's wife, a banker's wife, a librarian, and others.

THE
CUTTHROAT

PROLOGUE

NEW YORK, AUTUMN 1910

Good and evil resided in every man

"Medick is dead!"

Jackson Barrett crashed through John Buchanan's dressing room door, waving the Cognac bottle they kept for opening nights and bankable reviews.

Buchanan was blacking his face for tonight's *Othello*—his Moor, opposite Barrett's Iago. He tossed his greasepaint stick with a jubilant, "Best news we've had in a year!"

Nothing personal against Medick. That workman-like actor had struck it rich playing the dual title roles in the old Mansfield–Sullivan dramatization of Robert Louis Stevenson's *Dr. Jekyll and Mr. Hyde*. But his sudden death left the gold mine up for grabs, and they had a scheme to grab it with an all-new, modernized *Jekyll and Hyde* that would clean up on Broadway and launch the richest cross-country tour since *Ben-Hur*.

They banged glasses and thundered toasts.

"Barrett and Buchanan . . ."

"Present . . ."

"Dr. Jekyll and Mr. Hyde!"

The brandy barely wet their lips. They worked too hard managing the Barrett & Buchanan Theater Company to be drinking men, and their temperate habits kept them ruggedly youthful. Tall and broad-shouldered—"Lofty of stature," in the words of the *New York Sun* critic pinned above Buchanan's mirror—they bounded onstage like athletes a decade younger than their forties. Jackson Barrett was fair, John Buchanan, his near twin, was slightly darker, his hair more sandy than Barrett's golden locks. Both shimmered with the glow of stardom, and their intense blue eyes famously pierced women's hearts in the back row of the highest balcony. The ladies' husbands rated Jackson Barrett and John Buchanan as hearty men's men—fellows they could trust.

"I've been thinking . . ." said Barrett.

"Never a good sign," said Buchanan.

"What do you say we switch our roles back and forth—keep 'em guessing who's who. First night, I'm Jekyll, and—"

"Next night, you're Hyde. Sells tickets, and might even keep you from getting stale."

"Sells even more if we can talk Isabella Cook back on the stage."

"Rufus Oppenheim will never allow her."

Isabella Cook's husband held the controlling interest in the

Theatrical Syndicate, a booking trust with an iron-claw grip on seven hundred top theaters around the country. You could not tour first class without Rufus Oppenheim's syndicate, and you paid through the nose for the privilege.

"Why did the most beautiful actress on Broadway marry the spitting image of a bald bear smoking a cigar?"

"Money."

"She would never go with us even if Oppenheim let her," said Buchanan. "There's no *Jekyll and Hyde* role big enough for the 'Great and Beloved Isabella.'"

"Actually," said Barrett, "I've been tinkering with the manuscript."

"How?" Buchanan asked sharply, not pleased.

"I wrote a new role for Miss Great and Beloved—the beautiful heiress Gabriella Utterson—which makes her central to the plot. Gabriella sets her cap for our handsome young Jekyll. The audience sees the evil Hyde through her eyes and *fears* for her."

Buchanan understood immediately. His partner had gone off half cocked, per usual, but rewriting Robert Louis Stevenson's stuffed-shirt narrator into a beautiful leading lady was a crackerjacks scheme.

"Any other changes I should know about?"

"Added some biff-bang stuff," said Barrett.

"Like what?"

"An airplane."

"*Airplane?* What will an airplane cost?" They had warred over money since they opened their first theater down on 29th Street.

Barrett said, "Stage manager at the Casino says they're closing

3

He Came from Milwaukee. They'll practically *give* us their biplane if we pay for removing it from the theater. Meantime, you better bone up on your swordplay. We'll give them a duel they'll never forget."

"An airplane makes the play too modern for sword fights."

"The transformation potion makes Dr. Jekyll hallucinate. Jekyll and Hyde fight a Dream Duel."

"Jekyll and Hyde onstage together?"

"Brilliant, isn't it?" said Barrett. "Good and evil battle for each other's soul."

"Any more biff-bang?"

"Mr. Hyde escapes a howling Times Square mob on the subway."

"*Jekyll and Hyde* is set in London."

"London's old hat. I moved it to New York. Jekyll lives in a skyscraper."

Buchanan worried that erecting, striking, and transporting stage sets for a subway train would cost a fortune. Except a New York subway was not a bad idea if you subscribed to the Weber & Fields theory that audiences were more apt to respond in familiar, "realistic" settings. It worked for laughs. Could they put it across for melodrama?

"We'll cut down the subway for the tour."

"Don't patronize me with your cutting-down!" Barrett shot back.

"We'll be carrying sixty people on the road," Buchanan answered coldly, and they exploded into a red-faced, clenched-jaw shouting match.

"Melodrama is whipsawed! Why else are we attempting bloody *Othello*?"

"Cutting down *saves* money so we can *make* money."

"Movies are driving us out of the theaters, and theater audiences are nuts for vaudeville."

"Your free spending will kill us."

"Damn the expense! We're dead without spectacle."

Their stage manager stuck his head in the door with a finger to his lips.

"Angels," he whispered.

"Thank you, Mr. Young. Send them in."

The partners manufactured warm smiles for their investors.

Joe and Jeff Deaver, almost as tall as Barrett and Buchanan and considerably heavier than in their college football days, were heirs to their mother's locomotive factories and their father's love of showgirls. Decked out in capes and top hats, twirling canes, and trailing the scent of the perfumed blondes they'd parked in the hall, they could finance *Jekyll and Hyde* with a stroke of a pen.

"Your timing is exquisite!" boomed Barrett.

"I'll say. We just got invited to back *Alias Jimmy Valentine*. Broadway and a tour. They've got Vietor from England to play Valentine. And Lockwood to play Doyle. We're going to clean up."

"Not so fast," said Barrett.

"Why?"

"Opportunity has arisen closer to home," Buchanan explained. "Poor Medick is dead."

Jeff, the brains of the duo, asked, "Is your *Jekyll* ready?"

Barrett nodded, arousing Buchanan's suspicion that his partner's "tinkering" had included private negotiation with the moneymen. "We are ready to go."

"Do you have Isabella Cook?"

"We'll find a way."

"If you get Miss Cook on board, we say the heck with *Jimmy Valentine*," said Joe. "Don't we, Jeff? Vietor wants too much dough just 'cause he's English. And Lockwood's always getting chorus girls in trouble."

"Wait a minute," Jeff said. "Medick's young. What killed him?"

"They say he fell from a fire escape. Fourth floor."

"That's crazy. The man was terrified of heights. We had him in our *Black Crook*. Remember, Joe? They couldn't get him near the orchestra pit."

"Something's fishy. What was he doing on a fire escape?"

"Exiting a lady's back door," said Jackson Barrett, "pursued by a husband."

ACT ONE

SPRING 1911 (SIX MONTHS LATER)

Bell copied the strange crescent-shaped wounds
Strange cut marks on the body?

1

On the second floor of New York's finest hotel, the Knicker-bocker, at the corner of Broadway and 42nd Street, the Van Dorn Detective Agency's Chief Investigator sized up a new client through the reception room spy hole. The Research Department had provided a snapshot dossier of a "stiff-necked, full-of-himself Waterbury Brass King worth fifty million."

Isaac Bell reckoned they had their facts straight.

William Lathrop Pape looked newly rich. A broad-bellied man in his early fifties, he stood rock-still, gloved hands clamp-ing a gold-headed cane. His suit and shoes were English, his hat Italian. He boasted a heavy watch chain thick enough to moor a steam yacht, and his cold gaze bored through the front desk man as if the young detective were a piece of furniture.

Research had not discovered why the industrialist needed private detectives, but whatever William Lathrop Pape's troubles, he had pulled numerous wires for a personal introduction to Joseph Van Dorn, the founder of the agency. As Van Dorn was three thousand miles away in San Francisco, it had fallen to Isaac Bell to extend the favor requested by an old friend of the Boss.

"O.K. Bring him in."

The apprentice hovering at Bell's elbow raced off.

Bell stepped behind Van Dorn's desk, cleared candlestick telephones and a graphophone diaphragm out of his way, and laid down his notebook and fountain pen. He was tall and about thirty years of age, built lean and hard, with thick golden hair, a proud mustache, and probing blue eyes. On this warm spring day, he wore a tailor-made white linen suit. The hat he had tossed on Van Dorn's rack was white, too, with a broad brim and a low crown. His made-to-order boots were calfskin, well worn and well cared for. He looked like he might smile easily, but a no-nonsense gaze and a panther's grace promised anything but a smile were he provoked.

The apprentice delivered Pape.

Isaac Bell offered his hand and invited him to sit.

Pape spoke before the apprentice was out the door. "I was informed that Van Dorn would make every effort to be here."

"Sincere as Mr. Van Dorn's efforts were, they could not free him from previous obligations in San Francisco. I am his Chief Investigator. What can the Van Dorn Detective Agency do for you?"

"It's imperative that I locate a person who disappeared."

Bell picked up his pen. "Tell me about the person."

William Lathrop Pape stared, silent for so long that Bell wondered if he had not heard. "The person's name?" he asked.

"Pape! Anna Genevieve Pape," said Pape, and fell silent again.

"A member of your family?" Bell prompted. "Your wife?"

"Of course not."

"Then who?"

"My daughter, for pity's sake. My wife wouldn't . . ." His voice trailed off.

Bell asked, "How old is your daughter, Mr. Pape?"

"Eighteen."

"When did you last see Anna?"

"At breakfast on February twenty-seventh."

"Did she often go away for long periods of time?"

"Of course not. She lives at home, and will until she marries."

"Is she engaged?"

"I told you, she's only just turned eighteen."

Isaac Bell asked a question that he was reasonably sure he already knew the answer to. "When did you report that the girl was missing?"

"I'm doing that right now."

"But today is March twenty-fourth, Mr. Pape. Why have you waited so long to raise the alarm?"

"What does it matter?"

"It is the first question the police will ask when they get wind we're looking."

"I do not want the police involved."

The tall detective had a steady, baritone voice. He used it to speak soothingly as if explaining a disappointment to a child.

"Police involve themselves when the facts of a case indicate the possibility of foul play."

"She's an innocent girl. There's no question of foul play."

"Policemen suspect the worst. Why did you wait so long to raise the alarm if Anna's disappearance was unusual?"

Pape gripped his stick harder. "I suspected that she ran away to New York."

"What did she want in New York?"

"To become an actress."

Isaac Bell hid a smile. The situation was immensely clearer.

"May I ask why you have come to the Van Dorn Agency at this juncture?"

"She should have come home with her tail between her legs after a couple of weeks."

"Are you concerned for her safety?"

"Of course."

"But you still waited another week after those 'couple of weeks'?"

"I kept waiting for Anna to come to her senses. Her mother has persuaded me that we cannot wait any longer . . . Listen here, Bell, she was always a levelheaded child. Since she was a little girl. Eyes wide open. She's no flibbertigibbet."

"Then you can comfort your wife with the thought that a girl with Anna's qualities stands a good chance of a successful career in the theater."

Pape stiffened. "She would disgrace my family."

"Disgrace?"

"This sort of behavior attracts the newspapers. Waterbury is not New York, Mr. Bell. It's not a fast city. My family will never live it down if the papers get wind of a well-born Pape on the stage."

Bell's manner cooled. "I will have a Van Dorn detective familiar with the theater districts work up the case. Good afternoon, Mr. Pape."

"Hold on!"

"What?"

"I demand you personally conduct the search if Van Dorn can't."

"The agency parcels out assignments according to their degree of criminality. Mr. Van Dorn and I specialize in murderers, gangsters, bank robbers, and kidnappers."

At the moment, he was supervising investigations into train robbers derailing express cars in the Midwest, bank robbers crisscrossing state lines in autos, Italian gangs terrorizing the New York docks, a Chicago jewel thief cracking the safes of tycoons' mistresses, and blackmailers victimizing passengers on ocean liners.

"A temporarily missing young lady is not the line I'm in. Or are you suggesting she was kidnapped?"

Pape blinked. Obviously accustomed to employees obeying his orders and his whims, the industrialist looked suddenly at sixes and sevens. "No, of course not. I checked at the station. She bought a train ticket to New York— Bell, you don't understand."

"I do understand, sir. I was not much older than Anna when I went against my own father's wishes and became a detective rather than follow him into the banking business."

"Banking? What bank?"

"American States."

"You made a mistake," said Pape. "An American States banker faces a lot more lucrative future than a private detective. Take my advice: you're a young fellow, young enough to change. Get out of this gumshoe business and ask your father to persuade his boss to offer you a job."

"He is the boss," said Bell. "It's his bank."

"American States. *American Stat— Bell?* Is your father Ebenezer Bell?"

"I mention him to assure you that I understand that Anna wants something different," said Bell. "Your daughter and I have disappointed fathers in common— Now, by any chance have you brought a photograph?"

Pape drew an envelope from an inside pocket and gave Bell a Kodak snapped out of doors of children in a summer camp theatrical performance. Anna was a cherubic, expressive, fair-haired girl. Whether she was levelheaded did not show—perhaps a tribute, Bell thought with another hidden smile, to her thespian talent.

"Shakespeare," said Pape.

Bell nodded, engrossed in memories the picture brought forth. "*A Midsummer Night's Dream.*"

"How did you know?"

"They made me play Oberon when I grew too tall for Puck— Anna's a pretty girl. How old was she here?"

Pape muttered something Bell couldn't understand. "What was that, sir?" He looked up from the photograph.

The Brass King had tears in his eyes. "What if I'm wrong?" he whispered.

"How do you mean?"

"What if something terrible happened to her?"

"Young women come to the city every day," Bell answered gently. "They eventually find something they want or they go home. But, in either event, the vast, vast majority survive, enriched, even happy. I would not start worrying needlessly. We'll find your daughter."

2

Eighteen-year-old Anna Waterbury read *Variety* aloud to Lucy Balant, her roommate in Mrs. Shine's Boarding House for Actors. They had pooled nickels to buy the show business magazine and—like a sign from Heaven, thought Anna—*Variety* headlined the new *Dr. Jekyll and Mr. Hyde* tour about to cross the country on Barrett & Buchanan's private train.

"'Jackson Barrett and John Buchanan—matinee idols who ignite melodrama like dreadnoughts on a rampage—will trade title roles as they did on Broadway. The chief interest centers around the struggle between the good and evil halves of the same man. Isabella Cook portrays the innocent love interest tormented by Hyde. Miss Cook returns to the stage after two years' retirement, during which she was married and widowed by the late

Theatrical Syndicate chief, Rufus S. Oppenheim, who drowned when his yacht exploded.'"

Anna whispered, "Can I tell you a secret?"

Lucy was reading the Wanteds over her shoulder. "Look! 'Wanted for Permanent Stock. General businesswoman. Must be tall, young, experienced, and have good wardrobe. Join at once. Sobriety, wardrobe, and ability essential. Long season. Money, sure—'How tall is 'tall'?"

Anna said, "It's a secret."

"What?"

"You have to promise never, ever tell anyone."

"O.K., I promise."

"There's a man who's going to coach me to read for a role in a big hit."

"Is he a teacher?"

"No! Much better. He's a *producer*. A *Broadway* producer who knows someone in a big hit."

Anna's friend looked skeptical, or possibly envious. "Did he take you to Rector's?"

"Rector's? No!"

"*Anna!* A sport should at least treat a girl to a Beef Wellington. I mean, what does he want for 'coaching'?— Why are you laughing?"

"Because three weeks ago I wouldn't have known what 'a Beef Wellington' meant."

Anna Waterbury had learned so much so fast since coming to New York, Beef Wellington was the least of it. "I am," she said, "the only graduate in the history of St. Margaret's School for Girls who knows to ask whether a road offer includes train fare."

Not to mention who supplied costumes. And to dodge theatrical managers who got the artist, coming and going, by appointing themselves her agent. And to never, ever take a job with the circus. Not that anyone had offered her any job in anything, yet.

"Welcome to Broadway," Lucy fired back. She was jumpy, waiting to hear if she got the understudy part in *Alias Jimmy Valentine*, a big sensation based on an O. Henry story, which was sending a road company to Philadelphia. They had both tried out for it, but only Lucy had been called back for a second reading.

"No," said Anna. "He's not like that. He's a sweet old thing."

"How old?"

"I don't know—old as my father. He limps, on a cane. Besides, he's married. He wears a ring. He doesn't hide it. He's full of wonderful advice."

"Like what?"

"Give the star the center of the stage and stay out of his way."

"What's his name?"

"I can't tell you his name. He made me promise— Why? Because the cast would resent me if they knew he got me the part."

"What big hit?"

Anna dropped her voice even lower, and she looked around, though who else could fit in their tiny room? "This!" She waved *Variety*. "The spring tour for *Jekyll and Hyde*! I can hardly believe my luck."

There was a brisk knock at the door, and their landlady flung it open with an unusually warm smile. "Lucy Balant, you have a visitor."

Bouncing up and down beside Mrs. Shine, cap in hand, was a callboy from Wallack's Theatre. "Stage manager says to pack your bag!"

Lucy was out the door in minutes. "Good luck, Anna. Don't worry. It'll be your turn next."

Anna went to the narrow window and craned her neck to watch Lucy trotting alongside the callboy. She had a strong feeling that it really would be her turn next. What would she do if the nice old gentleman asked her to dine at Rector's? She knew in her heart that she did not have to answer that because he wouldn't. He really did want to help her. Although maybe after she got the part, he might ask her there to celebrate. Fair enough. As long as he brought his wife.

3

ALL CLOTHES WASHED GOOD AS NEW
THEATRE COSTUME OUR SPECIAL

Isaac Bell hurried out of the Chinese laundry.

A broad-shouldered hard case in an overcoat and derby blocked the sidewalk.

"Care to tell me why the Chief Investigator of a private detective agency, with field offices in every city worth the name, and foreign outposts in London, Paris, and Berlin, is personally sleuthing for one missing young lady?"

"I wondered when you'd show, Mike. Your plainclothes boys were pretending not to watch me exiting Hammerstein's stage door."

"I train them to dislike surprises."

Captain "Honest Mike" Coligney commanded the New York Police Department's Tenderloin station house. His precinct included much of the Theater District and the hotel and boarding-house neighborhoods where actors lived. Bell had worked closely with him years ago on the Gangster case, but operating on the same side of the law at sharply different angles made them competitors as much as allies. The policeman danced an elaborate ballet with the politicians who bossed New York City. The private detective was beholden to none. Coligney had six thousand cops backing him up, Bell had the Van Dorn Agency's ironclad guarantee: "We never give up! Never!"

"Haven't seen you in a while," said Coligney. "Where you been?"

"Out west."

"What brought you back?"

Bell gave him a copy of Anna's picture. Now that the captain had the police "involved," as Pape had put it, he intended to recruit extra eyes.

"Sweet-looking kid," Coligney said. "A hopeful actress explains why your sidekick Archie Abbott is hanging out in the theatricals' saloons. The blue-blooded Mr. Archibald Abbott IV having been a thespian before you brought him into the agency."

Bell remained reticent.

The captain probed drily, "It might even explain why Harry Warren's Gang Squad is knocking on rooming house doors, though I'm not sure how far detectives disguised as gangsters will get with rooming house landladies. But it still doesn't explain why *you* are gumshoeing personally—is the lassie's father a big wheel?"

"Not a Rockefeller or Judge Congdon, but big enough. Truth is, I had a couple of light days and felt sorry for the poor devil. He's self-important and self-admiring—the richest man in the Brass City—but Anna is his only child, and it became clear to me that he loves her dearly."

"Any luck?"

"Not a lot. I found a stage manager who sort of remembers hearing her read for a role. Archie found a callboy who told her 'no parts.' Harry found a landlady who thought she'd been looking for a room, three or four weeks ago. That would fit the time she left home, but if the name she gave was hers, she changed it for the stage."

"So did Lillian Russell."

"This one's become 'Anna Waterbury.'"

"Homesick."

Bell and Abbott had made the rounds of dance and music schools, and the cheap eateries patronized by young actors starting out and older ones on the way down, and Bell was now finishing up low-cost laundries in the theater neighborhood. They had shown Anna's photograph to landladies, young actors and actresses, and stage door tenders; a few thought they recognized her. In a tiny dressing room crammed with chorus girls at the Broadway Music Hall, Bell had found one who recognized her picture and recalled the name Anna Waterbury. So he was reasonably sure she was in New York, but still had no clue where.

"Hospitals?" asked Coligney.

"No Papes, no Waterburys."

"Morgue?"

"Any unidentified young women I should know about?" Bell

replied, doubting there were. He was neither especially concerned about young Anna's safety nor surprised he hadn't located her yet. New York was a huge city, and there were thousands of jobs for actresses in the vaudeville and dramatic theaters, in musicals and burlesque, and the road shows they spawned.

"None as of an hour ago," said Coligney. "Good to see you again, Isaac. Congratulations, by the way. I heard you finally persuaded Marion Morgan to marry you."

"Thank you. If there's a luckier man on the planet, I haven't met him."

"Lord knows what she sees in you."

"She's funny that way," Bell grinned back, and they shook hands good-bye.

"Say hello to Joe Van Dorn."

"Can I tell him you'll lend a hand?"

The captain nodded. "I'll pin up Anna's picture and have my sergeants mention her at roll call."

———

Two days later, running out of options and growing concerned, Isaac Bell mounted the front steps of a brick mansion on a dimly lighted cross street in the Tenderloin. The doorman stood six-four and weighed two-fifty. "Good evening, sir. It seems years since we've had the honor."

"Good evening, Skinner. Would you tell Mr. Sayers I want to see him?"

The doorman whispered into a voice tube.

Nick Sayers, handsome proprietor of the Grove Mansion

bordello—known as the "Ritz of the Tenderloin"—kept him waiting ten minutes. He was dressed in evening clothes and reeked of top-shelf cologne.

"Mr. Bell. Dare I ask? Business-business or pleasure-business?"

"Advice, Nick. In your office."

Sayers led him up the grand staircase and into his richly appointed office. He sat at his desk and offered Bell a chair. Bell took notice of a glass display cabinet filled with remarkably specific pornographic ceramic figurines. Sayers beamed proudly. "I've become a collector. Turns out, not every Staffordshire potter produces statues of spaniels—what sort of advice?"

"Who recruits girls at Grand Central Terminal?"

"Not the Grove Mansion."

"I am aware that you don't lure them personally, Nick. Who does it for you? Who ambushes pretty country girls when they step off the train? Who promises a cushy life?"

"Mr. Bell, I've really never felt the need to recruit. Young ladies come to the Grove Mansion as volunteers."

"Nick."

"Why don't I parade my girls by you? You can see with your own eyes that they could work in any house in New York. They work here because they want to."

"Nick. The Van Dorn Detective Agency was not founded yesterday. Cheap pimps hunt poor farm daughters who can only afford steamers and trolleys at ferry piers and trolley stops. High class resorts like your 'Ritz of the Tenderloin' troll Pennsylvania Station and Grand Central for the class of girls who can purchase a railroad ticket to run away from home. I am looking for one particular well-off girl. I know she came by train. I know she arrived at Grand Central because she journeyed from Connecticut. I want to know who to interview at Grand Central. And I am running out of patience."

"Patience?" Sayers got indignant. "Isaac! You helped me, a long time ago, and I helped you. I call us even steven."

"*Isaac* instead of *Mr. Bell*? Sounds like you're paying off ever-bigger friends at Tammany Hall."

"It would pay *you* to remember how to get along in this town. How dare you barge into my house, making threats?"

"Threats?"

Isaac Bell stood up, draped a big hand on the glass cabinet, tipped it forward, and slammed it down to the floor, shattering glass and smashing ceramics.

Sayers gasped in disbelief. "Do you know what those cost?"

"That was not a threat," said Bell. "Who is snagging girls at Grand Central?"

Sayers reached for his voice tube.

Bell said, "If you call Skinner, you'll need a new doorman. That's not a threat, either."

———

The bordello procurer at Grand Central ran his operation from Nyren's, a fancy station shop that sold French perfume, kid gloves, and silk scarves. Exquisitely dressed and barbered, he had the kindly, twinkly-eyed manner of an unmarried uncle. "May I help you, sir? Something for a young lady friend, perhaps?"

"I don't have a young lady friend."

Nyren delivered an indulgent wink. "Well, until you get one, why not something nice for your wife?"

"What I want," said Isaac Bell, "is a private conversation in your back room with each of your young gents who waylay girls off the trains and steer them in here."

The twinkle hardened with an edge like limelight. "I don't know what you are talking about. If you haven't come to make a purchase, please leave my shop."

"But first I want to talk to you, Mr. Nyren. I'm looking for this girl."

He held out Anna's picture.

Nyren pretended to study it. "I still don't know what you are talking about, but I never met this girl." Then, in an act that made the tall detective believe him, he dropped his mask long enough to leer, "I can assure you I never forget a pretty face."

"I will watch your shop for you while you round up your young gents. One at a time."

"I will call a policeman."

"I will, too," said Bell, "and it won't be one of the New York Central rail dicks you paid off. It will be his boss."

"Who the hell are you?"

"A friend of the young lady's family. Get them in here—now!"

Three swaggered into the shop, one at a time as Bell ordered. They were young, well dressed, and it was not hard to imagine a frightened girl falling for their polished manners and charming smiles. Bell greeted each politely. "I'm not here to put you out of business. I'm looking for one particular young lady and I would appreciate your help. My appreciation will take the form of a monetary reward."

"How much?"

"One hundred dollars," said Bell. The figure, two months' earnings for a day laborer, captured their attention. "Have you seen this girl?"

Two shook their heads. The third said, "I remember her."

"When did you see her?"

"Let me think . . . Month ago. Maybe five weeks."

The time was right, and Bell asked, "Did you speak?"

"Tried to. She wasn't buying any."

"What happened?"

"She just brushed past like I wasn't there and kept going."

"Did one of the other boys accost her?"

"No. Only me."

"How do you know?"

"I followed her out on the street."

"Did you really? Which way did she go?"

"Across 42nd."

"West?"

"Yes."

"How far did you follow her?"

"Fifth Avenue."

"Why'd you stop?"

"She was walking like she knew where she was going. Or knew what she wanted. So I figured, this is not a girl I could convert."

Bell remained silent, and the brothel recruiter added, "Want to hear something funny?"

"What's that?"

"I saw her a few weeks later—last week."

"Where?"

"Over on Broadway. She was strolling with an old swell. You tell me what she's about."

"What did he look like?"

"Old."

"Stooped over? Bent?"

"No. Tall guy like you."

"What color was his hair?"

"Gray."

"Beard?"

"No, just a mustache."

"What color were his eyes?"

"I don't know. I wasn't that close. Say, maybe I could go now? Maybe you could give me a piece of that hundred?"

"Maybe I could," said Isaac Bell. "You called him a swell. What was he wearing?"

"Homburg and a cape. Looked like he walked straight out of the operetta. Even had a gold-headed cane."

"Frock coat under the cape?"

"No. More like a pinchback."

"Pinchback?" Bell asked. "A bit up-to-date for an operetta."

"I thought so, too. Maybe the young lady took him shopping."

Bell passed him a one-hundred-dollar bill. "Here you go. Take a week off, give some poor girl a break."

"If I don't get her, some other guy will."

———

Four men followed Isaac Bell from Grand Central and paced him on the other side of 44th Street. Snappy dressers—presentable for the neighborhood, if somewhat flashy in two-tone shoes—they might have been out-of-town buyers just off the train, or junior advertising men, except for their socks. The modern breed of Gopher street gangster favored yellow hose. They were still there when he crossed Fifth Avenue. A traffic cop shot them a look, but he had his hands full sorting carriages from motor trucks.

Bell did not expect them to make their move on the block between Fifth and Sixth. Shared by garages and carriage houses, the Yale, New York Yacht, and Harvard clubs, and the Iroquois and Algonquin hotels, there were too many people. At Sixth Avenue, he crossed quickly under the El and stopped suddenly in the shadows of the overhead train trestle with his back to a stanchion.

4

The Gophers cut across traffic and blocked the sidewalk. Up close, scarred faces and missing teeth left no doubt they meant business. For reasons often debated by the Van Dorn Gang Squad, the shortest Gopher always did the talking.

"Friend of the family?"

Isaac Bell said, "Out of my way, boys."

The others took up the chorus and edged closer.

"Mr. Do-good?"

"Friend of the family."

"You're gonna learn—stay outta people's businesses."

The tallest made two mistakes. He forged ahead of the others and he lowered one hand to reach for his blackjack. Bell took advantage with a one-two combination that knocked the gangster to the pavement. Guard up—left hand and forearm protecting his chin and gut, right positioned to slough off a punch or throw his own—he bloodied a nose with a lightning jab and back-stepped as fast as he had waded in.

"Last chance, boys. Out of my way."

The short guy laughed. He thrust out his hand with a sharp twist and his blackjack slid from his sleeve into his palm. "Last chance? Gonna fight three of us?"

"Not while wearing my best suit."

Bell flared open his coat, revealing the use-polished grips of the Colt automatic in his shoulder holster. "I will shoot two and fight the last man standing."

———————————⬥———————————

Isaac Bell headed to the Bellevue Hospital morgue late the following afternoon, where he showed Anna's photograph to a recently appointed assistant coroner.

"I have no Anna Pape. And no Anna Waterbury."

"Any unknowns?" Bell asked.

The new assistant was working hard to modernize the obsolete institution that had been run for too many years by a commission of elected, often unqualified, and occasionally corrupt coroners. Improvements included making a record of the dead with photographs. He flipped through the file pages, and Bell agreed when he said, "No kids like this one—funny you should ask, though. We might have a younger woman coming in later. Sounded like a murder. One of the bosses went over himself."

"Where?"

"In the Tenderloin."

Bell asked for the address, caught the trolley across 34th Street, and strode swiftly down Eighth Avenue to West 29th Street. Captain Mike Coligney was standing outside a run-down building of flats. He was talking to a coroner Bell did not know personally and ignoring shouted questions from newspaper reporters held at bay by uniformed cops. Bell walked past, exchanged a private glance with Coligney, and waited half a block away until the official drove off in a Marmon.

Coligney greeted him gravely. "Sorry, Isaac, she could be your girl."

"Who found her?"

"The actor who lives here claims he came home from a month in the Midwest. He swears he didn't know her. We're holding him while we check, but it looks fairly certain he only left Pittsburgh this morning—the show he was in got canceled. She's been dead at least a day."

The reporters' shouts grew insistent. At an imperious glance from Coligney, his cops herded them farther down the street. He said to Bell, "I have six daughters. I won't have salacious speculation about a child from a good home. It's not that she was some unfortunate streetwalker."

"Did the neighbors hear anything?" Bell asked.

"Not in the flat. Not in the hallway. Not in the lobby. We're guessing she came under her own steam. In which case, she knew her killer."

"Unless she was carried in."

"We've got no witnesses to that. No, it looks personal. Vicious. Jealous rage."

"May I see her?" asked Bell.

Coligney hesitated. Bell said, "A fresh pair of eyes can only help."

"You'll write me a report."

"Of course. Thanks, Mike."

Coligney raised a cautioning hand. "I don't have to tell you not to touch anything. But just so you know before you go in there, Isaac. She's really been carved up."

5

Isaac Bell stood still and catalogued the location and condition of everything in the room. Personal possessions—Shakespeare plays on a shelf by an easy chair; busts and engravings of the actors Booth, Mansfield, Irving, and Jefferson; photographs of leading ladies, signed and framed; and a glass box stacked with programs—confirmed the actor's alibi as much as the punched train ticket he had shown Captain Coligney's detectives. It was more a home than a rented room, and it had been left neat as a pin, drapes drawn, bed made, wardrobe closed. Dust thinly layered tabletops, and a spiderweb linked the busts, but a landlady or a neighbor must have watered the house plant, a healthy geranium, during the month he was away. The windows were shut tight, and Bell guessed the air would smell musty if it weren't for the blood scent that lingered. He made a mental note that the killer had known the place was empty. The actor was lucky his show hadn't closed a day earlier or he'd be dead, too.

She was on the bed, on her back, still half in her overcoat. Her hands were positioned at her sides, open, one in a glove, the other bare. Her palms bore no cuts. She had not fended off the knife. Her face, too, was unmarked, neither cut nor bruised. But it was swollen, and her skin was tinged blue. With her cheeks rounded in death, she looked remarkably similar to the cherubic photograph taken when she was fifteen.

A circle of horizontal bruises around her neck paralleled the deep slice in her throat that had nearly cleaved her head from her torso. The absence of cuts on her hands, her blue-tinged skin, and the bruises gave Bell hope that the killer had strangled her before he went to work with his knife.

The tall detective moved at last and stepped deeper into the room.

Pools of blood had soaked her coat and the bedspread, but none had fountained onto the headboard and the walls, which Bell took as further evidence that her heart had stopped beating before arteries were severed. He counted ten crescent-shaped slices on her arms and legs; they varied in length, but were all shallow and had bled very little. Puzzled and curious, he copied them in his notebook.

(/) ⋑ ⋒ ⋓

He inspected her fingernails. Two were broken, but he was surprised to see neither the blood nor torn skin he would expect from her scratching her killer's wrists as she fought to live. For fought she must have, if only at the last moment. One of her boot heels was partly torn from the sole as she kicked against the floor or the bedpost.

Bell was inclined to concur with the cops that she had come to the flat voluntarily, but less inclined to assume it was for a tryst. Even discounting for a doting father's blindness, he thought that Anna's age, her sheltered upbringing, and a passion to succeed in the theater all suggested an innocent girl unlikely to strike up a liaison so soon after leaving home.

The cops had put great weight on the viciousness of the assault, characterizing it as the rage of jealousy. Or the anger of rejection, thought Bell. He was thinking she could have been lured to the apartment under a pretext that had nothing to do with a tryst. But he was painfully aware that when it fell to him to report to her father his daughter's fate, he wanted to soften the blow, no matter how slightly.

If only, he thought, I had found her in time.

———

"Stop right there," said Captain Coligney when he saw the expression on Isaac Bell's face. He raised a big hand that would have halted a freight wagon. Bell pounded down the front steps and brushed past him, heading for Broadway and Times Square.

"Leave him to us," Coligney shouted. "We'll get him."

"Not if I get him first."

Fifteen minutes after he left the house where Anna was murdered he was looming over the desk of the *New York Times* drama critic. "Mr. Klauber, I am Isaac Bell. Our mutual friend, Walter Hawley, introduced us at the Amen Corner shortly before he died." Walter L. Hawley had been chief political reporter of the *Evening Sun*.

"Bell? Certainly," Adolph Klauber drawled in a Louisville, Kentucky, accent. "In the insurance line, if I recall. What's up, Mr. Bell? You look mighty upset."

Bell said, "Within minutes, actors are going to telephone you to tell you that a young actress named Anna Waterbury lived in their boardinghouse. I want the address."

"I have no idea what you are talking about."

"Miss Waterbury was just murdered."

A blurted, unbidden *"What?"* died half voiced.

Fury had contorted the handsome features of the tall, powerful man looming over his desk. Klauber flinched and swallowed hard, in sudden fear for his own life. Then a transformation as startling as the critic had ever witnessed on any stage changed Isaac Bell's face again. Rage hardened to deliberate, measured, everlasting resolve. He spoke in a voice as cold as an Arctic sea.

"The vicious cutthroat who killed the poor girl slaughtered her so gruesomely that the newspapers will be printing extras. I am betting that some actor who knew where she lived will telephone you. Her neighbors will help me identify the cutthroat."

"Why would they telephone me?"

"Because before you became a critic, you were an actor,

Mr. Klauber. Who would you have telephoned when you were struggling for a place in the theater? The police? Or a famous drama critic who used to be an actor and is therefore sympathetic to the backstage standpoint."

"I hope—no, I trust—I would not have been so crassly ambitious."

"You forget the indignities suffered, the disappointments, and the poverty. From what I've seen the past few days, the theater is a hard life, and it's easy to get lost."

"Well," Klauber conceded, "everyone's got to make a living somehow."

His telephone rang.

———

Isaac Bell bounded up the front steps of Anna Waterbury's boardinghouse—two time-battered, nineteenth-century town houses merged into one, mid-block, on a cross street off Broadway. He knew he would be lucky to have five minutes before cops and reporters besieged it. The front door was flung open before he could knock. A pair of vaudeville dancers, the woman in swirls of silk, the man in white tie, looked crestfallen.

"You're not Mr. Klauber."

"Mr. Klauber sent me," Bell lied. "We need your help. What are your names?"

"Heather and Lou," said the woman, who was an extraordinarily beautiful brunette with long dark hair.

"Heather and Lou, how well did you know Anna?"

"Only from the supper table," said Heather.

"Do you recall the last time you saw her?"

"Yesterday. She never came home last night."

"Did she leave with anyone?"

"She left alone."

Bustling up behind the dancers came their landlady, Mrs. Shine, a round woman with suspicious eyes and a work-worn face. She looked appalled when Bell asked whether she had known Anna, and she protested that she ran an orderly house and she could not be held responsible for what her boarders did away from the house.

"Did she have a boyfriend?"

The landlady crossed her arms. "Not on this premises."

"Would any of your other boarders know whether she had a boyfriend?"

"Only Lucy Balant. They shared a room."

"May I speak with Lucy?"

"If you take yourself to Philadelphia," said the landlady, and one of the hovering dancers explained, "Lucy is an understudy in *Jimmy Valentine*—"

"Oh my Lord," groaned the landlady. "Look at them!"

From one direction pounded a phalanx of police, from the other a mob of reporters. Uniformed cops were trailing plainclothesmen. The reporters were shouting questions.

Isaac Bell hurried uptown to the Knickerbocker. He wired instructions to the Philadelphia field office and several other offices around the continent, issued orders to every detective in the bull pen, then raced across town to Grand Central Terminal, where he caught a train to Waterbury, Connecticut.

He was in the Brass City in less than two and a half hours, but the newspapers had beat him to it. No one answered the telephone when he called from the Waterbury Station, and when he got to the Pape home, a three-story brick mansion flanked by stone turrets, he found reporters milling outside the spiked fence.

A thug in a black coat and fedora guarded the gate, and two flanked the front door—Pape Brass company cops, Bell assumed. He palmed his Van Dorn badge to shield the flash of gold from the reporters. "Mr. Pape is a client. If he wants to see me, tell him let me in the back door."

He received the polite "Wait here, please" that he expected. Private cops treated Van Dorns with kid gloves, hoping to be remembered next time the agency's Protective Services branch was hiring. The guard hurried back. "Walk around the corner. One of the boys will take you through the side gate."

Bell was ushered down a service alley and in the servants' entrance. A liveried butler led him through the house and across an immense drawing room dominated by a pipe organ. He knocked on the door to a library that doubled as Pape's home office and left Bell face-to-face with the grieving father.

"I can only say how sorry I am, sir. I promise you that we will never give up until we bring her killer to justice."

"She'd be alive if you had found her."

6

Isaac Bell brought the New York papers from a Bridgeport news-boy who ran onto the train when it paused in the station. All hewed the same line—guided, Bell was certain, by Captain Coligney—that an innocent young woman of a good family had been lured or forced to the room where she was murdered. None raised the possibility that Anna might have known her murderer.

Deprived of the salacious, the papers fell back on a tried and true comparison to the ultimate evil. Back in 1888, nearly twenty-five years ago, a string of murders in London were a sensation on both sides of the Atlantic. To Bell's day, in 1911, reporters routinely likened them to any unsolved knife attack against a woman.

Police at work on the Anna Pape case suspect a moral pervert similar to Jack the Ripper whose gruesome murders in the Whitechapel district of London startled the world.

———————

"The cops reckon a boyfriend," Bell told a hastily organized squad of his best available detectives. He had wired others who were out of town to report to New York, but he would manage with these for a start.

"A boyfriend is my instinct, too. Or at least someone she knew and trusted. There's no evidence, so far, that she didn't go to the flat voluntarily. And the way he cut her up strongly suggests jealous rage. That said, we have no one who witnessed her arrival at the flat, no one who saw her being carried, dragged, or marched into the building. Would they have? Probably, but no guarantee, particularly late at night."

"Any sign of knockout drops?" asked redheaded Archie Abbott.

"The *assistant* coroner conducted the autopsy, which means it was scientifically sound. Chloral hydrate is swiftly metabolized, but he found no alcohol in the contents of her stomach, either."

The detectives nodded their understanding. The taste and odor of chloral hydrate were masked by alcohol, so it was a reasonable bet the killer had not slipped the victim knockout drops in a drink.

"Chloroform?" asked Harry Warren. The grizzled Gang Squad chief was one of Bell's closest confidants.

"The assistant coroner told me that the odor would have dissipated by the time her body was discovered. I certainly didn't smell it. But the autopsy revealed something unusual. Her neck was broken. Which takes a mighty strong hand. Anna was petite, but it does suggest we are looking for a big bruiser who doesn't know his own strength. Nonetheless, the main point is this, gents: it is imperative that we establish whether she went there voluntarily, vital that we confirm whether she was acquainted with her killer or was attacked by a stranger. If it was personal, we will discover his name. If it wasn't personal, then a vicious cutthroat is prowling the city and may kill again. Either way, I want him in the electric chair."

"Why would she go with the man if he wasn't a boyfriend?" asked a young detective still on probation.

"Hope," answered Bell.

"Hope for what? That he'll become a boyfriend?"

That drew some smiles, which faded when Isaac Bell said in an icy voice, "Anna wanted to be an actress. She hoped for a role in a play."

———   ———

Lucy Balant walked home to her shabby hotel, exhausted. She had never been so tired in her life. She hadn't spoken a word of *Alias Jimmy Valentine* yet, hadn't set a foot onstage except to rehearse lines with the stage manager for the roles she stood by for. But that didn't mean she didn't work. They paid her, fed her, and housed her, and in return the company required her to do any job needed. Skilled with a needle, she assisted the wardrobe mistress. Long days started very early in the morning, repairing costumes and washing them in the theater's old-fashioned laundry, cranking them through the wringer, then racing up six flights of stairs to the roof to pin them on clotheslines, and ironing them when half dry.

She plodded up the stairs and into her room, shut the door, and leaned against it for a moment of peace and quiet in the dark. This was their last night in Philadelphia, then on to Boston, where maybe one of the regular actresses would get sick, or quit, or fall off the stage and break her neck.

"Lucy?"

She jumped, her heart leaping into her throat. A tall figure was in her room, standing in the shadow between the bed and the wardrobe.

"Don't be afraid." A woman's voice, thankfully.

A raven-haired woman in her twenties stepped into the light spilling through the window. "I have to talk to you."

"How did you get in here?"

"I let myself in."

Lucy's heart was still pounding. "I locked the door when I left."

"I picked the lock. Lucy, my name is Helen—"

"Picked the lock? You forced your way into my room. What are you talking—why are you here?"

"I must talk to you. My name is Helen Mills. I am a Van Dorn detective. There is no reason to be afraid."

"I *am* afraid. What are you doing in my room?"

Mills had recently been promoted to full detective—the first woman for the Van Dorn Agency—after graduating college. Quick to see opportunity and quicker to act, it only occurred to her belatedly to put herself in Lucy's shoes. How would she or any woman alone feel if the door to her hotel room turned out not to be the protection she thought it was?

"I am sorry. This case is so important, I forgot my manners."

"If you ever had any to start with— Case? What case? Why didn't you just wait in the lobby? Or you could have found me at the theater."

"I am sorry," Helen apologized again. "But I wanted your full attention."

"You have it. So what do you want?"

Helen Mills said, "I have terrible news and I need your help. Your roommate Anna is dead."

"*What?* No! She was fine when I left New York."

"Anna was murdered."

Lucy staggered back a step and struck the bed, which nearly buckled her knees. "No, she . . ."

"I have to ask you some questions. Your answers could help us find the man who murdered her. I'm sure you're upset."

"How would you feel?"

"I would be very upset . . ."

"What do you mean murdered? What happened? Who's the man?"

"We don't know, yet. If you can manage to answer my questions, you can help us find him."

"But why? That doesn't make sense. She's a really nice girl.

She wouldn't hurt anyone." Still in her coat and shaking her head, Lucy sat on the bed. "She read for my part. If she'd gotten it instead of me, she wouldn't have been killed."

"Did she have a boyfriend?"

"No."

"Would she have told you if she did?"

Lucy said, "I would have known it. All she cared about was getting a role. That's all she wanted. That's why she left home, and it didn't sound to me like her home was bad. I think she had a wonderful home."

"Did she have a man who was hoping to be her boyfriend?"

"No one I saw."

"Was there any man she might have gone with to an apartment?"

"I doubt that," said Lucy. "She was Miss Innocent. I'd be amazed if she ever kissed a boy."

Helen said, "But for some reason she went to an apartment with a man."

"Alone?"

"Apparently."

"Well, that's a surprise, I must say. A huge surprise— Oh . . ."

"What?"

"No, it couldn't be. He was too old."

"Who was too old?" asked Helen.

"Some old man, a Broadway producer, was coaching her to read for a role."

"Can you describe him?"

"No, I never saw him. She just told me about him."

"How old?"

"She just said 'old.' He limped. I think he used a cane. And he was married. Or, at least he wore a wedding ring. She really thought he was going to help her get a role."

"Did she read for the role?"

"I don't know. She said he knew someone important in the show. She was sure she would get the job."

"Did she say in what play?"

"*Dr. Jekyll and Mr. Hyde.* The spring tour. Barrett & Buchanan are taking it on the road."

———

Isaac Bell was expecting her to wire a report. Instead, Helen Mills went straight to the Broad Street Station and took the train to New York City. Racing uptown from Pennsylvania Station, she stopped at the Almeida Theatre, where *Dr. Jekyll and Mr. Hyde* had been playing before it went on tour, then hurried to the Van Dorn field office at the Knickerbocker.

Bell was issuing orders in the bull pen and detectives were rushing out. Ordinarily, they would welcome her with big greetings, but tonight all she got were grim nods. Bell sent Harry Warren on his way and conferred quietly with Archie Abbott, who had been his best friend since they boxed in college. An actor before his socially prominent mother demanded he quit the stage, Archie knew the ins and outs of show business.

Finally, Bell beckoned her to join them.

Helen Mills had apprenticed under Isaac Bell and become his protégée. Mr. Van Dorn had ordered her on the Philadelphia posting to broaden her experience. She hadn't seen Bell in months, and the first thing she noticed was a face so joyless, it looked hacked from granite. She exchanged a quick glance with Archie, who confirmed with a nod that Bell was deeply shaken by Anna Waterbury's murder. She went straight to business.

"I found Lucy Balant."

"A wire would have saved time."

"Wires can be confusing. I thought this was too serious a case not to report in person."

Isaac Bell raised an eyebrow and gave her a knowing look. Helen Mills possessed a strong drive to be in the heart of the action. Not a bad quality in a detective. At least when tempered with common sense. "Go on," he said. "Report."

She told Bell what she had learned and concluded, "It seems to me that it's a question of how old that producer was. Too old to be strong enough to kill?"

"Young people," said Bell, "see everyone as old. The middle-aged recognize middle age. And the old see everyone as young. Anna was only eighteen."

"Young enough," said Archie Abbott, "to believe a man who claims he can pull wires to get her a role."

Bell said, "For all we know, he's only thirty-five and limps because he got shot in the Spanish–American War or hit by a trolley."

Archie said, "He picked the right show to lure the poor girl. *Jekyll and Hyde* is a sensation, packed with modern scenic effects. Barrett & Buchanan are going to clean up with that tour."

"I saw it with my father," said Helen. "Women were fainting in the aisles."

"Who played Hyde? Barrett or Bu—"

Bell cut them off. "Helen! Before you go back to Philadelphia, go to the Almeida and ask did Anna Waterbury read for a part in *Dr. Jekyll and Mr. Hyde*."

"I stopped on my way here," said Helen. "They're rehearsing a new play. *Dr. Jekyll and Mr. Hyde* has already left for Boston— Do you want me to go to Boston?"

"No, I'll wire the office." Bell signaled an apprentice who rushed to his desk. Bell handed him a copy of Anna's picture. "Run this over to Grand Central. Put it on the night mail to Boston. On the jump!" To Helen he said, "The Boston boys will have it in the morning—what's the matter?"

Helen Mills said, "Talking to Lucy made me realize something. If the murderer wasn't Anna's boyfriend or didn't even know her, what happens to the next girl he catches alone?"

7

"Would you tell me your name, miss?"

Most girls in the business made up a name. But Lillian Lent had decided that if she was giving away everything else for two dollars, why stop at her name, if acting friendly with a decent sport could lead to a buck or two tip. This sport, decked out in an old-fashioned cape and limping on a cane—and doffing his topper, no less—had nice manners. He even looked her straight in the face as if he remembered he was talking to a human being. He might disappoint her, but she bet he'd be charitable, so she raised her head—he towered over her—to look him back in his eyes, and answered with the biggest smile she could smile without showing her rotten teeth, "I am Lillian."

"What a lovely name. It suits you."

"Thank you kindly, sir."

"What is your family name?"

"Lent—like the holiday—but I'm not religious."

"Lillian Lent. Alliterative. Very pretty. It suits you. When did you come to Boston, Lillian Lent?"

"How do you know I'm not from Boston?"

"Your accent sounds like Maine."

"Oh. I guess it does. I've been here a couple a three months. Maybe four."

"Did you grow up on a farm?"

"Potatoes. Now you know why I came to Boston."

"Shall we go for a walk, Lillian?"

She had read him wrong. She had assumed by his manners and his costly boots that he would spend money for a room. But at least out of doors, on a chilly spring night, went quick. No doubt about that. She let him steer her into the dark of the Common, saying, "A walk it is," and still hopeful about a tip.

When Chief Investigator Bell's orders clattered in on the private telegraph, detectives in the Van Dorn field office atop Boston's South Station drew straws. Who would hold down the fort? Who would conduct interviews in a theater full of actresses and showgirls? They used matches for straws.

James Dashwood had learned magic tricks and marksmanship from his mother, who had been a sharpshooter in Buffalo Bill's Wild West Show. He palmed a long match before they drew.

———

The street and sidewalks were blocked by railroad express wagons lining up to enter an alley between two theaters. Stagehands and teamsters were loading in for the marquee that promised

TOMORROW NIGHT
ALIAS JIMMY VALENTINE
Direct from **NEW YORK**
and **PHILADELPHIA**
"Top O. Henry Short Story Topped Onstage"
—*VARIETY*

Dodging horses, sidestepping manure, Dashwood passed under the next marquee, which proclaimed

JACKSON BARRETT & JOHN BUCHANAN
Present
DR. JEKYLL and MR. HYDE
Direct from **BROADWAY**
Featuring the Height of Mechanical Realism
Two Sensational Scenic Effects

He breezed past a sign on the ticket window that read

OPENING NIGHT SOLD OUT

and into the lobby, where he learned from an advance man, buttering up the *Globe* drama critic, that there weren't any showgirls. *Dr. Jekyll and Mr. Hyde* wasn't a musical. But a bright-eyed kid arranging the opera glasses concession assured him they had plenty of actresses.

"I'm trying to run down a girl who read for a role in New York. Who should I ask?"

"Stage manager. Mr. Young."

"Where's he?"

"Running rehearsal."

"Why are they rehearsing? I thought they already played in New York."

"We're squashing Broadway sets to fit a Boston stage. If they don't rehearse, the actors will crash through flats and fall into the orchestra pit."

"What orchestra pit? It's not a musical."

The kid looked at Dashwood like he'd just got off the boat. "We still need music. *Incidental* music. How we gonna introduce scenes and fire up drama?"

The young detective slipped inside the empty house and waited while his eyes adjusted to the dim lighting. Rows and rows of seats were empty, except for two large codgers in silk top hats, and a lanky fellow with a tangle of long hair and a scraggly beard.

Dashwood eased quietly down the rows and sat when he was close enough to distinguish faces on the stage.

Beautiful actresses were rehearsing getting strangled.

"Say, kid?" he whispered to the opera glasses boy, who was hustling down the aisle with an armload of programs. "How come both guys are strangling them?"

"Mr. Barrett and Mr. Buchanan exchange the roles of Dr.

Jekyll and Mr. Hyde. They have to rehearse both as villain and hero."

Jackson Barrett and John Buchanan actually looked quite similar—so alike, they could pass for brothers. They were big, vigorous men in their early forties and Arrow Collar model handsome, except when one did the strangling. Then, while the stage lights grew faint, his whole stance changed. Hunched low, expression transformed, Mr. Hyde appeared smaller yet, in some mysterious way, even stronger, and left no doubt he would make short work of the girls.

"Who are the rich guys?"

"Angels."

"What?"

"Our investors—Mr. Deaver and Mr. Deaver—the moneybags."

"And who's the scraggly fellow over there?"

The boy looked where Dashwood had nodded. His cheery expression darkened. "The troublemaker."

Dashwood looked more closely. "The troublemaker" was younger, early forties, than his appearance suggested. "What's he doing here?"

"Snuck in like you."

A woman screamed.

The cry of abject terror whipped Dashwood's head around. She wasn't on the stage but somewhere in the dimly lit rows of empty seats. The detective was up in a flash, running to help, a hand plunging for the pistol under his coat. She screamed again. Now he saw her across the empty rows. She stumbled, wracked with convulsions, clutched her breast, and collapsed into the aisle.

"Miss Gold!" thundered a strong voice from the stage.

Mr. Hyde had straightened up to John Buchanan's full height.

The fainting victim scrambled to her feet. "Yes, Mr. Buchanan?"

"One piercing shriek will suffice, Miss Gold."

"I'm sorry, Mr. Buchanan. I thought the moment required—"

Jackson Barrett strode forward and cut her off in tones as thundery as his partner. "Young lady, we plant you in the audience to 'faint from terror,' to encourage the rumors that our grisly Mr. Hyde will so overly stimulate Boston ladies that they swoon. The 'moment requires' that you convince potential ticket buyers—*not* overly distract the audience that's already purchased tickets to see me and Mr. Buchanan and Miss Cook onstage."

"Yes, Mr. Barrett."

"Get back on the floor."

"Stretcher bearers," roared Buchanan. "Enter and exit swiftly."

Actors, clad in white like hospital orderlies and a nurse, raced down the aisle. They rolled Miss Gold onto their stretcher and hauled her away, with the nurse trotting alongside taking her pulse.

The rehearsal resumed.

An incredibly beautiful actress entered, and Dashwood recognized the famous Isabella Cook, whose picture was on every magazine stand. She seemed to glow in the light. Buchanan burst from the shadows, hunched as Mr. Hyde, and growled at her. Before she could recoil, the shabby man with the long hair jumped from his seat, shouting,

"Those are my words! I wrote that."

Barrett and Buchanan advanced to the edge of the stage,

shoulder to shoulder, and peered into the lights. "Who's that out front?"

"I wrote that. You stole my words."

"Good Lord," shouted Barrett. "It's Cox—again. Out, damned liar!"

Buchanan ordered, "Remove that fool from this theater."

"I wrote that. Those are my words."

"Mr. Rick L. Cox, you are a lunatic, get OUT of our theater!"

Ushers stormed down the aisle and dragged Rick L. Cox out the doors.

"Mr. Young!" demanded Buchanan. "How did he get in here?"

Young, whom Dashwood had already determined was the stage manager, ran to them, wringing his hands. "I am terribly sorry, Mr. Barrett, Mr. Buchanan. It won't happen again."

"Bloody well better not."

"Crazed lunatic."

The stage manager turned to the gaping cast and stagehands. "Ladies and gentlemen, may we resume, as we are *raising the curtain in six hours*?"

Rehearsal continued.

Dashwood established from a purloined program that the stage manager's full name was Henry Booker Young. Almost as tall as Barrett and Buchanan, and nearly as handsome, the rail-thin Young was bounding around in shirtsleeves and vest, listening to the stars, and hurrying down to the orchestra pit to confer with the conductor. When he came out into the house to check the lighting, Dashwood trailed him back up the steps and through a door beside the stage.

Backstage was busier than a farm at harvest.

In a single glance about the high, narrow space, James Dash-wood saw crowds of actors and stagehands, enough rope to raise sails on a square-rigger, and a gang of cussing carpenters attempting to assemble half a New York City subway car. Overhead in the towering flies floated a full-size biplane—another "sensational scenic effect," Dashwood surmised. Riggers were struggling with ropes, trying to keep it from swaying, and Dashwood had a sudden insight that illusion in the theater was forged with heavy objects.

He made himself invisible in the folds of a curtain and waited for a lull in the activity storming around the stage manager. At last, Henry Young announced, "Lunch, ladies and gentlemen. Back in half an hour."

Actresses, actors, and stagehands stampeded into the wings, and James Dashwood found himself alone with Henry Young. He followed him onto the stage and froze, transfixed by the auditorium. It looked as if each of the thousand seats was an eye staring at him.

He edged sideways into the far wing and bumped into a table arrayed with knives, clubs, swords, and blackjacks. It looked like the aftermath of a police raid on a street gang. But when he picked up a gleaming dagger, he discovered it was made of rubber painted silver.

"Put that down!" shouted the stage manager, running full tilt from the opposite wing.

"Sorry, I—"

Young snatched the rubber dagger from his hand and placed it reverently where it had been. "This is a property table, young man. The props are laid out in the order the actors will pick them up. Never, ever, ever molest a property table. Who are you? What are you doing here?"

Dashwood straightened his shoulders and stood taller. "I am Detective James Dashwood, Van Dorn Agency. May I ask you a question?"

"About what?"

"Do you recall a young actress named Anna Waterbury reading for a role before you left New York?"

"No."

Dashwood showed him Anna's picture. "Do you recall seeing her?"

"No."

"Is it possible someone else heard her read for a role?"

"*No one* reads unless I conduct the reading."

"So you are quite sure you didn't see this actress?"

"I am positive. All character bits for actresses and actors were filled long before we left New York."

"There was no reading in New York?"

"None! Excuse me, young man, I have an opening night in five and a half hours."

"Thank you, sir. I appreciate the time you gave me." Dashwood extended his hand, and when he had the stage manager's clamped firmly in his, he said, "You know, sir. You look so familiar."

Henry Young preened, and admitted, "I trod the boards years ago. Perhaps you saw me in a play."

Insulting a subject was no way to get him to talk freely, so James Dashwood did not confess that he spent his small amounts of free time and money at the movies.

"I'm afraid I haven't been to a play since high school."

"I toured high schools— Now, young man, as I said, *Dr. Jekyll and Mr. Hyde* opens in Boston tonight—provided a hundred disasters are set straight in the next five hours. Good-bye."

Dashwood wired New York.

ANNA NEVER READ JEKYLL

Then the detective burrowed into the file drawers that contained the Boston field office's collection of wanted posters. Apprenticing for Isaac Bell, James Dashwood had learned the power that came from memorizing criminals' faces. He was sure he recognized the *Jekyll and Hyde* stage manager, and he wondered whether he had seen Henry Booker Young pictured with a price on his head.

8

An old woman walking a dog found Lillian Lent's body the second morning after she died.

The Cutthroat, who had murdered her, slipped among the morbid, who were watching the police detectives, cops, and reporters, and edged close. They had kicked aside his cape, with which he had so lovingly covered her, and had thrown over her instead a soup-stained tablecloth. That said all that had to be said about so-called human decency.

He moved away and edged toward the bench on which her life had become his before he suddenly had to drag her corpse deep into the bushes. A trysting couple had interrupted him before he could continue with his blade. This morning he had been unable to resist the impulse to attempt to recover the moment by inhaling the atmosphere.

The wind stirred the leaves under the bench. Suddenly he saw the white blur of a handkerchief. He patted his pocket, but even twenty paces away he knew it was his by the gleam of pure silk. White as snow, except for the red splash of his embroidered initials.

He searched his coat, found a half-empty packet of cigarettes, rubbed the wrapper against the inside of his pocket, then strode to the bench and knelt to retrieve his handkerchief.

"What have you got there?"

A sharp-eyed cop had followed him.

"What is that you're holding?"

"I noticed something that could have been dropped by the man who killed the poor girl," the Cutthroat answered.

"Hand that over!"

"I presume officers of the Boston Police Department read Mark Twain."

"What?"

"*Pudd'nhead Wilson*? Twain's plot turns on the science of fingerprint identification."

He rose with the cigarette packet clasped in his handkerchief and held it before the cop. "Don't touch it! Here, give me your helmet. I'll drop this inside, and your detectives can retrieve it at the station house without smudging the fingerprints."

The cop whipped off his helmet and turned it over like a bowl. The Cutthroat dropped the cigarettes inside.

"Thank you, sir."

"The least a citizen can do," said the Cutthroat. "Remember, don't touch it. Leave that to the experts."

He pocketed his handkerchief and sauntered off.

———————

James Dashwood got a long-distance telephone call from Isaac Bell.

"Lillian Lent, the girl killed in the Common, was she cut up?"

Dashwood wondered how the Chief Investigator had caught wind of the murder of a lowly prostitute two hundred miles from New York, but he was not surprised. "No. Just strangled."

"Do you know that for sure, James?"

"I saw her at the morgue with my own eyes, Mr. Bell. Only strangled."

"No mutilation?"

"No blood."

Dashwood listened to the telephone wires hiss. He waited, silent, knowing that the Chief Investigator did not clutter thinking time with small talk.

"How did you happen to be at the morgue?"

"You had your Anna Waterbury killed in New York, Mr. Bell. I figured it was worth checking for a connection. I spoke with the coroner. He confirmed there wasn't a mark on Lillian except for the bruises on her throat."

Again, a long silence. Finally, Bell asked, "Did you check her fingernails?"

"That's the one strange thing. She didn't scratch him."

"Any broken nails?"

"Several, but none that looked freshly broken."

"No skin under them, no blood?"

"No."

"Might she have been wearing gloves?"

Dashwood said, "She was not a girl who could afford gloves. Besides, she died quick. It looks like her neck was broken."

"Broken?" asked Bell. "By a blow?"

"No. The coroner said it happened while she was strangled."

"A strong man."

"Probably. But she was a tiny little thing. Wisp of a girl."

"But otherwise not a mark on her?"

"No cuts."

"Thank you, James. It was a long shot. Send me your full report. Immediately."

Isaac Bell hooked the earpiece, jumped to his feet, and paced the detectives' bull pen. Fact was, he could pace from 42nd Street to the Battery and back, but none of his leads, if they could be called leads, had gone anywhere. As time passed, it looked increasingly unlikely that his detectives would turn up a witness who saw Anna with whoever got her inside the flat where she died. Equally unlikely was the prospect of finding a witness— other than the procurer he had already interviewed at Grand Central—who saw her with any man anywhere during her weeks in New York.

He told the Van Dorn operator to place a long-distance call to the Philadelphia field office.

"Helen, I want you to go to Waterbury, Connecticut. Get Anna's mother to talk to you. Find out if the girl kept a diary. If she did, read it."

"To find if she had a boyfriend, who might have followed her to New York?"

"Exactly."

"I thought you were sure she didn't."

"I'm not sure of anything anymore, including whether the murder was personal. So we're back to the question we ask about every crime: Who had motive?"

———

"Who had a motive?" asked Joseph Van Dorn.

"A boyfriend, or a disappointed suitor, or a lunatic," said Bell.

"In other words," growled the Boss, "you've learned nothing about him."

The powerfully built, red-whiskered founder of the Van Dorn Detective Agency was a hard-nosed, middle-aged Irishman who had immigrated to America, alone, at age fourteen. Prosperous now by his own hand, "the Boss" had been born with little more than the charm and natural good cheer to cloak his fierce ambition and a deep hatred of criminals who abused the innocent. His manner, that of a friendly businessman, had surprised many a convict who found himself manacled facedown on the floor, having allowed the big, smiling gent to get close.

Isaac Bell had apprenticed under Joseph Van Dorn. The Boss had introduced the banker's son to the lives lived by people he dubbed "the other ninety-seven percent of humanity" and had trained a champion college boxer in the "art of manly defense" bred to win street fights with fists, guns, and knives. To say that

Isaac Bell would march into Hades with Van Dorn on short notice would be to underestimate his gratitude.

"Your report states that Mike Coligney's plainclothes boys found her body."

"The actor whose home was the apartment where the girl was murdered used his landlady's telephone to call the police."

"As well he should, for a police matter," Van Dorn said sharply with a sharper glance at his Chief Investigator.

Bell said, "He called the police because he had no way of knowing that Anna Waterbury's father hired the Van Dorn Detective Agency to find his daughter."

"What do you mean by that?"

"I mean that the client believed in us and trusted us. The Van Dorn Detective Agency is morally bound to find her killer."

Joseph Van Dorn shook his head. "The police have the men—patrol officers and detectives and their informants."

"We are more qualified to find the guilty man and build a case that sticks."

"It is a police matter," said the Boss. "Leave it to the police. They know the neighborhood."

"I've already sent Helen Mills to Waterbury to persuade Anna's mother to let her read the girl's diary."

"What for?"

"In case," said Isaac Bell, "the murderer didn't live in the neighborhood."

9

When the Springfield, Massachusetts Christ Church choir practiced for Easter service, every singer cocked her ear to hear Mary Beth Winthrop set the standard for the first sopranos.

"Lift up your heads,
O ye gates,
and be yet lift up,
ye everlasting doors . . ."

Tenors and basses responded,

"Who is the King of Glory?
Who is the King of Glory?"

Mary Beth Winthrop raised her eyes to the stained-glass rose window and prayed:

Faster. Put on some steam.

Glaciers rumbled at a quicker tempo than choirmaster Fluecher conducting the boys through endless "Who is the King of Glory"s.

Faster, please.

Mr. Fluecher heard a note he didn't like and stopped them dead. Rapping his knuckles on his music, he compared the tenors' pitch to a derailing freight train.

A fire. A small fire in a wastepaper basket.

The smoke would drive them out of the church and in the confusion no one would notice her gallop to the Shubert Theatre. *Dr. Jekyll and Mr. Hyde*, which had come to Springfield for a week, straight from Boston and New York, was leaving today for Albany. But not before Barrett & Buchanan replaced the soprano who sang "Amazing Grace," *a cappella*, in the funeral scene. A piece of a biplane had fallen on the poor girl and a wonderful opportunity had blossomed only five blocks from Christ Church at the Shubert.

Right now, at this very moment, they were hearing singers try out for the role while Mary Beth—who sang in perfect pitch always, "and even would in a locomotive factory," Mr. Fluecher claimed when he held her up as an example to the others—was stuck in choir practice. Not only could she outsing each and every one of them, she could also act circles around any girl in Springfield.

Maybe her yellow hair was not as long and thick as she would like, which wasn't to say it was stringy. And she knew she wasn't as pretty as the girls who couldn't sing on pitch. Not with her round moon face. Except, when she looked closely at pictures on sheet music and magazines, the stars' faces were as round as dinner plates—a shape that caught attention and projected their voices. So it didn't matter not being as pretty. She would get the part. If she weren't stuck in choir practice.

At last, it was over, and she ran all the way to the theater.

The sight of pieces of a New York City subway car rolling from the stage door alley on a freight wagon told her she was too late. *Dr. Jekyll and Mr. Hyde* was leaving town. Company members were walking to the railroad station, the stagehands were striking the sets, and the Shubert's manager was directing assistants on ladders who were changing the marquee:

MATINEE TOMORROW
ALIAS JIMMY VALENTINE
Direct from **NEW YORK** and **PHILADELPHIA**
"Top O. Henry Short Story Topped Onstage"
—VARIETY

Mary Beth Winthrop wandered away, numb with grief, until she sank to a park bench and wept. She had missed the reading. Some other girl got the role.

"Are you quite all right, miss?"

She looked up. An older gentleman with a kind face was leaning over her, balanced on a cane. "What's the matter?" he asked, and when her tears flowed harder, he sat beside her and offered a snowy handkerchief with his initials embroidered in red. "Here, miss. Dry your eyes."

She did as he said, and sniffled, "Thank you, sir."

"Can you tell me what's the matter?" he asked again, and Mary Beth Winthrop found herself suddenly pouring out every hope and dream in her heart to a complete stranger. He listened intently, nodding, never interrupted. When she was done, he asked, "Would you tell me your name?"

"Mary Beth."

"What a pretty name. It suits you. Don't worry, Mary Beth. You'll get another chance."

"In Springfield? Never. Nothing like this ever comes to Springfield. *Jekyll and Hyde* was my only way out of here. I'll have to stay home and marry some stupid—"

"No, no, no. I meant you'll get another chance today."

"What do you mean? For *Jekyll and Hyde*?"

"Of course."

"But they're striking the sets. They're leaving."

"I'll arrange it."

"Are you in the company?"

He smiled. "No."

"Then how can you arrange it?"

"Do you know what an angel is?"

"I'm not sure what you mean."

"In the theater, an angel is a man who invests money in a show—puts up the cash. So, no, I am not a member of the *Jekyll and Hyde* company. But they regard me as their friend. Their very, very good friend. Now, do you understand?"

"Yes."

"Are you ready?"

"Yes. Yes!"

"Then come with me."

He walked her to a small hotel.

"We'll go in the back way. The stage manager stays in the annex. But he wants it private."

"Isn't he loading the train?"

"He'll be saying good-bye to an old friend, if you know what I mean, before he joins the train. But before his old friend joins him, we—that is to say, you—will sing for him. Are you ready?"

"Yes."

"Did you bring your music with you?"

"Right here."

"Good. In we go now. Just let's make sure we are not spotted. Because he will be very unhappy if we inadvertently give him away. And you do not want to sing for an unhappy man— Oh, by the way, if you are shocked, you have every right to be. But please remember, not everyone in the theater behaves this way. There are plenty of happily married, faithful thespians—and even some stagestruck angels." He tugged off his glove and showed her his wedding ring.

Mary Beth clutched her music and followed him up the alley. He opened a door and led the way up a narrow back staircase, opened another door, glanced down a hall, then touched his finger to his lips for silence and started down it, with Mary Beth close behind. He opened the door with a room key, slipped in, and beckoned her to follow. It was a small room, barely large enough to hold a bed and a steamer trunk, where she would have expected an armchair.

On the trunk was the familiar red and white wagon call card you displayed on a door or in the window to signal the Adams Express driver of a delivery to be picked up. The call card partly covered an address written on a shipping label:

—DALE, ARIZONA TERRITORY. PPP RANCH, ATTENTION
RANGE BOSS PETERS

He closed the door, tossed his cane on the bed, and shrugged his cape off his shoulders.

"Look at me," he said.

Mystified, she looked up and sucked in a startled breath. She had not realized how compelling his gaze was. His eyes were a stony shade of blue, and they pierced hers with the concentrated force of bottled lightning. "Where . . ." she started to ask. Where was the stage manager? Her eyes drifted back to the address label. She recognized the sender's name, a deacon in her own church. "Where—"

He snapped his fingers.

"Look at me!"

The rigor in his voice rivaled the force of his eyes, and for an awful moment she felt that she had no choice but to obey. At the edge of her vision she saw his hands fly at her face.

Quick and athletic, the young woman dodged instinctively, whipping her head back and away from his hands. Only when she tried to scream and could not make a sound did she realize that he had tricked her into exposing her throat.

———— • —— • ————

Half the sport, half the pleasure of the game, was to plan the plan. Plan, anticipate, hope. And savor, knowing they would never catch a master of self-discipline and restraint. This time, the Cutthroat had planned as painstakingly as he had for Anna Waterbury in New York. Then all he had had to do was wait. And hope for the exact right candidate to come along. God bless her, she had. Unlike Lillian—when he found himself stalking Boston Common on sudden impulse—there would be no interruptions in Springfield, no lovers rutting in the dark, no unfinished job, no dog walkers, no cops.

The room was paid in advance, booked for a week. It was situated at the end of the hall in the back of the house. The hotel across the alley catered to salesmen, who were out working all day, carousing in saloons half the night, and stumbling home so blotto they would not notice a pig slaughtered next door. The room had its own private bathroom with a deep porcelain tub longer than the girl was tall.

10

———— ·—· ————

The express wagon driver swore to anyone who would listen that his horses knew how to read. Or if his team could not read, they at least had a fine eye for the shape and color of the Adams call card. He never had to tighten the reins to stop when they saw the red and white rectangle hanging from a doorknob.

A heavy steamer trunk bound for the Arizona Territory was waiting to be picked up, the charges prepaid. He wrestled it into the wagon and continued his rounds until he saw the company's one-ton power wagon, which ran on a twenty-eight-cell Exide electric battery and bore the sign THIS WAGON CARRIES INTER-STATE COMMERCE TRAFFIC ONLY.

He hailed the driver, and they transferred the Arizona trunk. "Heavy."

They noticed the return address and laughed. "Bibles."

The power wagon delivered the trunk to the freight depot attached to Springfield's Union Station, where it was put aboard an Adams Express car on the Albany-bound Boston section of the Lake Shore Limited. The train was broken up in Albany, the Chicago-bound passenger coaches hooked to the Lake Shore, the Adams Express car shunted to a New York Central fast freight headed for St. Louis, via Buffalo, Cleveland, and Indianapolis.

The fast freight was hauled by Mikado 2-8-2 locomotives especially suited to speeding on the flat, water-level line. They were scheduled to be replaced with freshly watered and coaled engines every two hundred miles. But the first Mikado never made it past Herkimer, New York. Steaming at forty miles an hour, it was suddenly switched off the main line. It jumped the tracks before the surprised engineer could hit his air brakes and plunged down the embankment into the Mohawk River, dragging five express cars with it.

Scant moments behind it, the New York Central's 20th Century Limited extra-fare passenger flyer was overtaking on the next track at eighty miles an hour. Like a cracking bullwhip, the caboose on the back of the wrecked train had been flung off its rails onto 20th's track. The rocketing Limited's engineer saw it in the beam of his electric headlamp. He slammed on his air brakes, threw his Johnson bar across its full arc to reverse his drivers, and prayed.

It was no coincidence that a top Van Dorn detective like white-haired Kansas City Eddie Edwards was riding in the express car on the 20th Century Limited. Isaac Bell had his best railroad specialists hunting a gang of train robbers, and Edwards was headed for points west, riding free. Van Dorns were welcome guests in the rolling fortresses when crack passenger trains carried fortunes in gold, jewels, bearer bonds, and banknotes. Amenities were sparse—a Thermos flask, a mail sack for a mattress, a canvas bag of hundred-dollar bills for a pillow—and sleep was interrupted to draw guns at station stops, but the famously tightfisted Mr. Van Dorn liked saving money on train fares. He also wanted his men rubbing shoulders with express agents, who had the latest information on criminals in the robbery line.

The instant the 20th Century Limited's brakes and back-spinning drive wheels brought the speeding train to a grinding, clashing halt, Edwards grabbed a riot gun. The conductor pounded on the locked door. "Fast freight on the ground."

Edwards piled out with the train crew to help, still gripping the riot gun in the event that thieves had caused the wreck. The veteran detective's instincts were proved right by the sudden crackle of rifle and pistol fire. The express agent ran back to guard the 20th's express car. Eddie Edwards ran toward muzzle flashes in the dark.

He established that three or four train robbers were raking the wrecked train with gunfire and that a single express agent was firing back from an overturned car. Then he leveled his pump-action weapon in the direction that would do the most good and opened up. The train robbers had the advantage of numbers and their rifles' longer range. Detective Edwards had a rapid-firing weapon and ice water in his veins.

———————

An all-roads rail pass personally endorsed by Osgood Hennessy, the president of the Southern Pacific, was among Isaac Bell's most valued possessions. He was greeted warmly on a New York Central & Hudson night mail racing out of Grand Central, and he arrived at the Mohawk River crash as dawn was breaking.

A wreck train was lifting a caboose off the track with a crane. Freight cars lay half in the water. Crates and trunks were scattered on the riverbank. Hundreds of yards of track had been torn into heaps of twisted steel and splintered crossties. The entire site was littered with spilled clothing, paper, and shattered barrels spewing excelsior. Clumps of those thin poplar-wood shavings that had cushioned the barrels' contents, tossed on the wind like miniature tumbleweeds.

Eddie Edwards greeted him with the lowdown.

"They chocked a switch frog with iron wedges. That shunted the fast freight onto that siding. As she was steaming at forty miles per hour, she jumped the tracks. And that's just the first thing they did wrong."

"What else did they do wrong?"

"Derailed the wrong train. They thought they were robbing the Twentieth Century, which was coming along next. She was doing eighty, and if they'd derailed her, she'd have flown across the river and halfway to Canada."

"That makes no sense," said Bell. "The bunch we're tracking never made that kind of mistake."

"They're not ours," said Edwards. "Just some amateurs who went drinking until it sounded like a good idea."

"I wondered about them working so far east."

"I got three of them chained to a tree. To call them criminals would be an insult to the outlaw classes. Sorry you came all the way up here."

"Might as well have a look while I am," said Bell.

Edwards showed him the switch frog jammed open with metal wedges. They worked their way across the torn-up siding and down the embankment. The wreck gang would have its work cut out for them, laying a new siding so they could position their crane to lift five express cars out of the river. There was paper everywhere. An empty steamer trunk floated, turning lazily on still water. Suddenly caught in an eddy, it drifted into the main current, sinking deeper and deeper. Barrels floated after it.

"What's that white thing?"

"Looks like a mannequin. For a show window."

"There's another."

A half dozen of the wax fashion display forms floated from a partly submerged railcar. "Like they're going swimming," said Edwards.

Isaac Bell peered intently at the debris along the riverbank and suddenly strode toward it. Edwards hurried after him. "What do you see? Is that another one?"

"It's not a mannequin."

It was the body of a petite blond woman, her throat and torso horribly butchered. Bell counted ten crescent-shaped cuts on her limbs.

"What are those cuts?" asked Edwards. "Like crescent moons."

"Same as he did to Anna Waterbury," said Bell. "Identical." Mystified, he showed Edwards his notebook and copied these in under them.

(/ Ɔ ∩ ∪

"Same killer?"

"Same monster." Bell covered her body with his coat.

"How the heck did she end up here?" asked Edwards.

"Which car did she come out of?"

The detectives wrote down the car numbers they could see.

"Syracuse," said Eddie Edwards, "is the Eastern Region Office."

Two hours later the Van Dorns were poring through timetables and manifests with the chief dispatcher for the New York Central's Eastern Region, which covered lines from New York City and Boston that converged at Albany, where the fast freight train had been made up.

"The New York Central & Hudson Railroad," said the dispatcher, "serves half the people in the nation. Of that half, three-quarters are on lines that could have conveyed the poor girl's body to Albany."

He pointed at a map that covered an entire wall and shrugged apologetically. A legend on top listed thirty-six cities, towns, and regions to which the railroad took passengers on through cars. "Are you sure she was not inside some container?"

"We don't know," said Bell. "Her body fell on the riverbank. Whatever she was inside of smashed open and drifted away."

"But with no address label, how are we to ascertain where she started her journey?"

"We will eliminate all places from which those five cars did not come."

"They came from Albany. They were loaded in Albany. The contents could have come from anywhere served by our lines, as far south as New York, as far east as Boston, and from any of the express companies. No, I am terribly sorry, Mr. Bell. But without a proper address label, I cannot help you."

"Find out whether any of the cars were shipped and sealed intact by an express company."

"I will try."

———

Bell fired off a telegram in Van Dorn cipher to Grady Forrer, who ran Research.

ALL PETITE WOMEN MISSING THIS WEEK
NEW ENGLAND
NEW YORK

———

Isaac Bell learned from Eddie Edwards, whom he had instructed to stay with the New York Central dispatcher in Syracuse, that one of the smashed cars derailed into the Mohawk

River belonged to the Adams Express Company. It had originated in Boston, hooked to the Boston section of the 20th Century Limited, and stopped in Worcester, Springfield, Pittsfield, and Chatham on its way across Massachusetts.

Van Dorn Research turned up a newspaper story about a Springfield girl who had not come home from choir practice. Her name was Mary Beth Winthrop.

The morning mail brought a photograph.

As had happened with Anna Waterbury, her attacker had not marked her face, and Bell recognized her instantly. He raced to Springfield. At the Adams Express office in the freight depot, he presented the credentials of an insurance investigator with Dagget, Staples & Hitchcock, a venerable Hartford, Connecticut, firm that was willing to legitimize masquerades by top Van Dorns in exchange for sound and very private detective work. Bell asked for a list of every item put aboard the express car that fell in the Mohawk River.

Ironically, the display window mannequins he and Eddie Edwards had seen floating in the river had been shipped by a Springfield factory. The mannequin crate could have had room for a body, but a telephone call to the factory eliminated the possibility.

"We pack 'em tight," said the manager. "So they don't bang into each other."

The only other item shipped that day large enough to hold a body had been a steamer trunk bound for Scottsdale, in the Arizona Territory. The express company clerk looked puzzled.

"What is it?" asked Bell.

"I hadn't noticed before. No reason to—the freight was pre-paid. But the shipper was old Deacon Price."

"I would like to meet Deacon Price."

"You'll have something of a wait. He was buried last week."

———

Isaac Bell hurried back to New York and assembled the detectives he had recruited to hunt Anna Waterbury's murderer. As was Van Dorn custom, they had adopted an informal moniker: the Anna Squad.

Bell said, "Not only did the killer assume an innocent man's identity to ship the trunk, he also rented the room where he lured her in the deacon's name. So any trail for the trunk has gone as cold as he intended. However, despite the effort he made to put time and distance between him and the body, we've been dealt something of an even break by finding this poor girl weeks or even months ahead of his schedule."

"How will that help us, Mr. Bell?"

In what did not appear to be an answer at first, Bell said, "Similarly, Anna Waterbury was discovered by chance sooner than he had intended when the occupant of the apartment where he killed her returned home to New York earlier than expected."

Detective Harry Warren, the Gang Squad chief, spoke up. "If it's true that these killings in New York and Springfield are connected, if they were committed by the same man, then he's had lousy luck twice—an actor fired and a train derailed. What are the odds of that kind of coincidence?"

Isaac Bell said, "You've put your finger on it, Harry. The question we must answer is, how many times has he had *good* luck?"

"Good luck?"

Warren and several others looked puzzled. Grady Forrer, chief of Research, nodded blankly. But Helen Mills, whom Bell had reassigned to New York after she managed to read Anna Waterbury's diary, which put a stop to boyfriend talk, and young James Dashwood, whom he brought down from Boston, both raised tentative hands.

"That is a terrible thought, Mr. Bell," said Mills.

"Yes," said Isaac Bell. "How many of his victims do we not know about?"

Dashwood said, "You're suggesting the possibility of many murders, Mr. Bell."

Silence settled over the bull pen.

Isaac Bell broke it.

"I am not suggesting, I am *asking* how many. And I am asking every operator in our Anna Squad, how many more before we catch him?"

Isaac Bell got home to Archie and Lillian Abbott's East 64th Street town house after midnight. Built only four years ago as a wedding gift from Lillian's father, railroad baron Osgood Hennessy, it had included within its limestone walls a private apartment for Archie's mother. She had lived there until she left to be with Archie's younger sister, who had borne twins. Now it served as Isaac and Marion Morgan Bell's home on the occasions they found themselves both in New York.

Marion had just gotten in herself, having worked late directing a two-reel comedy at the Biograph Studios. Her straw-blond hair was still pinned up high on her head so it didn't get in the way when she looked through the camera. The effect was majestic, revealing her graceful neck and setting off her beautiful face like a golden crown.

They agreed each was starving and met in the kitchen. Bell mixed Manhattan cocktails, sliced bread and toasted it on the gas range, while Marion melted cheddar cheese with ale, Worcestershire, mustard, and an egg for a Welsh rarebit.

She was a well-educated woman, with a Stanford University law degree, and with experience in business, before she began making moving pictures. Bell often relied on her incisive mind to talk out thorny cases, as she had unusual powers of observation and a way of approaching problems from unexpected angles.

"What about the girl in Boston?" she asked when he had filled her in on the grisly Mohawk River discovery.

"Lillian. The prostitute."

"You're sure your murderer didn't kill her, too?"

"Dashwood looked her over at the morgue. She was not cut."

"None of those strange crescents?"

"Not a mark on her."

"Only strangled? . . . Was her neck broken?"

"Yes."

"Do I recall correctly that Anna's neck was broken, too?"

"Yes."

"And am I right in assuming that both girls' necks were broken 'accidentally'?"

"So to speak. Both were small girls, and he would appear to be very strong. The bruises on their throats indicated that he meant to strangle them. There are better ways to break a neck, if that's your intent."

Marion pondered that silently, and they went on to discuss other things, including the fact that Helen Mills had discovered nothing about any boyfriend in Anna's diary; that Anna, Mary Beth, and Lillian shared a similar petite build and hair coloring; and the mysterious crescent-shaped symbols carved on Anna's and Mary Beth Winthrop's bodies.

Later, when his wife had changed into a silk peignoir that matched her green eyes, and Bell was watching with growing interest as she let loose her hair, Marion suddenly said, "But . . ."

"What?"

"But what if the murderer was interrupted just after he strangled Lillian? What if someone came along before he could . . . do what he wanted with his knife?"

"Then we would have three murders in a row," Bell answered soberly. "And be one closer to counting how many."

"How many victims he has already killed?"

"Exactly."

"How will you do that?"

"I've got to figure out how to get Mr. Van Dorn to gather our forces."

"What will it take to convince him?"

"More evidence."

11

Isaac Bell banged a perfunctory knock on Joseph Van Dorn's door and shouldered through it. The Boss glanced up from his desk, took one look at his Chief Investigator's expression, and spoke into his candlestick telephone. "I will call you back later." He hooked the earpiece, and asked testily, "What's on your mind, Isaac?"

"I'm ready to broadcast an All Field Offices Alert."

Van Dorn shook his head. "Field Offices Alerts are as urgent as 'All hands on deck' in a hurricane. But ordering every operator in the agency to drop everything to act on orders from the top is disruptive—even excusing those engaged in gunplay. That is why we seldom issue them, and then only for the most pressing matter."

"We have evidence of three similar murders of young girls in three separate cities," said Bell. "I'm not waiting for a fourth."

"*Two* possibly similar murders," Van Dorn shot back. "And one unlikely link in Boston. I said last week, Isaac, and I'll say it again, it's a police case. Let the police handle it."

"It's gone beyond the cops."

"Why?"

"Three murders in three cities," Bell repeated. "Local cops rarely talk to local cops in the next precinct, much less neighboring cities. And never across state lines."

"What are you driving at?"

Bell replied to Van Dorn's question with a question of his own: "How do you get us federal government contracts?"

"By spending ridiculous amounts of time buttering up government officials in Washington while the rest of you have a fine time being private detectives."

"Those officials are buying something priceless from you. Priceless and unique."

"What is that, may I ask?"

"The Van Dorn Detective Agency's broad overview from our field offices all across the country. Cops don't have that overview. Without it, they can't see patterns. They can't connect related crimes. They can't fit pieces of a puzzle together. They don't have the pieces."

"The Justice Department's—"

"No, sir," Bell interrupted. "At this moment, there are only two types of national forces that can put the pieces together— newspapers linked by national wire services and private detective agencies with a continental reach like ours."

"Newspapers?" Van Dorn leveled a meaty finger at the heap of cuttings that Bell had ordered sent to him from Research. "Have you seen this drivel?" He snatched up one and read aloud in a voice steeped in scorn.

> "The killings of the Broadway stage actress Anna Waterbury and Springfield church choir singer Mary Beth Winthrop, whose mutilated body was found in the Mohawk River train wreck, appear to be the brutal work of a madman as methodical and cunning as Jack the Ripper."

Van Dorn crumpled it in his fist and picked up another.

> "The case looks like Jack the Ripper all over again, the murderer seemingly affected with an insane mania to mutilate bodies as had the notorious Whitechapel Fiend."

He threw it down and read from a third.

> "The detectives seek a woman hater of the Jack the Ripper type."

"Natives tom-tomming in the jungle make more sense than journalists."

"That is precisely why I wanted you to read them," said Isaac. "The newspapermen are often on the scene. But they report little more than what the cops tell them. While the cops don't know what's going on next door. That leaves only the Van Dorn Detective Agency to collect and share evidence that can stop a murderer preying on young girls who are alone. Defenseless orphans."

"Anna Pape and Mary Beth Winthrop weren't orphans. Lillian Lent, in Boston, probably wasn't, either."

"Any hopeful young woman who leaves the bosom of her family to try to be an actress—or any poor farmer's daughter who falls to prostitution like Lillian Lent—is, in effect, an orphan. Alone with no protector."

Joseph Van Dorn said nothing.

"And no one knows that better than you," said Bell.

The Boss glowered dangerously.

The Chief Investigator and his old mentor knew each other as well as any men who had stood shoulder to shoulder in battle. Van Dorn knew that Bell had not finished arguing his case. Not only not finished but was about to play his "hole" card.

"Orphans," Bell repeated. "No father, no husband, no big brother to look out for them," adding with a sudden quirk of his lips, "No Captain Novicki."

Joseph Van Dorn shook his head, helpless to stifle the smile that softened his flint-hard eye. "Low blow, Isaac."

Back when Captain David Novicki was a junior officer on a sea-battered steamer jam-packed with immigrants, he had taken the orphan boy Joseph Van Dorn under his wing. When the ship finally landed in Boston, Novicki had found Van Dorn a family to live with outside the slums. He had looked in on him on subsequent voyages back, steering him into school and away from trouble. Nearly four decades after that fateful crossing, they were still fast friends. Joseph Van Dorn credited his immense success in the detective business to David Novicki, as Isaac Bell credited Van Dorn for his.

"Here's another low blow," said Bell. "We both know they're not paying clients."

"I never thought they would be."

Bell returned his smile. Then his handsome features hardened and his eyes grew cold, and he said firmly, with no reservation, "We're the only ones who can stop him, Joe. Van Dorns can hunt everywhere in the country. And we never give up."

"O.K.! Send the blooming thing."

———————

Isaac Bell telegraphed the All Field Offices Alert on the private wire, ordering detectives across the continent to scour their cities and surrounding regions for similar unsolved murders in recent years. He instructed them, as he had Research, to pay particular attention to disappearances of petite blond women. And he called for a fresh look at past discoveries of skeletons and body parts.

Bell followed up with personal telephone calls to offices within the limits of the long-distance system. It had been extended just this year as far west as Denver.

Field offices that Bell could not reach by long-distance received long letters sent by Morkrum Printing Telegraph.

Bell went to Grady Forrer's rabbit warren of back rooms to assign the Research Department the task of tracing news reports of unsolved killings. "I have a question: When did this start?"

"What do you mean, Isaac?" asked Forrer.

"Was Anna Waterbury his first victim?"

"Good question." Grady Forrer looked around at his army of unkempt bleary-eyed researchers. "You heard Mr. Bell. Do you have any questions for him?"

"I do, Mr. Bell," said a scholarly-looking, middle-aged researcher. "The victim's name was Anna Genevieve Pape. Why do you always call her Anna Waterbury instead of Anna Pape?"

"Because she wanted to be Anna Waterbury," said Isaac Bell.

12

"There isn't a body buried in L.A. that Tim Holian can't jab with a spade."

The subject of the oft-spoken compliment—Timothy J. Holian, the formidable chief of the Los Angeles, California, Van Dorn field office—shambled in and out of city agencies, perspiring freely, on a hot, dry spring day. He wore a battered panama hat that most private detectives would have long since handed down to a gardener, a greasy necktie, and an ill-cut sack suit hung heavy with pistols. He limped, having taken four bullets from the German spy Christian Semmler's gunmen, two of whom he'd shot dead, in the blazing Thief case shoot-out that had all but annihilated the Los Angeles field office the year before.

The compliment referred to metaphorical bodies—the secrets behind scandals. There wasn't a government clerk in the city's morgue, hospitals, and police stations who wouldn't do the Van Dorn a favor for cash or valuable information that could be used against enemies. If flesh-and-blood bodies were what Tim Holian wanted, flesh-and-blood bodies Tim Holian would have.

He soon shambled back to the office with lists of young women who had disappeared, lists of petite blond murder victims, lists of nameless bodies, and lists of mutilations. These he coordinated with lists his detectives had compiled from interviews with homicide cops and newspaper police reporters. Even after culling the unlikely from the likely, they still had a chilling number of strangled victims—six in the past three years, four of them hopeful actresses, one prostitute, and one librarian walking home alone.

Tim Holian telegraphed the results to New York, care of Chief Investigator Isaac Bell. He followed up by composing a personal letter for Bell. He was still writing it when the company wire rattled out a query from Bell himself:

EXPLANATION

Holian wired a shortened version of his letter, wherein he speculated that the extraordinary number of possible victims might testify to the lure of the filming of movies, a fast-growing business that drew so many young people to Los Angeles. This drew a second query from Bell.

WHY NONE BEFORE 1908?

Tim Holian wired back that 1908 marked the beginning

of a flood of movie makers from the East Coast. Then he speculated:

MAYBE KILLER MOVIE MAN

Bell did not reply.

——— · ———

Charlie Post, chief of the one-man Denver field office, took a fresh look at an awful murder that occurred only last year. The eviscerated body of a doctor's wife had been found in a gold smelter. She was from a prominent Colorado family, and her husband had been swiftly tried, convicted, and hung for the crime. The entire incident would have been a comedy of errors if it hadn't been tragic.

Whoever had killed her—and Isaac Bell's All Field Offices Alert had raised new doubts in a case that Post had never liked— had thrown her body into the smelter's charge hopper. Under ordinary circumstances, it would have boiled to oblivion. But labor and owner hatreds being ferocious as they were in Denver, saboteurs had drawn the furnace fires to ruin the smelter. The molten ore had cooled, and when the killer dumped her body, it bounced on a hardened mass of ore and slag, where it was found the next morning by scab laborers imported to break the strike.

"Clearly," the prosecutor had told the jury, "this doctor knew less about the smelting business than he did about surgery. Having butchered the poor woman like he was taught back east in medical school, he was tripped up by his ignorance of Colorado's most important industry."

Convinced more than ever that the case stunk, and emboldened by Bell's alert, Post raided his emergency expense fund to bribe a coroner's assistant to let him see photographs of the body.

"Son of a gun."

Her arms and legs were stippled with the shallow crescent-shaped slices that Isaac Bell had ordered him to look for. He wired New York. Then he found a saloon. The murderer was Bell's man. The doctor was innocent. And the best Charlie Post could hope for, as he raised a glass to toast—"Right and wrong"—loudly enough to catch the attention of the floor manager, was that husband and wife were reunited in Heaven.

———————

"Telegram from Texas Walt Hatfield on the Western Union line, Mr. Bell."

"Texas Walt Hatfield is a movie star. He doesn't work for us anymore."

"Whatever you say, Mr. Bell. But he still knows the Van Dorn cipher."

Bell looked over the typewritten lines of code and deciphered them in his head. Texas Walt—who had been masquerading as a stunt performer on the Thief case when movie makers hired him away to play cowboy parts—had not bothered to save money by reducing a telegram to a few words. The once famously terse Texan was no longer laconic, having gotten used to booming his movies in *Photoplay* and *Motion Picture Story*

Magazine. As Bell read his wire, he could hear his old friend's Texas drawl, which had grown more pronounced when he became a Western star.

> *Howdy, Isaac Old Son,*
>
> *Rode the train to Albuquerque, New Mexico, yesterday. I had caught wind of a poor little dance hall gal cut up real bad last October. Then I caught wind of your All Field Offices Alert and it struck me she might be up your alley. Turned out, she probably is. Not only carved-up but decorated with them little half-moons you was asking about. Hope it helps.*
>
> *Happy Trails.*
>
> *Your good friend, Texas Walt Hatfield, former ranch hand, former Texas Ranger, former Van Dorn detective*
>
> *P.S. Near as I can tell, she's the only one in Albuquerque. I looked into the other killings in town. All stemmed plausibly from misunderstandings between tetchy acquaintances.*

———————

Horace Bronson, chief of the San Francisco field office, who had just returned home from a stint running the Van Dorn overseas outpost in Paris, was greeted by a Morkrum printed telegram from his old friend Isaac Bell. This called for a three-track investigation. Bronson sent his apprentices to San Francisco's theaters and his seasoned operators to the Barbary Coast brothels. He himself killed two birds with one stone by visiting his friends among the police to establish that he was back in town while inquiring about missing young women and unsolved strangulations.

After wiring Bell his office's initial assessment, Bronson, too, wrote a letter.

> . . . I am somewhat amazed by how many and how long. Obviously, not every one of these girls' murders were committed by the same person. But many at least could have been, and they go back ten years or more. And the terrible thing, my friend, is this: one or two a year adds up to relentless slaughter.

Isaac Bell forwarded the Los Angeles, Denver, Albuquerque, and San Francisco reports to the detectives of the Anna Squad with a terse cover letter.

> The Anna Squad is now named the Cutthroat Squad.

13

Connections trickled in from the field offices, and Isaac Bell saw hints of patterns.

Some bodies were draped under bloodstained capes. The capes were alike, but not identical, yet all were standard factory-made items that could be purchased in ordinary department stores. The murderer could easily replace them without being traced.

Fair-haired young victims like Anna Waterbury, Lillian Lent, and Mary Beth Winthrop turned out to be mostly actresses in theater and vaudeville and the circus, but some were prostitutes. What these poor souls had in common was what he had told Van Dorn: these were girls on their own, without family or husbands to protect them.

Of the mutilated bodies, many had their necks broken.

Coroners and cops recalled strange marks carved in the girls' skin.

Bell told Joseph Van Dorn, "I stood in with the Herkimer County coroner. The man barely noticed these cuts. When I remarked on them, he wrote them in his notes as 'superficial stab wounds.' It never occurred to him she was already dead before he took out his knife."

"What do you suppose they mean?"

"I'm racking my brains. I have no idea."

"I think they're a calling card," said Van Dorn.

"Some sort of message," Bell agreed.

"Lunatic."

"But no less dangerous for it, and too slick to get caught."

———

Another pattern formed, the most disturbing yet. Some bodies had been hidden in old cellars, abandoned buildings, and deep woods.

"How many were never found?" Bell wondered aloud.

Van Dorn said, "You've got a monster on your hands, Isaac."

"A monster who travels. He's left victims in Kansas City, San Francisco, St. Louis, Chicago—the list keeps growing."

"A traveling man," mused Van Dorn. "A salesman? Or a railroad man? How long has this been going on?"

Bell answered bleakly, "The Chicago field office just found one of his capes in an abandoned lake boat. Inside was a skeleton."

———◆———

"How long" became almost unbelievable when Grady Forrer brought Bell a clipping from the *Brooklyn Eagle* dated July 24, 1891. The paper made the usual Jack the Ripper comparison, though to be fair to the writer, this killing went so far back that it was not long after the London rampage.

"If this is him, too, he's been killing girls for twenty years."

———◆———

"What do you suppose drives him?" Marion asked late at night. Bell had staggered in at two o'clock and sat with her in bone-weary silence.

"No motive of the sort we understand. He's not killing for gain, or revenge, or love. He's just doing what he feels like doing."

"A wild animal."

"I've been calling him a monster. The trouble is, believing he's a monster doesn't get me any closer to stopping him."

"That would be the same as calling him evil, wouldn't it?" Marion asked.

Bell agreed. "It's not enough to think he is evil. In fact, it's not even helpful."

Marion said, "I'm beginning to understand why the newspapers keep referring to Jack the Ripper. He's like an explanation for the unexplainable."

"Even though we don't know a thing about Jack the Ripper."

"What *do* we know about him?" asked Marion.

Bell had already observed that the further back Research delved into newspapers, the more recent the memory of Jack the Ripper, the more their reporters invoked the connection. Now he asked Grady Forrer for information on the actual Jack the Ripper. Forrer had anticipated the request. Waiting for him was a thick packet of yellowed clippings from the *Sun*, the *World*, the *Herald*, and the *Times*. The top sheet's headline read

CARNIVAL OF BLOOD CONTINUES
POLICE PARALYZED

"What do they boil down to?" Bell asked.

"Theories," Grady told him, "all unfounded. Speculation, all imaginative. Conjecture, all fanciful. Guesses, all hopeless. Jack the Ripper is said to have been a nobleman or a surgeon or a Freemason, or a Polish radical, or a merchant seaman, or a leather worker, or a butcher. All that is known for sure about him is that eventually he stopped killing women in London. Although exactly when he stopped—whether 1888, or 1889, or 1891—is hotly debated. Also debated is why he stopped. Did he kill himself? Did he die of natural causes? Did he get bored? Did he immigrate to Australia? Did he flee to Brazil? Did he settle down to a quiet life in the country?"

"Do they debate whether he ever stopped at all?"

Grady shrugged. "The consensus seems to be that if he didn't die, at some point he must have run out of steam."

Bell slung the clippings under his arm and found an empty desk in the bull pen.

————⟡————

"Where is the Boss?"

"Went downstairs for supper."

Downstairs was the palatial dining room of the Knickerbocker Hotel. An orchestra played. Every table was taken and conversation was animated. Bell waved to Enrico Caruso, who was dining with coloratura soprano Luisa Tetrazzini, but continued on a beeline toward Joseph Van Dorn, who was reading the menu at a corner table with his back to the wall. Bell eased onto the banquette, catty-corner to him, with his back to the other wall.

"Welcome," said Van Dorn. "We haven't broken bread in a long time. How are you?"

"Intrigued," said Bell.

"Good Lord. We better order first." Van Dorn looked up, and the table captain came running.

"Cocktail?" asked the Boss.

"Not yet," said Bell.

Van Dorn ordered a Manhattan.

"With Bushmills Irish Whiskey, Mr. Van Dorn?"

"Always— You're sure nothing for you, Isaac?"

"I am sure."

Van Dorn ordered oysters and roast beef.

"And for you, Mr. Bell?"

"Pollo Tetrazzini."

He waited for Van Dorn's drink to arrive and toasted him back with water when the Boss said, "Mud in your eye."

"O.K.," Van Dorn said. "Spit it out. What intrigues you?"

"There are a hundred theories about Jack the Ripper."

"At least."

"The one I find most intriguing is that he stopped killing prostitutes in London twenty-three years ago when he escaped to America."

"I've heard that."

"What do you think? Did he come here?"

Van Dorn shook his head. "One version had him killing an old woman on the Bowery, if I recall. Didn't make much sense. She wasn't young and she wasn't a prostitute."

"I read about it," said Bell. "It didn't seem at all like his other crimes."

"And yet you're 'intrigued.'"

"Not by that murder. No, what intrigues me is a question: Is it possible that the reason Jack the Ripper was never caught was he fled London in 1888 or 1889 and landed in America? Maybe in New York. Maybe Boston. And laid low for a while."

"Far-fetched," said Van Dorn. "How long do you think he laid low?"

"The first killing I've found that could be him was in Brooklyn in 1891. But the question is, is he killing again?"

"Now? 1911? That *is* far-fetched."

Bell agreed it was far-fetched.

Van Dorn's oysters were served on a bed of ice. He heaped a few of them on Bell's bread and butter plate. "That's exactly the kind of speculation we get in the newspapers."

"Agreed," said Isaac Bell, and challenged his own question: "Besides, wouldn't the Ripper be too old by now?"

Joseph Van Dorn raised a bushy red eyebrow. "Too old?" he asked silkily.

"We're talking about a murderer who committed his crimes twenty-three years ago."

Van Dorn said, "I suppose that from your perspective, a man past forty looks ancient."

Bell said, "You and I both know that past age forty, criminals who haven't been jailed tend to slow down."

Van Dorn signaled the waiter. "You see that soup ladle on the sideboard?"

"I beg your pardon, Mr. Van Dorn?"

"That big long one."

"Yes, sir. I see it."

"Bring it here."

The mystified waiter delivered the ladle.

Van Dorn asked Bell, "Tell me, young fellow, how would you characterize the poor devils who will soon not see the sunny side of *fifty* again? Decrepit? Flea-bitten? Feeble?"

With a cold smile for his Chief Investigator, the Boss hefted the heavy silver serving tool in his powerful hands and tied the handle in a knot.

"Too old?"

Bell swept to his feet in a fluid motion as swift as it was graceful.

"Thank you for your oysters," he said, and glided from the dining room.

"Isaac!" Van Dorn called after him. "Where the devil are you going?"

"England."

ACT TWO

LONDON (SIX DAYS LATER)

Set a thief to catch a thief

14

"Fact-based truth, Mr. Bell," Joel Wallace told Isaac Bell. "High-and-mighty Scotland Yard never nailed Jack the Ripper."

When Americans ran into trouble abroad—businessmen swindled, tourists with daughters excited by shady suitors, art collectors worried that bargain-priced Rembrandts and Titians might have been lifted from their rightful owners—the lucky ones landed in Jermyn Street at the Van Dorn Detective Agency's London field office.

Joel Wallace ramrodded the outfit. He was a short, rugged man in a loud suit, and he had made the Van Dorns a formidable presence in the capital city of the British Empire. The stuffier sort of Englishmen might be put off by his cocksure manner, but his brash ways assured Americans that Wallace was an aggressive detective they could count on, and word soon got around the expensive hotels and four-day ships: See Joel Wallace. The Van Dorns'll set you straight.

"The Ripper ran circles around Scotland Yard. They won't love a Yank reminding them."

Which was precisely why Isaac would not want to present himself as Chief Investigator of a private detective agency. Better to let the high-and-mighty peer down their noses at a humble insurance sleuth who was indulging an eccentric hobby on his day off.

"Toyed with the coppers," said Wallace. "Played tricks on 'em. You're looking at his biggest joke right across the street—Metropolitan Police H.Q."

It was a cold spring day, and the rain that greeted Bell's ship at Southampton Docks and pelted the boat train was soaking London. Canvas topcoats were in order, for the walk past the cherry blossoms of St. James's Park and across the Whitehall government district to the Victoria Embankment. Backs to the Thames, they faced New Scotland Yard, a double-wing, four-story building striped in horizontal rows of stone and brick. Soot-black Parliament buildings loomed just upriver. Scarlet trams rumbled on Westminster Bridge. Big Ben was striking two o'clock.

"New Scotland Yard—built the same year the Ripper started killing. One guess what the workmen found where they were laying the foundation."

"Half a body," said Isaac Bell. Five days steaming across the Atlantic Ocean in the Cunard liner *Mauretania* had been time to reread and ponder Research's newspaper clippings and memorandums word by word. A phrase from the inquest stuck in his head. The butchered woman found in Scotland Yard's cellar had been "well-nourished." Hardly a description to fit the alcoholic prostitutes Jack the Ripper had murdered in the Whitechapel slum.

Bell was also intrigued by the coroner's estimate that she had been dead as long as two months before her torso was discovered. If she was Jack the Ripper's victim, could she have been his first?

"Nowhere near half a body," Wallace corrected brusquely. "A third, at most. Torso, no arms, no head. Wrapped up in her dress."

"Her dress?" asked Bell. "Or a man's cape?" At the inquest, the cloth was described as "satin broche." He had checked with Marion. Lightweight satin broche made dresses. But heavier broche weaves were fashioned into capes.

"Good question, which I can't answer," said Wallace. "Who knows what happened to the evidence so long ago. Seeing as how Scotland Yard insisted the Ripper hadn't killed her—some other murderer did her. A couple of weeks later they dug up her arm. The Yard still swore it was coincidence." He laughed. "Like some other Londoner just happened to be stashing chopped-up women under H.Q. that year."

"Why would Scotland Yard lie?"

"How could they admit it was the Ripper? First, they can't nail the louse. Then he rubs their faces in it. Bad enough to have her body dumped in their cellar—a body never identified, by the way—but dumped by Jack the Ripper? Too much, Mr. Bell. They might as well admit they missed the boat."

Bell asked, "How corrupt were the cops back then?"

Like any field office chief worth his salt, Joel Wallace had made many friends in many walks of life. "From what the old-timers tell me, they didn't have their hands out as much as ours, but they kowtowed to the upper crust even more. Still do. A so-called gentleman has to go to a lot of trouble to be suspected as a criminal, much less arrested." He mimicked an upper class English accent: "'Our sort doesn't do that sort of thing . . .' At any rate, the newspapers thought Jack the Ripper buried his victim there. So did everybody in London. So did most of the cops, but not the bosses. Listen, he had turned the town on its ear. They'd believe anything, and they were scared."

"What do *you* think, Joel?"

"He'd have to be one heck of an athlete to carry even half a dead body into an unlit construction works in the middle of the night."

"Why bother?" asked Bell. "Why risk getting caught or breaking his neck in the dark?" For a criminal who made a practice of not getting nailed, taking that kind of chance made no sense.

"My personal theory? Jack the Ripper had it in for the Police Commissioner."

"Why?"

"Revenge for Bloody Sunday. There was a working class mob in Trafalgar Square. Socialists, radicals, and the Irish— England's three favorite bogeymen in one conveniently located riot. The Commissioner ordered a billy club charge. Cavalry blocked the exits."

This was news to Bell, who had had Grady Forrer's Research

boys go back only to the first Ripper killing. Proof—not that he needed it—of the value of traveling to the scene. "When was Bloody Sunday?"

"Year before," said Wallace. "Ten thousand men and women attacked by club-swinging 'bobbies.'"

"Does that make him a Socialist, or a radical, or Irish?"

"He could have been trampled. Or just an outraged witness. Don't forget why Britons hate each other's guts. Most are starving in filthy slums. The Army rejects four out of five recruits 'cause they're sick and underfed. Can you imagine eighty percent of American boys stunted by starvation? Sure, we've got poor folk, but ours can hope—better times next year. These miserable devils are stuck at the bottom forever. It's a cruel nation, Mr. Bell. Jack the Ripper probably figured to get some back by making the honorable Police Commissioner look like a fool."

"Or toying with the cops just to show he was smarter. 'My funny little games,' he wrote to the Central News Agency."

"*If* he actually wrote that letter. The Yard and the papers got hundreds of letters claiming they were from Jack the Ripper."

"He wrote it," said Bell. "Look at the order of events. The Yard posted copies, hoping someone would recognize the handwriting."

"No one did, and he never got caught. Fact-backed truth, he *was* smarter."

"I'll see you later," said Bell, and stepped into the street. "Meantime, find me someone who was at the postmortems."

"Coroner?"

"Anyone who saw their bodies."

"Sure you don't want me to go in there with you?" asked Wallace. "The inspector who my friends set you up with is a prickly son of a gun."

"I prefer to appear harmless," said Bell.

Good luck with that, thought Wallace as he watched the tall detective mount the front steps of New Scotland Yard like an angry lion.

———

Police constables picked for imposing height and remarkable breadth guarded the entrance. Silver buttons fastened their high-collared navy tunics. Eight-pointed Brunswick stars glistened on their helmets.

Isaac Bell presented his card.

While he waited for his appointment to be confirmed, he turned around casually and cast the eyes of a dazzled tourist upon the barge-filled river, the busy bridge, Westminster Palace, Big Ben, the bustling street. The sweep of his gaze broke infinitesimally, just long enough to signal Joel Wallace.

The rail-thin man in a bowler hat and guard's coat loitering outside the office on Jermyn Street had made a second appearance in St. James's Park. Now he was strolling nonchalantly along the Thames Embankment. A possible coincidence, but unlikely, as he had engaged in some camouflage by changing his scarf from blue to green.

London was Joel Wallace's town. It was his job to find out who was shadowing the Van Dorns. Chief Investigator Isaac Bell had bigger fish to fry in Scotland Yard.

———————

"Insurance, you say, Mr. Bell? What firm do you represent?"

Bell had already presented a business card, and the Scotland Yard inspector had taken his time reading it. But the angry lion Joel Wallace had observed had glided into the depths of its cage as Bell tamped down his own impatience to present the picture of an earnest citizen deferring to the majesty of the police. He answered, politely, "Dagget, Staples & Hitchcock."

The inspector twirled Bell's card in his fingers. Joel Wallace had chosen him because he had joined Scotland Yard in 1885, three years before Jack the Ripper's rampage. That made him a man in his late fifties and facing retirement, and probably not happy about either. "Prickly" was putting it mildly. He was haughty, arrogant, and deeply disdainful—and in no mood, as Bell had presumed, to do the Chief Investigator of an American private detective agency any favors.

"From Hartford." He let the card fall to his desk. "In Connecticut." He pronounced it *Con-nec-ti-cut* in the English manner, emphasizing syllables Yankees ignored. "Why have you come to Scotland Yard, Mr. Bell? Or should I ask, why did you prevail upon an associate of a Home Office undersecretary to ask me the favor of granting you an interview?"

Isaac Bell managed a cordial smile. "I just crossed the pond aboard the *Mauretania*. I'm on the trail of a Chicago jewel thief who calls himself Laurence Rosania. Perhaps you've encountered him in London?"

"I can't say I have."

Bell mentioned a recent unsolved burglary at the Ritz Hotel.

The inspector returned bland assurances that investigations were closing in on the actual thief, who was certainly not Rosania.

Bell said, "I'm seeking certain connections between the victims and the thief."

"I should think the loss of valuables to a criminal would be connection enough."

"Fraudulent claims. Rosania lifts your wife's necklace and you claim insurance on her bracelet as well." He produced a photograph. A remarkably elegant figure for one so young, Rosania was gazing blasély into the camera.

"This was taken upon his incarceration in the New York State prison at Sing Sing. Unfortunately, he gained a pardon and promptly went back to his ways. I'm fairly certain he has worked the liners, and I can't help but wonder whether upon disembarking popped up to London to crack a safe, then home free on another ship."

"That would take nerve."

"Rosania knows no shortage of nerve."

"Are you requesting Scotland Yard's assistance in the matter?"

The deferential citizen permitted himself a nonplussed laugh. "No! Of course not. It's not the sort of case I'd expect the police to grapple with. Conspiracy and all, if you can imagine. Far too complicated."

"Too complicated?" The inspector bristled. "Then what the dickens are you doing here?"

"I just landed from the *Mauretania*."

"You've already said that."

"Aboard ship, I encountered a ring of operators in the smoker who should interest you."

"Jewel thieves?" the inspector asked, with an expression that combined a smirk and a sneer.

"Blackmailers," said Bell. When he spotted them working up their racket in the First Class Smoking Room, he had seen a golden opportunity to get Scotland Yard on his side.

And indeed the inspector's smirk faded. "Whom were they blackmailing?"

"I don't know if you are familiar with the expression 'badger game' over here, but it involves maneuvering the blackmail victim into a compromising situation where he fears exposure."

"I have heard of the badger game."

"I deduced that they were working the badger game on a rich old geezer."

"Did you happen to 'deduce' the victim's identity?"

"His name is Skelton. I believe you would know of him as the Earl of Milton."

The inspector sat up straight. "Do you have proof of this?"

Bell pulled from his pocket five Kodak snaps of shipboard gatherings. He fanned them on the inspector's desk like a royal flush. "Of course, you recognize Lord Skelton. This man here is the ringleader. The young lady with her hand on Skelton's arm is the one who inveigled her way into the poor old duffer's stateroom. This surly bruiser pretended to be her angry husband."

"Why would they let you take their pictures?"

"They didn't know I had a camera."

"How did you conceal it?"

The tall detective smiled, a trifle less cordially. "How I conceal my camera could be called an insurance investigator's trade secret."

Yet another of the joys of being married to a beautiful film-maker.

"The extortionists persuaded Skelton to withdraw money from his London bank and pay them off at the Savoy Hotel this afternoon."

Isaac Bell tugged his gold fob chain and drew forth a Waltham music pocket watch. The lid was engraved with a speeding 4-4-0 locomotive that sparked memories of his first encounter with the Van Dorn Detective Agency. It hinged open at his touch and chimed George M. Cohan's "Yankee Doodle Dandy."

"Three o'clock," Bell said over the music. "They'll be at the Savoy any minute. As *Mauretania* is a British liner, I believe the blackmailers land in your jurisdiction."

The inspector thought so, too. Detectives were summoned urgently.

Isaac Bell filled them in on pertinent details including—thanks to the estimable Joel Wallace—the number of the room where the shakedown would take place. He declined a half-hearted invitation to tag along on the raid, claiming, "Anonymity is priceless in insurance investigation."

Alone with the now beaming inspector, Bell got down to business. "May I ask you a favor?"

"Name it."

"If you would indulge a hobby of mine," he opened with a self-deprecating smile. "A sort of 'Sherlock Holmes' hobby."

"Sounds like a busman's holiday."

"Perhaps for a real detective, but for me it promises excitement I don't often find in the insurance business."

"What sort of Sherlock Holmes case excites you?" the inspector asked with unconcealed condescension.

"I've become obsessed with solving the identity of the long-ago mysterious perpetrator of the Whitechapel murders—I am referring, of course, to Jack the Ripper. I am fascinated by the case."

"Many are."

"It's an astonishing mystery."

"You could say that."

"Would you happen to know anyone I could interview who served Scotland Yard that long ago? Acquaintances who might recall details of the case not found in the newspapers?"

"You flatter me. *I* was serving then. Still only a constable."

"A *young* constable," said Bell, laying it on thick. "I'd never have guessed. Well, this is my lucky day. Do you have a theory?"

"Of what?"

"The mystery of how the greatest police detectives in history never caught the cruelest murderer in England?"

"There is no 'mystery.' The solution is simplicity itself."

"I am all ears," said Isaac Bell.

"The Whitechapel Fiend committed suicide."

"When?"

"He drowned himself in the Thames in December 1888. Three weeks before Christmas. One month after committing his last outrage."

15

———————

"Who was he?" asked Isaac Bell.

"His name was Druitt," said the inspector. "Montague John Druitt, a barrister of good family. It was recognized by senior investigators that his brain had collapsed under the weight of accumulated horror. You see, the armor that deflects emotion in the lower classes wears thin as men advance up the scale. Druitt being of good family, his outrages were more than he could bear. He had no choice but to do the gentlemanly thing and hurl himself in the river."

"I see . . . But how does your theory explain—"

"It's not a 'theory,' Mr. Bell. It is fact. Just as it is a fact that if Druitt hadn't killed himself, we'd have very soon had him dead to rights."

"You mean that Scotland Yard was closing in on him?"

"It was only a matter of time."

"Fascinating . . . But how does your . . . 'fact' explain the Ripper murders *after* Christmas?"

"The Ripper's last murder was committed November ninth, 1888."

"Kelly."

"Kelly?"

"His victim of November ninth, 1888. Mary Kelly."

"Of course. Learning the prostitutes' names must go with the hobby."

Incensed, Bell said coldly, "Remembering their names reminds me that defenseless women were murdered."

"Quite. At any rate, that one was Montague John Druitt's fifth and final murder. His body was pulled from the river at the end of December. There were no Ripper murders after November ninth."

"How do you explain the murders in 'eighty-nine and 'ninety that exhibited markedly similar maniacal butchery?"

"Those were committed by other murderers."

"Also never solved?" Bell asked.

"Correct."

"Did you actually work on the case?"

"No."

"Would you know anyone I could interview about his suicide? Retired policemen possibly? Perhaps a constable who saw the Ripper pulled from the water? Or a detective who investigated subsequent murders similar to those that the barrister who killed himself had committed?"

"Why are you harping on them? Those murders were wholly unrelated to the Whitechapel outrages."

Isaac Bell mastered his mounting anger to answer like an innocent hobbyist. "It would be a feather in my cap—and what a boon to my insurance business to establish friendships for life in Scotland Yard—if I were somehow able to turn up definitive proof that Jack the Ripper drowned in the Thames."

"Ancient history," scoffed the inspector. "Stories of a quarter century past. Think of it, man. It's been twenty-five years."

"Twenty-three," said Isaac Bell. "Tell your retired friends I'll buy dinner for anyone who's got a story."

The inspector stared long and hard. Then, without a hint of a smile or degree of warmth in his eyes, he said, "You'll get more out of that lot standing drinks."

"Montague John Druitt. Oh, aye, governor, I remember Druitt."

"Did you actually meet him?" asked Isaac Bell.

The Red Lion in Parliament Street was a loud public house, blue with tobacco smoke, a short way from the House of Commons. Back in New York, Bell would have called it a cop saloon. It was crawling with constables and detectives. Even the elderly potboy collecting empty glasses looked like a pensioned-off bobby. It was conveniently around the corner from the Canon Row Station in the back of Scotland Yard, and the landlady was a looker who had young and old eating out of her hand.

The former constable drafted by the prickly inspector to meet with Isaac Bell had served his entire career in Scotland Yard's

Whitechapel H Division, retiring as a sergeant. He had asked for a pint of "mild" but had accepted happily Bell's offer to splurge on "brown and mild."

"Did I meet him? Face-to-face, I did. He looked like a scrap of wet canvas. Been in the water a month. If his family hadn't raised the alarm, we'd never have identified the poor sod. His brother recognized bits of his clothing."

"Poor sod? You mean Jack the Ripper?"

"If you say so, guv."

Bell looked at him sharply. He was a shrewd old man, the sort who chose his words carefully, and Bell heard a private message in his "If you say so" answer. The tall detective was couching his next question when he was interrupted by a sudden clanging of electric bells. A fire alarm, he thought, but no one in the pub took notice except two men at the bar who downed their drinks and belted out the door. The ringing continued, shrill and urgent.

"What's that about?"

"Division bell. Ringing a vote in the Commons. Members have eight minutes to get inside the chamber before the door-keepers lock it up. The bells are all over the district, in pubs and restaurants and hotels. Those two will make it. No need to find their trousers."

"Would you join me in another?"

"Don't mind if I do."

The barmaid drew more mild ale, filling their pints halfway and mixing in bottled brown ale.

"Cheers, guv."

"If not the Ripper, who?" asked Bell.

"How do you mean?"

"I get the impression that you don't fully accept Yard's solution that Barrister Druitt was Jack the Ripper."

"Before you read too much into your impression, mind you, the list of 'official' suspects reported by the assistant chief constable of the Criminal Investigation Division included the suicide."

"Who else was on the list?"

"A Polish Jew named Kosminski."

"What made Kosminski a suspect?"

"He lived in Whitechapel."

"That's the only reason?"

"He was a foreigner. And a Jew. And in and out of the lunatic house. It added up. In the mind of the assistant chief constable."

"Any more?"

"A Russian confidence trickster called Ostrog."

"Another foreigner," said Bell. Joel Wallace's assessment of Scotland Yard was beginning to sound generous.

"Another regular guest of the lunatic house and Her Majesty's prisons," said the old man, and fell silent as he sipped his beer. The division bell finally stopped ringing.

"Did the C.I.D. assistant chief constable favor one suspect over the others?"

"He was not in the habit of confiding in constables, which was still my rank in 1888," the old man answered drily. "But I do know, guv, that he struck from the list the insane medical student, and the doctor avenging his son who died of the clap, as well as a duke, a peer of the realm gone to ground in Brazil, and a horny painter."

"Who was the woman buried in New Scotland Yard's cellar?"

"No one knows."

"Isn't it odd she was never reported missing?"

"London's gigantic. Still, she couldn't have been from White-chapel. Someone would have said, 'Oh, that must be Maud or Betty, she's gone missing.' No one did."

"Unlike when Barrister Druitt was pulled out of the river."

"Right you are, guv. His family had reported him missing. It was in the record. They had people to identify his clothing . . . I thank you for the brown and milds, governor. I'm going to tod-dle along home now. Past me bedtime."

"Do you know anyone who could tell me more about the girl in the cellar?"

The old man scratched his chin and eyed Bell speculatively. "Well, if you really care about her . . ."

"I do."

"I'd talk to Nigel Roberts."

"Who's Roberts?"

"Retired early from the Yard. Used to be C.I.D."

"H Division?"

"Detective sergeant."

"Where would I find him?"

"Lincoln's Inn Fields. He got himself made keeper of the Lock Museum. What would you call that in America? Manager?"

"Or curator. It's after hours. Where would I find him? Right now?"

"He lives at the museum. They gave him a wee room up in the garret. But I would stay right where you are, if I were you."

"Why?"

The old copper downed the last of his beer, licked his

mustache, and flashed a yellow-toothed grin. "Word's out, a Yank is asking about the Ripper. Nigel Roberts could never put old Jack out of his mind."

————

"Mr. Bell, I presume?"

It was late, and the Parliament members who had run off to vote had returned, looking triumphant, when a striking figure with long white hair and glittering spectacles sidled up to Isaac Bell at the bar. He looked haggard but good-humored, and Bell had the impression of a man vaguely surprised to have awakened one morning to find himself old. There was a restlessness to him, a sign of the sort of impatience that Bell looked for in a top-notch detective.

"Mr. Roberts?"

Roberts returned a cheerful nod. "Servants are addressed by their surname in England. Better call me Roberts."

"Why does a retired Criminal Investigation Division detective call himself a servant?"

"Coppers are 'housekeepers.' Which is to say, Scotland Yard keeps the wrong element out of the right element's houses."

"Is that why you retired early?"

"No. Sir-ing my governor because he sucked up to Commissioners born in Mayfair finally reminded me of a lesson I learned as a boy—but ignored when I joined the Yard."

"What lesson?"

"Power pollutes. Obedience enslaves."

"Sounds like you were born in Whitechapel," said Bell.

"Close enough."

"How did you escape?"

"A rich silk mercer died back in Shakespeare's day. He left his fortune to found a school for penniless boys."

Bell said, "I saw you in the pub when I came in. Were you waiting for me?"

"Word got around you were asking about the girl in the cellar."

"Sounds like the Jack the Ripper case is still alive."

"To me it is."

"Did Jack the Ripper put her body there?"

"The newspapers said he did."

"I've read them."

"Everyone in London thought so, too. Do you know about the dog?"

"The Commissioner's bloodhound," answered Bell. The newspapers had had a field day when the Police Commission tried to track whoever had left the body in New Scotland Yard with a bloodhound.

"Not that dog. While the Commissioner was traipsing after his hound, a private citizen let his dog loose in the cellar. The Yard had searched high and low, but the dog dug up the girl's leg buried a few inches under where they had looked."

"It was *her* leg?"

"The Met surgeon conducting the postmortem thought so."

"How long had it been there?"

"Around two months. The general consensus was he went to the cellar twice. Buried her leg first, then dropped off the bundle with her torso sometime later."

"Is it possible that our cellar girl was a foreigner?"

"What makes you ask that?"

Bell said, "According to Mark Twain, London is a city of 'villages.'"

"Hundreds," said Roberts.

"The newspapers printed stories about her body being found in New Scotland Yard. And yet no one stepped forward to claim her body. No one said, 'Oh, that's my missing daughter, or girl-friend, or cousin.'

"In actual fact, a girl from Chelsea went missing back in July. Her mother thought it was her. Her description fit the well-fed torso—a healthy young woman—and her mum had the impression that her daughter had taken a housemaid job in a rich man's house. But there was no head to identify. Nothing to discourage the Yard from insisting that the Whitechapel Fiend was a home-grown working class fiend who restricted his depravities to penniless, drunken prostitutes. Much neater that way. Besides, who can be disappointed in our police if all the Ripper is killing are fallen woman who will die soon of drink anyhow? In the end, she is just another mystery."

Bell asked, "Could she have been his first victim?"

"The one who started him off? What a marvelous question. She could be, except for one wide-open question."

"What question?" Bell asked, and Roberts said exactly what Bell had told his Cutthroat Squad back in New York. "How many bodies did he hide so well, they were never found? All we do know is that our cellar girl's killing predated Jack's first 'of-ficial' victim."

"Polly Nichols. August thirty-first."

"You've been bit by the Ripper. You know the dates."

Roberts signaled the barmaid and ordered two whiskeys.

"Why don't we raise our glasses, Mr. Bell? To our Lady of the Cellar, a living girl who lost her life to the Ripper—or another monster like him. And then we'll drink to the Yard that made nothing of her dying but a mystery."

Bell tossed back the whiskey and signaled for refills. "I wonder why she was different than his other victims."

"Other *known* victims. How do you mean different?"

"Well-fed. Not poor. What if he had known her personally . . ."

Roberts shrugged, apparently uninterested in that line of inquiry, and Bell changed the subject.

"Have you ever heard of symbols being carved into his victims' bodies?"

"What do you mean by symbols?"

"Not wounds that would kill, but . . . signals . . . *ritualistic* marks that might indicate something, send a message. Or a code."

Roberts asked, "What did they look like, the ones you heard of?"

Bell had a curious feeling that the former police detective was testing him. He opened his notebook.

(/ ⊐ ⋂ ⋓

Roberts tugged his specs down his nose and studied the marks over them. "No. I recall no shapes like that."

Bell asked, "Did Jack the Ripper ever drape his victims in a cape? A man's cape."

"No, he covered their bodies with their own dress or apron."

"Did—"

Roberts interrupted. "Mr. Bell, you look like a man who could do with a haircut."

The observation was as inaccurate as it was incongruous, and Bell said, "Just had one on the boat."

"Would you consider a shave?"

"What are you talking about?"

"I'm going to send you to Davy Collins. Tell him I said to tell you a story."

"Who is Davy Collins?"

"A tonsorial practitioner in Whitechapel."

16

———————

Davy Collins's barbershop had a red and white pole by the street door, which was wedged between a dark pub, where men and woman drank in silence, and a tiny grocery with empty shelves. Its twisting stairs were so narrow, it seemed a miracle that his red leather reclining chair had been carried up them. An ornately coiffed barber sporting an elaborate curlicued mustache greeted Bell in an Italian accent so thick, he sounded like a vaudeville comic mocking immigrants.

"I am looking for a barber named Davy Collins," said Bell.

"Eet eez my Enga-lish-a name."

"Do you know Mr. Nigel Roberts?"

"Meesta Roba-sa eez retire-a cop-a."

"He says for you to tell me a story."

"What-a kind-a story?"

"A Jack the Ripper story."

The barber picked up a gleaming razor and demanded in harsh Londonese, "Who the bloody deuce are you, mate?"

Bell said, "I'll tell you who I am if you'll tell me why you pretend to be Italian?"

"Englishmen treat the barber from sunny Italy kinder than Davy Collins of Whitechapel by way of Ireland."

"I'm American. I'm kind to everyone."

Davy Collins laughed. "Fair enough. What story you want to hear?"

"A true one."

"The only true one I have is about the time I saw the Ripper."

"You actually *saw* him?"

"With these eyes."

"When?"

"It was the ninth of November, 1888."

Mary Kelly, thought Bell. The murder that the inspector had insisted was Jack the Ripper's last. "Night or day?" he asked.

"Dead of the night. Past four in the morning."

"What were you doing out?"

"Looking for a place to lay my head. I was knackered. Hadn't a penny. I was peddling a magical hair-growth elixir, but no one was buying." He flourished his razor again. "Suddenly I thought, to hell with the baldies, what did they ever do for me? Somehow find a way into haircutting instead of hair growing. That night, at four in the morning, I fell upon an honest trade, haircutting instead of hair growing. Took me two years of saving pennies to buy my razors."

"At four in the morning, was there light to see?"

"Whitechapel was blacker than a mine in those days."

"Then how did you see him?"

"When there is no light, your eyes see more."

"But not a man's face."

"A man's frame," said Davy Collins. "The shape he cuts. How he moves."

"A silhouette?" Bell asked dubiously.

"When he ran from the rents where Mary had her room."

"But only a silhouette," said Bell. He was getting nowhere, wasting his time. Roberts, for some reason, had played him for laughs.

"Until he ran through the light."

"What light? You said there was no light."

"At the end of the street was a lamppost with a light."

"In *Whitechapel*? Gas. Flickers."

"Like a candle in the wind—but bright, compared to the dark."

"How far away was the lamppost?"

"Fifty feet? Maybe less."

"What shape did the man cut?" asked Bell.

"Bounding like a hare."

"What do you mean by a 'hare'?"

"He ran like a boy. Fearless. Sure on his feet."

"But he couldn't have been a boy. How old? would you guess."

"I don't have to guess. I saw with these eyes. He was barely into manhood."

Which today, Bell thought, if true, would make London's

Jack the Ripper *his* Jack the Ripper—a killer no older than his early forties.

"Did he appear to be a strong man?"

Davy Collins shrugged. "All I know is, he was quick."

"Did you follow him?"

"Why would I? I didn't know why he was running. They didn't find poor Mary until the morning."

Bell shook his head. "Wait. If they didn't find Mary Kelly until the morning, then why was the Ripper running? What scared him?"

"The knock at the door."

"What knock at the door?"

"The fellow who came to collect the rent."

"At four in the morning?"

"She was behind in her rent," said Davy Collins. "Dodging the landlord."

"Did you see the collector?"

"No. But he would knock whenever he saw a light. That's why the Ripper ran. The knock surprised him."

"Did her room have a second door?"

"Not bloody likely."

"Did he go out the window?"

"How would I know, guv? I'm just speculating."

———————

"The shadow waited until you came out of the Yard," Joel Wallace reported when Isaac Bell got back to Jermyn Street.

"I saw him," said Bell. "He followed me to the Red Lion."

Wallace nodded. "I reckoned he was about to go after you, but then I think he spotted me because he suddenly hopped a tram."

"You let him ditch you?" Bell hid neither his surprise—Wallace was top-notch—nor his dismay.

"The man knew his business. Timed it perfectly. Left me standing on the bridge with egg on my face."

"Is he a cop?"

"Too slick. More like military."

"Military?"

"There's a war brewing. London's full of dreadnought spies—Germans, mostly, but Frogs, Japs, Eye-talians, and Russians, too—tripping over each other looking to lift new battleship plans."

"Was he shadowing you or me?"

"You," Wallace answered firmly. "I'm not working up any spy cases."

"Neither am I," said Bell. "Besides, even Scotland Yard never suspected Jack the Ripper was a German spy."

"Maybe whoever sicced him on you thinks you're up to something else?"

Bell pondered that. It was the more likely scenario.

"I locked horns with Lord Strone last year—Secret Service Bureau, Military Intelligence."

"The Thief case," said Wallace. "But Archie said you worked things out."

"I thought we did. Trouble is, Strone knows I'm not a Dagget, Staples & Hitchcock insurance investigator."

"Spies think like crooks," said Wallace. "Don't trust nobody."

"I tangled with Naval Intelligence once. But that was years ago. Long before Mr. Van Dorn made me Chief Investigator . . . Do you know anyone to look into Strone?"

Wallace nodded briskly.

"Make it clear we don't want to put the agency on the wrong side of the Secret Service Bureau—unless they give us cause."

"Understood, Mr. Bell."

"And cable Archie in New York. Strone keeps an estate in Connecticut."

"I'll get right on it . . . Look, Mr. Bell, I'm sorry I let the guy ditch me."

"Did you do any better with the postmortems?"

———

Joel Wallace had done much better with a postmortem witness, producing a Harley Street surgeon who had been a coroner's assistant back when he was a medical student. It had been his job to take notes. The doctor had a sharp memory and a cold eye, and he presented Bell with grisly details in abundance.

Bell asked him to comment on the speculation at the time that Jack the Ripper was a medical student.

"They gave him far too much credit for surgical skills. His dismemberments struck me as the work of a deer stalker who had experience butchering game. Or even an actual butcher. It was clear he used a large knife, whereas an anatomy student would have been trained to use a small dissecting blade. No, this chap knew where to separate an arm from the shoulder at the joints, or a leg from the hip, but that doesn't take a surgeon. Clearly, he was strong—he would have to be to wrench limbs apart the way he did."

"What about his ability to remove organs?"

"Again, he's earned far too much credit. His method of removing organs was to slash open the general area and tear loose what he was after."

"Did you see any symbols cut in the skin?"

"Symbols? What sort of symbols?"

"Did he carve shallow marks on the victims?" Bell described the crescent shapes he had seen carved on Anna Waterbury's and Mary Beth Winthrop's corpses.

"No crescent shapes," said the surgeon.

"None? I don't mean *wounds*. Marks."

"But they weren't crescent-shaped," said the surgeon.

"You did see them?"

"I saw L-shaped marks. Like this— May I?" He reached for Bell's notebook and fountain pen, turned to a blank page and drew:

L L L

Bell shook his head . . . Unless . . . "Could a slip of the blade make an L look like a crescent?"

"No, the L's were sharply defined by straight lines. L-shaped cuts, made with two strokes of the blade, on perpendicular courses. If that's what you mean by a symbol."

"That's what I meant. But not that shape."

"You could say the same about the V-shaped cuts, too."

"V-shaped cuts?"

The surgeon drew:

V V ⊀ ⊀ ⊿

Bell flipped pages in his notebook.

(⟋ ⊐ ⋂ ⋃

"No," said the surgeon. "Not at all like yours. L's and V's. Yours look like horns."

The British Lock Museum occupied a three-story brick row house several doors down from the Sir John Soane's Museum in Lincoln's Inn Fields. The hall porter invited Isaac Bell to browse the collection while he went in search of "Keeper Roberts."

Bell roamed the centuries-spanning displays of safes, hand-cuffs, door locks, and keys with an expert's appreciation. He admired a working model of an Egyptian pharaoh's pin tumbler lock and examined skeptically a German chastity belt. Drafts-man's drawings detailed the workings of the 1861 Yale cylinder pin tumbler that had elevated lockpicking to a fine art.

A thief-catcher lock—which Bell had heard of but never seen—was accompanied by an eighteenth-century lesson book for accountants. The book warned auditors tallying the estates of the deceased to beware of safes armed with spring-loaded manacles to trap a thief who tried to pick the lock. This one protected a strongbox, left open to show springs that had the power to shatter wrist bones.

A lock dubbed un-pickable caught his eye. The museum challenged the visitor to try, and even supplied a set of picks. Isaac Bell was using his own when Nigel Roberts walked in.

"You're wasting your time, Mr. Bell. No one has ever succeeded in picking that lock."

"It's got a lot of pins," said Bell, who maintained a light pressure on his turning tool, which he had inserted vertically to leave room for his pick. "Or it could be because they tried it using your tools."

He lifted the final pin and increased pressure on his turning tool. The un-pickable lock rotated open, and he looked Roberts full in the face.

"Davy Collins thinks that Jack the Ripper was as agile as a young man. Which you could have told me yourself, if you cared to. You also could have told me that Davy himself admitted he was 'speculating.' Whoever he saw running wasn't necessarily the Ripper."

"Who are you, Mr. Bell?"

"'Power pollutes,' you told me. 'Obedience enslaves.' Who do you obey?"

"No one."

"What game are you playing?" asked Bell. "Why did you send me on a wild-goose chase?"

The tall detective and the white-haired old man locked angry eyes.

"Those girls he slaughtered aren't my 'hobby,'" said Roberts. He started blinking behind his spectacles. "They are not pieces in a game."

Isaac Bell recalled that the retired constable at the Red Lion had told him, "Nigel Roberts could never put old Jack out of his mind."

Despite the games, Bell had to concede that something about Roberts rang true. Did he find the murderer as repulsive as Bell did? Did he truly care about the women the Ripper had killed so long ago?

"Calling him a monster," said Bell, "or naming him the Whitechapel Fiend, somehow denies that he was a human criminal."

"It also somehow denies that the girls were human beings," said Roberts. "And that makes me almost as angry as their tarting up their failure to catch him with a word like 'mystery.' It makes the Ripper seem like an unstoppable force of nature instead of the product of incompetent investigators."

"Jack the Ripper is not my hobby, either," Bell said bluntly. "I am not an insurance investigator on a busman's holiday."

"Then what's your interest— Don't worry. I won't tell. Besides, they wouldn't listen."

"O.K.," said Bell. "But tell me something first. A professional operative has been shadowing me since I got to London. Is there anything in the Jack the Ripper case that my asking questions would get me shadowed?"

"We've already established that Scotland Yard did not solve at least five murders by the same killer, plus ten or more after he supposedly drowned. Were they incompetent or did they prefer not to? If they were incompetent, they don't want to be reminded. If corrupt, then they don't want you to expose them."

"But I don't think the shadow is a cop," said Bell.

"Why?"

"I know cops. This guy is different. Besides, the inspector helped me talk to retired coppers. He must have known if I came to the Red Lion, I would meet you."

"Undoubtedly," said Roberts.

Convinced that Roberts knew nothing about the shadow, Bell palmed his Van Dorn badge and showed it to the old man.

"I am Chief Investigator of the Van Dorn Detective Agency. I am hunting a murderer who operates similarly to your Jack the Ripper."

"Do private detectives investigate murder in America?"

"Ordinarily, murder is a matter for the police," Bell admitted.

He told Roberts about his role in Anna Waterbury's death.

"I let her down," he said. "I let her father down. I will make amends the only way I can—by strapping her killer in the electric chair."

"I wish you the best of luck," said Roberts. "But I fail to see similarities to Jack the Ripper, who killed many, many women."

Bell described the subsequent murders of Lillian Lent and Mary Beth Winthrop.

Roberts grew excited. He demanded details.

Bell reported the patterns: fair, petite young women; their necks broken; their bodies wound in capes. He gave him the murders turned up by his All Field Offices Alert: the slaying in Albuquerque that Texas Walt unearthed; Tim Holian's account of girls killed in rising numbers that paralleled the movie business shift to Los Angeles; Bronson's raw assessment of relentless slaughter in San Francisco.

Roberts asked, "Are you saying that your murderer operates *similarly* to Jack the Ripper? Or are you saying that he is actually *one and the same*, Jack the Ripper?"

"I was told at the Yard that Jack the Ripper drowned himself in the Thames."

"I do not believe you left America in the midst of a murder investigation to study the habits of famous killers. I ask you again, are you speculating that your man is actually Jack the Ripper?"

"Whether he is hinges largely on how old he was when he killed in London. Was he as young as Davy Collins suggests? Keeping in mind that no one knows for sure whether Davy Collins saw the actual Ripper or someone else."

Roberts shook his head and marveled, "It doesn't seem possible . . . But now I see why his age is so important to you." Abruptly he smiled and looked satisfied. "You're ready for Barlowe."

"Who is Barlowe?" Bell was wary. It sounded like Roberts was back to his games.

"Wayne Barlowe was a newspaper artist who drew for the *Illustrated News*. You'll have seen his drawings in your research. Try to get him to tell you a story. Tell him I told you to ask him to tell you a story. If he asks which story, tell him the one I never believed."

"Will his story tell me the Ripper's age?"

"I was told that Wayne Barlowe interviewed a woman who

saw Jack the Ripper up close. I asked, repeatedly, whether what I heard was true. Barlowe won't tell me. In fact, he cut me off. You may have better luck, not being with the Yard."

"Will he tell me the Ripper's age?" Bell repeated harshly.

"With any luck, you can tell his age yourself."

"How?"

"When you see the Ripper's face."

17

The Cutthroat walked on a railroad track with a girl in his arms.

"I love American rivers," he told her.

The Ohio River was tearing alongside them in the dark. It made a sound that seemed to blend far-off thunder and the slither of an enormous snake.

"Your rivers are mighty compared to the Thames."

He laughed softly. "Even in flood, the Thames can't hold a candle to your rivers. Yours drain mountains—ours mere hills—and valleys as broad as all England."

Swelled by melting snow and spring rains, they uprooted trees, smashed steamboats, scoured soil, and swept drowned cattle, men, and women to distant oceans. A floating body raced on the surface, pummeled by waves and driftwood. A body that sank was hurtled over the river bottom in a corrosive slurry of mud and water.

"The Mississippi is my favorite," he said. "But we'll make do with the Ohio tonight— Not to worry. It will take you to the Mississippi in a week or so."

Scraped, battered, and unrecognizable where the rivers joined at Cairo. A month or so later, seagulls would feast in the Gulf of Mexico. "Show me no body," he told her, "and I'll show you the perfect crime . . . Let me count the ways."

Fires—that'll teach her to smoke in bed. Fresh-dug cellars before they cement the floor. Shallow graves where only coyotes sniff her out. Played-out quarries. Smelters. Oil refineries. Distilleries. An overgrown mine shaft in Pennsylvania once, where, judging by the stink, someone else had the same idea. "But this is true, my dear—for crisp, clean, ease of disposal, nothing beats a river."

His night vision was superb, and he walked sure-footedly toward an abandoned coal wharf where riverboats took on fuel before the railroads put them out of business. Suddenly he stopped, cocked his ear, and listened hard.

"Do you hear that?"

Voices singing:

> *"Put your arms around me, honey, hold me tight.*
> *Huddle up and cuddle up with all your might.*
> *Oh, babe . . ."*

The Cutthroat spotted them in the starlight, stumbling toward him on the train tracks. A pair of drunks harmonizing, or so they thought, Collins and Harlan's hit Victor recording from *Madame Sherry*. Strapping men, he saw as they drew closer, work-hardened day laborers, young, quick, and barely slowed by the booze. Even though they were having trouble remembering the words:

> *"When they look at me, my heart begins to float,*
> *Then it starts a-rockin' like a motorboat.*
> *Oooh-ooh, I never knew any gal like you."*

They finally noticed him ten feet in front of them, lurched to a halt, and looked him over.

"Whatcha got there, mister?"

"The young lady had a bit much to drink," said the Cutthroat. They snickered.

The bigger one said, "So now you're gonna have a bit much of her."

"What did you say?"

"I said, you're carrying her down the tracks into the dark so you can have her before she comes to." He turned to his friend. "You know somethin', Vern? Seeing as how there's two of us and only one a him, we're going first."

He turned back to the Cutthroat. "You can have seconds."

"Thirds," said Vern.

The Cutthroat opened his arms. The girl fell hard, audibly cracking her head on one of the rails. The cape he had wrapped around her flew open.

"What did you do that for?" the bigger drunk howled. "You want to kill her?"

"Ain't gonna be no fun dead . . ." said Vern. His voice trailed off as he moved closer.

"Jimbo, you see what I see?"

"Oh, man, she fell on her head, busted her neck."

"Look again, you idiot. She was already dead."

Jimbo leaned over the body. He fumbled a match from his clothing and raked it across his belt buckle. The Cutthroat closed one eye and slitted the other. Sulfur flamed, half blinding them both.

"I'll be damned. He cut her head almost off."

"And look what he did to her—"

The Cutthroat's cane hung from a strap looped around his wrist. When the match went out, he drew his sword from the cane and whipped the bloody blade to the bigger man's throat. "Do exactly what I tell you, Jimbo."

Jimbo's hands shot up in the air. "Easy, mister. Easy. Take it easy. We're not telling anyone, we're just going to—"

"Do exactly what I tell you, Jimbo. Are you ready?"

"Yeah, yeah, just don't—"

"Punch that man in the mouth as hard as you can."

"What—"

"Don't hold back. If you hold back, I will slash your throat wide open." He could have said "like hers" but did not have to. Jimbo had seen plenty in the flare of the match. *Now!*

The smaller man didn't move. He just gaped in disbelief. Jimbo's fist struck him full in the mouth, knocking in teeth, and slamming him half conscious on his back.

Jimbo said, "I'm sorry, Vern. He made me—"

"Turn around, Jimbo."

"You said you wouldn't stick me."

"I will not 'stick' you. Turn around!"

The Cutthroat swung his cane with all his strength. Reinforced with steel, heavier than it looked, it caved a shard of bone into Jimbo's temple, dropping him on top of his groaning friend. The Cutthroat sheathed his sword in his cane and picked up a chunk of heavy track ballast in each hand and pounded at both men's heads. When they were dead, he felt in their clothing for their rotgut bottle.

He raised it by the neck, high to the stars, and smashed it down on Jimbo's shattered temple. Broken glass and whiskey sprayed the bodies. Then he stepped back and cast a shrewd eye on his handiwork. Whether or not a train ran them over in the dark, if Sherlock Holmes himself discovered them in the daylight, even the great detective would deduce that Jimbo and Vern had killed each other in a drunken fight.

He wrapped the girl in his cape again and lifted her tenderly into his arms and continued walking to the coal wharf, marking its location by ghostly shadows that trees growing out of the long-abandoned structure thrust against the stars. Closer, he saw the silhouettes of mooring bollards. The dock planks were rotten, and he took care to walk where underlying joists would take their weight.

Her hair was bright as straw, and when he lowered her into the Ohio River, the water splayed it like a halo. Air captured in the cape held her afloat. An eddy formed a patch of still water beside the wharf, and it took a while before the current bit a hold and swept her into the dark.

"Good-bye. You were everything I hoped for."

18

"Poor Detective Roberts."

Wayne Barlowe laughed.

Isaac Bell had found the illustrator's loft in a spacious Chelsea garret with a skylight in the north-sloping roof. While retired Scotland Yard C.I.D. Detective Sergeant Roberts could pass as an artist, with his long silver hair and glittery spectacles, the actual artist Wayne Barlowe resembled a policeman—squat as a fireplug, with an expressionless face pockmarked like a firing squad wall.

"What do you find funny about 'poor Detective Roberts'?" asked Bell. Barlowe had already struck him as another game player like Roberts, and the tall detective was fed up with game players.

"Just when Roberts is finally on the verge of giving up identifying the 'greatest monster of the Victorian Age,' Mr. Isaac Bell, insurance adjuster and amateur sleuth, arrives from America with a beguiling theory that the 'greatest monster' is going strong abroad."

Barlowe had works in progress on several easels, blank sketch pads on others. On the biggest, he was drawing, in fine-lined pen and ink, a sperm whale ramming a boat with its head and splintering another with its tail. Bell had never seen a whale more malevolent, and he said as much, reckoning that such skills might reproduce accurately a description of Jack the Ripper's face.

Barlowe ducked his head modestly and thanked him for the compliment.

"Nigel Roberts heard a rumor that you interviewed a woman who saw Jack the Ripper up close. I've studied your drawings in the newspapers, but I have never seen one that includes his face."

"I never drew his face."

"But did you hear him described by the woman who saw him?"

"The rumor is true."

"May I ask why you won't tell Roberts what she said?"

"Roberts thought I was daft. But Roberts was a copper. So he couldn't speak to the people who trusted me. He obviously did not admit it to you, but the fact is, I did tell him what she said. I just wouldn't draw it."

"What did he look like?"

"What did he look like?" Barlowe mused. "Angelic."

"*Angelic?* Are you joking?"

The sketch artist picked up a pencil in his blunt fingers and walked to another easel. In seconds, a face was alive, its features and some hints of character distinguished by a few swift lines.

"A boy?"

"Handsome, isn't he?"

Bell shook his head in disbelief. "A choirboy."

"As I said, angelic."

Bell stared, shaking his head. "Do you think he really did look like this?"

"Had the young woman ever made the acquaintance of a Bible, she'd have sworn on a stack of them. She truly believed he looked like this, even though he scared the daylights out of her."

"How did he frighten her if he looked so innocent?"

"He cornered her in Hanbury Street."

"That's where he killed Annie Chapman," said Bell.

"Same exact place. Number 29 Hanbury Street. An alley leads into a backyard. Chapman was next. First time he tried it was this girl. Grabbed her throat in both his hands."

"How did she get loose?"

"I don't know if you have any conception of the life these women live. It's no better now than back then. You can see it in any slum street that hasn't been cleared. And many that have . . . The girl had wandered all night in the rain, seeking clients to raise the price of a bed to sleep in but spending it on drink instead. Out in the rain to earn the money again. By the time the Ripper cornered her, she was soaked to the skin. Dripping wet, head to toe. His hands slipped. She ran."

Barlowe tossed his pencil on the easel tray and stalked back to his whale.

Set in the back of the house away from street noise, the atelier grew quiet but for the occasional, distant huff of locomotives crossing the Battersea Railway Bridge and the scratching of Barlowe's steel pen.

"What was her name?" Bell asked.

"Emily."

Bell pondered what he had heard. "I think I understand why you never drew his face."

"And why is that, Mr. Bell? I would like to know. Because I have asked myself a thousand times, could I have stopped the Ripper from killing God knows how many more girls if I had?"

"No one would believe that this handsome boy would hurt anyone. In fact, they would even find it impossible to believe he would patronize a prostitute."

"Not when he could have any girl in London with his smile. My editors would have laughed me out of their office."

Bell saw that Barlowe was deeply distressed and thought he knew why. The tall detective moved closer and arrowed the full force of his probing gaze into the artist's eyes. "Or, were you afraid you might finger the wrong man?"

Barlowe stared, silent for a full minute, before he whispered, "What if . . ." He paused to compose himself. "What if in her terror and panic, she imagined another face? A different face. A boy she might have admired from a distance? Or a handsome young gentleman—it seems a gentleman's face, wouldn't you agree?—a youth in clean clothes and utterly unattainable? Couldn't even the poorest creature experience a romantic crush? . . . But . . . What if he were recognized—this innocent, whose face I sketched for the newspapers and posters? If the mob didn't kick him to death, they would hang him from a lamppost."

"Didn't you think to ask her again later, after she calmed down?"

"Of course! I waited a week. I went to her regular spots. Couldn't find her. Spoke with a woman who had known her. She told me that Emily was afraid the Ripper would come back for her. She was so frightened that she kept running. She left Whitechapel. Left London—half mad with fear, she must have been. I was told later that the poor thing ran all the way to Angel Meadow."

"Where is that?"

"Manchester. And if you think Whitechapel is rotten, you should see Angel Meadow. Thousands of workers' tenements built on top of a paupers' graveyard. Twenty-five years back, it was even worse. Engels, who you may recall wrote the *Communist Manifesto*, and had seen a thing or two, called it Hell on Earth."

"Were you there for the newspapers?" Bell asked.

"I wrangled a commission. But I went looking for Emily."

"Did you find her?"

"Easily. She was famous, having come from exotic London. Slum dwellers' lives were so tightly circumscribed in those days. The Manchester folk called her London Emily."

"Did you ask her?"

"She saw me coming and she let out a shriek and ran for her life."

———————

"I need something to take to Manchester," said Isaac Bell.

Joel Wallace unlocked the two-inch oak door to the closet that housed the field office arsenal.

"What part of Manchester?"

"Angel Meadow."

"The poor folk are too beaten down to trouble you much. But for the gangs—they call them scuttlers—I recommend a U.S. Marines' landing party."

"I was thinking more in terms of an alley gun." Bell was opting for close-quarters stopping power that wouldn't mow down innocents.

"Number 4 lead bird shot," said Wallace, "will change minds up to five yards." He handed Bell a double-barreled derringer. Bell practiced loading the two-inch .410 cartridges into the stubby pistol until he could reload without taking his eyes off his target.

———————

Bell settled his hotel bill with the Savoy's cashier and exchanged pound notes for a sack of shiny half-crown coins. In an old-clothes shop at St. Katharine Docks, he bought a sailcloth sea-bag, a pair of rugged trousers, a rough wool undershirt, a frayed jacket bursting at the elbows, a pair of heavy boots that the shopkeeper said came from a steamship stoker's widow, a length of rope for a belt, and a sweat-stained stoker's cap that he inspected closely for lice.

He hailed a hansom to Euston, and changed clothes in the station lavatory. His disguise passed early tests with flying colors. The train ticket clerk assumed without asking that he was traveling third class, and a porter who bumped into him barked, "Make a lane, mate," instead of, "Beg your pardon, governor."

Drawn by the new Prince of Wales class 4-8-0 locomotive, the Manchester Limited glided from the station. Bell's train, a local destined to make many stops, chugged after it, accelerated in fits and starts between dark, seemingly endless walls of slab-sided brick factories, and lumbered suddenly into open fields that seemed impossibly green in contrast to the city. The fields were speckled with snowy sheep and, as the train continued north, were laced by narrow canals.

In four and a half hours, the train passed through factory towns on the outskirts and arrived in Manchester, an industrial city of immense modern cotton mills and a thousand tall chimneys. The opulent railroad station, banks, stock exchange, and sumptuous hotels and palaces, were monuments to the yearly weaving of eight billion yards of cheap checked gingham cloth that made "Cottonopolis" so wealthy that the only city richer in the world was London.

Isaac Bell walked to the slums. It was raining hard. The last time he had seen smoke so thick was Pittsburgh's infamous oily "black fog" that hurt to breathe.

Twelve pence made an English shilling, twenty shillings a pound. For fifteen pounds, grandees like the Earl of Milton and Lord Strone could charter a private train. Or a village could pay a schoolteacher's salary for a year. The prostitutes Jack the Ripper murdered had been hoping to earn four pence to sleep indoors.

Isaac Bell's half crowns—two and a half shillings—equaled thirty pence, and word raced like fire through the narrow lanes and fetid alleys that ringed the thundering mills. A tall sailor with yellow hair was handing out "two-and-six" to anyone who could tell him anything about an old woman known as London Emily.

Astonishment on the slum dwellers' faces told Bell that a single shilling would have done the job. Work in the mills was sporadic, depending on the markets, and low-paying. There were lines outside the workhouses that traded a night out of the rain for a day of work, breaking rocks or picking oakum out of old hemp rope. The Salvation Army soup kitchens were crowded.

He described London Emily as short and thin, with gray or white hair. Even if she had been only sixteen when Jack the Ripper attacked her, from what he saw of Angel Meadow, twenty-three years in the slum would have long since turned her into an old woman.

A pale creature dressed in a ragged shawl tugged his sleeve. "I'm her. I'm London Emily."

19

Isaac Bell shook his head. "I'm sorry, but you're half a foot taller than she was on her best day."

Against his better judgment, Bell gave her a half crown. It was a mistake that he would not make a second time. Flocks of old women descended from every point of the compass. Fights broke out as they struggled to get near him.

Bell took off at a long-legged run down lanes and through alleys until he lost them. But soon another flock gathered.

He was thinking he had to come back another day in a different guise when he heard a frightened cry. "Scuttlers."

The women scattered.

The street gangs had come hunting for the sailor with half crowns.

Bell had not seen a bobby since he entered the slum and did not expect to meet one now. They came at him from two directions. It took a moment to realize they were separate groups who had spotted him simultaneously and would fight for the right to attack him. Swinging spiked pickax handles, short, thin, scarred, and tattooed men and boys exploded into bloody battle. The winners dispersed the losers with a bombardment of dead dogs and rats, stomped the fallen with nail-studded clogs, and charged Isaac Bell.

Bell had already fished the derringer out of his seabag. Waiting for the leaders to close within fifteen feet, he braced against the recoil and fired one barrel. The hail of lead pellets knocked the legs out from under four men leading the charge. The remainder gazed into the as-yet-unfired second barrel and cocked their skinny arms to throw their clubs.

Bell fired his second barrel and ducked the only club they managed to launch. His hands flew. He broke the gun open, pulled the spent shells, loaded in fresh ones, flicked it shut, and took deliberate aim.

A flicker of motion in the corner of his eye made him jump back and protect his head as the body of another dead animal plummeted down from a rooftop. The scuttlers charged. Bell fired, backed into a wall, and fired again. In New York, he would expect Number 4 lead shot at point-blank range to send the toughest Gophers fleeing—the same for a mob of strikebreakers in Colorado. The scuttlers were more hopeless, more accustomed to pain, or more anesthetized by booze, and when the bird shot only penetrated a half inch into their flesh, they charged again, bloody and limping.

Bell tried to reload. The lead scuttler swung a spiked club.

Hands busy on the gun, eyes on the threat, Bell stepped into the charge, kicked hard, snapped the barrels shut, fired twice, and reloaded. The man he kicked was writhing at his feet. Two more were down on the greasy cobblestones, pawing at their legs and trying to stand. Bell took aim and walked toward the rest.

There was ice in his eyes, and even the bravest broke and ran.

Bell vaulted a wooden fence. He had seconds before they regrouped.

———

He tore through twisted rows of reeking backyards, vaulted another fence, sidestepped an open sewer, and emerged in a section of the dense slum where no one had heard the gunfire. Or maybe they had, for the lane he found himself in was empty of people, and the silence was so deep that he could hear the hollow roar of gingham looms shaking wooden floors behind the high stone walls that guarded the mills.

An old woman poked her head from a window with no glass.

Staring at Bell, she disappeared, then reappeared in an alley. She edged closer, stepped into the lane, then edged back, restless as a cat. She was tiny, her wrinkled skin pale, her hair white. Bell stepped toward her. She glanced about fearfully but stood her ground. When she opened her mouth to speak, he saw she had no teeth. That lack could be what slurred her tongue so badly that he could barely hear her. Addiction to laudanum—a tincture of opium suspended in alcohol—was the likelier cause, and laudanum would also explain her restlessness.

"What did you say?"

"London Emily. I hear you're giving two-and-six fer London Emily."

"So did everybody in Angel Meadow."

"I'm London Emily."

"A dozen ladies told me the same. How can I believe you?"

"'Cuz I know what they don't."

"What's that?"

"I know what yer gonna ask me."

Intrigued, though not yet hopeful, Bell said, "Go on. What do you think I want to ask you?"

"Jack the Ripper."

Bell shook his head. "Everyone knows that London Emily ran from the Ripper."

The old woman stepped closer to Bell and spoke in a stronger voice. "Not in Manchester."

"What do you mean?"

"I never told a soul. He'd-a found out."

Isaac Bell moved subtly to corner the old woman. Would she scream when he showed her Barlowe's sketch of a face that had been emblazoned in her memory before the Ripper attacked and long after the night of mind-rending terror? Would she run at the sight of the man who nearly killed her?

He pulled the stiff protective envelope from his seabag and carefully slid the sketch from it. London Emily fixed her eyes on it. She stiffened under her shapeless shawl. She stared. She broke into a toothless smile.

"Do you recognize him, Emily?"

She whispered.

Bell asked, "What did you say?"

"So handsome."

———

"Do you remember?" Bell asked gently. "Where did you see him?"

"Hanbury Street."

"Do you remember what number?" He was making a conscious effort now to quiet his excitement.

Emily nodded vigorously. "Number 29."

"What did he say to you?"

"He asked me, 'What's your name?'"

Bell waited. She said nothing more. He asked, "What did you tell him?"

She stared at the sketch with a half smile.

"What did you tell him when he asked your name?"

"I told him, 'Emily.'"

"What did he say?"

"He said, 'What a lovely name.' He said it suited me."

"What did you say?"

"I said, 'Thank you, sir.'"

"What next?"

"We went in the backyard and he grabbed me by the neck."

She was getting agitated again, and Bell tried to ease her mind. "Was he really this handsome?"

"Oh, aye. Even more."

"Emily," Bell asked gently. "Could you have confused him with a memory of a different man? Some man you had known before? Or seen on the street?"

"Who could forget such a beautiful face?"

"Was he really this young?"

She shrugged. "I was young."

"Are you absolutely sure he was the Ripper? Not someone else? Not a different handsome man?"

"Not someone else."

"Even though you had only seen him once."

"Not once! Not once! What do you mean?" she asked indignantly.

Bell felt the ground reel under his boots. He himself had speculated. Had the Ripper known his first victim? Obviously, Emily was not the woman buried under Scotland Yard. But was she someone else he had known, too?

"You saw him *before* you saw him in Hanbury Street?"

"Of course."

"Do you remember where you saw him?"

"Oh, aye."

"Where?"

"Wilton's."

"Wilton's? What is Wilton's?"

"Wilton's Music Hall. In Wellclose Square. I went if I could find a penny or a man to pay my way."

Isaac Bell felt as if the black sky had fallen on his head.

A young girl's crush, just as Wayne Barlowe had guessed. If not the angelic gentleman the illustrator had proposed, could a handsome actor have caught her eye? All the more dazzling in limelight and theater makeup?

"He was an actor?"

"No."

"No?" Bell's hopes soared as quickly as they had fallen.

"They never let him act—except once he carried a spear."

"Then what did he do at Wilton's?"

"Everything. He wore a sandwich board to tout the show. He ran for beer. One day, I watched him paint the scenery in the backyard. He sold sweets and passed out programs. Sometimes, he was a callboy, knocking on dressing room doors. And he stood right at the elbow of the prompter himself."

An all-rounder, thought Bell. A boy-of-all-work assigned every job that needed doing in the theater. But how deep was their connection?

"Did he hand you a program?"

"I couldn't get in that night. I had no money. By the time I earned it, he was gone."

"Did you help him paint scenery in the yard?"

Emily's face fell. "He chased me off." She grew restless, her hands fluttering.

Bell asked, "How often did you see him on the stage with a spear?"

"Once."

"Only once?" How did one sighting on the stage stick him so deep in her memory?

"And once when he carried a lantern."

"So only twice?"

"Twice."

"But you said you went often."

"He wasn't always there."

Bell was aware that laudanum addicts were prey to halluci-nations. As hallucinations went, her handsome callboy was a doozy.

"Emily, would you like to keep his picture?"

"Yes, please."

Bell helped her work it inside the envelope. She hid it in the folds of her shawl.

"Where do you live?" he asked.

"They give me a cot at the Salvation Army. I help in the kitchen."

"I'll walk you home," said Bell.

"Why?"

"Because I am going to give this sack of half crowns to the Army commander to be sure you're taken care of."

Emily got a crafty look in her eye. "If you give it to me, I can take care of myself."

"I would rather give it to someone I can trust to keep you safe."

"You think I might spend it on laudanum."

"No 'might' about it," said Bell so firmly that she dropped the subject with an abject nod.

At the door of the soup kitchen, she blurted, "Don't tell no-body what I said."

"I won't."

"He'll come for me."

"Don't worry," said Isaac Bell, hearing his own words ring hollow, "I'll make sure he doesn't . . . Emily? What was the callboy's name?"

"Jack."

"Jack? Do you remember his last name?"

"Spelvin."

"Jack Spelvin?"

"Handsome Jack."

20

"Here's a strange one," said Harry Warren, reading from the Research Department report that Isaac Bell had ordered sent every morning to the Cutthroat Squad.

Helen Mills, James Dashwood, Archie Abbott, and several other detectives in the New York field office bull pen not of the Cutthroat Squad looked up from their work.

"What's strange?"

"Woman throat slashed and carved up in Cleveland."

"Sounds like our man."

"Except she was a six-foot-tall brunette."

"Prostitute?"

"Banker's wife."

"Crescent carvings?"

"None reported."

"Shouldn't Cleveland send a man to the morgue?"

"Already did. No carvings."

"Sounds like a coincidence."

"Who wants to tell Mr. Bell it's a coincidence?"

A profound silence settled over them—the Chief Investigator took a dim view of coincidences in general and an even dimmer view of coincidences offered as explanations. The silence was broken suddenly by James Dashwood, who was thumbing through a pile of old issues of *The Clipper*, the actors' weekly that listed jobs.

"There you are!"

"Who?"

"Stage manager I told you about. For *Jekyll and Hyde*? I knew I recognized him." He held up *The Clipper*. "Henry Young." He pointed to a line drawing of an actor playing a villain in an 1897 melodrama.

"That's not a wanted poster."

"I know. But now I know he was working in a Syracuse stock company in the late nineties."

Joseph Van Dorn burst into the bull pen. Last heard from, the Boss was in Washington, and the detectives jumped to their feet. "Who's heard from Isaac?"

Archie Abbott said, "He had Joel Wallace cable me to check up on Lord Strone. He's the—"

"British spy. What does he want with a British spy?"

"To see if Strone's still in business."

"Is he?"

"He's kind of disappeared on his yacht."

"That's all you've heard from Isaac?"

"Well, he cabled Marion when he arrived in London."

"Maybe we should install his wife down here to keep up with him."

Van Dorn stormed off. Looks were exchanged. The Boss was losing patience with the Cutthroat Squad.

Archie Abbott waited until the front desk telephoned that Van Dorn had gone downstairs for a late breakfast. Quickly, he stood up and gathered his things. "See you tomorrow."

"You're going home at ten in the morning?"

"I've got tickets to see *Jekyll and Hyde* again."

"It closed. It's on the road, remember?"

"I'm seeing it in Columbus."

"You're going all the way to Ohio to watch a play?"

"Lillian invited Marion Bell. Marion missed it in New York, and now she misses Isaac, so we're taking her with us."

"Still, a long ways to go for a play."

"My father-in-law is lending us his train."

Detectives who rode to work on streetcars rolled their eyes.

"It will get us there in time for the curtain," Abbott explained blithely. "On the way home, we'll tuck into bed for a good night's sleep."

Harry Warren said, "Of all the girls I could have married, why did it never occur to me to nail one whose father owns a railroad?"

"Numerous railroads."

Marion Morgan Bell hung back a step when Lillian and Archie walked down the center aisle and the audience craned necks for a glimpse of the famously beautiful railroad heiress and the man who had been the New York Four Hundred's most eligible bachelor before he fell for her. As Isaac put it, "Detective disguises don't come better than man-about-town who married well."

They were the last to take their seats. The orchestra began to play, and the curtain rose on a set that depicted a light and airy apartment in a New York City skyscraper, an up-to-date image that captured the attention of every Columbus lady in the audience. The story moved with great speed, and when night transformed the apartment for Mr. Hyde's entrance, the modern home seemed deeply sinister. It was impossible to tell whether Barrett or Buchanan was playing Hyde, so convincingly evil was the character.

But only when women began gasping and crying out did Marion realize she was not as caught up in the play as the rest of the audience. She glanced at Lillian, a brave and steady young woman. Lillian looked terrified. Even Archie, who had seen it before, appeared so riveted that Marion half expected him to pull a pistol to protect them.

As it raced on, as a huge airplane swooped over the stage, as Hyde leaped on the roof of a speeding subway car, as the utterly compelling Isabella Cook came within inches of destruction—prompting more than one man to start from his seat to help her—Marion wondered why she was not quite so engaged as the others. The answer was simple, and no fault of the brilliant production. She so admired every bit of craft that was stirring the audience that her mind had shifted to the technical details of how she could re-create and embellish those effects on film.

The play ended to standing ovation, shouts, and cheers.

Lillian said, "Let's go backstage and meet the actors."

"No," said Marion. "Not me."

"Why?"

"I want to see them as I saw them."

A little pout started to form on Lillian's face, but it melted into a smile. They were very close, with Marion sometimes in the role of big sister. "I know what you mean. You're right. Let's remember them as we saw them."

Archie said, "I sense a 'Marion plot,' don't I?"

Marion Morgan Bell clutched the program in her fist. "I am going to make a movie of Barrett & Buchanan's *Dr. Jekyll and Mr. Hyde*."

Isaac Bell rode the London & North Western back to London, retrieved his clothing from Euston's baggage office, and changed in the lavatory. Then he telephoned Joel Wallace from a coin-operated call box. The box he chose was at the end of the row, with cut-glass windows overlooking the station's Great Hall.

Wallace asked, "How'd you make out in Manchester?"

"Found out why they hate each other. Otherwise, a bust. The poor girl fell for a good-looking theater callboy who may or may not have been the guy who tried to kill her. That's who she remembered . . . Any more cables from New York?"

"Testy one from the Boss."

"Another 'Report now'?"

"'Report immediately.'"

"What does Research say?"

"No new bodies since you sailed. Except a tall brunette they don't think counts."

"Missing girls?"

"Chicago, Pittsburgh, Columbus."

On Bell's orders, Grady Forrer's boys were querying field offices daily for reports of missing girls who resembled the fair and petite murder victims.

"None out west?"

"None we hadn't heard about earlier."

Bell pondered the report. Missing girls, no bodies. Young women disappeared for all sorts of reasons. But this murderer so often succeeded in hiding his victims.

"Have you ever been to Wilton's Music Hall?"

"In Whitechapel? No, the Methodists took it over for a mission twenty years ago. Why?"

"Just a thought. Ever hear of a guy in the theater named Jack Spelvin?"

"On the stage?"

"Could be anything—an all-rounder, or even a scenic designer, director, actor, manager."

"Not here in London. I think I heard of a *George* Spelvin back home. Not *Jack*. Why?"

"Emily's crush," Bell answered distractedly. His eyes roamed the train travelers crisscrossing the Great Hall.

"What's the word on Lord Strone?"

"Out of business," said Wallace. "The Secret Service Bureau gave him his walking papers."

"Are you certain?"

"As certain as I can be about spies. Cabled a fellow I bank on to confirm. He cabled back that Strone's gone fishing in Florida."

"We'll see about that," said Bell. "I've got another job for you."

"When?"

"Right this minute. On the jump!"

Isaac Bell took an escalator deep underground to the tube train and rode east for several stops. He returned to the surface at Moorgate. A misty drizzle mingled with the coal smoke. It was hard to see fifty feet ahead. He walked into the East End and onto Bishopsgate, a busy commercial street jam-packed with wagons and double-decker horse trams that cut through the Whitechapel district that Jack the Ripper had terrorized.

The Range Riders, a Tom Mix Western, was showing at the Electric.

Bell bought a ticket. The movie theater sat more than a hundred and was so recently built that he could smell the paint. He found a seat in the back row. Before the Western started, they showed a Picture World News Reel of "Old King Teddy's"—King Edward VII's—funeral processing through London. Bell grinned with delight. Wait 'til he told Marion that the newsreel she had shot a full year ago—five hundred and twenty feet of what the movie people call topical film—was still playing in the theaters.

A man in a bowler and a long black coat entered from the curtained lobby and took a seat one over in the row in front of Bell. In the light flickering from Marion's film, Bell saw he was in his thirties and impeccably dressed. He had walked ramrod straight, and he sat similarly stiff and upright. Neither his bowler and walking stick, nor his civilian topcoat, could disguise the proud badge of lifelong military service.

Isaac Bell leaned forward and whispered in his ear, "My wife made this film."

The icily supercilious retort matched his posture: "Are you addressing me, sir?"

"Why did you follow me from Euston Station?"

"I beg your pardon."

"You and I caught the Tube to Moorgate. Then we walked— London Wall on to Broad Street, Liverpool, and up Bishopsgate. We could have taken London Wall direct to Wormwood and Bishopsgate, but I wanted to be absolutely certain it was you again before I punched you in the nose."

21

The shadow jumped up and sprinted from the theater.

Bell pounded after him.

Coattails flapping like a startled crow, the shadow fled through the lobby and out the door. He shoved through the rippling wall of pedestrians blocking the sidewalk and plunged over the curb into the truck and wagon traffic inching along Bishopsgate High Street. Isaac Bell was catching up when a burly man in a tweed coat and workman's cap shot a scuffed, lace-up boot in his path. Bell tripped and went flying headlong into the street, rolling on his shoulder when he hit the cobblestones and tumbling under the ironshod wheels of a giant hay wagon trundling fodder to the horse-tram stables.

Bell heard shouts of alarm. Traffic came to a standstill. People reached under the wagon and helped him to his feet. He looked around confusedly, retrieving his hat and assuring pass-ersby that he was not injured. He could see neither the shadow nor the backup operator waiting to trip him. But Detective Joel Wallace's broad back was disappearing into a lane on the far side of Whitechapel, hot on the trail.

Isaac Bell chased after Joel Wallace, who was following the man in the bowler hat. The operator in tweed had peeled away early on, scurrying up Bishopsgate without looking back. The Van Dorn stayed with his boss as the man negotiated the ill-clad crowds on greasy cobblestone streets littered with scrap paper and horse manure. Bell caught up when Wallace stopped behind a cart with a broken wheel that was blocking the sidewalk.

"Heck of an acrobat," Wallace said over his shoulder, his eyes fixed on an alley. "For a moment there, I thought he really got you."

"Ran off with the circus once— Where'd he go?"

"Ducked into that beer house. We're looking at the back door. Ought to be out any sec."

The drizzle changed abruptly to cold rain that poured down from the dark sliver of midday sky that showed between the houses. "Here we go! No, that's not him— Wait, who is that?"

"Quick-change artist," said Bell. "Turned his coat inside out."

Their quarry edged from the alley, wearing what appeared to be a light-colored canvas raincoat. He looked around the lane and stepped briskly away.

"I'm getting me one of those," Joel Wallace whispered.

As the Van Dorns trailed the shadow through Whitechapel, trading the lead, and several times removing their hats and exchanging them with one another, it occurred to Isaac Bell that Jack the Ripper would not have worn gentleman's clothing when he haunted these streets. Certainly not after the first killing. Even procuring prostitutes, he would have stood out like a sore thumb. He had to have blended with the poor. Or had Ripper outfitted himself with a shabby variant of the shadow's reversible coat?

"Spotted us!" said Bell. The man had glanced over his shoulder at just the wrong moment and glimpsed Joel Wallace sprinting for a doorway. He ran.

"Get him!" So much for following him back to whoever gave him his orders. They would have to interrogate him instead.

Ironically, they caught up with the shadow on Hanbury Street, and when he sidestepped into an alley, it was not Number 29—but close. Bell tore in after him and grabbed him by his canvas collar.

"I beg your pardon. What do you think you are doing, sir?"

"Interviewing you."

"Do you know who I am?"

"I will when I'm done."

"I am a police officer."

"No you are not," said Bell. "Police officers work shifts. They spell each other. You're shadowing me around the clock. You followed me around London; you followed me to Manchester. About the only place you didn't follow me was into Angel Meadow, where I could have used a hand. Now you're following me in London, again. All by your lonesome. That makes you a freelance. If you're freelance, I want to know who's paying you. If you're working for Military Intelligence, I want to know what the blazes you think you are doing shadowing an American citizen on legitimate business."

Bell lifted him an inch off the ground and shook him hard. "Which is it?"

"I could have you shot!"

Bell lowered him until his feet touched the mud, loosened one hand, and drew his derringer. "I'm better fixed for shooting."

He let the operator peer into the immensity of twin barrels, each nearly half an inch wide. "Who are you?"

The man dropped his gaze. "Freelance."

It was almost certainly a lie, but Bell went along, asking, "Who are you working for?"

"Military Intelligence."

Bell regarded him sternly. "That is ridiculous. I have nothing to do with Military Intelligence, if such a thing even exists."

"I'd expect you to deny it."

"Deny what?"

"We know who you are."

Bell tightened his grip and backed him hard against the bricks. He pressed the barrels to his cheek. "Tell me who I am."

"We know who you are, *Mr. Isaac Bell*. What we don't know is who you are spying for. The United States or Germany. Or both."

Bell snapped his fingers in sudden comprehension. "Abbington-Westlake."

The operator's eyes widened. He recovered in an instant and

desperately tried to backpedal from his mistake. "I have no idea who you're talking about."

"Tell that underhanded rat I know he's your boss," said Bell, and stalked away.

Joel Wallace trotted after him.

"What the heck was that about?"

"Commander Abbington-Westlake, British Admiralty, Naval Intelligence Department, Foreign Division."

"Fancy name for 'Royal Navy spy.' Told you, it was dreadnoughts."

"I caught him snapping Kodaks of ours in the Brooklyn Navy Yard. Back in aught eight."

"Wha'd you do to him?"

"Promised I'd throw him off the Brooklyn Bridge if he tried it again. He turned out to be very helpful." Bell shook his head. "Abbington-Westlake is one of those operators who acts like he's a stuffy old duffer before his time. Behind the bumbling front he's slick as ice. Should have thought about him first time around. I just assumed he was too sharp to make this stupid a mistake."

"Like I say, spies don't trust nobody."

"The thing is," Bell mused, "he is such an insider . . . If anyone knows what the Yard won't tell me about the Ripper, it's Abbington-Westlake."

"Will he talk to you?"

"Not unless he sees a payoff."

"What can you offer him?"

Bell thought hard for a full minute. "We need a German."

"Where do we get a German?" asked Wallace.

"I'll get the German. You find out which of Abbington-Westlake's London clubs he'll eat lunch at tomorrow. Can you do that by midnight?"

Wallace nodded. "Bank on it."

"Report to me in Lincoln's Inn Fields."

"At midnight?"

"I'll need you to stand lookout."

"What'll I be looking out for?"

"The cops."

"Why?"

"Because it won't do me or you any good if Metropolitan Police constables arrest the Van Dorn Detective Agency's Chief Investigator."

"For what?"

"Burglary."

"Fact-based truth," Joel Wallace agreed. But he blinked like a man whose head was spinning. "Mind me asking what're you planning to break into?"

"The Lock Museum."

22

At seven o'clock, the bar at the Garrick Club emptied out as actors hurried off to the West End theaters to dress for the evening shows. The few who remained nursed their drinks with an eye to keeping them going until some prosperous soul offered to buy a round for a player "at liberty."

The obvious candidate was a tall, amiable American in an expensive white suit. He was a guest, the barman confided to the members, who had presented a letter of introduction from The Players, an actors' and writers' club in New York that had a reciprocal membership arrangement with the Garrick.

Sadly, the guest was already buying whiskeys for James Mapes, a handsome leading man whose great mane of wavy hair was laced with silver. Despite his years, Mapes, whose mane might once have been as golden as Isaac Bell's, still cut a commanding figure. Only his frayed cuffs suggested that he had been refusing to play character roles for longer than he should.

"'Reckless,' the critics call me," he told Bell. "'Deluded.' Granger—the cruelest of those scribblers—actually wrote of my last *Count of Monte Cristo*, and this I quote from memory, 'Mapes ought to have switched to character parts whilst Queen Victoria reigned.'"

"Why would the critics pile on like that?" asked Bell sympathetically.

"Because they're right! Who wants to see an old warhorse making love to a filly?"

"Half the men in the audience."

Mapes laughed. "Ah, you're a generous soul, Bell. Yes, sir. Generous." He peered into the diminished contents of his glass.

"Would you join me in another?" asked Bell. "Not to worry, it's on the firm."

"Then I thank you, and I thank the firm."

Bell signaled the barman, who poured fresh doubles.

"Cheers! . . . Mr. Mapes, have you ever played a German?"

"Not in donkey's years. Way back when I was too young to carry leads."

"What sort of Germans did you play?"

"Villains. Heavies. *Vhut utter Shermans ah zere?*"

They took their drinks and wandered through the handsome club, which was hung with oil paintings of members, present and deceased, in famous roles, and decorated with costumes and stage props. Bell pointed out an empty space. "Waiting for you, perhaps?"

"More likely, my friend Vietor. He's made a 'sudden smash sensation' in *Alias Jimmy Valentine*."

"O. Henry's safecracker story. My wife and I saw it on Broadway."

"What did you think of Vietor's reformed criminal?"

"I believed Jimmy Valentine intended to go straight. Even though I knew the short story, he had me worried for his fate."

"He asked me to coach him in the role," said Mapes. "Subduing the dark side of Vietor's character was like pulling teeth. Now he's touring your provinces, raking it in hand over fist. Hope for us all! When last I last saw him in New York, he was cadging drinks at the Waldorf-Astoria. Now he's ready to return to England, equal parts rich and famous."

In the well-appointed library, Bell found the privacy he was seeking. He had spent an hour in it earlier, poring through a collection of old programs, but had had no luck finding any from Wilton's Music Hall. "Do you know anyone in the theater named Jack Spelvin?"

"No."

"He was a callboy at Wilton's back in the eighties."

"You're sure you don't mean *George* Spelvin?"

"*Jack.*"

Bell wondered whether Emily could have confused the name of the boy she fell for. It seemed unlikely. "Did you know George Spelvin?"

"There is no George Spelvin. It's a pseudonym, a *nom de guerre*, when we don't want the audience aware we're on the stage. Rather more commonly used in America."

"Is it used in London?"

"Occasionally. The language volleys of back and forth; actors who tour across the pond end up speaking almost similar English. Here, we're more likely to bill ourselves as Walter Plinge instead of George Spelvin."

"But not Jack?"

"Never heard of a Jack Spelvin."

Bell had to wonder. The Ripper loved his games. Maybe Emily's callboy actually was the same man who tried to kill her, a murderer with a sense of humor.

"I gather," said Bell, "he was a sort of boy-of-all-work."

"Excellent means for an apprentice seeking a toehold on the stage," said Mapes. "Callboy, prompter, assistant stage manager, a walk-on, and up you go. Or if he discovers he's got a head for business, he'll shift to the front of the house—sell souvenir programs, rent opera glasses, assist the treasurer in the box office. By now, Jack Spelvin could own a bloody theater—though you can be sure he'd have changed his name from Spelvin."

Mapes gazed mournfully into his glass, which was empty again, and Bell realized he had better get to business before any more whiskey went down the hatch. "Mr. Mapes," he said, "it is my honor to offer you a job. It's only a one-night stand, but it will pay equal to a full month on the West End."

"May I presume wardrobe is included?"

"My tailor will fit you for whatever suit of clothes, shirts, ties, hat, and coat you decide that you need for the role. The costume, of course, is yours to keep."

"Railway tickets?"

"It will be right here in London. We will go by cab," said Bell, keeping to himself that the entire job would likely take place inside a cab.

"Why me?"

"The role demands a charismatic actor with nerves of steel."

Mapes considered the prospect. "'Nerves of steel' implies some possibility of danger."

Isaac Bell looked him in the eye, and the actor saw the American's amiable expression harden perceptibly as he reassured him with a promise. "You will never be out of my sight."

"When will the curtain rise?"

"You've got a busy morning with my tailor. Curtain rises tomorrow evening at eight."

"Do you remember Nellie Bly?" asked the Cutthroat.

The girl—her name was Dorothy—was silent.

"Famous newspaperwoman? . . . No?"

Dorothy lay on her back beside an empty steel oil drum in the warehouse of a Cleveland refinery. She was wrapped head to toe in his cape. He had left her face showing. Her blue eyes had popped open, staring at a sky she would never see.

"What am I saying? Nellie Bly was famous before you were born." He glanced again at the girl. Still staring, still silent.

"Beautiful girl. Nellie had a lot of nerve. She got herself locked up in a lunatic asylum once just to report on what it was like to be locked up in a lunatic asylum. She wrote a book about it: *Ten Days in a Mad-House*. I always wondered—did Nellie worry that her editor would forget to get her out? What if he fell off a train or died in a fire while she was still locked up? . . . But the reason I ask is, Nellie went on to be a wealthy business-woman. Not only that, she became an inventor. In fact, she invented this astonishing new kind of barrel."

He slapped the steel drum and it gave a melodious boom.

"That's right—an easily sealed fifty-five-gallon oil barrel that never rots or leaks and is strong enough to hoist onto ships and railcars and be transported anywhere in the world. John D. Rockefeller is forever in her debt. And so am I. For another 'perfect crime.'"

He scooped Dorothy into his arms and lowered her into the barrel. He banged on the head and sealed it tight with a simple wrench.

"See, Dorothy? All gone."

———

Clocks were striking midnight in London.

Across the street from the wrought-iron-fenced lawns of Lincoln's Inn, the windows were dark in all three stories of the Lock Museum. Lights out except for a garret dormer in the roof, which told Isaac Bell he had assumed correctly that there would be no hall porter guarding the front door at this late hour. If the porter lived in a servant's room in the cellar, he had gone to bed, since no lights showed in the tradesman's entrance under the front steps. But the light in the window garret indicated that Nigel Roberts was home, either awake in his room or, hopefully, falling asleep reading in bed.

Isaac Bell hurried up the front steps and pretended to knock at the door. He held his other hand at waist height, assessing the lock, first with his turning tool, then with a pick. He waited, looked around, and pretended to knock again. With only the gardens across the street, no one could see him from a window. Still, he pantomimed disappointment, descended the steps slowly, and walked around the corner onto Gate Street.

Joel Wallace was waiting inside a two-wheeled hansom cab. The cabby, seated high up behind the passenger box, was an ex–Royal Marine who drove regularly for the Van Dorn field office. His horse was feeding from a nose bag.

"How's the lock?"

"Brand-new Yale."

Joel Wallace groaned. "Why don't you just borrow the thief catcher? I bet Roberts would lend it to you."

"He'd be happy to help," Bell agreed. "But if it goes sour, the old boy's out of his job. And his home." He took out his watch. "Time. I've got twelve-ten."

Joel Wallace moved his ahead twenty seconds. "Twelve-ten."

"Bring the cab around the corner at twelve-fifteen."

"You can't jimmy the Yale and lift that strongbox in five minutes."

"If I don't, I'll have a bobby wondering why I'm hanging around the Museum's front steps at midnight." He jumped out of the cab. "Five minutes. I'll pass you the box on the garden side. Don't stop. I'll catch up at the office."

Bell hurried around the corner and up the steps. The lock was a standard six-pin, new and well made, probably by an English firm licensed by the Yale company. He reinserted his turning tool, put on light pressure, and worked in his pick. He found the pin that was most out of alignment in its hole—the candidate to be picked up first. He lifted it, which allowed the pressure on his turning tool to rotate the cylinder tube slightly. Then he felt for the next pin made to bind most tightly by the cylinder's rotation.

He heard footsteps on the sidewalk, the measured tread of a big man in heavy shoes. At this hour in this wealthy district, a firm stride and menacing swagger announced a police constable on patrol.

23

Isaac Bell stood tall and kept working his picks at waist level.

He lifted the third pin, and the fourth. Two to go. But the fifth and sixth were both binding. Rushing to unlock the door before the bobby reached the steps, he had applied too much torque with his turning tool. He eased it slightly, prayed, and got one pin to go up, freeing the cylinder from all but the final pin. The footsteps stepped behind him.

"Good evening, sir."

The constable's imperious tone demanded an immediate response. The lack of the deference ordinarily accorded a well-dressed gentleman implied that a housebreaker with a brain in his head would dress the part to blend in with the residents of the neighborhood—wouldn't he, sir?

The sixth and final pin resisted the pick.

"Good evening, Constable," Isaac Bell tossed over his shoulder, shielding his hands with his torso.

"Have you business here, sir?"

"No."

"Then what are you doing?"

The sixth pin finally let Bell lift it. He increased pressure on his turning tool and the Yale clicked open. He palmed his picks, turned the doorknob, and faced the constable. "I am a guest."

"Seems a late hour for a visit to a dark house."

"I am staying the night," said Bell. "The British Lock Museum hopes to acquire my father's collection. They've put me up in the director's suite."

He stepped inside the front hall.

"As I was dining late at my club, they lent me a key. Good night, Constable."

"Good night, sir."

Bell closed the door on the officer's salute, locked it, and glided silently from the front hall. The collection room was lit dimly by the gleam of a streetlamp that penetrated the curtains. Bell went straight to the German chastity belt, guided by reflections off its glass case.

The thief-catcher strongbox was next to it. He closed the lid carefully, pocketed the key, and slung the heavy box under his arm. He counted a full two minutes and then glided to the front window to check the street.

He could not see the constable.

Joel Wallace's hansom cab rounded the corner at a quick trot. Bell had no choice but to ease out the door, hoping the constable had moved on, close it behind him, and hurry down the steps. He crossed to the garden side of the street, let the cab overtake him, and passed the strongbox into Joel Wallace's hands.

"Where did the constable go?"

Joel Wallace pointed.

Bell went the other way.

———

"And then the Frenchman said to me . . ."

Commander Abbington-Westlake was holding forth at the long and raucous members' table in the dining room of the Savile Club in Mayfair. A wine bottle stood beside each of the dozen men at lunch. When its contents drained low, a white-coated steward replaced it from the member's personal stock.

Formed by wealthy writers and artists, and currently occupying a pleasant house on Piccadilly, the Savile prided itself on a distinct absence of stodginess. This would have surprised the many who had fallen for Commander Abbington-Westlake's pomposity act, proof that, as espionage masquerades went, stuffed shirts were as likely to be underestimated as drunkards. He was a large, round man, with fleshy cheeks, an officer's mustache, and hooded eyes. His plum-toned voice carried.

"So the Frenchman said to me, 'I've learned enough about you English to know that one is in deep trouble when a gentleman addresses one as "sir."'"

He paused for a significant glance up and down the table and twitched a bushy eyebrow. "I replied, 'You are correct, sir.'"

The dining room echoed with laughter, cries for new bottles.

After lunch, he joined the others for cigars and bustled into the bar, calling, "A very large brandy, my good man."

"Make it a double," said Isaac Bell, materializing from a dark corner. "The commander is buying."

Abbington-Westlake covered his surprise. "How the devil did you get in here, Bell?"

"My introduction from the Yale Club of New York City was greeted hospitably."

"Standards are falling everywhere."

"Especially in the quality of shadows."

"All right!" said Abbington-Westlake. The bar was crowded with after-lunch cigar smokers. "Perhaps we should—"

"Find a quiet place to talk about why you're having me followed?" asked Bell.

"I said, 'All right!'"

The club had a little patch of garden in the back. They sat there and smoked.

"Why have you tackled me here in my own club?" Abbington-Westlake asked aggrievedly. "It's not done, Bell. Not at lunch. What is it you want?"

"In addition to calling off your shadows?"

"They're off. What do you want?"

Bell said, "I told you years ago, that behind a scrim of amiable bumbling, upper-crust, above-it-all mannerisms, and a witty tongue, you are extremely well informed about your fellow spies."

"Competitors," said Abbington-Westlake. "Not fellows."

"Then what made you leap to the absurd conclusion that I am spying for the United States?"

"Or freelancing for German Kaiser Wilhelm's intelligence

service," Abbington-Westlake shot back. "Can you blame me for being suspicious in a dangerous world? Why wouldn't the Van Dorn Detective Agency go into the spy business? Pinkertons spied for your President Lincoln."

"Don't tar me with the Pinkerton brush," Bell said coldly. "Van Dorns are not company cops and strikebreakers. Nor are we spies."

"Bell, England is staring down gun barrels. The Hun is on the march. He's building dreadnoughts faster than we are. Why wouldn't I expect the worst?"

"Why didn't you just ask what I was up to?"

"Would you have admitted it?"

"Of course. We're on the same side."

"What side? Your government is maddeningly neutral."

"The United States steers clear of Europe's squabbles. But when push comes to shove, we stand against tyrants. The British Empire is greedy, but the king of England is not a tyrant. The Russian tzar is a tyrant. So is the German kaiser."

"Then tell me what you're doing in London. And spare me your masquerade about Jack the Ripper. Really, Bell, it seems below you."

"I'll do better than tell you. I'll show you."

"Show me what?"

"Someone I found."

"Whom have you found?"

"A German who wants to sell a secret."

"What secret?"

"A new fire-control device."

Abbington-Westlake's eyes went opaque as Bell was betting

they would. Naval cannon range and speed of fire were increasing rapidly, demanding radically improved methods for the dreadnought battleships to aim their big guns. "Why would you share your treasure with me?"

"You're better placed in London to do something about it. And I have no doubt you will do the gentlemanly thing and share it with us."

"No doubt," Abbington-Westlake lied. "Where is this Hun?"

"He has promised to meet me in a cab at Charing Cross."

"When?"

"Eight o'clock tonight."

"Do you trust him?"

"He's scared and greedy," said Bell. "All he wants is to get his money and board the first boat back to Germany."

Abbington-Westlake's expression hardened. "So the reason you are sharing this is you expect me to put up the money."

"I don't need your money," said Bell.

"Really? Oh— Well, I stand corrected . . . Bell, this is all quite unusual."

It occurred to Isaac Bell that this was as enjoyable as fly-casting for trout. It was time to set the hook. He said, "I think I made a mistake. I thought this was for a Navy man. Now it strikes me I should speak with a fellow I know at the Foreign Office."

"Not if you're expecting immediate action."

"Then Military Intelligence."

Abbington-Westlake regarded him shrewdly. "I regret to inform you that your old friend Lord Strone has been put out to pasture."

"Leaving only you?"

"To your great good fortune," said the commander. "I will have that cab surrounded by twenty picked men."

"No," said Bell. "Not one. This German is as sharp as they come. He's survived twenty years' spying in London and you never caught him. You don't even know his name. He'll spot your picked men in a flash. We will keep it simple—you, me, and him."

"How did you stumble upon him?"

"Sheer luck," said Bell.

"I thought so. How?"

"I was closing in on a Japanese. The German beat me to him. He wrecked everything I'd been working for. I lit out after him and caught up."

"So you made your luck."

"Exactly as you would, Commander. Shall we shake hands on it?"

Abbington-Westlake extended a soft pink hand. Bell gripped it hard. "Just so we understand each other, sir, I will spot your 'picked men' just as I spotted your shadow. Don't try to slip them past me."

"Wouldn't have dreamed of it."

Fog was thickening when Isaac Bell pulled up in front of the Charing Cross railroad station in a closed carriage, a roomy cab that Londoners called a growler. He opened the door and beckoned Commander Abbington-Westlake. The Navy spy was dressed identically to the hordes of City bankers rushing home in bowlers and raincoats, with one exception. Instead of an um-brella, he carried a walking stick with an ivory knob carved to resemble the head of a crocodile.

Bell moved over to make room on the seat beside him. Abbington-Westlake climbed in, and the Van Dorn driver set his horse at a quick trot up the Strand.

"Wait. Where are we going?"

"Our German changed his mind at the last minute. Trafalgar Square."

"But—"

"But your picked men are at Charing Cross?"

"Of course not."

"Good. Because I suspect this fellow is going to run us in circles until he feels safe."

At Trafalgar Square, a flower girl tapped the window and handed Bell a scrap of paper.

Bell read aloud, "'Berkeley Square.'"

"How did that girl distinguish this cab from a hundred others?"

"The same way the German will. The driver has a white rib-bon tied to his whip."

The horse trotted up Cockspur to Pall Mall, up Pall Mall and across Regent Street to Piccadilly, where it turned at the Ritz Hotel onto Dover and down Hay Hill into Berkeley Square. It stopped abruptly. James Mapes flung open the cab door and climbed heavily inside with a strongbox under his arm. He was dressed in a fine suit of clothes, a rabbit-felt fedora, and the lat-est Burberrys waterproof. Bell could almost hear Joe Van Dorn's howls of protest over his expense sheet.

"Took your time," Mapes said in an accent so heavy that Abbington-Westlake, straining to see his face in the dark, said, "What was that?"

"He said," said Bell, "we took our time."

"Damn right, we took our time, and we'll continue to take our time until we're convinced you have something of value."

"Vere ist der muny?"

"Where are the fire control plans?"

Mapes patted the strongbox. "In der buks."

"Open it."

"Show der marks."

Bell passed him an envelope. "Give me the key."

Mapes pulled a key from his pocket but held on to it and used it like a letter opener to slit the envelope. Suddenly a shadow loomed out of the fog. The driver knocked a warning, but he was too late, and the shadow took the shape of a constable's helmet. A truncheon rattled the window.

"Ist der trick!" Mapes shouted. *"Schweinhund!"*

Bell snatched the key from his hand, but Mapes held on to the envelope as he pushed open the opposite door. Bell lunged for him, blocking Abbington-Westlake's attempt to trip him with his walking stick. Mapes tumbled out, eluding Bell's grasp, and ran into the gardens of Berkeley Square.

The constable lumbered after him, blowing his whistle. Abbington flung open his door.

Bell pinned his arm. "Let him go."

"He'll escape."

"We have his strongbox," said Bell. "There'll be coppers all over us." He called to the driver, "Get us out of here!"

The horse galloped onto Fitzmaurice Place, rounded the curve into Curzon Street at a speed that caused the top-heavy growler to career on two wheels. The driver regained control before it fell on its side. Cracking his whip, he wove in and out of lanes. Suddenly they emerged into the flurry of Piccadilly traffic just west of the Ritz, where they blended in with a hundred other growlers, hansoms, and petrol motor taxis. At the edge of Green Park, he pulled under a streetlamp haloed by the fog. It cast soft light on Bell's and Abbington-Westlake's faces.

"Why is he stopping?"

"To give his horse a breather," said Bell.

"Shall we have a look in the box?"

"Be my guest," said Bell. He handed over the key.

——— — ———

"*Wait!*"

"Why?"

"Funny feeling," said Isaac Bell. He leaned in and studied the box carefully. "I think it's a trick."

"What trick? I fail to see a trick. I see a strongbox filled with priceless information."

"Let's see your torch."

Bell switched on the flashlight and played the beam over the lock and the keyhole.

"What do you see, Bell?"

"Give me your walking stick."

24

Gingerly, Isaac Bell inserted the key partway into the strong-box lock.

Then he poked at the key with Abbington-Westlake's walking stick.

"What the devil are you doing?"

"Let us pretend that you are turning that key," said Isaac Bell. He turned the stick around and used the ornate knob to shove the key deeper into the lock. It engaged with a sharp snick. A sudden explosion of noise resounded in the closed cab like a thunderclap. The crocodile disintegrated, spraying Bell and Abbington-Westlake with splintered wood and ivory.

"What?" gasped Abbington-Westlake.

His shattered stick was pinned in the iron jaws of the wrist manacle that had sprung from the box.

"I had a funny feeling it was a thief catcher," said Bell.

"A what?"

"Thief catcher. I read somewhere that accountants had to look out for them when they audited a dead man's estate."

Abbington-Westlake pulled what was left of his stick from the manacle. "This could have been my arm."

"What's in the box?" asked Bell.

"You open it," said Abbington-Westlake. He jumped when the lid squealed on rusty hinges. Bell switched on the flashlight, fixed the beam on the manacle springs, then played it inside.

"Empty!" said Abbington-Westlake.

"No. Here's something."

The tall detective and the English spymaster stared. The box contained a single sheet of paper. Abbington-Westlake snatched it up. A steel-pen drawing depicted the ninety-eight-gun wooden battleship *Dreadnought* that had fought Napoleon's navy one hundred and six years ago at the Battle of Trafalgar.

"Of all the bloody cheek."

"He's got a sense of humor," said Bell.

"The Hun will stop at nothing."

Isaac Bell hung his head as if equal parts embarrassed and apologetic. "I am sorry I let you down, but he really pulled the wool over my eyes . . . If it makes you feel any better, he got my money."

Abbington-Westlake recovered quickly. "I suppose I would be somewhat more irritated if that had shattered my arm. As it is, I'm in your debt."

"You can pay me off easily."

"How?" Abbington-Westlake asked warily.

"Tell me about Jack the Ripper."

"Bell, will you drop this bloody charade?"

"No, you're wrong about the masquerade. I was trying to do two things at once. Back in America, I am tracking a monster who is killing girls and I am increasingly sure he is the same man."

Abbington-Westlake shook his head. "I am sorry to disappoint you, Bell. He is not the same man."

"Do you know for sure?"

"I'll confide in you the solution to the Whitechapel Mysteries. It was proved for a fact who the Ripper was. He drowned himself in the Thames."

"Stop! Next, you'll name suspects, from an insane medical student, to suicides, to a doctor avenging his son, to a royal Duke, to a peer of the realm hiding in Brazil, to a famous painter, to a maniacal immigrant Pole."

"All right. All right," Abbington-Westlake rumbled on. "Look here, Bell. I don't mind sharing a confidence with a man of your integrity . . . Give me your word as a gentleman it will go no further."

"My lips are sealed," said Isaac Bell.

"I have photographs. I will show them to you in gratitude for saving my wrist."

"Photographs of what?"

"Mortuary photographs of his victims' bodies."

"Where did you get them?"

"That's neither here nor there."

"How did you get pictures?"

"I'll show you— Driver! Whitehall. Number 26."

Abbington-Westlake tossed his broken cane in an elephant-foot umbrella stand and turned up the lights in a windowless office in the back of the Old Admiralty Building. He unlocked a closet, twirled a combination, and opened a Chubb fireproof safe. From it he pulled a thick manila file.

"Of course I didn't believe your story about looking for the Ripper. But I sent around for these anyway, reasoning that I should bone up. Do you recall that you asked a certain Harley Street surgeon whether the Ripper carved symbols on his victims? Yes, yes, yes, of course I know you talked to him. I just didn't believe why, at the time. Look at these L-shaped marks. Not crescent-shaped. They're L-shaped."

He flipped through photographs of mutilated bodies and tossed each to Bell.

Bell said, "The surgeon insisted a slip of the blade could not make an L look like a crescent." Indeed, the L's were sharply defined by straight lines.

L L L

"The V-shaped cuts, too."

"Look at these."

V V ⚔ ⚔ ⚔

"Squares, don't you see?"

"They're not square."

"Not *that* kind of square. The stone mason's square. His ancient instrument of measurement."

"Masons?" Bell asked, not entirely sure he had heard right.

"These are signs of the Freemason. The Masonic Brotherhood."

"What do the Masons have to do with murdering girls in Whitechapel?" asked Bell. Was there anyone in all of England who didn't have a lunatic theory about Jack the Ripper?

"Clearly, the fiend was sending a message."

"What message?" asked Bell.

"Invert the V. What do you get? You get a compass. The compass is a mason's drafting tool."

⚔ ⚔

"These V slashes, like the L's, mock the police. He is saying, I am a Freemason."

"Why?"

"To throw the police off the scent and besmirch the Brotherhood. Whom, obviously, he hated."

"Why would he hate the Masons?"

"Who knows how he thinks?"

"Are you a Mason?" asked Bell. He reckoned that Abbington-Westlake probably was, if England was at all like the United States, where half the men in the country had banded into one fraternal order or another. Masons, Odd Fellows, Elks, Owls,

Knights of Columbus—the list was endless, and many Americans claimed brotherhood in more than one of them.

Abbington-Westlake did not admit to being a Mason, saying only, "That's neither here nor there. Point is, old boy, he didn't send that message on your bodies. Our man carved L's and V's, not crescents. So our Jack the Ripper is not your murderer."

"Unless he changed the message."

Abbington-Westlake crossed his arms triumphantly over his chest like a man who had won an essential argument. "There you have it, Bell."

"There I have what?"

"The question you must answer: What do the crescents mean?"

25

What the Cutthroat meant by the crescents was a question that Isaac Bell was acutely aware he had to answer.

"There's another question much more vital," he told Abbington-Westlake.

"Oh?"

Bell watched the naval commander for signs of a lie, no easy task with a man so good at it. For the answer to this question was core to the reason he had come to London. "Why is Scotland Yard so bent and determined that Jack the Ripper stopped killing in 1888?"

Abbington-Westlake sighed. "How should I know? I'm a simple practitioner of naval espionage."

"Commander, you are cynical. And you are treacherous. But

what makes you most dangerous is that your ambition is served by first rate ingenuity. If you saw any hint of Scotland Yard being vulnerable on this issue, you would mine it for every ounce of advantage you could wring out of it to hold over their heads. What caught your attention? What made you smell blood in the water?"

Abbington-Westlake lit a cigar without offering one to Bell, got it going, and puffed smoke. "Do you recall, old boy, what I taught you years ago about the rules?"

"Something about don't tell the servants and don't frighten the horses?"

"Top marks for retention."

"Or was it 'don't tell' the horses?"

"Now, Bell . . ."

"Now, Commander." Bell fished the broken cane out of the elephant foot and shook it under Abbington-Westlake's nose. "You seem to have forgotten that this could have been your arm. Come clean."

"Truth is, I looked into it, on a purely informal basis, for the Home Office."

"Why?"

"Favor for a chap I was at school with."

"I don't believe you."

"The Home Office oversees Scotland Yard."

"I know that, but I don't believe you. You did it on your own, figuring to gain leverage for the next time Naval Intelligence wants a favor from the Yard. You don't ask favors, you collect debts."

"All right, Bell. There were hints of irregularities in the

investigations. And, frankly, the reasons for the irregularities came down to clumsy attempts to cover up sheer incompetence."

"My field office chief suggested that the day I arrived in London."

"Joel Wallace is a bright fellow. Yet another reason I suspected you were spying."

Bell asked the key question that had brought him to England: "Can you tell me whether Jack the Ripper killed more women in London after 1888?"

"London and the suburbs," Abbington-Westlake answered blandly.

Isaac Bell drew a deep breath. "After 'eighty-eight?"

"'Eighty-nine, 'ninety, and the first half of 'ninety-one."

"Why did the Yard deny it?"

"If they said he was dead, the case was closed. The most they could be charged with is incompetent detective work on only five killings. Subsequent murders could be blamed on copycats until the fiend finally ran out of steam or vanished."

"What happened in the second half of 'ninety-one?"

"Vanished."

"Not a trace?"

"Not a trace."

"Any idea why?"

Abbington-Westlake shrugged. "In my humble opinion? Same reason he shifted operations to the suburbs. Wisely not pressing his luck in London. How long could he count on Scotland Yard bungling? By mid-'ninety-one, he probably reckoned it was time to stop pressing his luck in England."

"Thank you," said Isaac Bell. He headed for the door. "Tell me one more thing, Commander."

That drew another elaborate sigh. "Now what?"

"Why should I believe you?"

An uncharacteristically bleak expression crossed over Abbington-Westlake's face, and his poignant reply reminded Bell of a shaken Captain "Honest Mike" Coligney the day they found Anna Waterbury's body in the actor's flat on West 29th Street.

"Because I have three daughters."

"I never thought of you as a family man."

"It sneaked up on me," said Abbington-Westlake. "When I wasn't looking."

"I thank you for your help," said Bell, and headed for the door.

"On the contrary," Abbington-Westlake replied in cold, measured tones, "thank you, Mr. Bell, for spending more time with me while we sorted out what you are up to."

The door opened, swinging inward. The tall, thin shadow Bell had cornered in Whitechapel entered.

"Not so fast, Mr. Bell."

Behind him were his heavyset partner in tweed, whom Bell had encountered outside the Electric movie theater, and another, who had the height and heft of a Marine sergeant out of uniform. They crowded into Abbington-Westlake's office, blocking the door.

Isaac Bell gave them a quick once-over and looked at Abbington-Westlake.

The British spymaster said, "I do not like being hoodwinked nor made sport of."

"I would think by now you've gotten used to it," said Bell. To the shadow and his men he said, "Gents, get out of my way."

They spread out, left and right, with the shadow in the middle.

Bell looked the shadow over again, and admitted, "You surprise me. I hadn't realized you're more of a fighting man than a spy."

"I restrained my better instincts on orders. My new orders mesh with my instincts. Are you familiar with the Gurkha fighters' *kukri*?" He took a leather sheath from his coat and pulled out of it a foot-long curved knife made of heavy steel. It looked like a boomerang with a razor's edge.

His men whipped service revolvers from their coats, cocked them, and aimed them at Bell's head. Bell looked at Abbington-Westlake. "I seem to be the only one who doesn't know his new orders. Care to fill me in, Commander?"

"We'll start with your accomplices. The agent who pretended to be a German, and the agent who pretended to be a police officer, and the agent driving your growler."

"I hailed the growler on Oxford Street. The bobby was an unemployed potboy. The German is a Dutch tulip salesman."

"Their names?"

"Didn't catch them."

"My offices," said Abbington-Westlake, "are in the back of the building and encompass the rooms above, below, and next to this one. You may yell in outrage. You may scream in pain. You may weep with dismay. No one will hear you. And, frankly, if by a miracle they do, I will send them packing with a word. We will start with your accomplices and work our way slowly to what you are really up to. Enjoying a bit of vengeance on the way."

———————

Isaac Bell opened his hands and addressed Abbington-Westlake. "I'm embarrassed. Not only did I fail to see that this fellow who's been following me around is an actual fighting man, I also fell for your pomposity act. It never occurred you were vicious as well as unpleasant."

"Slashing with the Gurka *kukri* requires a very fine touch as its primary purpose is to sever bone and muscle."

"With a single blow," said Bell. "I'm familiar with the *kukri*. It is the Nepalese weapon of choice for beheading people who annoy them."

"Reginald has that fine touch," said Abbington-Westlake. "He can use it as a skinning knife. I've seen him flay a man's arm from wrist to shoulder, removing a layer so thin you could read your morning paper through it. Name your accomplices."

"Now I'm really embarrassed. I completely forgot to ask."

"Hold his arms," said the shadow.

"Wait!" said Abbington-Westlake. "Take his gun."

Isaac Bell had been trying to distract the gunmen with bravado and sarcasm while weighing his chances of shooting both with a quick draw of his Browning before they shot him. As practiced as he was at clearing his holster and firing fast, the odds were abysmal. Even if he managed to shoot them both, the *kukri* knife would take his head off.

"I am opening my coat slowly," he said, "to hand you my automatic, butt first."

He did. Abbington-Westlake took it and swung it like a club. The heavy barrel raked Bell's forehead and smashed his hat to the floor. Head ringing from the blow, Bell heard the spymaster say, "I'm informed he carries a derringer in his hat."

They fished it out.

"Take his arms."

Isaac Bell stepped back and played his last card. "Do you know what makes a fighting man?"

The man with the knife answered with cold certainty, "It takes fatal wounds to stop him."

"Then you'll forgive me." Bell dove to his left. For the barest fraction of a second, he caught all three off guard. He hit the floor rolling, tucked his knees, and got his fingers inside his boot and around his throwing knife. The gunmen were recovering, tracking him with their pistols, and the shadow was raising the *kukri* for a killing blow.

A gun went off, thunderous in the small room, the slug throwing splinters from the floor into Bell's face. He hurled his blade underhand. A flicker of steel and light disappeared in the shadow's throat.

Bell saw a gun sight-line up with his head. He was moving forward, reaching. The *kukri* fell from the shadow's hand. Bell caught it and slashed with all his might.

A hand grasping a pistol fell to the floor.

The other gunman gaped, horrified, and when Bell lunged at him, he whirled out the door. Still moving, Bell whipped around with the knife drawn back to slash.

Abbington-Westlake screamed, backpedaled as the blade whistled through the air, and dropped Bell's Browning. Bell snatched it off the floor and sprang to his feet, breathing hard.

"This is your mess. Clean it up, stay out of my way, and we are even."

"*Even?*" Abbington-Westlake gestured at his fallen men, one squeezing his tweed sleeve to his bloody stump, the other clutching his throat. "How are we even?"

Isaac Bell picked up his derringer and his hat.

"You still have two hands, don't you?"

26

Isaac Bell stalked into the British Lock Museum with the thief-catcher strongbox under his arm. "I found this with a note attached that said return to Lost & Found care of keeper Roberts."

What happened to your face?"

"Slipped shaving."

Nigel Roberts closed both arms around the heavy chest and lugged it to its spot beside the German chastity belt. "I'd have lent it to you."

"I would not have you lose your job and your home on my account."

"It's the Ripper's account."

"I thank you for all your help. Maybe I can pay you back.

Abbington-Westlake has a theory that the Ripper was sending messages to, quote, 'besmirch the Freemasons.' What do you think?"

Nigel Roberts's eyes glittered. "I'll look into it. But I will tell you right off, it would be far more complicated than the spy supposes. And much, much more interesting."

"I hope I haven't sent you down a rabbit hole."

"I like rabbit holes."

Maybe it wasn't as lunatic as it sounded, and Bell had a strong feeling that the old cop would devote the rest of his life to investigating the Freemason angle. No doubt that if there were such an angle, Nigel Roberts was the man to nail it down.

Bell extended his hand. "I've got to catch the boat train."

"Are you convinced the killer who murdered your Anna is Jack the Ripper?"

"I'm pretty sure he's a man in his forties. I'm pretty sure he never stopped killing. I am pretty sure he is carving a message into these poor girls' bodies that says who he is. But the only fact I know for sure is that until I decipher his message, he's still on the loose."

———

Bell stopped at the Jermyn Street office on his way out of London.

"What happened to your face?" Joel Wallace asked.

"Ran into a door. I want you to see what you can turn up on Jack Spelvin."

"Who?"

"The Wilton's Music Hall callboy Emily remembered."

"Oh, yeah. But I thought she was confused."

"Just in case I'm the one confused, I'd like you to find out where Mr. Jack Spelvin was acting in 1889, 'ninety, and the first half of 'ninety-one. And where did he go from there?"

"Tall order, Mr. Bell."

"Do you have any friends in the music halls?"

"Couple of chorus gals, of course, but, uh—"

"Start with them."

Joel Wallace shrugged dubiously. "Before their time."

Bell said, "Maybe their mothers remember him."

27

Aboard the Jekyll & Hyde Special highballing to Toledo and Detroit, Jackson Barrett and John Buchanan were ensconced in their private cars, Buchanan closeted with the company treasurer, Barrett entertaining a clutch of newspaper reporters with a bottomless whiskey bottle and a font of theater stories.

"Mr. Barrett?" asked an attractive woman representing a Chicago paper. "You alternate the roles of Jekyll and Hyde, seemingly at random. Do you ever forget which role you are playing?"

The big baritone voice lowered conspiratorially: "Well, I'll tell you. When in doubt, I glance into the wings and steal a look at Mr. Buchanan. If he's made up like Hyde, I know I'm Jekyll."

The reporters laughed, and scribbled.

The company publicist, standing guard, beamed.

The Boys, as he called Barrett and Buchanan, had always been geniuses at booming a tour, but for *Jekyll and Hyde* they were outdoing themselves, and the bookings more than made up for the expense of freeloading journalists. On this leg of the tour, they had even attracted a wire-service writer, whose nationally published articles would boost ticket sales in Chicago, Cincinnati, St. Louis, and Denver, all the way to San Francisco.

Barrett took a sip from his teacup, having apologized for not joining the drinkers with a solemn, "Duty calls at eight-thirty." A second sip, and he added, "If Mr. Buchanan looks like Jekyll, I am almost certainly Hyde."

"But how do you slip so effortlessly from Jekyll into Hyde?"

"*Slip?* One never *slips* from Jekyll into Hyde. One *emerges* from Jekyll into Hyde!"

It was not all a bed of roses. One crotchety writer—a failed thespian, Barrett had no doubt—asked, "What, exactly, happened that stopped the show last Thursday in Columbus?"

The publicist answered smoothly, without mentioning the dread Rick L. Cox by name. "A man in the audience suffered some sort of attack of agitation. He became so disturbed that he began shouting while the actors were performing. The theater's house manager decided, cautiously but wisely, to lower the curtain while the ushers attempted to calm the man and until he could be escorted from the auditorium."

The crotchety writer checked his notebook, and asked, "What did the man mean by shouting, 'Those are my words! I wrote that'?"

Barrett stepped in. "Mr. Buchanan and I asked that very same question after the show. We were informed that the poor fellow was so confused that he literally didn't know his own name. The doctors ordered him removed to an asylum, where they could examine him thoroughly. I'm afraid that is all we know at the moment." He shook his head, and those nearest thought they saw his eyes mist with tears, an arresting sight in such a leonine head.

"Isn't it a sad reminder that the mask of tragedy is not worn only on the stage?"

They were nodding reflectively when John Buchanan strode in from his car, bellowing, "Forgive me, lady and gentlemen of the press, forgive me. Mundane duty called. When our generous backers catch up in Toledo, they will expect an accounting of our production, accurate to the penny . . . Are you enjoying the Jekyll & Hyde Special?"

"Yes, sir, Mr. Buchanan."

"You run a mighty hospitable train."

"Can I ask you, Mr. Buchanan? Examining your tour schedule, I note that after one week each in Toledo and Detroit, you will play a full extra week in Cincinnati, which is longer than you're scheduled for St. Louis and Denver. Are you at all nervous about committing to such a long run in Cincinnati?"

"Not in the slightest. We've always encountered the most astute audiences in Cincinnati. And it's good for the company to settle in now and then for a longer run."

Jackson Barrett stole a look at the Chicago lady's notebook and winked at the publicist. Her opening sentence would practically pay for the train.

> Two of the handsomest actors that ever graced the
> modern stage are heading for Chicago with hope in
> their hearts and charm to burn.

The wily old publicist nodded a clear signal that The Boys better toss a coin to choose who would thank her at an intimate supper after the show.

Buchanan finished his answer.

Barrett picked up the cudgel.

"Cincinnati is a splendid omen for the continued success of *Jekyll and Hyde*. The Civil War general who commanded the troops that saved Cincinnati from Confederate invasion was named Lew Wallace. I am sure that each and every one of you remembers that when he retired in peacetime, Lew Wallace wrote a famous novel called . . . Lady? Gentlemen?"

"*Ben-Hur*," they chorused.

"The novel that inspired the play *Ben-Hur*."

"The most successful play in the history of the American theater."

"Which," Barrett fired back, "launched the most lucrative road show ever!"

"At least," said Buchanan, "until the good people of Toledo, Detroit, and Cincinnati buy their tickets."

More scribbling, more grins from their publicist.

The clock struck the hour, and things got even better.

Isabella Cook breezed into the car in a diaphanous tea gown. Two qualities struck anyone who had only seen her on the stage. Up close, she was tiny. And, seen in person, her big, round eyes were bigger, her bow lips more sensual, and her aquiline nose straighter than seemed possible on a mortal.

"I hope I am not interrupting."

The male reporters leaped to their feet. The lady from Chicago wrote,

Isabella Cook's melodious contralto voice sounds as if Our Maker had chosen it to harmonize with each and every one of her beautiful features. The winsome blonde wears her hair in the modern style of the heiress Gabriella Utterson, who is key to the terrifying plot of *Dr. Jekyll and Mr. Hyde.*

Barrett and Buchanan had risen with a flourish, exchanging a private glance. Say what they could about their leading lady—and they could say plenty—the "Great and Beloved" never missed an entrance nor any opportunity to boom a show in which she had negotiated a percentage of the take. Another glance said, Worth every penny.

"My dear, how good of you to stop in."

"Come sit between us."

And she did, prompting the first question, which started, of course, with condolences.

"With the greatest sympathy for the recent loss of your husband, Miss Cook, may I ask you, as a recent widow, do you find it terribly difficult having to perform night after night in such an arduous role?"

Isabella smiled bravely. "It would be much harder, if not impossible, without the firm shoulders of Jackson Barrett and John Buchanan to rely on, and to lean on, and, I am grateful to say, occasionally weep on."

The lady from Chicago wondered how to couch the big question in her readers' hearts. "Would it be fair to say they make you feel a little less lonely?"

Isabella Cook smiled at one, then the other. "More than a little."

Now—how to ask?—which of the handsomest actors that ever graced the modern stage made the widow feel the most less lonely? But the male reporters were growing restive, and whiskey had made one cocky.

"Jekyll or Hyde?"

Isabella obliterated him with an innocent, "My favorite Jekyll and my favorite Hyde do everything necessary to make the show go on."

Their stage manager entered on cue. "Excuse me, Miss Cook. Excuse me, Mr. Barrett, Mr. Buchanan . . ."

"Yes, Mr. Young?"

"You scheduled a principals' rehearsal."

The actors rose as one. "Duty calls, gentlemen and lady. Mr. Young will see you back to the dining car."

But before the reporters could drain their glasses and close their notebooks, it suddenly all went to blazes. "Just one more question, please?"

The wire-service reporter, an old man reeking of whiskey and nickel cigars, had yet to speak. He had come aboard at Columbus. The publicist didn't know him, and they had assumed he had been put out to pasture, covering theater news. He had put a dent in the whiskey, and had nodded amiably at the actors' jokes. Now, just as they were wrapping things up, he had a question.

"Have you run into any difficulty selling tickets owing to the reports of murdered women?"

28

Jekyll and Hyde's publicist stood, wild-eyed and speechless, in the swaying car.

John Buchanan said, "What?"

Jackson Barrett asked, "What do you mean?"

All three of the showmen noticed belatedly that the old man reeking of whiskey and nickel cigars had the crafty eyes of a seasoned police reporter with a nose for a big story. Or the cynicism to create one. "What I mean," he said, "is that since you've been on tour, young girls have been getting murdered and mutilated. I'm curious whether the horror of these crimes has affected ticket sales?"

"Why would it?" blurted Barrett. Buchanan tried to stay him

with a gesture, which would have been futile if Isabella Cook had not laid her hand on his arm.

"Well, you boys may be too young to remember, but when I was a young pup reporter in New York, Richard Mansfield's *Jekyll and Hyde* company came back early from London with their tails between their legs. They had opened to wonderful reviews, as good as they got here. 'The curtain fell upon a shock of silence,' said the *Telegraph*, 'followed by a roar of sympathetic applause.' But then Jack the Ripper started murdering. Girl after girl, like is happening here. London audiences stopped buying tickets. As if they were saying, Too much blood in the street. Who wants to see it in the theater, too?"

Buchanan said, "We've noted no falloff in bookings."

"No empty seats?"

"None," said Barrett, and the publicist finally got a hold on himself to claim, "The wraps are actually increasing."

The "wrap" was the money taken in at the box office, counted when the curtain went up, stacked in brick-size packs wrapped in paper, and delivered under armed guard to the Jekyll & Hyde Special's steel safe, to be divvied up at prescribed intervals with the Deaver brothers.

"Why do you suppose your ticket sales have not been affected yet?"

"Audiences love the play," said the publicist, "because it is a piece with class written all over it, and it has a great plot."

"What about *Alias Jimmy Valentine*?" asked Barrett.

"What about it?"

"*Jimmy Valentine*'s been dogging us in every city we've played. Why blame us? Why not blame them?"

The wire-service man pounced with a cold smile. "Because *Alias Jimmy Valentine* doesn't have murdered girls in its show."

"Nonsense," said Buchanan.

"Fact is, I hear in many quarters that *Dr. Jekyll and Mr. Hyde* is jinxed."

"Nonsense," said Barrett.

"Add it up—Mr. Medick, the previous holder of the rights, tumbled to his death from a fire escape. Poor Miss Cook's husband, the late Theatrical Syndicate booking trust magnate, Rufus S. Oppenheim, was blown to smithereens, along with his yacht, before you opened in New York. And now all these girls are getting murdered. Is there anything you would like to say to reassure audiences?"

The other reporters had pencils poised.

Buchanan stepped forward before Barrett could speak. "Yes. Please write that John Buchanan and Jackson Barrett hope that their play will offer audiences a respite from the cares of the world."

"Tell 'em it has an exciting plot," said the publicist. "They'll kick themselves if they fail to see it."

The reporter wrote down both answers, and turned to Barrett. "Mr. Barrett, have you anything to add?"

"Our hearts go out to the poor women and their families who loved them, and we pray the killer is arrested very soon."

———

John Buchanan was red-faced and seething when he finally got Jackson Barrett alone in his Toledo dressing room. "Did you have to say that to that infernal reporter?"

"Say what?"

"'Our hearts go out to the poor women and their families who loved them, and we pray the killer is arrested very soon.'"

"Somebody had to say it."

"Did you hear what our publicist said? Did you hear what I said?"

"Yes. That's why I said what had to be said."

"You gave that reporter exactly what he wanted. You made a direct connection between those murders and our show. That story will dog us around the country, slashing sales just like Jack the Ripper did to Mansfield."

"Nonsense! We live in modern times," said Jackson Barrett. "Jack the Ripper was a Victorian fiend. We don't have fiends in the twentieth century. Our audiences will mob the box office for blood and gore."

"Is that a fact? Would you like to hear what that son of a bitch reporter said when he barged back into my private car after the others left?"

"If it will make you happy, of course I would like to hear what he said. What did he say?"

"He asked, 'How will we answer a murder victim's father and mother who claim that our *Dr. Jekyll and Mr. Hyde* provoked her killing?'"

"'Provoked'? Ridiculous. It's a *play*."

"'Ridiculous'? Tell that to Richard Mansfield."

"Mansfield died in aught seven."

"I know that," shouted Buchanan. "But in London, according to that bastard reporter, that was the main thing that killed

Mansfield's box office. People asked, did the play provoke Jack the Ripper?"

"Absurd."

"I know it's absurd. You know it's absurd."

"That reporter knows it's absurd."

"But what if ticket buyers don't know it's absurd? What if they blame us?" Buchanan sank in a chair and put his head in his hands. "We are sunk . . . Jackson, how in blazes can we get around this?"

Barrett grinned the way he did whenever he came up with a big idea. "Tell you what. We have an airplane, right?"

"What airplane?"

"Flying over the stage. The one you said cost too much. Fortunately, I prevailed. Audiences love it."

"So what?"

"So we paint an airplane red. We paint 'Jekyll' and 'Hyde' on the wings. We fly it over the city where we're playing. A billboard in the sky."

"It's not a real airplane. It's a stage prop."

"We rent a real one that looks like ours. With an aviator to fly it."

"That would cost a fortune."

"We'll save a fortune in billboard passes. Why give free tickets to shopkeepers who put our ads in their windows when we have a billboard in the sky?"

Buchanan took a deep breath. A billboard in the sky was a bold idea. If the publicist could make hay with it, it might actually save them.

"I know a pilot."

"Wire him!" said Barrett.

"Her."

"Oh, one of your ladies?"

"No, it's not like that. She's happily married, she has children, and I know her father."

"Ugly, too, I presume?"

———————

"*Driver!* Stop. Head for Chelsea."

Isaac Bell was on his way to Waterloo Station to take the boat train to Southampton Docks. Acting on sudden instinct, he ordered the cabby to make a detour.

"Ain't you got to get to your ship, guv?"

"I'll be quick, and triple your fare when you get me to the station on time."

Wayne Barlowe was working in his loft, putting finishing touches on the whale.

"What happened to your face?"

"Slipped in the bath."

"Did you find Emily?"

"She loved your sketch," said Bell, and told him about Jack Spelvin. "Did you ever see Spelvin perform at Wilton's?"

"No."

"You'd remember his face if you had?"

"Of course."

"I gave her your sketch. Could you make me another?"

As happened on their last meeting, Barlowe's hands flew without hesitation.

"How is she?" he asked.

"Alive—barely. She seems to have landed in some sort of safe berth at the Salvation Army. How long she'll stay there will depend on whether she goes back to the laudanum."

The sketch was in Bell's hands in moments, a near replica of the first. He asked, "Could you draw another of him when he's older? The way he'd look today, if he's still alive."

"Are you assuming that Spelvin was not an innocent actor?"

Bell said, "I have to consider every possibility. Including if Emily was not hallucinating, Spelvin was not innocent."

Barlowe hesitated. "I have to consider twenty years of variables, twenty years of events, that changed him. Drink, tobacco, illness, accident, grief."

"Joy," said Bell. "If it is he, I doubt he feels grief."

"I'm asking you, is he Jack the Ripper?"

"Draw him like he is the Ripper," Bell said brusquely. "I want to see what he might look like now. Start with what people saw when he was young—bounding like a hare, handsome, angelic—and imagine he's been lucky, no illness, no accidents, few disappointments."

Barlowe picked up his pencil reluctantly. He worked for a few minutes and handed Bell a sketch of a pleasant-looking, somewhat elegant man in his forties. The face lacked the eye-catching qualities of Jack Spelvin in his youth.

Barlowe said, "It's too general, Bell. Do you see what I mean? He could be anyone."

"You are too modest," said Isaac Bell. "Far too modest."

"What do you mean?"

"You are an artist."

Barlowe had captured the face of a chameleon.

Twenty-three years after the so-called Jack Spelvin mesmerized Emily, this man in his forties could indeed be anyone—almost invisible in one instant, bland in another, and striking in the next. A girl might not even notice him until he was ready to be noticed. She might see him as innocuous. Or harmless. Or intriguing. Or dazzling.

He would choose.

29

The Cutthroat dipped an artist's brush in a vial of spirit gum. He painted the adhesive on the lace backing of a gray mustache made of human hair. Then he dipped the brush again and coated the skin above his upper lip, exhaling through his nostrils to dispel the nauseating odor of alcohol and pine resin. To make the glue dry faster, he fanned it with an old souvenir program stolen the night that Mansfield's *Dr. Jekyll and Mr. Hyde* opened its ill-fated London run at the Lyceum.

He had carried it everywhere in his vagabond life and cherished the illustrations of scenes from the play. An ordinary paper program the theater gave away would have disintegrated years ago, but the souvenir was printed on strong silk. Though mottled from the oil on his fingertips, and drips of spirit gum, the colors had never faded. Every page transported him back to a haunting night of melodrama, mastery, and death.

He tapped the brush handle to his lip. When it stuck to the spirit gum and lifted the skin, it was ready. He pressed the mustache to his lip and held it firmly. The coupling of gum to gum felt warm for a few moments and then it was on good and tight. He tested the mustache in the mirror with a gentle, fatherly smile. It flexed naturally.

He grayed his hair, dabbing in pressed powder with a densely bristled goat-hair makeup brush. Old-fashioned gold wire-rimmed spectacles aged him further, while their tinted glass shielded the fire in his eyes. He worked a wedding ring on his finger; few married men wore a wedding ring, and the girls took it as a sign of extreme fidelity. His detachable shirt cuffs— instead of up-to-date sewn-on cotton—were as behind the times as his specs and made of stiff celluloid that protected his wrists from their fingernails.

Before he stepped out into the night, he gazed upon the program cover.

Richard Mansfield in
Dr. Jekyll and Mr. Hyde
A Souvenir of the Lyceum Theatre
Lessee and Manager, Mr. Henry Irving
August 8, 1888

The Cutthroat felt his heartbeat quicken. He had scrounged pennies for the cheapest seat in the back of the Lyceum. The play was a culmination of an obsession that had deepened nightly since he first feasted on the Robert Louis Stevenson novella and the lightning bolt of recognition that the story struck. It was an entirely new way to regard what every man knew in the darkest part of his heart. Everyone knew that good and evil resided in every man. Everyone knew he had to resist evil. Until *Jekyll and Hyde* promised what everyone wanted: the means to have both.

There had been rumors of a play. An American actor was said to have bought dramatic rights from Stevenson. Then came word it had opened in New York to magnificent notices. London was next, and opening night from even the cheapest seat in the house was everything the Cutthroat had hoped for.

And more. In Mansfield's adaptation, Hyde attacked women as well as men. For the Cutthroat, everything he wanted fell into place. It took only a few short hours after the curtain fell for him to murder a woman who denied him. By a miracle and some good luck, he didn't get caught. A cask of spoiled wine in the St. Katharine Docks storehouse, where he paid for his bed as the night watchman, preserved the body while he got rid of it in pieces.

He would be more careful next time. He would plan. Savor. Anticipate. Returning to the theater repeatedly, he had prepared for that next time. Prostitutes were safest, he decided, the nature of their bargain being privacy. It was safer to kill them in their places, leave their bodies, and sleep safely in his own place. Three weeks later, he killed his first prostitute. Set off by the play, he let the demon in him come and go. In between, he led a blameless life. He was in every aspect Jekyll and Hyde. But unlike Jekyll, he needed no secret potion to become Hyde. The play was his potion.

But suddenly he was punished. Returning to the Lyceum one evening, he found the theater dark and shuttered. The Mansfield play had failed, driven out of business by his own Jack the Ripper murders. The audience had dried up. Who wanted to watch a play about horror when the horror of real-life killings gripped London? He would wait three long years before he saw *Jekyll and Hyde* performed in New York.

He tested the mustache with another smile, took one of the capes hidden under a false bottom in his trunk, and swirled it over his shoulders. He snatched up a walking stick and strode into the dark streets at a jaunty pace. When he saw her, fair-haired in the glow of a streetlamp, he slowed his pace and transformed the walking stick into an old man's cane by the simple act of leaning on it.

She looked him over, saw he was old and rich, and gave him a hopeful smile.

"Would you tell me your name, miss?"

30

Isaac Bell had fired off two final cables to New York before he boarded his ship at Southampton. To his Cutthroat Squad:

    LUSITANIA
    PILOT BOAT

To Grady Forrer in Research:

    MURDERED GIRLS
    MISSING GIRLS
    TRAVEL PATTERN

Lusitania flashed past sail-driven pilot boats as she raced along the Fire Island coast at her twenty-five-knot service speed. Slowing at last for the first time since she put to sea at the

Needles, the four-stack Cunard liner stopped beside the light-ship *Ambrose* at the entrance to the channel. The steam-powered Sandy Hook pilot boat *New York* launched a heavily laden yawl in the lee of *Lusitania*'s cliff-like black hull. The yawl's oarsman rowed to the ship. The harbor pilot climbed her rope and wood Jacob's ladder.

An agile quartet of Van Dorn detectives clambered after him. *Lusitania*'s assistant purser, as lavishly tipped as the pilot-boat crew, took them directly to Isaac Bell's stateroom.

"Grab a seat. The Cutthroat Squad has four uninterrupted hours, until the tugboats land us at 13th Street, to think out loud. I expect bright ideas to spark others."

Archie Abbott, Harry Warren, James Dashwood, and Helen Mills crowded onto chairs and the edge of the bed. Grady Forrer leaned quietly against the bureau. Bell paced.

"The question is no longer whether Anna Waterbury's mur-derer is Jack the Ripper. The question is how has he managed not to get caught for the twenty years he's been murdering women in our country?"

"But is he Jack the Ripper?" asked Harry Warren.

"Here's what he might look like if he is."

The ship's photographer had made copies of Wayne Barlowe's aged drawing. Bell passed them around.

"This could be any gent in his forties," said Archie Abbott.

"A rather handsome 'any gent,'" said Helen Mills. "Out-standing."

"But not unique."

"Looks like a grown-up altar boy," said Harry Warren.

"This eliminates men who look older and younger," said Dashwood. "He's not thirty. He's not fifty."

"Why don't we print these up like wanted posters?" asked Mills. "Warn street girls about a man who looks like this."

Isaac Bell thought of Wayne Barlowe, caught in a similar bind, refusing to draw the angelic and possibly innocent youth for the police posters, and second-guessing himself ever since. "No," he said. "Archie's right. This drawing could be many gents in their forties. If we print these up, we'll get bullies forming lynch mobs and a bunch of innocents dancing from their necks."

"That's a valid point," said Helen. "But the girls he's killing are innocent, too."

Bell said, "I'll consider it after we isolate the city he's operating in. Meantime, a better angle is to decipher the crescent shapes he carves in the bodies."

"Did the London Ripper do this to his girls?"

"He cut symbols. But they were different. We need to know what his crescents mean."

"How come no one's seen him attack?" asked Helen. "No one's even heard a scream?"

"Three reasons," said Bell. "One, he's a predator. That means he's extraordinarily alert and aware of his surroundings. Probably the last time he had to run was the night when a con man named Davy Collins caught a glimpse of him in 'eighty-eight. Two, he never frightens his victim before he has complete control of her. He's made an art of putting her at ease. Three, America is a big continent. When he arrived, he reckoned he'd never get caught if he kept moving around. If the Van Dorn Agency hadn't been working up the Anna case, no one would have noticed the connection between her and Lillian Lent in Boston and Mary Beth Winthrop in Springfield. Fortunately, we *are* working the case, so the All Field Offices Alert turned up a slew of his killings. We know he's still in business. We know what his victims look like. And I'm betting he looks something like this picture."

"He's killed girls in twenty cities," said Harry Warren. "How does he get around?"

"Precisely what we will focus on," said Bell. "How does he travel? Why does he travel? What line is he in?"

———————

"A drummer," said Archie Abbott. "Who travels more than a traveling salesman?"

"He's an executive," said Helen. "He travels city to city visiting his company's factories."

"He's a bank robber," said Harry Warren. "The new breed that cross state lines in autos."

Bell shook his head. "He's been murdering since 1891. How'd he cross state lines before autos?"

· "Covered wagon."

Isaac Bell did not smile. The detectives exchanged wary glances. The stateroom fell so silent, they could hear stewards hustling luggage in the corridor and the faint piping of pilot whistles as *Lusitania* crept toward Quarantine.

"Sorry, Isaac."

"A circus performer," said Archie Abbott. "They're always on the move. Or a vaudevillian."

Now Bell had his people where he wanted them—the best minds in the agency, working full steam at turning speculation into facts. He looked at Abbott. "If he had been a London music hall actor, could he play vaudeville here?"

"Why not? Music is music, and the jokes work the same: Set-up. Premise. Punch line. Was he on the bill?"

"I have no playbills or programs from back then. The music hall isn't even a theater anymore."

"What's his name?"

"Jack Spelvin."

"Sounds like he had a sense of humor. Spelvin's a pseudonym."

"The Ripper liked his games." If the crescent cuts were the murderer's idea of a joke, thought Bell, what was the punch line?

"He could be a hobo," said Harry Warren. "Stealing rides on freight trains."

"Except," said Helen Mills, "where does a hobo get cash in hand to show the girl?"

"But what if he isn't *stealing* rides? What if he's a railroad man?" said Warren. "They're on the move. Brakemen invented the red-light district with their red lanterns."

Bell said, "I find it difficult to imagine a railroad man dressing in a cape and homburg to convince Anna Waterbury he was a Broadway producer. Though he could be an express agent." The well-paid operators who guarded the express cars could afford to dress like dandies, and often did.

"Union organizers travel," said Harry Warren.

"An engineer," said Helen Mills. "They travel for work. So do specialist doctors and surgeons. So do actors. As we just said."

"A private detective."

Everyone stared at Archie Abbott.

Bell nudged them back on track. "There are three or four hundred thousand commercial travelers in the country. If he is a traveling salesman, then he's probably a commission man. They make their own schedules. Union organizers, engineers, and specialists who travel might number in the low thousands. Archie, how many actors are there?"

"All told? Maybe thirty thousand."

"All men?"

"Men, maybe twenty thousand."

"Not exactly what I'd call narrowing down," said Harry Warren.

That was followed by a deep silence. Helen Mills broke it. "Speaking of a cape and homburg, how did Jack the Ripper dress in London?"

"That was a long time ago, and it depends on who thinks they saw him. The illustrators mostly agreed on a gentleman's cape and top hat, but that was the image they expected of a man who could afford to pay a prostitute."

"In other words, we don't know what he does, and we don't know how he gets around."

"We can assume," said Bell, "that he must be of some means to afford to dress well and travel. Unless he is wealthy and doesn't have to work, whatever his job, it almost certainly requires him to travel."

"Right back where we started," said Harry Warren.

"Not quite," said Isaac Bell. "We're miles ahead of where we started." He looked at Grady Forrer, who remained silent through the speculation.

"We have a pattern," said the Research chief. "We can match our pattern to the travels."

"What pattern?"

"His route," said Isaac Bell. "Tell them, Grady."

Forrer ticked cities off on his enormous fingers. "New York, Boston, Springfield, in the order petite blond girls were murdered. Albany, Philadelphia, Scranton, Binghamton, Pittsburgh, Columbus, in the order girls disappeared. Ten days ago, a girl was reported missing in Cleveland."

"He's back to doing an expert job hiding bodies," said Bell. "Or luck's on his side, again."

Grady Forrer tugged a map from the folds of his tent-size coat and unrolled it on the stateroom bed. The route was marked in red. Looping north from New York to Boston, the red line meandered over the densely populated northeastern section of America, crossing each other occasionally, the size of the cities diminishing as it progressed westward.

"Why did you circle Cincinnati?"

The big manufacturing and trading city on the Ohio River nudged the Indiana and Kentucky borders a hundred miles beyond the westwardmost Columbus.

"Cincinnati breaks the pattern. There's a girl missing in Cincinnati who resembled his other victims. But she disappeared months before Anna was murdered. A singer at the continuous vaudeville house. Happy in her job, according to the other performers. No hint that she was about to run, nor any reason why she would."

Bell gestured at the map. "Before all these?"

"An anomaly," said Grady Forrer. "But anomalies sometimes make a point. So I circled her."

"What's her name?"

"Rose Bloom."

"*There's* a stage name," said Archie Abbott.

"Actually, she was born with it, a pretty little Irish girl—There you have it, gents," Forrer said. "And lady," he added with a courtly bow to Helen Mills. "Two questions for you to contemplate: What takes our man on this route? Which is to ask, what's his line? And where is he headed next?"

"Three questions," said Isaac Bell. "Can the Cutthroat Squad detect where he is headed next *before* he kills some poor girl when he gets there?"

31

Prospering for a century on a big bend of the Ohio River, Cincinnati was accustomed to spectacular arrivals. Eight thousand steamboats had landed in the single year of 1852, with priceless cargo, and with ambitious passengers eager to share in her boomtown riches. In the dark days of the Civil War, Cincinnatians improvised a pontoon bridge of coal barges for fifty thousand Union troops who had arrived in the nick of time to block a Confederate Army invasion. And when the Kaiser's brother—the much-loved Prince Henry of Prussia—arrived on his American tour, the police had to shoo adoring mobs off the roofs of his train cars while the United German Singing Societies serenaded him.

But no arrival could prepare Cincinnati for the Jekyll & Hyde Special.

For days in advance, newspaper writers described the show train in awed detail—Jackson Barrett and John Buchanan's private cars, decorated to the actor-managers' personal taste; the leading actors' and actresses' lavish staterooms; the dormitory cars, stacked with Pullman berths, for players, stagehands, carpenters, electricians, clerks, publicists, accountants, and musicians; the dining car, "the heart of the train that serves mouthwatering repasts all round the clock"; the freight cars that carried the elaborate sets; and the express/baggage car, with its monumental steel safe for the box office receipts, guarded by a heavily armed, ice-eyed agent of Van Dorn Protective Services, the trusted subsidiary of the famous detective agency that furnished house detectives for first class hotels, and as jewelers' escorts, bodyguards, and for discreet assistance to William Howard Taft's Secret Service squad when the president ventured from the White House—ten gleaming red cars in all—cannonballed from city to city by a high-wheeled Atlantic 4-4-2 Deaver-built locomotive that was, her engineer confided to the *Cincinnati Enquirer*, "a good steamer and rides easy."

Telegraph operators relayed its progress as it thundered south through Detroit. Would the Jekyll & Hyde Special deliver actors, scenery, and musicians in time to stage the show for their first-night curtain?

No one knew that Barrett and Buchanan had deliberately scheduled a close-run arrival to build suspense and encourage the Cincinnati, Hamilton & Dayton Railroad to clear tracks for their special rather than risk the wrath of a city that loved its theaters. Betting pools sprang up in saloons, beer gardens, and gentlemen's clubs, and fortunes changed hands for side bets on the precise moments it would tear past intervening stations.

Suddenly, when it was ten miles out and no greater excitement could be imagined, a blood-red biplane—the spitting image of the airplane everyone had heard was in the play—soared over the city, skimmed the river, and swooped under the Roebling suspension bridge.

The most unlikely event tripped up the Cutthroat.

This sweet little dancer's upturned nose was as sensitive as his.

"I smell spirit gum."

He had stuck to his rules. He had practiced self-discipline and restraint. He had planned. He had anticipated. He had hoped. But still he was tripped up: Little Beatrice's nose was as sensitive as his. In Cincinnati, of all places, despite laying extraordinarily elaborate groundwork.

"Is that a false beard?"

She actually reached up to tug it. He recoiled, jerked his head away from her hand.

"It is, isn't it?" She laughed, and stood on tiptoe to inspect it closely. "That's the best one I've ever seen." Her laughter died as she considered the oddity.

He was quick, he reminded himself. He had better be. The

suspicion of danger had narrowed her eyes. Still, he was confident that he held the advantage. She was only operating on instinct. He had at his command decades of know-how.

"Why are you wearing a false beard?"

"To hide . . ." he said, then cast his eyes down as if too dismayed to complete his thought. He could still control her.

"From what?" she asked sharply. Her voice had an unpleasant edge, a grating noise that he longed to silence. But he couldn't silence her before he coaxed her to join him inside his cottage. It was next to the river at the end of a dark lane. The last girl he had brought here, Rose—Rose Bloom—had entered willingly. But Rose had not smelled spirit gum, nor noticed anything to trip him up.

It was all too easy to imagine how the cottage would look to a girl who was already wary: remote, tucked away in a storehouse district, the only dwelling on the lane. He had had the front porch painted a warm yellow so that it looked welcoming and had installed an electric light on the front porch, and had left another burning inside. Pleasant, lived-in, welcoming, a cosy cottage on the outskirts of town, with a rowboat dock convenient to the Ohio.

"For you," he answered.

"I don't understand."

She stopped walking abruptly and looked around as if noticing for the first time that the street was devoid of people. They had just reached the storehouses at the corner of his lane. They could smell the river. "What do you mean from me?"

"Not *from* you," he stammered. "To protect you. To hide my face."

"From what?"

"Scars. I was wounded horribly in the Spanish War." The false beard was so gray, it was nearly white, which would make him rather too old to have fought in the 1898 War. But hopefully for a girl so young, a war of thirteen years ago could have been fought a hundred years in the past. Ancient history. Civil War. Revolutionary War. War of 1898.

She said, "Oh." Still standing there, still gazing around—looking for help, he feared—she said, "Well, so am I."

He searched her pretty face by the streetlamp. "Scarred?"

"From a fire."

"Where?"

"Where you can't see."

"Can't see? I saw you dance on the stage."

"The corset covers it. A lamp exploded when I was a little girl. It looks horrible. I'll never let anyone see."

"You poor thing."

"Well, you're a poor thing, too."

"Aren't we a pair?"

"If you say so."

"I *do* say so. And I promised you supper. My housekeeper will be quite put out if we let it get cold."

"Is she there now?"

"She better be. Who do you think serves supper and washes the dishes?"

Still, she hesitated.

He took a chance and went for broke. "You know, Beatrice, in all my days of booking national tours, I've never met a dancer who wasn't famished after her show."

That got him a grin that wrinkled her pretty nose, and suddenly they were friends.

"I'm starving!"

He shrugged his cape off one shoulder and offered his arm.

"Step this way."

———————

Late that night, he propped Beatrice in a kitchen chair while he ate a cold supper. Just before dawn, he tied his cape around her, gathered her in his arms, and climbed down the steep stairs to the dock. The river smelled rank. The fierce current was so loud, he could barely hear her splash.

"Good night. You were lovely."

How wrong he was about that.

32

Isaac Bell jumped off the extra-fare St. Louis Limited at Cincinnati and headed straight to the morgue in City Hospital. The talkative coroner, who greeted him on the front steps, started apologizing for the condition of the old building. "Dates back to the 1860s. We're building a fine new hospital across town."

"May I see the girl?"

A barge hand had spotted her butchered body jammed under an Ohio River wharf. The Van Dorn field office had already reported a dancer missing from the continuous vaudeville house where she worked, the same theater where the singer Rose Bloom had disappeared months earlier.

Beatrice Edmond had told a friend she was trying to land a

part in a road company, but she had not said which one. The field office chief had found no one who had seen her at any of the Cincinnati theaters where tours were playing—not *Tillie's Nightmare*, the Marie Dressler show at the Bethel, nor *Alias Jimmy Valentine* at the Lyric, nor *Dr. Jekyll and Mr. Hyde* at the Clark, and surely not *Salome* at the German.

"Her cape snagged on a wharf," said the coroner, "or she'd have drifted to New Orleans before anyone noticed."

"May I see her?" Bell asked again. Twenty-to-one, "her cape" was a standard department store item and twice the size a tiny girl would wear.

"Not much to see. The current banged her around, and the city sewage is as corrosive as you'd ex—"

A racket in the sky cut him off in the middle of a sentence.

BLAT! BLAT! BLAT! BLAT! BLAT! BLAT!

Isaac Bell looked up, astonished. He recognized the sound instantly, but the last thing he expected to hear over Cincinnati was the staccato blast of a rotary airplane engine at full throttle. A red streak of lightning shot past the hospital fifty feet above the Miami Canal and vanished in the direction of the Ohio River.

"Bet you don't know what that is," said the coroner.

Bell was an avid airman and knew exactly what it was. "A new Breguet Type IV tractor biplane with a Gnome rotary engine. But what's he doing here?"

"Advertising! That's—"

BLAT! BLAT! BLAT! BLAT! BLAT! BLAT! drowned him out again.

The Breguet skimmed the mansard roof of the four-story

hospital so close, it sent tiles flying, and Isaac Bell could not help grinning in envy of the lucky pilot. Then he saw the advertisement painted on the underside of the wings touting the show that Anna Waterbury had hoped would have a place for her:

JEKYLL

on the left wing and

AND HYDE

on the right.

The red plane flashed by trailing castor oil smoke that smelled like someone had blown out candles.

"First airplane that ever flew over Cincinnati," said the coroner. "Booming *Dr. Jekyll and Mr. Hyde*. Tickets are going like hotcakes. I'm taking the wife on Saturday.

"Come on in," said the coroner. "I have her on the table."

———————

Later, Isaac Bell wandered Cincinnati's theater district, reading marquees and playbills and collecting programs. He stopped in front of the vaudeville house. Beatrice Edmond's name was still on the bill. Her cape *had* been too big.

He took the theater programs to the two-room Van Dorn field office on Plum Street. The chief—Sedgwick, an eager young detective they had hired away from the Police Department and who had gained a reputation in New York for snappy telegrams in the middle of the night—was working late. Bell spread the programs on a table and opened his notebook.

( ) ⊃ ∩ ⋃

He juggled the symbols in his mind, inverted the crescent moons, angled some horns, and tried to group them in patterns. Then he took out his fountain pen. He was sketching freehand in the margins of the theater programs when, reaching for another, he suddenly saw the crescent shapes as Jack the Ripper carved them.

———————

"I need your private wire."

"Want me to send for you?"

"I remember my Morse."

Bell sat at the key and tapped out orders to New York in cipher.

```
CINCINNATI
ON THE JUMP
FORRER—LINK ROAD SHOWS TO MURDERS MAP
DASHWOOD—ASSIST CINCINNATI FIELD OFFICE
BRING RIPPER WARNING POSTERS
ABBOTT, MILLS, WARREN—ON THE QUIET
```

"Why on the quiet?" said a voice over his shoulder.

"Hello, Joe." Bell stood up and shook Joseph Van Dorn's enormous hand. "I thought I heard you come in."

"New York told me you were here. I caught the B&O from Washington."

"Why?"

"To determine where your investigation is going."

Isaac Bell's face lighted in a triumphant smile.

"It is going to town with bells on."

"Why on the quiet?"

"I'm disguising my operators."

"As what?"

"I'll show you."

Bell led Van Dorn to the table where his notebook lay open among the programs.

(/ ⋑ ⋒ ⋓

One by one, he pointed to the crescents with his pen.

"Here's a smile," he told Van Dorn.

"So?"

"Here's a frown."

"If you say so."

"Mouths! Eyes!"

"Isaac!" Van Dorn exploded. "What in blue blazes are you talking about?"

"Mouths. Upturned and downcast. Eyes. Upturned and downcast—the raw ingredients."

"OF WHAT?"

ACT THREE

BACKSTAGE

33

CINCINNATI

The Deaver brothers were getting jumpy.

"Explain, again," Jeff demanded. "Who is Isaac Bell?"

"Mr. Bell," said Joe Deaver, "is a Hartford, Connecticut, insurance executive who—"

"We don't need insurance! We won't own anything to insure if *Jekyll and Hyde* closes on the road."

Jeff hadn't shaved or left their hotel suite in days. It had fallen to Joe to go out into the world, where, as luck would have it, he had been approached by a potential savior.

"A *rich* Hartford, Connecticut, insurance executive who's put together a syndicate of investors to finance shows in the theater. He's got some cockamamie idea to produce a musical play based on Robert Louis Stevenson's *Treasure Island*. We're invited to the Queen City Club for lunch. We don't want to keep him waiting. Get dressed!"

"We were going great guns," moaned Jeff. "The show was making money hand over fist."

"It also spends money hand over fist, which was fine as long as we filled the theaters. Now that we're playing to some empty seats . . ."

"If Mother catches wind of this," said Jeff Deaver.

"Don't say it," said Joe Deaver.

While the theatrical angels appeared fabulously wealthy to working actors and three-dollar-a-day stagehands, they actually existed on an allowance. It was generous enough to live large, but under the authority of Grandfather's will, which compelled them to take the Deaver family name instead of their father's, their mother held the purse strings. Since Mother blamed the theater for the showgirls who had seduced Father repeatedly, she would never release the next year's allowance if she learned that they had lost this year's investing in *Dr. Jekyll and Mr. Hyde*.

"I will slit that damned reporter's throat and shove his leg through it," said Jeff.

Joe had no doubt that Jeff would kill the reporter if opportunity arose, or he might even create the opportunity. "Don't," he said. "Even Mother would catch wind of *that* newspaper report."

Mother was holed up in the family's Lower Merion Main Line estate. The only visitors to her fifty rooms and two hundred acres—which Joe and Jeff dreamed of one day inheriting to subdivide—were her bankers and her priest.

"What's this about *Treasure Island*? We don't have any money for another play."

"Which is why," Joe explained patiently, "we will maneuver Mr. Isaac Bell into buying into our investment in *Jekyll and Hyde*. If these murdered girls sink us, we'll at least get some of our money out."

"But why would Bell invest in *Jekyll and Hyde* when the papers are full of murdered girls?"

Joe Deaver said, "Partly to involve Barrett & Buchanan in his pipe dreams for *Treasure Island* and partly to secure employment in *Dr. Jekyll and Mr. Hyde* for a friend."

Jeff Deaver grinned. At last, a motive he could understand. "Sounds like the insurance man fell for an actress."

"Helen," said Joe. "An attractive brunette who knows how to wear a gown. Bell claims she was a scholarship girl at Bryn Mawr who got taken under the wing of one of his investors."

"A likely story."

Joe shook his head emphatically. "Bell is as straitlaced as you'd expect of an insurance man. And I'm sorry to say Helen doesn't come across as your average chorus girl on the make."

"What part does she want?"

"Mr. Bell believes she should replace Barbara."

"Barbara? No! Barbara makes a crackerjacks job of it. How do we know Bell's friend is up to doing 'general business-woman'?"

Joe was running out of patience. He answered sharply.

"Your Barbara is paid twenty bucks a week to dust Jekyll's library in one scene; speak the line 'Mr. Hyde hasn't come home yet, Dr. Jekyll' in another; and get strangled any evening one of the regulars catches a cold. If Isaac Bell will cover half of our investment, I *guarantee* his friend Helen will be up to it."

———————

A Baltimore & Ohio fast freight from Pittsburgh slowed to enter the Cincinnati yards. A hobo dropped from a boxcar. A railroad detective ran after him with a billy club.

"Come here, you!"

Harry Warren did as he was told. His clothes were grimy, his hands and face smeared with coal soot, but a cop with a sharper eye might have noticed that he was fitter, stronger, and better fed than most who rode the rails.

"Where you think you're going?"

"Hoping for Frisco."

"You got yourself a long walk. And a busted head for stealing rides." The yard bull whipped his billy skyward. "Tell your friends Cincinnati is off-limits."

"Do you really want to try that?"

Warren's tone was almost conversational. He waited for the yard bull to reconsider, but the man swung at him anyway. Seasoned hickory whistled. Parting the air that Harry Warren's skull had occupied an instant earlier, the brutal blow ended up as a wild swing angled across the rail cop's torso. When it smacked the gravel by his left foot, he was off balance, with his right side exposed.

Four inches of lead pipe had materialized in Harry Warren's hand. He gauged his opportunity and applied the pipe to the yard bull's skull well above his vulnerable temple with a force precisely calculated to flatten him facedown, head ringing, and legs too shaky to try to stand for several minutes.

"Which way's the Lyric Theatre?"

"Huh?"

"The Lyric. Where they show *Alias Jimmy Valentine*. It's about a detective trying to mistreat an innocent safecracker."

An angry thumb gestured a route into the freight district.

Having ensured that he would be remembered as a tough who rode the rails if someone asked questions later, Harry Warren made a quick tour of streets clogged to a standstill by horse- and mule-drawn wagons, exasperated teamsters, and motor trucks belching blue exhaust. He breakfasted on sausages in saloons and washed them down with German beer. He met some local hard cases, and passed a pint of whiskey to a city cop; you never knew who'd come in handy later.

Quickly absorbing the nature of the city—skilled craftsmen packing saloons midday, their women working low-paying jobs in the factories—he worked his way to the section where they showed movies, vaudeville, and plays.

The Clark Theatre's electrics ballyhooed

DR. JEKYLL and MR. HYDE
Direct from **BROADWAY**
JACKSON BARRETT & **JOHN BUCHANAN**
Present
The Height of Mechanical Realism
Two Sensational Scenic Effects

Posters out front showed a red airplane and a speeding subway.

Warren headed next door to the Lyric.

ALIAS JIMMY VALENTINE
Direct from **NEW YORK**
"Top O. Henry Short Story Topped Onstage"
—*VARIETY*

"Nate Stewart's expecting me," he told the old guy at the stage door and gave a name trusted by the wrong element in Hell's Kitchen. "Tell him Quinn's here."

The head carpenter had received a telegram of introduction from a New York guy who knew Harry Warren as Quinn. A boy was sent running. Nate Stewart hurried out with a welcoming handshake.

"How was your train?"

"Free," Harry Warren replied, with an us-against-the-bigwigs grin that said he saved his ticket money for better things. "Still got room for a sceneshifter?"

"You timed it perfect. The sons of guns at *Jekyll and Hyde* poached my top hand when their feller lit out for the Oklahoma oil fields."

———————

Lucy Balant loved the Dow Drugs pharmacy at the corner of Fifth and Vine, just down the street from *Alias Jimmy Valentine*. It had a Becker's "iceless" soda fountain—the latest thing to chill syrups, soda water, and ice cream mechanically instead of with ice—which made drinks ambrosially colder on a hot day. The fountain was surrounded by an octagonal marble counter and sixteen stools that had a rapid turnover, since it was near the train station. So for an actress who finally had a steady job, even if it was only as an understudy, and could afford a treat, it was perfect to drop in for a quick ginger ale. Plus, the soda jerkers made darned sure mashers didn't bother a girl alone.

A tall, dark-haired lady detective took the stool beside her the second it was empty. "I hope you remember me, Lucy."

"Vividly. What are you doing in Cincinnati?"

"Hunting Anna's killer."

"Because of what happened to the vaudeville dancer?"

"The same man."

Lucy shuddered. "It was horrible. Like hearing about Anna all over again. Have you seen those posters?"

"Did he look familiar?"

"He just looks like a guy. A well-off, older guy."

"I keep hoping the poster will help. Doesn't the picture remind you of anyone?"

"But it could *be* anyone."

"Anyone in your show?"

"I suppose he looks a bit like Mr. Lockwood, and even a little like Mr. Buchanan or Mr. Barrett—I finally got to see *Jekyll*, the first act— It could even be Mr. Vietor. But of course it isn't."

"Does the man on the poster remind you of any man backstage at either show?"

"No. Why are you asking about the shows?"

"What about *Jekyll and Hyde*'s stage manager?"

"Mr. Young? I've never seen his face."

"Your theaters are next door."

"They say he never leaves the theater. Sleeps on a cot. Why are you asking about these men?"

"Because both their road shows toured in cities where women were murdered or went missing."

Earlier that morning—in an elegant forest-green railcar parked on a private siding in Union Station—Grady Forrer had unrolled the map the Cutthroat Squad had last seen five days ago in Isaac Bell's *Lusitania* stateroom. Bell, Archie Abbott, and Helen had weighted the curling corners with pocket pistols.

Three new lines intersected with the red line that depicted the Cutthroat's trail of death across the Northeast and Middle West. Cities were now marked with the letters M or D. A yellow line looped from New York to Philadelphia to Boston and stopped in Albany, New York. A green line and a blue line ended beside the red in Cincinnati.

"What's the short yellow line?"

"*The Pharaoh's Secret*, a musical that closed in Albany. They sold the sets to a carnival and sent the actors home. Obviously, the murders and disappearances—M marks murders, D, disappearances—continued. The green line is *Alias Jimmy Valentine*. The blue is *Dr. Jekyll and Mr. Hyde*."

Helen Mills repeated for Lucy Balant the gist of what Isaac Bell had said.

"In one of these companies is a vigorous killer in his early forties who came from England in the heyday of touring theater. He's had twenty years to make a career in America."

"He's an *actor*?"

"He could be any man in the theater. Actor. Director. Stage-hand. Manager. Angel. Scenic designer. Rigger. Electrician. Carpenter."

"Mr. Vietor—our Jimmy Valentine—is English."

"So I hear."

"But he is very nice . . ." Her voice trailed off. "Of course he would be if he was tricking girls—"

Helen Mills interrupted urgently. "I am not saying it's him. Please don't jump to that conclusion." Just like Isaac Bell had warned. Do not condemn an innocent to a lynch mob.

Lucy Balant pondered what she had heard. The soda jerker, who was sweet on her, asked if she wanted another ginger ale. She shook her head and he went away.

Helen Mills said, "Please look at me, Lucy."

Lucy turned to her.

The detective said, "I will do anything to stop this Cutthroat. But I need to operate in disguise and I can't do that if you suddenly blurt out, 'I know Helen. She broke into my room in Philadelphia. She's a private detective.'"

"You'd be trusting your life with me."

"You knew Anna Waterbury. She was not just a story in the newspaper, was she?"

"She was a nice girl."

"There you have it."

"Does your boss know you're talking to me?"

"No," Helen lied. Isaac Bell had been reluctant to let her operate in Cincinnati but had concluded he had no choice if he was going to plant a woman inside one or both of the touring companies. They had come up with a story to deal with the fact that Lucy Balant knew she was a Van Dorn detective.

"I'm working this case on my own. No one knows I'm here. I took time off— Actually, I quit."

"What do you live on?"

"I've saved my money since I was an apprentice."

"Helen, you're taking all kinds of chances."

"Worth it if I catch him."

"Do you mind me asking what your disguise will be?"

"Not at all," said Helen, relieved that she had put over the story. "I don't want to shock you if we bump into each other. I will masquerade as an actress reading for "general businesswoman" jobs in *Jekyll and Hyde* and *Jimmy Valentine*."

Lucy said, "Ours is getting antsy to go back to New York."

"I heard."

"I wanted it," said Lucy. "The stage manager keeps saying I'm too short. But you're really tall. Have you ever been on the stage?"

"In school."

"Good luck with *Jimmy Valentine*. You'll need it, because you sure won't get *Jekyll and Hyde*."

"Why not?"

"I hear that the boyfriend of the girl who has it is a *Jekyll and Hyde* angel."

"Mine's a bigger angel."

Lucy's big eyes grew enormous. "You have a boyfriend who invests in the theater?" An up-from-under glance unspoken asked, is that how you can afford to quit your job?

Helen stuck to her story that she was working alone. "He's not my boyfriend. I just met him on this investigation. He's married. But he's actually very nice. And when people assume he's helping me for the wrong reasons, he sets them straight."

Lucy nodded. "You have to be careful on the road. That's for sure." She gave a rueful laugh. "The awful joke is, the nicer they are, the more careful they are, too. So you end up with both of you being careful and no one making the first move. Which reminds me, Helen, speaking of moves: When you read for *Jimmy Valentine*? Look out for Mr. Lockwood."

"A grabber?"

"He thinks he's irresistible."

"Thanks for the warning. What do you hear about grabbers at *Jekyll and Hyde*?"

Lucy Balant grinned. "Girls *hope* Mr. Buchanan will grab them. But he refuses to have anything to do with actresses. Nice as can be, but strictly business. They say he goes with rich ladies because they don't need anything from him."

"And Mr. Barrett?"

"Oh, Mr. Barrett! I was introduced to him at a cast party in Chicago. He did that older gentleman thing where he bows over your hand. Then he looks in your eyes. He had me blushing like I was fourteen." Lucy fanned her cheek with her napkin. "But, not a chance. Everybody says he's all business, too."

"What about your Jimmy Valentine?"

"Mr. Vietor is a gentleman. He's been coaching me, actually. There's a part that might come open if the girl takes a job in New York. I might be able to get it. Or at least read for the stage manager when Mr. Vietor thinks I'm ready."

"Now you warned me, Lucy. And I must warn you. Be very, very careful who you ever go with alone. Particularly a man in his forties. Anna was not the only petite blonde this Cutthroat killed."

"Mr. Vietor's only in his thirties."

"But don't actors sometimes 'adjust' their age?"

"Mr. Vietor wouldn't bother. He's so handsome, who cares how old he is?"

34

"When did you first join forces, Mr. Barrett and Mr. Buchanan?"

The *New York Sun* assistant theater critic—a natty gent with gin on his breath and a flawlessly knotted bow tie—had caught up with the *Jekyll and Hyde* company in Cincinnati.

Barrett and Buchanan were sipping coffee in the Clark Theatre green room, where they had agreed to submit to "just a few questions." Ticket sales were tapering off, and they could use all the help they could get. Their publicist was standing by warily, ready to pounce if the critic turned unfriendly or The Boys' banter got out of hand.

"Mr. Barrett was a callboy," Buchanan answered, "where I was appearing in *Hamlet*, and—"

Barrett interrupted. "I was the *prompter*, the callboy's superior. Mr. Buchanan carried a lantern in *Hamlet* to indicate it was night, and it was my job to remind him to hold the lantern overhead and not block the audience's view of Mr. Otis Skinner, who happened to be playing Hamlet."

"When Mr. Barrett wasn't prompting, he was painting scenery," said Buchanan. "On occasion, he presided over the opera glasses concession."

The reporter smiled uncertainly. "You gentlemen have different recollections of your early years."

"What did you say your name was?" asked Barrett.

"Scudder Smith. *New York Evening Sun.*"

The publicist interrupted. "I'm wondering why you don't look familiar. I thought I knew everyone on the *Sun*."

"The *Sun* hired me when I contracted with the *Denver Post* and Mr. Preston Whiteway's *San Francisco Inquirer* to publish stories that coincide with the opening of seat sales for road shows coming to their cities."

"Whiteway?"

Smith took a letter from his coat pocket with *Sun* letterhead. "Here. Sorry, I should have shown you this earlier. My introduction from Mr. Acton Davies. You'll see he mentions Mr. Whiteway."

The publicist handed it back with a much-warmer smile. Davies was the *Sun*'s chief critic and the acclaimed biographer of the theater's legendary Maude Adams. Preston Whiteway's *San Francisco Inquirer* anchored a fleet of newspapers, and he also owned Picture World, motion picture news reels seen in movie houses and vaudeville theaters across the continent.

Barrett said, "Well, Mr. Scudder Smith of the *Sun*, the *Post*, and the *Inquirer*, what other questions may we answer?"

"When did you become partners?"

"Eons ago," boomed Buchanan. "When was it, Jackson? It must have been aught three."

"Aught four," said Jackson Barrett. "We produced a road tour of *The Admirable Crichton*. I was Crichton. Mr. Buchanan played Lord Loam."

"How many years after your *Hamlet* was that?"

"Mr. Skinner's *Hamlet*," said Barrett. "Mr. Buchanan's lantern."

"Ten years," said Buchanan.

"So you first met in 'ninety-four. Seventeen years ago."

"Seems longer," said Barrett.

"I could not help but notice how convincingly you conducted your sword fight. I fully expected blood to flow. I could have sworn you were fencing with real sabers."

"That is because we do not *fence*. We duel."

"To me it looked like a real fight to the death."

"Real sabers make real noise," said Buchanan. "The clang of steel arrests the senses."

"And draw real blood," Barrett added, "which keeps us on our toes."

"How did you learn such swordsmanship?"

"The way we learn everything," Buchanan answered bluntly. "Study. Practice. Rehearse."

Barrett said, "We take to heart the great showman David Belasco's advice to actors. We never idle away the night hours in clubs and restaurants. Nor do we lie abed in the morning."

"But who taught you to fight so convincingly?"

"A deadly duelist."

Pencil poised, the reporter asked the duelist's name.

"We pledged never to reveal his identity."

"Why not?"

"Few who lost to him survived the experience."

Scudder Smith's smile congealed as if he was unsure whether his leg was being pulled. He noticed their publicist shoot the actors a warning glance not to mock the press.

Mock away, thought Smith.

"Are there strains in this fraught production?"

"'Fraught'?" said the publicist. "What fraught?"

"Are you dredging up that wire-story nonsense?" asked Barrett.

Scudder Smith said, "Everyone's read about the *Jekyll and Hyde* jinx—launched in blood—Medick falling to his death and Miss Cook's husband's yacht exploding. And wherever you play, girls disappear or die."

Buchanan's cheeks and forehead reddened. "Women are murdered all the time."

"And disappear often," Barrett added. "Can't say I blame them, judging by their male prospects."

The publicist lied manfully: "Here's a fact for Acton Davies. And Mr. Preston Whiteway, too. Ticket sales are up since that wire-service article. I hate to sound cold and heartless, but lots of folks are drawn to bloodshed."

Scudder Smith jotted his notes in practiced shorthand. *Here it comes, boys, both barrels:* "If that's true," he said, "then business is about to boom."

"How do you mean?"

"My newspaper's Research Department put together a map of all the murders and disappearances."

"So?"

"Then they mapped the route of your tour. Guess what? The maps match."

"What are you talking about?"

"Maps of bloodshed. Often when you play a town, a girl disappears or dies."

Barrett said, "But we played head to head with *Alias Jimmy Valentine* in most venues. Go talk to them."

"I have appointments to interview Mr. Vietor and Mr. Lockwood as soon as we wrap up our conversation with just a few more details."

"You can't print that nonsense."

"I wouldn't dream of it," said Smith. "At least not yet."

Buchanan spoke in a voice trembling with emotion. "We are carrying eighty people. *Eighty people* whose jobs depend on this tour continuing."

Scudder Smith said, "I sympathize with every one of them. I've lost many a job in my life."

Jackson Barrett said coldly, "I hope you'll remember that when you get closer to 'yet.'"

"Of course I will," said Scudder Smith. "I am not a stone. Where did you say that *Hamlet* was playing when you met?"

"A godforsaken hole out west," said Buchanan. "In the endless wastes between Denver and San Francisco."

"Mr. Skinner warned those who would jump ship, 'The Rocky Mountains are littered with the *bones* of actors attempting to get home to New York.'"

"Where, exactly, out west?"

"Butte, Montana. In a tent."

"Of course, you'd already acted in New York before you met? Both of you?"

"If a platform stood a single step above the sidewalk and had a bedsheet for a curtain, we played it," said Jackson Barrett.

"What year did you first act in New York?"

John Buchanan swept to his feet, saying, "You've entertained us far too long, Mr. Smith. Thank you for your time. We are so glad you liked our play."

The publicist opened the door.

Smith closed his notebook and stood up with a gleam in his eye that suggested the morning's work was done. "Oh—I almost forgot. Sorry. Just one more question. Where were you gentlemen born?"

"Under a cabbage leaf."

"In a stork's nest."

Scudder Smith laughed dutifully. "But our readers would love to know more about your backgrounds."

"They may read about them when we write our memoirs," said Barrett, and they swept Smith out the door.

"If you're in need of a ghostwriter," Smith called over his shoulder, "I'm your man," and added for the publicist, "Why wait 'til they're old men? Let their admirers read the memoirs of spectacular actors in the full tide of life."

The publicist walked him to the stage door, musing, "I could imagine paying a ghostwriter."

"I don't come cheap."

"We would match your rate—provided the *New York Sun*,

the *Denver Post*, and the *San Francisco Inquirer* never print the phrases 'map of bloodshed,' 'murdered girls,' 'launched in blood,' nor the word 'jinx.'"

———————

Scudder Smith went straight to Central Union Station. In a far corner across the passenger hall an unmarked doorway led to the private car platforms. A burly railroad cop blocked the way.

"Where do you think you're going?"

Smith showed him his badge.

"Sorry, sir. Say, would you happen to know, is Van Dorn hiring?"

"Protective Services is always on the lookout for good men," said Smith. "Best way to get noticed, put on a clean shirt and polish those shoes."

He walked out under the train shed, keeping an eye peeled for anyone watching from the other private cars parked on the siding. Fortunately, those cars blocked the view from the long Jekyll & Hyde Special parked far away. At the end of the row was a luxurious car, enameled a rich forest green. Curtained windows gleamed like crystal; loops of telephone, telegraph, and electric wires snaked into the station's systems; and a flinty-eyed conductor in a uniform decorated with gold piping guarded the door.

The front compartment, paneled in rosewood, was furnished like a millionaire's rolling office, with a desk of quartered oak, a comfortable leather armchair, a telegraph key, and a glass-domed stock-ticker machine. Neither the desk nor the chair were in use. Chief Investigator Isaac Bell was on his feet, about to spring.

"What do you think of them?"

"Mighty full of themselves," said Scudder Smith.

"Is either a murderer?"

"Hard to tell."

"Is either undeniably innocent?"

"I wouldn't go that far."

"How'd they react to the map?"

"Stopped cracking jokes— Of course, if they're what they say they are, then the map hits them right in the wallet."

"Where were they born?" asked Bell.

"They dodged that like in every article we read about them. It's a practiced duet."

"Did they say how they mastered the saber?"

"They claim they took lessons from a deadly duelist on the lam. Thing is, a bit of mystery never hurt a show business career."

"I dislike mysteries."

"Like P. T. Barnum says, 'Always leave 'em wanting more.'"

"Are they coy or are they lying?"

"Anna Waterbury was not the first thespian to rewrite her past," said Smith, regretting it instantly as fire exploded in his old friend's eyes. Better change the subject. "I wonder if I might wet my whistle?"

Bell directed him to the sideboard with a brusque nod. Scudder Smith poured gin and tossed it back. "I must admit, I enjoyed myself. I miss my newspaper days."

"Did you detect a trace of an English accent in either of their voices?"

"No more than any actor," said Smith.

Bell nodded grimly. He had heard many an American actor affect an English-sounding drawl with upper-crust pretensions, often at a volume to project expression to the balcony seats. "Actor speak," Archie Abbott dubbed the stagy elocution delivered with faithful diction, exquisite inflection, and commanding posture.

"I set it up to take another shot," said Scudder Smith. "I got the publicist interested in me ghostwriting their memoirs. Or do you want Helen or Archie?"

"It's my turn," said Bell.

35

As they did most evenings in every city they played, Jackson Barrett and John Buchanan walked home to their train after the show. At the station tonight, just inside the private platforms entrance, a tall, lean, golden-haired young gentleman in a white suit touched the brim of his hat in a friendly salute.

"Good evening, Mr. Barrett and Mr. Buchanan. I am Isaac Bell, and I would be honored if you would join me for supper in my car."

Bell gestured toward a palatially fitted dark green and gold car, which the actors had already noticed was cut several notches above the other millionaires' train cars parked overnight in Cincinnati.

Buchanan demurred. "Thank you, Mr. Bell. But it's been a long day."

"It's been many long days for me," said Bell, "but I am at last in a position to make a lucrative proposal." He gestured again to the car, adding, "I know I can't lure you with champagne, but my cook grills one of your favorite dishes—Maryland rockfish."

"How'd you find that out?" asked Buchanan.

Bell answered with an easy grin, "I am new to the theater, but by exercising due diligence on behalf of my syndicate, I learned that actors are famously hungry after a performance—ravenous after a brilliant one—and that you two have a particular preference for rockfish. Though we Hartford Yankees call them striped bass."

Barrett asked, "Where'd your cook get rockfish fresh in Cincinnati?"

"He traded the champagne you don't drink for iced beauties from a St. Louis express."

"I am persuaded," said Barrett.

"Me, too," said Buchanan.

Bell led them into his car. A first course of chilled Gulf shrimp and Maine lobster was laid out on a candlelit dining table set with silver, crystal, and Staffordshire bone china decorated with scenes from Shakespeare.

As Archie Abbott had predicted, Barrett and Buchanan tore into the shrimp and lobster in appreciative silence. Bell watched in awe as they tackled striped bass, asparagus tips, and new potatoes Parisienne as avidly, and it was only over Baked Alaska that Jackson Barrett finally asked, "What lucrative arrangement are you proposing, Mr. Bell?"

Bell said, "I had lunch with your angels, as theater folk call them, and concluded I would rather approach you directly."

"In other words, they weren't interested?" asked Barrett.

"They were more interested in persuading me to share in *Dr. Jekyll and Mr. Hyde*."

"Why?"

"Come now, gentlemen, that wire-service story is no secret. I'm sure you'll weather it, but the Deavers' desire to spread the risk and get some of their money out is reasonable. I personally have little doubt that your *Dr. Jekyll and Mr. Hyde* will tour for many years."

"From your lips to God's ear," said Buchanan.

"But at some point, I imagine, you would want to move on."

"Where?"

"A new show," said Bell.

"Leap from a sure thing into the pit of speculation?" said Buchanan. "No thank you, sir. The only new show I'd do would be made with the wave of a magic wand instead of money—but still sells tickets for money."

"First rule of the stage," Barrett chimed in. "Cherish your hits. When you close a good play, you miss it forever. You've been immortal—a god—until the curtain comes down on your final performance. Next morning, you're knocking on a banker's door with your hat in your hand."

Bell said, "My syndicate will pay for you to make a new play. You will have no concerns about raising money."

"Why us?"

"Your modernized *Jekyll and Hyde* demonstrates that Robert Louis Stevenson is as sure a financial thing as the original was twenty-five years ago. You're the men to do it next for *Treasure Island*."

"Didn't we hear Julie Goodman is writing a *Treasure Island*?" Buchanan asked Barrett.

"It doesn't matter what Jules Eckert Goodman is doing," Bell said dismissively. "Ours is a musical play."

"A musical? What a strange idea."

Bell returned a thin smile. "Our due diligence went beyond rockfish. You've done musicals. And they made money."

"Well, we didn't lose any," Buchanan admitted.

Bell said, "Critics and audiences applaud your alternating roles in *Jekyll and Hyde*. They will love *Treasure Island*. You'll be Long John Silver one night, Mr. Barrett, and Squire Trelawney the next."

The actors regarded Isaac Bell with shrewd expressions that told the tall detective that he had lassoed their attention. Time to act on Archie Abbott's advice: The language of the theater is cash.

"*Treasure Island* will make you rich. Royalties for the script alone could run as much as fifty thousand—*before* you count your profits from the Broadway production and the road show."

"There is one big, insurmountable problem with *Treasure Island*," said Buchanan.

"I see no problem. Mr. Stevenson's widow accepted our offer for the rights, and a million boys and girls who loved the book are now adults who will line up to buy tickets."

"The problem is, *no girl in the story*," said Barrett. "No romance. No hope of hero and heroine falling in love. A musical *Treasure Island* must have a romantic angle if it's to play to bigger audiences than children's Christmas pantos."

"But there *is* a girl," said Bell.

277

Barrett laughed. "What are you proposing, bring young Jim Hawkins's *mother* on the voyage?"

Buchanan joined the laughter. "Jim's mother falls for Long John Silver. Silver is reformed by love and turns his Spyglass Tavern into a Methodist mission."

"Dr. Livesey is your girl," said Isaac Bell.

The actors' eyes lighted up like double eagle gold pieces.

Barrett said, "Change Squire Trelawney's sidekick to his fiancée."

"No women doctors in the eighteenth century," Buchanan protested.

Bell said, "Your modernized *Treasure Island* will be taking place in the *twentieth century*—here-and-now 1911, just like *Jekyll and Hyde*."

Barrett said, "No pirates in 1911. The Royal Navy exterminated them."

Isaac Bell looked them both in the eye. "We have no shortage of cutthroats in 1911."

Barrett and Buchanan exchanged a glance.

Buchanan said, "True," and Isaac Bell smothered his impulse to level a gun in their faces and demand, "Tell me what is true."

"But with no pirates," Jackson Barrett asked, "where did the lost treasure come from?"

Bell was ready for that one. "The Spanish–American War."

"Yes!" Barrett said, suddenly excited. "They lifted the treasure when the *Maine* blew up in Cuba."

"Long John Silver betrayed Cuban rebels," said Buchanan, and the actors chorused the 1898 battle cry: "Remember the *Maine*!"

Bell asked, "Can you persuade Miss Isabella Cook to play Dr. Livesey?"

"Miss Cook will demand a share."

"Whatever agreement you made that makes her happy in *Dr. Jekyll and Mr. Hyde* will be fine with me— Which reminds me, I want to see your production again before I report to my investors."

"You will be our guest tomorrow evening."

"No thank you, I will buy my ticket. This is strictly business. But there is a favor I would ask you."

"Name it!"

"If we decide to go forward with *Treasure Island*, I would like to spend time with your *Jekyll and Hyde* company— backstage, and aboard your train when you leave for the West."

"You'll find it quite dull, Mr. Bell," said Buchanan. "Strictly business."

"Melodramas are short on the 'chorus girls' of lore," said Barrett.

"I'm recently married," Bell grinned back at him. "No need of chorus girls. But I'm obliged to learn enough ins and outs of the theater arts to protect my partners."

"Let's hitch your car to our train," said Jackson Barrett.

"Ride along to San Francisco," said John Buchanan.

"You'll be our caboose."

"I could not ask for more," said Isaac Bell.

36

The Cutthroat brushed spirit gum on his upper lip and cursed out loud. He had just shaved, his skin was raw, and it stung like the devil. It would sting even worse when he removed the mustache, this time an enormous affair trimmed in the walrus style. He fanned the lace backing with his souvenir program and fixed it under his nose.

He was dressed in blue-striped overalls over a red-checked shirt, which he had bulked up with horsehair padding. Now he perched a battered derby on his head and wire-rimmed spectacles on his nose. Pipe cutters, wrenches, hacksaw, files, and a gasoline blowtorch arrayed in a wooden toolbox completed the portrait of a master gas fitter. He even had a card from the

Cincinnati Gas and Electric Company emblazoned with the motto "Heat with gas, light with electricity." The company was expanding, enjoying great success with modern, up-and-coming customers like the Van Dorn Detective Agency on Plum Street.

He hefted the toolbox on his shoulder, sauntered out of his yellow cottage by the river, walked to the streetcar stop, and rode into the center of town. Off near Plum Street, he walked to the Van Dorn office on the ground floor of a substantial-looking building. The private back door was down an alley, but he walked in the street entrance.

They had one wall plastered with wanted posters—including a copy of the imaginatively aged one of himself that had riveted his eye in the red-light district. The sharp-eyed young detective, working in vest and shirtsleeves, had a pistol in a shoulder holster. He jumped up from his desk with an eager-to-help smile.

"Hello there. What can I do for you?"

"I'm supposed to check your meter."

The detective opened a door to the cellar stairs. "Give a shout if you need anything."

"Thank you." The Cutthroat paused on the steps to look at the wall of posters. "Do you think you'll catch all those guys?"

"That's our job."

"Do you?"

"What?"

"Catch them all?"

"We never give up."

"Never?"

The Cutthroat studied his poster. He recognized the hand of a newspaper illustrator back in London. A decent artist, but the likeness wasn't specific. He was tempted to stand beside it, yank off his walrus mustache, and ask, "Look familiar?"

———————

He could use every tool in his box. Theater lights were all electric now, but he had learned gas fitting back in his apprentice days when footlights, wing lights, and border lights burned "town gas." Here in Cincinnati, it was the new and abundant and more potent "natural," taken from the ground instead of manufactured from coal.

He found the live-gas inlet pipe, found the master cock, and closed it. He removed the meter from the inlet and outlet pipes. The inlet and outlet holes were supposed to be tightly corked to keep air away from the residual gas inside the meter. Instead, he left them open and laid the meter on the cellar floor, directly under the service pipe, which would get you sacked in a flash by any supervisor who noticed. Then he bridged the inlet and outlet pipes with a prethreaded length of lead pipe, in which he had drilled a microscopic pinhole. He opened the master cock. The gas that leaked slowly through the pinhole would gather in the cellar.

Air entering the uncorked meter would form a highly volatile mix with the gas inside it. He slipped the end of a long length of slow-burning fuse in one of the holes, uncoiled it along the cellar wall, and lit the fuse. When the slowly smouldering flame finally ignited the air–gas mix in the meter, that small explosion would set off the rest of the accumulated gas as powerfully as a blasting cap exploded dynamite.

He climbed the stairs and closed the door.

"What's that I smell?" asked the detective.

The Cutthroat plucked the blowtorch from his box. "I had to sweat a pipe."

"Hope you didn't fire that thing up to look for a leak," the detective joked.

The Cutthroat laughed along with him. "Believe it or not, no matter how often we warn the public not to, people still light a match when they smell gas in the dark. Sorry about the stink, it will dissipate before you know it."

———

Isaac Bell tipped his hat to Isabella Cook.

The actress was drinking tea in a wicker peacock chair in the Palace Hotel's Palm Court. Other ladies were wearing wide-brimmed, flower-and-feather-heaped Merry Widow hats that were getting tangled in the high-back chairs. Miss Cook sat, unentangled and stylish, in the latest Paris fashion: a Paul Poiret turban hat. Instead of merely framing her lovely face, the close-fitting turban made it all the more beautiful by allowing her eyes, her bow lips, and her aquiline nose to emphasize themselves.

"I have been looking everywhere for you, Miss Cook."

"Purchasing a ticket will bring you near for three more nights at the Clark Theatre. After that, you may enjoy repeat performances in St. Louis, Denver, and San Francisco."

Bell said, "I can't risk shouting my proposal in the theater. The audience would lynch me for interrupting your performance."

She looked him up and down with a small smile and a shrewd eye. "It looks to me like they'll have their hands full if they try. Who are you, sir?"

Bell swept his hat off his head. "Isaac Bell. May I sit with you?"

"What do you want, Mr. Bell?"

"I have a proposal that will make you rich and happy."

"I fell for that line when I married."

Bell said, "I offer my condolences. I know you were widowed last fall."

She ignored his condolences, and asked, "Is yours a financial proposal?"

"It is."

"Sit down, Mr. Bell." She beckoned a waiter, and Bell ordered tea. They shared small talk about Cincinnati and the pleasures and tribulations of traveling, she on the stage, Bell selling insurance to banks and railroads and timber barons. She asked where he lived when he wasn't traveling.

He answered truthfully as it meshed with his Dagget, Staples & Hitchcock insurance cover. "My wife and I have a house in San Francisco."

"New-built since the earthquake?"

"One of the few that survived on Nob Hill."

She looked suitably impressed by Nob Hob, and Bell said, "I read in the Chicago papers that you are close friends with Mr. Barrett and Mr. Buchanan."

"We've worked together in the past. And we're having a fine time at present. The Boys are serious businessmen and spectacular showmen—a rare combination in the theater."

"Where are they from?"

"The *thee-ah-tore*!" Miss Cook emoted with a devilish smile, and Bell, who had liked her immediately, liked her more. "Born in a properties trunk."

"Both of them?" he asked, going along with her joke to steer her toward the mystery of where they were born.

"Where else would they be born, Mr. Bell? Some dreary inland city? Some soul-smothering small town bereft of art and theater?"

"I read in the magazines that you're from a small town."

"I know of what I speak. Though I confess, had I been born in a grand city, I might have aspired to no higher station than the youngest president of the Ladies Garden Improvement Society."

"Certainly the most compelling," said Bell.

"Are you flirting with me, Mr. Bell?"

"No, ma'am. I never flirt with beautiful women."

Mobile eyebrows joined the smile. "Why not?"

"I am faithful to my wife."

"Pity . . . What is your offer?"

"I've suggested backing a new play for Barrett & Buchanan. I hope you will find it engaging, too, which is why I was asking about their background. As fiscal agent for my syndicate, I am obliged to know the nature and background of potential partners."

"Their 'nature and background' is an open book. They've been on the stage their entire lives, and have a reputation for as much honesty as can be found in most producers. Seriously, Mr. Bell, had there ever been a hint of fraud, I would not be in business with them. No, I think you can rest easy on that count. They are what they appear to be—undefeated men of the theater."

"It sounds like you admire them."

"I admire survivors who succeed with a minimum of damage to others. The theater is not easy. They do it well. Which is why I don't care where they were born. For that matter, I don't know why *you* care. Now, tell me about your proposal. That's what got you seated beside me."

"I am obliged by my principals to conclude arrangements with Barrett & Buchanan first. After that, I have the deepest hope that you will be interested, too."

"Before you waste your time, let me caution you: I will not work *for* them," she said. "I will work *with* them."

"That goes without saying," said Bell. "The sensation you've made of *Jekyll and Hyde* guarantees that you would be a principal, too."

"Then I look forward to answering more due diligence questions."

"Well, I'm curious about one thing. It seems strange that the actor Medick and your husband, Rufus Oppenheim, died within days of each other."

"Strange? Bizarre, is more like it. None of this—a sensational run on Broadway, a first class tour, my 'triumphant return'—would have happened if they didn't."

"Why not?"

"Medick owned tour rights to Richard Mansfield's *Dr. Jekyll and Mr. Hyde*. Barrett & Buchanan backers would never invest in their new version while Medick was still making a go of it on the road."

"No wonder you say 'bizarre.' Is it true that Medick fell from a fire escape?"

"Pursued by a husband, went the story. Medick was a renowned, shall we say, 'swordsman,' hated by grooms, cherished by brides."

"Like John Buchanan?" asked Bell.

"Where did you get that idea?"

"Due diligence includes weighing gossip."

Isabella Cook shook her head. "Mr. Buchanan never dips his pen in the company ink. He conducts his escapades where they are nobody's business—far from the stage, and higher up the social scale, where smirking moralists are shunned."

"I'm relieved to hear it. Is Mr. Barrett as sensible?"

"In my experience," she said, "Mr. Barrett, too, steers clear of actresses— How did we get on escapades, Mr. Bell?"

"Two freak deaths back-to-back—Medick's fire escape and your husband's yacht."

"I almost died, too, speaking of bizarre, but the tender had just taken me ashore to have lunch at the Knickerbocker. I heard the explosion as I stepped onto the pier. I turned and saw a nightmarish sight—where the boat had been—a horrible ball of fire. Sheer luck I had the appointment. Not that 'luck' is a word one uses around death."

"Who were you meeting for lunch?"

"The Boys. Jackson and John wanted me to persuade Mr. Oppenheim to let me return to the stage. Which, of course, he never would have. Men are impossible that way, aren't they? How long have you been married, Mr. Bell?"

"We will celebrate our first anniversary next week."

"Do you allow your wife to support herself in her own career?"

"She was in the habit long before I met her."

"What does she do?"

"She makes movies."

"Really? I often sneak into afternoon shows. Great fun. I'm sure I've seen hers."

"She is Marion Morgan Bell."

"Marion Morgan! Of course. The filmmaker who married an insurance man. *You're* the insurance man—but not so staid as the label implies—I love her films."

"She'd love to get you in one."

"I cannot imagine working with movie manufacturers," Isabella Cook replied coolly. "On the stage, I play to my audience—not some faceless entity snipping bits of celluloid."

"Marion is too lovely to be a faceless entity. She's a knockout— Forgive me! That was thoughtless."

"Whatever do you mean?"

"Rhapsodizing about my marriage when you just lost your husband."

Isabella Cook brushed the back of Bell's hand with her fingertips and raised cool, clear eyes to his. "Rufus Oppenheim was a dog."

———————

Back in his railcar, Isaac Bell wired New York:

```
SPEED UP INVESTIGATING
MEDICK FIRE ESCAPE
OPPENHEIM YACHT
```

He was grasping at straws.

If only he could come up with some way to distract the Cutthroat. Make him look over his shoulder. Throw him off balance, before he killed again.

37

"Miss Mills," said the *Alias Jimmy Valentine* stage manager. "I want you to read these lines with Mr. Douglas Lockwood, who plays Detective Doyle."

Helen Mills nodded eagerly.

Lockwood was tall and handsome, with a stern manner that fit the character of Doyle, the detective determined to send reformed safecracker Jimmy Valentine back to prison. He took Helen's arm firmly in his strong hand and stood very close.

He spoke his line.

Helen spoke hers. "Yes, Mr. Doyle."

The stage manager asked them to do it again. Still holding her arm, Lockwood repeated his line. Helen repeated hers. Then

Lockwood addressed the stage manager as if Helen was not standing on the stage between them.

"She's a bit green. Stiff as a board, actually. Perhaps not hopelessly . . . What time is it? I'll tell you what, let me rehearse her a little. I'll bring her back shortly."

"Half an hour, Mr. Lockwood."

"Come along, dear. Bring your script."

Lockwood led her through the wings and back to the principals' dressing rooms and opened a door with his name on it. It was comfortably sized, with a lighted mirror for putting on makeup, a washstand with running water, and a couch.

"Sit there. Now, here's the thing, dear. If you're going to put this part across, you've got to give the impression that you are attracted to Detective Doyle. He's a breath of fresh air in your constrained life, and, frankly, quite exciting compared to the boys who hang about trying to court you. So when you say, 'Yes, Mr. Doyle,' you must say it as if you are happy—delighted, even—to agree to whatever he proposes . . . O.K.? Now, let's try it. Here, I'll make it easy, I'll sit next to you."

He sat close to her, took her arm firmly, and spoke his line.

Helen said, "Yes, Mr. Doyle."

"No, no, no, no." Apparently baffled, and sounding impatient, he ran his fingers through his hair. Then he patted her shoulder.

Helen Mills said, "I think I could relax a little if you just talked to me for a moment. Tell me about yourself."

Lockwood smiled, and asked in a husky voice, "What do you want to know?"

"Oh, I don't know . . . Where were you born? You sound as if you're from England."

"Well, that's very sweet of you to say, but I'm afraid my birthplace is not quite so romantic."

"I read in a magazine that you're from London."

"You're confusing me with my fellow star. Mr. Vietor is from England."

"Oh, my gosh, I'm so sorry," Helen said. In fact, Grady Forrer's researchers had queried the magazine's editor, who stood by the story but offered no actual proof.

"Sometimes publicists exaggerate."

"Where were you born?"

"Jersey City. Just across the river from New York. You're not from New York, are you?"

"Oh, gosh, just a little town you never heard of, in Maryland."

Lockwood sighed. "You Southern girls are just so exciting, I lose all control around you."

"Please let go of me, Mr. Lockwood."

"Now, dear, just relax and get into the mood of your line. You are, after all, saying *yes*."

"My 'yes' does not go backstage."

"It better if you want to get on the stage," he said curtly. "Now, come on, dear, we don't have all afternoon. I can get you this part with a snap of my fingers."

"If you don't take your hands off me, Mr. Lockwood, I will floor you."

He reached toward her blouse with one hand while attempting to get up her skirt with the other. "You can't floor me. I'm bigger than you are."

She could hear Isaac Bell. *"You're a strong girl, Helen. Never give up. Go straight at him."*

"What if he's too big to fight?"

"Feint. Throw him off."

Helen laughed loudly.

"Are you laughing at me?"

Lockwood suddenly got a mean look on his face. He raised a hand to slap her.

That left him wide open.

———

"Thank you for reading, gentlemen," said Henry Young. "We will be in touch."

Four actors smiled gamely, thanked the stage manager, and headed up the aisle of the empty theater.

"Mr. Abbott, could you stay a moment longer?"

Archie Abbott approached the stage.

Henry Young, tall and rangy as a stork—a powerful stork—stood in front of the stylish *Dr. Jekyll and Mr. Hyde* set. One eye was twitching with anxiety. A role had opened up when a *Jekyll and Hyde* actor was lured back to New York to read for a new play by Paul Armstrong—the toast of the town for his *Jimmy Valentine* and glad to do Joseph Van Dorn a favor. The stage manager needed a replacement desperately or he would be going on himself.

"More than only a moment, I hope," Abbott said, with a professional smile that projected cheerful confidence in his talent, sober habits, and a willingness to work hard.

"Mr. Abbott, I remember you from some years back, do I not?"

"You have an astonishing memory, sir. It was back in aught two. I read for you for a road tour of Mr. Belasco's *The Heart of Maryland*."

"The Midwestern spring tour, I believe it was."

"I didn't get the part."

"You were too young. As you might be, I fear, for this role. Keep in mind that Mr. Pool has been Mr. Hyde's butler for over twenty years."

"As much as it pains me to say it, sir," said Archie Abbott, "I sincerely believe I can play a man in his fifties."

"I have other reservations."

"May I hear them," asked Archie Abbott, "that I might put them to rest?"

"The way you just 'elocuted' that statement is my next reservation. You do call up the impression of being to a high manner born. Will we be asking too much of the audience to believe that you are a butler?"

"The best butlers I know can more easily pass for a gentleman than most so-called gentlemen. Granted, some in the audience may not know from personal experience that a gentleman's butler is expected to bring a cool head and a keen eye to his tasks, but all will appreciate his positive attitude."

When Henry Young still looked dubious, Abbott promised, "But I have no doubt I can give the impression of servility."

The stage manager remained silent.

Abbott decided this conversation would have ended already if he weren't a serious contender for the part. "You mentioned other reservations, sir?"

"I find it difficult to believe that you really want the part."

"I want it very much, sir. I need this job."

"But," the stage manager said, "I've heard that you married well."

"An heiress," said Abbott.

"*Extremely* well."

"A lovely heiress," said Abbott. "Kind, generous, intelligent, extraordinarily beautiful, and destined to inherit many railroads from a doting father, who is an old man with a weak heart."

"Then why do you want a small role in a play that is leaving godforsaken Cincinnati for ever more godforsaken points west?"

"She came to her senses."

———————

"The girls in the *Jimmy Valentine* company told me that Mr. Vietor claims he entered boarding school in Bedford in 1888," Helen Mills reported to Isaac Bell.

"Bedford's seventy miles north of London. Hour and a half on the train."

"The trouble is, Mr. Bell, Vietor says he was twelve at the time."

"*Twelve?*"

"He was still in school in 'ninety-one, age fifteen. Which would make him thirty-five today. Not in his forties."

"When did he come to America?"

"First time was 'ninety-seven."

"At twenty-three."

"He made a name for himself in London first. Back and forth ever since, touring."

Bell said, "I'll cable Joel Wallace to check at the Bedford School, but it could take forever. He must be lying about his age. If Mapes was right, Vietor's got to be in his forties."

"And there is something else, Mr. Bell. He's coaching Lucy Balant for a bigger part. I warned her not to be alone with any man. Including him. I'm not sure she'll listen."

Bell said, "I'll tell Harry Warren to keep a close watch on him. Who else in the *Valentine* cast?"

"The actor who plays Detective Doyle is definitely lying about his age. He claims thirty-two. A girl who knew him well swears he's *fifty*-two. And he told me he was born in Jersey City, not London."

"How do you rate him?"

"He sounds English to me, but, like Archie says, most of them do. But he's nowhere as young as thirty-two. Fifty, if he's a day."

"What makes you so sure?"

"His slow reflexes."

38

A life in the theater, both on the stage and behind the scenes, had taught Henry Booker Young the protocol for conducting a reading for a part to be won by an angel's protégée. An air of business as usual was expected of the stage manager. But brusque impatience was to be leavened with kindness. And talent, no matter how sparse, was to be noted and somehow praised. Particularly when the angel—the tall, handsome, and, to Young's eye, dangerous-looking Mr. Bell—was sitting on the edge of his seat in the front row of the otherwise empty house, watching like a mother falcon.

"Can you tell me about your work on the stage, Miss Mills?"

Helen Mills answered in a rush. "I was Nora in *A Doll's*

House, Gwendolen Fairfax in *The Importance of Being Earnest*, Candida in *Candida*, and—"

"Where did you perform these roles?"

"Bryn Mawr."

"The college."

"Yes, Mr. Young."

"Have you performed with any legitimate companies?"

"This will be my first."

"Have you ever read for any legitimate companies?"

Helen looked flustered.

"Well, have you?"

"I read for *Jimmy Valentine*."

"How did you make out there?"

"I decided against taking the part."

Young smiled thinly. "That would jibe with a story making the rounds about Mr. Lockwood's broken nose. Was it you, Miss Mills, who socked the star?"

"I'm afraid I lost my temper."

Young sounded sympathetic: "It is not easy to be an attractive girl in the theater. However, I would caution you to ponder precisely how much you are willing to sacrifice to go on the stage." He was stepping so far beyond the unspoken boundaries of awarding a job to an angel's protégée that the angel himself stiffened visibly.

Isaac Bell made him nervous. While seemingly typical of the wealthy men who pursued actresses, something about him seemed off. He was so much more fit and alert than layabouts like the Deaver brothers. And Bell seemed truly concerned for the girl's well-being, almost a fatherly concern—though if he were her actual father, he would have been no more than nine or ten years old when she was born. Maybe it was true that Helen Mills was the niece of one of his investors. Maybe Tennyson was thinking of stage managers when he wrote: "Theirs not to reason why, / Theirs but to do and die."

He plowed ahead, determined for some perverse and unsafe reason he could not quite put his finger on, to shield her from disappointment. "Women of privilege rarely make a go of it in the theater. Give me a shopgirl for the ferocious ambition and hard work the stage demands."

"Don't worry about privilege, Mr. Young. I was a scholarship girl in college. I grew up in a mill town without a pot to— I mean, a penny to my name."

"Excellent," said Henry Young. He had been misled by the young woman's striking poise. "The general business you will read for will include occasionally appearing as a housemaid, wielding a feather duster, in Mr. Hyde's library, and standing by to be strangled on a regular basis. See if you can put this over."

He handed her a page of playscript. "Take your time. Tell me when you're ready."

"I'm ready."

"Go on, then."

She rolled the paper into a cylinder, which she held like a feather duster, lowered her eyes as if timid or dazzled by her employer, and read, "'Mr. Hyde hasn't come home yet, Dr. Jekyll.'"

"You'll do."

"Do you mean I get the role?"

"You will be paid twenty dollars per week, take your meals

on the train, occupy an upper berth in the Pullman car, and buy your own clothes."

Isaac Bell cleared his throat. It sounded like a growl.

"All right, Mr. Bell, we'll provide costumes, and she may descend to the first lower berth that becomes available."

———————

James Dashwood talked his way into the Clark Theatre and wandered around asking for Henry Young until he found him.

"Detective Dashwood."

"You remember me?"

"I'm a stage manager, I can never forget a face even when I want to. It was in Boston. You were wondering whether Anna Waterbury read for me, and you thought you had seen me before. Did you figure out where?"

"Syracuse. Obviously, I didn't 'see' you: I was still a kid out west when you were the Syracusan Stock Company's treasurer."

"You must have seen an old wanted poster."

"Do Barrett and Buchanan know?"

"All of it. The ticket fraud. The gambling that drove me to the fraud. The foolish going on the run. The arrest. The prison sentence."

"Why did they hire you?"

"They say I learned my lesson."

"So they trust you."

"I've never given them reason not to."

Dashwood raised a skeptical brow.

Young said, "They are decent men, Detective— Now, if

you'll excuse me, I have to load eighty people and two sensational scenic effects featuring the height of mechanical realism onto a railroad train."

———————

Isaac Bell gathered the Cutthroat Squad in his car.

"We've infiltrated both tours and narrowed the field of suspects. Harry Warren and Grady Forrer exonerated the *Alias Jimmy Valentine* head rigger, Bill Milford, and scenic designer, Roland Phelps, who grew up in New York and were definitely living in the city during the Ripper's rampage in England— Milford in the Tenderloin, Phelps in his family's Washington Square town house.

"Helen Mills has eliminated the actor Lockwood, from *Alias Jimmy Valentine*, by establishing that he is neither strong enough nor quick enough to overwhelm his victims. On the other hand, she has learned that Lucy Balant is getting 'coached' by the star of the show, Mr. Vietor. Her roommate, Anna Waterbury, was coached by the Cutthroat. So we keep the book open on Mr. Vietor. Fortunately, *Jimmy Valentine* will catch up with us in St. Louis the day after tomorrow.

"Meanwhile, Grady discovered the Deaver brothers spent their college years, in the late eighties and early nineties, in England after being kicked out of schools in Pennsylvania and Massachusetts. But the time I spent with them convinced me that neither Joe Deaver nor Jeff Deaver has the brains not to trip himself up for twenty *minutes*, much less never get caught in twenty years."

"Are you sure it's not an act, Mr. Bell?"

"Edwin Booth could not put over such an act. Now, what about Mr. Rick L. Cox, the lunatic writer?"

"Cox," said Forrer, "was locked up in a Columbus asylum *before* Beatrice Edmond was murdered in Cincinnati."

Bell said, "Scudder and I couldn't pry much out of Jackson Barrett and John Buchanan."

"Opaque," Smith interrupted. "No clue that either's from London."

Dashwood relayed Henry Young's claim that Barrett and Buchanan trusted their stage manager not to defraud them.

"Go back and find out what he has on them. What's his leverage? Somehow they have each other by the short hairs."

Archie Abbott said, "Gossip says Henry Young rarely leaves the theater 'til it's time to board the train to the next city."

Bell wrapped it up. "We are down to Barrett, Buchanan, Vietor, and Young— Back to it, everyone! See you tomorrow in St. Louis!"

They were trooping out of the car when an explosion rattled the windows.

"That was close."

Isaac Bell said, "Better see if we can help. Go first, James, you're the detective. The rest, remember to act like regular helpful citizens."

They hurried into the station hall, Dashwood in the lead.

People were crowding out the front entrance. From there,

they saw a pillar of smoke lit orange by flames rising several blocks over. They joined the mob running toward it. Bell forged ahead, with a sinking feeling it was on Plum Street. He caught up with Dashwood, and they reached Plum just as teams of wild-eyed fire horses pulling steam pumpers thundered toward the smoke. It was gushing from the field office's shattered front door and windows and from the building next door.

"Our chief works late most nights."

Bell shoved through the crowds. He skirted the firemen, who were stringing their hoses and raising ladders to the next-door windows, and cut down the side alley. The back door had been blown open. He ran into the dark, shouting for the chief.

"Sedgwick! Jerry Sedgwick!"

No one answered. Bell soaked a hand towel in the lavatory, covered his mouth and nose, and ran up the hall to the front office. The interior was demolished. Plaster had fallen from the ceiling. The cellar door was open. Flames were leaping from the stairs.

He pushed into the front room, where a wall of smoke and flame stopped him short. Through it, he thought he could see a figure slumped over the desk. At that moment, the firemen finished tying into the city hydrants. Hose water blasted through the windows, scattering glass and dropping flames to the floor. The smoke shifted. Jerry Sedgwick was there, coughing violently and trying to stand.

Bell got halfway to him before the water stopped. By the time he reached the chief's desk, flames were jumping to the ceiling again, and the wet towel he pressed to his face had dried stiffly in the heat. Bell slung Sedgwick over his shoulder and tried to retrace his steps. But the smoke was suddenly so dense, he could not see the way. The water streams sprayed again, knocking down smoke. The respite was brief, the smoke thicker. He was running out of air.

"Mr. Bell!"

Dashwood was calling.

"Mr. Bell! *Isaac!*"

Bell staggered toward the sound of his voice.

He saw Dashwood reaching for him and, behind the young detective, the alley door. He pushed Sedgwick into Dashwood's arms. In the alley, half a dozen deep breaths of cool, fresh air had the eager chief gasping, "I'm O.K. I'm O.K."

"Hospital," said Bell.

"No! I'm O.K. I gotta talk to you."

"Talk in the ambulance," said Bell.

The Cutthroat Squad had swung into action, quietly bribing an ambulance crew for their help and the police to clear a path. Once inside the motor wagon, Bell asked, "You sure you're O.K.?" Sedgwick had lost his eyebrows and most of his hair.

"I mined coal when I was a kid. This was nothing compared to that. Mr. Bell, he blew us up."

"Who blew us up?"

"Gas fitter said he was from Cincinnati Gas and Electric, and I fell for it, hook, line, and sinker. Little while ago, I smelled something funny and went down to check. He had unhooked the meter and laid a slow fuse. That's what I smelled. I went to put it out, but I was too late. It blew me back up the stairs. What I don't know is, who he was and why he did it."

Bell exchanged a glance with Dashwood.

Dashwood said, "Sounds like he knows we're here?"

"Not the Cutthroat Squad," Bell said after a moment's reflection. "More likely, our wanted poster set him off. And now we know something else about him."

"What's that?"

"He's a counterpuncher."

When the Jekyll & Hyde Special started out for St. Louis, Bell joined the closing-night cast party in the dining car. While pretending to trade small talk, Archie Abbott explained the gas-fitter connection to the Cutthroat.

"If we're right that he's had backstage experience, it's no coincidence that he's a gas fitter. These days, lighting effects are all electrical. But theater electricians also manage water effects, like rain and floods. That's because plumbing and gas fitting are similar trades and used to fit pipes to light theaters with gas."

"He's an actor, first and foremost," said Isaac Bell. "It's one thing to know how to be a gas fitter, but to *impersonate* a fitter—to costume himself and portray himself as a workman so believably that he could fool an operator as sharp as Jerry Sedgwick, inside our field office, which has his face on a wanted poster—the Cutthroat has got to be one heck of an actor."

39

"My so-called St. Louis Express was late," said Marion Morgan Bell. "I missed the show, and I haven't even changed, but I hoped I could catch you before you left the theater."

Isabella Cook was removing makeup in her Grand Opera House dressing room.

She inspected the tall blonde and liked what she saw. Stylish in a traveling outfit of tweed jacket, boot-length straight skirt, and a snug cloche hat, Marion Morgan had forthright sea-coral green eyes and a sure-footed smile—clearly a woman like herself who got things done and done right.

"Your husband claimed he was faithful to his wife. One look and I'm not surprised."

"Sounds like you tested him."

"It would have been a mug's game. Have you eaten?"

"On the train, thank you."

"Would you like a glass of wine—I'm having several."

Her maid poured a glass of Billecart-Salmon Brut champagne for Marion and topped off Isabella's, who said, "Your telegram was the first I've ever had that offered immortality."

"Isaac wrote me that you expressed a low opinion of 'movie manufacturing.' I wanted to capture your attention."

"You have it. What's your pitch?"

"There will come a day when the last men and women who were thrilled by you tonight in St. Louis will pass from this earth and take their memory of your performance with them. But if you allow me to film your performance, it will live forever."

"But *I* won't live forever."

"But we will both live longer than we can imagine when we're this young. Isaac was just in London and he saw my film of King Edward's funeral procession. I haven't been in London in a year, but it's still showing in the movie theaters. If you let me film your performance in *Dr. Jekyll and Mr. Hyde*, you can see your Gabriella Utterson again and again, year after year, for the rest of your life—and so can your audience."

"They'll get bored after the second decade."

"Not of the performance I saw in Columbus," said Marion, and Isabella Cook laughed.

"Are you always so persuasive?"

"Only for good causes."

"Do you have your Isaac wrapped around your finger?"

"We wrap each other."

Isabella Cook sighed. "I'll bet you do . . . Would he happen to have a brother?"

Marion shook her head, with a small smile. "He's an only child. His mother died when he was a little boy . . . I want to move the play out of doors, beyond the confines of the stage."

"Why?"

"When Mr. Hyde stalks your Gabriella in a storm, I want beautiful Central Park buffeted by a gale."

"Why?"

"Death is a thief. It steals our joys. When we take Gabriella Utterson out of doors, we will see her joy in the sun, in the rain, in the snow and trees and sky—the joy she will lose if the evil in Jekyll and Hyde takes her life."

"How do you go about 'buffeting'?"

"I haven't done any yet, but while I was shooting a comedy at Biograph last month, a scenic designer, Mr. Sennett, invented a wind machine that I'm going to try."

"What is a 'wind machine'?"

"An enormous propeller spun by an airplane motor."

"Pointed at the *actors*?"

Marion Morgan smiled. "Did I promise it would be easy?"

Isabella Cook laughed.

"What do say, Miss Cook?"

"I am leery of any performance I can't control. Technically, Mr. Barrett and Mr. Buchanan direct the play. But I do nothing on that stage that I don't want to. I am an intelligent woman who trusts her instincts. But when your camera stops rolling, the show is only half done. I won't be around when you make the final decisions pasting up the film the audience sees."

"Of course you'll be around."

"What do you mean?"

"I'm also an intelligent woman who trusts her instincts. My instinct tells me that you make decisions for the good of the show. Editing is a painstaking process. You may stand beside me as long as you can bear it."

Isabella Cook put down her glass. She shook her head. "Why don't we discuss this in the morning?"

Marion looked crestfallen.

Isabella Cook said, "Let me guess. You don't want to see your Isaac if you can't tell him you talked me into this."

Marion nodded.

Isabella Cook said, "I have a hotel suite for when I'm bored with the train. Stay the night there. We'll talk in the morning—but no promises."

"Good morning, Mr. Bell!" cried the stage door tender at the Olympic Theatre, where *Alias Jimmy Valentine* was breaking St. Louis box office records. "How may we help you this morning?"

Expecting to have to talk his way into the star's dressing room, Isaac Bell found himself greeted like royalty. News traveled fast in the theater, and angels backing new musicals were not turned away from stage doors.

"May I see Mr. Vietor?"

The door tender snapped his fingers. "Quinn!" he called to a sceneshifter, slouching nearby. "Take Mr. Bell to Mr. Vietor's dressing room."

Harry Warren tugged his forelock. "Right this way, Mr. Bell."

Bell tipped him a dollar. "Here you go, pal."

"Mighty generous, sir." Quinn pocketed the dollar and banged on Vietor's door. "Mr. Isaac Bell to see you, Mr. Vietor."

The curly-haired Vietor flung his door open with a handsome smile. He was nearly as tall as Bell, and as tight and slim. He had a big voice. "Mr. Bell, I've heard so much about you. Do come in."

Bell said, "I bring regards from a mutual acquaintance, James Mapes."

"Mapes. Oh, cheery Mapes. What a happy soul. Did you see him in London?"

"We had drinks at the Garrick."

"How did my name come up?"

"Mapes indicated an empty space on the portrait wall that was waiting for you."

"Cheery Mapes. What a sweet thought. Come in, come in. Would you have a drink?"

"Thank you, no. I've got a long day ahead. Don't let me stop you."

"I'm the same way. Can't touch a drop until the show is over. Sit, Bell. Sit."

Bell took the armchair. Vietor perched on a stool at his makeup table. Turning half away from Bell, he studied the mirror. Bell wondered, why did he put on stage paint so early? Finally, Vietor glanced away from the glass, opened a drawer, and took out a silk jewelry sack.

"Have you seen the show?"

"In New York. I told Mapes I truly believed that your Jimmy Valentine was going straight."

Vietor untied the drawstrings, fished out a gold ring, and began fiddling with it.

"Did Mapes tell you he coached me?"

"He sounded very proud of your success," said Bell. "He believes it's your Jimmy Valentine that will put you on the wall at the Garrick."

Vietor watched the ring fly between his fingers. "I'll bet he said I was a dark soul."

The actor's manic excitement had bounced unexpectedly from exhilaration to contemplation, and Bell saw an opportunity to draw him out. "Mapes said, 'Subduing the dark side of Vietor's character was like pulling teeth.'"

"Ha! He loves that silly phrase— How old do you think I am?"

Bell studied him closely. "Forty-six."

"My Lord! Where did you get that idea?"

"You're not thirty-six."

"Sad but true. See this?" Vietor held up the ring. "My grandmother's wedding ring. She must have been a huge woman, big as a house. See?" He worked it onto his left ring finger. "And my hands are not that small."

Bell recalled that Anna Waterbury had told Lucy Balant that

the "old" Broadway producer who coached her wore a wedding ring. "Do you wear it?" he asked.

"Not really." Vietor looked in the mirror again. He turned fully toward it. He found Bell's eyes in the reflection. "The past catches up."

"What past?" asked Bell, with the strong feeling that he was about to hear a confession.

"The lies."

"What lies?"

"Well, I'm not about to blurt it out to a complete stranger."

"You've already started."

"Ha! I suppose I have."

His door flew open and a very pretty petite blonde burst in. "Mr. Viet— Oh, I'm so sorry, I didn't realize."

Vietor sprang to his feet. "That's all right, dear. Come in. Meet Mr. Isaac Bell. We have a mutual friend in London. Mr. Bell, Miss Lucy Balant, a very talented young actress."

"Mr. Bell! How nice to meet you. You're the angel— Oh, I beg your pardon, that was really silly of me."

"I've been called worse things," said Bell. "Pleasure to meet you, Miss Balant."

"Now, Lucy, could you come back in ten minutes? Mr. Bell and I have a little bit more catching up to do."

Lucy said good-bye, and closed the door behind her.

"Well, there you have it." Vietor tossed the ring high, caught it nimbly, and eyed Bell through it like a spyglass.

"Have what?"

"Forty-six. You called it spot on—I don't give a *damn* that I'm old. A girl as bright and wise as she will never find a man her own age worthy of her, much less able to match her spirit and cheer her to victory. I will take care of myself, hurl myself into physical culture. I won't die young. I won't require a nurse. Bell, you've been so helpful, I should make you my— No, we'll do it in London. Mother's there, can't travel anymore. Mapes'll be best man. But I do hope you can come."

"What?" asked Isaac Bell.

"I'm going to marry that girl. There! I've said it. Mr. Bell, your jaw has dropped."

Isaac Bell laughed out loud. He stood up and offered his hand. "May I congratulate you, sir? I wish you and the young lady all the happiness in the world."

He could have added, Thank you, Mr. Vietor. Thank you, Lucy Balant. The Cutthroat Squad is down to three men in one show.

———————

Isabella Cook eyed Marion Morgan over the rim of her coffee cup. Neither woman appeared to have slept soundly.

"Where would we make this movie?"

"Los Angeles."

"*Los Angeles,*" the actress groaned. "After months on the road? Must we?"

"The light is perfect, and it rarely rains. I can take pictures three hundred and twenty days a year in every imaginable location. And, by the way, women can vote in California."

"I hope I wouldn't have to stay there long enough to vote."

"I will go ahead and have everything waiting. If all goes well, I'll have you on your way to New York in two weeks."

"Only two weeks?" Isabella Cook brightened. "I'll pretend I'm visiting my husband in Hell."

"Longer, of course, when you stay for editing . . . May I ask Isaac to approach Mr. Barrett and Mr. Buchanan on behalf of his syndicate?"

"That will take some persuading. They can be grimly hidebound and staunchly old-fashioned. But here's the trick—tell your Isaac that the one thing The Boys love more than money is credit. They're clever businessmen, but they are actors at heart. Actors love credit. Immortality tops the bill."

Reckless? asked the cautious voice that kept him free.

Aren't detective posters warning prostitutes about you?

Not in St. Louis. A most satisfactory boom back in Cincinnati probably made detectives think twice about posters. Besides, the socialite who had aroused his interest was no girl of the streets but a country-club lady of the suburbs.

I'm not reckless.

Still, unplanned murders, like rich food and strong drink, were luxuries best indulged in measured doses. Impulse doubled the odds of capture. But tonight felt like one of those nights when the excitement was worth taking chances, a night to "test his mettle" on a woman of higher rank.

Undisciplined?

What are you doing?

Petite and blond. A wealthy young lady. Good taste said let

her go. Caution said let her go. Wisdom said let her go. But she had run and been hiding and now he found her again, his Emily. He hungered for the moment he saw the shock in her eyes.

James Dashwood watched an alley off Market Street that led to the Grand Opera House's stage door. This late in the evening, he hoped to ambush Henry Young if he left to sleep on the Jekyll & Hyde train after the final curtain. Suddenly he got a surprise.

The scraggly-haired writer, the lunatic Cox, whom Dashwood had last seen in Boston shouting, "I wrote that!" wandered up Market and stopped at the mouth of the alley. There, he lurked as if building courage to charge the stage door.

Dashwood walked up to him. "Hello again, Mr. Cox. What brings you to St. Louis?"

The writer straightened up to his full height. Many inches taller than Dashwood, he stared down at the young detective with smouldering eyes. "Hello *again*? What do you mean 'again'? Do I know you?"

"We met in Boston."

Rick Cox shook his head emphatically.

Dashwood said, "At a rehearsal for *Dr. Jekyll and Mr. Hyde.*"

"Were you one of the ushers who threw me out of the theater?"

"No. But I did see it happen. What brings you to St. Louis? Last I heard, you were locked up in Columbus."

"I got out."

"Out the front door or over the wall?" Dashwood's mild joke had the effect he desired. A small smile softened the writer's angry face.

"Front door."

"When was that?"

"Few weeks ago."

Back to five suspects, thought Dashwood. He had to keep him talking. "How'd you manage that? They just let you go?"

"They couldn't keep me when I stopped paying."

"Paying? Paying for what?"

"It's a private asylum. Barrett & Buchanan paid for the first week. I paid an extra couple of days myself. I reckoned I needed more time to calm down."

"Where'd you get the money?"

"Royalties. Barrett & Buchanan pay me a percentage—a small percentage, a pittance—so I don't sue 'em for stealing my story."

"Which one stole your story? Barrett? Or Buchanan?"

"Both."

Dashwood said, "I don't understand. If you get money, they didn't exactly steal your story."

"But they get the credit. And I can't live with that anymore."

James Dashwood said, "May I buy you a drink?"

Suspicion hardened Cox's features again. "Why?"

"I'm a Van Dorn private detective," said Dashwood, watching for a reaction.

Cox leaned closer. "Are you really? Are you working on a case?"

"I was taking the night off, when I saw you."

There were many saloons around Union Station. They entered one with prosperous-looking patrons. Cox said, "This will be on me."

"No, I invited you. It's on me."

"I may be Barrett and Buchanan's patsy, but I'm still better paid than a gumshoe. Even a Van Dorn."

Cox ordered whiskey. Dashwood asked for beer.

"Mud in your eye."

Dashwood sought Cox in the mirror behind the bar and, when they locked gazes, said, "I don't see the payoff. How is shouting in theaters going to get you credit?"

Cox tossed back his whiskey and juggled the glass in his hand as if weighing the wisdom of a refill. "I've been asking myself the same question. So far, all shouting's gotten me is arrested and thrown in the bughouse."

"Then what were you doing hanging around the theater tonight?"

"Just calming down . . . trying to figure things out . . . planning on how to get the credit I deserve." Cox glanced outside the windows where crowds of people were suddenly sweeping along the sidewalk toward the train station. Curtains had descended and theatergoers were hurrying home to the suburbs. Something caught Cox's eye and riveted his attention.

"I have to go. Meet me here tomorrow for lunch. Thanks for the drink."

"You paid," said Dashwood. "Thank *you*."

"Lunch! Tomorrow."

Cox pushed through the swinging doors. Dashwood lost sight of him in the crowd.

———————

"Sleep tight," said Isaac Bell's conductor, which struck Bell as an unusually personal remark coming from the taciturn old geezer.

"Good night, Kux."

He showered in the marble bathroom, poured two fingers of Bushmills, and carried the whiskey into the owner's stateroom at the back of the car. The lights were low, the bed had been turned down, and his heart soared.

"Don't be frightened. It's only me."

"Marion!" Bell scooped her into his arms. "Where did you come from?"

"New York."

"This is wonderful. Why didn't you tell me you were coming?"

"I had a business meeting. If it didn't go well, I might have wanted to slink off by myself."

"I'm glad it went well."

"It went *very* well. Isabella Cook agreed to be in my movie."

Bell let go of her. "Which movie?"

"What I told you: *Dr. Jekyll and Mr. Hyde.*"

"No," said Bell.

"No? Why not?"

"It's too dangerous. Fifty-fifty odds one of The Boys is the Cutthroat. If not, he could be their stage manager. I don't want you anywhere near the *Jekyll and Hyde* company until we have him in chains."

"Isaac, if I can make this movie, I can tell Preston Whiteway and Picture World to go jump in a lake."

"I thought you told him that when you made *The Iron Horse*."

"I didn't burn that bridge, and I'm glad I didn't. I've had no luck putting a four-reeler together on my own. *Jekyll and Hyde* is the best shot I've had since."

"I won't put you in danger."

"I won't let go of this opportunity. I'm sure nothing will happen to me."

"I'm sorry. That's not good enough."

"But I know, I just can't put it in words."

Bell said, "Why don't we sleep on it? Talk it over in the morning."

"I'm not tired."

"You're not? Neither am I."

Reckless? the Cutthroat asked again.

The theater train, a limited-stops express that ran on the suburban commuter line, pulled out of Union Station at ten minutes to midnight. Forty minutes to Tuxedo Park. Forty minutes to decide.

Reckless?

Maybe I was in my younger years.

Undisciplined?

Do you take me for a fool? Discipline is second nature now, my sturdy watchman, ever-vigilant, acutely observant.

He had sharpened the instincts he had been born with. He had grown so sharp at gauging menace, so skilled at covering his tracks, that the odds of getting captured had long ago shifted in his favor.

Reckless? It would be impossible to be reckless. And he had the advantage tonight of operating on familiar territory, for to his eye the Midwestern cities were all similar, with the theaters short train rides from the wealthy suburbs. Cincinnati was the first place he settled after sailing from England on an ancient "half clipper" cotton ship. It was returning empty to New Orleans. The other passengers joked that they were carried as ballast, but her captain was pocketing the ticket money and could care less about his name or whether he owned a passport or landed in New Orleans disguised as a sailor.

A showboat—a theater on a Mississippi River barge—brought him to Cincinnati, where he met a woman with money. After she died, the yellow cottage on the river had been his to visit intermittently for nearly twenty years.

He knew the territory. The theater train carried a gay crowd of mostly younger people who could afford to sleep late the next morning. That they all knew each other—Tuxedo Park being a town of prosperous businesses that benefitted from proximity to its powerhouse neighbor on the Mississippi River—made it even riskier as he would have to pry her loose from the clods vying for her attention.

I know the risk.

He took a seat at the back of the car a couple of rows behind her and imagined the opening sequences of the drama. It started with a curtain-raiser on a quiet suburban pavement that was darkened by the spring-budding trees filtering the streetlamps. She would say something like, "You look familiar."

And they would start to walk down tree-lined streets that grow increasingly dim and narrow.

"Would you tell me your name, miss?"

They were turning into a lane when the curtain crashed down.

The imagined encounter evaporated. A man, who had entered the car from the vestibule behind him, leaned close and whispered,

"I know who you are. You thought you could evade me. I want my credit."

40

The Cutthroat caught a glimpse of long, stringy hair.

He stood up, brushed past Rick Cox, and whispered, "Follow me."

He pushed through the vestibule door onto the open platform between the cars. Cox caught up with him in the near darkness. Faces lit only by the glow from the cars ahead and behind, ears half deafened by the thunder of the engine and the wheels clattering on track joints, they stared at each other. Cox's weirdly mobile features reflected a dozen questions. He blurted one.

"Why are you wearing a false beard?" Cox glanced back at the car at the gay crowd in the bright lights and for a second, the Cutthroat saw, he fixed on the petite blonde with the musical voice. It all dawned on the lunatic in a flash. "Oh . . . No . . . You!"

He reached to tug the Cutthroat's beard.

The Cutthroat blocked him with his cane. As he did, he twisted the head, yanked out the blade, and rammed it deep into Cox's belly. He had murdered many, many more women than men. But their internal anatomy was the same, at least when it came to organs that mattered. He gripped his weapon with both hands and used all his might to drag it up through the sternum.

He checked that no one was coming from either car. Then he stepped over the side chains, pulled the body under them, leaned out into the slipstream and held on with one hand while he pulled Cox with the other. Calling on almost superhuman strength, he lifted Cox's body beside him, swung it high and far, and yanked it in from the arc of the swing and under the wheels.

You are brilliant.

The lunatic hurled himself under a speeding train.

Brilliant.

He retrieved the cane he had dropped, sheathed his blade, and waited outside in the vestibule while the train slowed for Tuxedo Park. The passengers hurried out of the car. He followed them from the lavish stone station, wrapping his cape tightly closed to cover the blood that soaked his coat and trousers. Ahead, he could hear the blonde laughing with her friends, escaping him again.

Leaving him still hungry.

———————

"Isaac!" Marion said in the night.

Bell came awake in an instant, reaching under the pillow, eyes glittering like cobalt. She had turned on a light.

"I know why I know the Cutthroat won't hurt me if he is in the *Jekyll and Hyde* company."

Bell let go of the gun, sat up, and put an arm around her shoulder. "Tell me."

"You think it's highly likely that the Cutthroat is in the *Jekyll and Hyde* company."

"Likely enough to make it too dangerous."

"He won't hurt me. He can't hurt me. Because if he wants to have the movie made, he needs me alive."

Isaac Bell broke into a broad smile.

"Are you laughing at me?" she asked.

"No. I am, as always, grateful for your wisdom. But this time even you don't fully understand what you've reckoned."

"I told you, you don't have to worry about me."

"Thanks to you, I don't have to worry about *anyone*."

"What do you mean?"

"You've come up with the ideal way to distract him. If the Cutthroat is Barrett or Buchanan or Henry Young, he won't hurt *anyone* because he won't risk getting caught until after you finish the movie in Los Angeles. That gives me the entire tour across the West to nail him before he murders another woman."

41

"Immortality, Mr. Bell?"

Barrett and Buchanan eyed Isaac Bell skeptically over their coffee cups. Their train had just crossed the Missouri–Kansas line and was passing through oil fields littered with abandoned derricks.

"Next, you'll sell us the Brooklyn Bridge."

"On top of *Treasure Island*."

The tall detective found no humor in their banter. Not when he knew that these men were two of his three suspects. The odds were, one of them had slaughtered Anna Waterbury and Lillian Lent and Mary Beth Winthrop and how many more girls who had died in terror.

"A movie will make your performances live forever."

"We weren't aware you were involved with motion pictures, Mr. Bell."

"My wife is a filmmaker. Marion Morgan Bell."

Both actors' eyebrows shot upward. Buchanan said, "You are married to Marion Morgan? She made *The Iron Horse*. You saw it, Jackson, about the western railroads."

Barrett was studying Bell closely. "So you are not a complete stranger to show business, Mr. Bell."

"I believe I can persuade her to immortalize your production of *Dr. Jekyll and Mr. Hyde* in a big film. Three full reels. Maybe four."

John Buchanan shook his head. "Absolutely not. If the audience can watch a movie, why would they come to our show?"

"They can read *Dr. Jekyll and Mr. Hyde*. But they still come to your show."

"Interesting," Barrett said. "It is something to consider."

"Someday in the future," Buchanan added vaguely.

Bell said, "You would have to do it immediately after your last performance in San Francisco. It can be made fast and inexpensively only while your company is still together, your scenery and costumes intact."

"Who will pay for it?" asked Buchanan. "You're talking about carrying the entire company during the process, not to mention what cameras and that sort of thing cost."

"My syndicate will put up the money in exchange for half the profits. Your movie rights to your play will keep the other half."

"This will take some pondering."

"Why?" asked Bell. "It was your idea."

"Our idea? What are you talking about?"

"Mr. Barrett, you said you wished your play would not disappear. And, Mr. Buchanan, you wished you could sell tickets to a production that cost nothing to make. Didn't you?"

"Wishes."

"I'm offering you your wishes. If you must ponder, ponder two unique facts about movies. One, a movie preserves your play—and, particularly, your performances—for the ages."

Barrett nodded.

Buchanan said, "Yes, yes, immortality. There's where you started. What is the other unique fact?"

"An all-new kind of 'magic wand' profit never seen before in the history of the theater. Speaking in round numbers, let's say your play wraps eight thousand a week, provided you crowd the theater. But your play costs you seven thousand a week in salaries and expenses. Each and every week, whether or not you crowd the theater."

Bell watched Barrett and Buchanan exchange raised eyebrows, again. The Hartford insurance man had learned a thing or two.

"To make your movie will cost you nothing. When it plays in every movie house in the country, it will bring in twenty, thirty, fifty thousand a week. Every week. While your cost every week will remain zero."

"I like that," said Buchanan.

"Money and immortality," said Barrett. "Very tempting, Mr. Bell."

"Your idea, gentlemen. All I did was listen to you. But speed is of the essence, unless you're willing to go to the expense of starting from scratch with a whole new company, scenery, and costumes."

Barrett and Buchanan looked at each other and traded silent nods.

"What's the next step?"

Isaac Bell stood up. "We shake on it, and then I will do everything in my power to talk my wife into it."

"If she won't," said Barrett, "we'll find someone else."

Bell jumped at the chance to make Marion bulletproof.

"That won't be necessary. We have already discussed it."

"Was talking her into it a negotiating ploy?"

"Guilty," said Bell. "It's a terrible insurance man habit. The customer wants his steel mills insured for the lowest premium. I sympathize but must 'clear it with my underwriters,' who are real skinflints. Fact is, there's really no one else to film your play better than Marion, and she is so excited about moving it out of doors, beyond the confines of the stage. When Mr. Hyde stalks a girl through the storm in Central Park, she will fashion a wind machine to buffet the trees. And you will fight your Dream Duel in a hurricane."

"I, for one, will send my understudy," said Buchanan.

"Me, too," Barrett grinned. "Poor Mr. Young will have his hands full standing in for both of us."

"Is Mr. Young a fencer, too?" asked Bell.

"Enough of one to spell us on occasion."

Barrett said, "But, seriously, if for some reason your wife can't—"

Isaac Bell answered firmly, "If Marion Morgan Bell can't

make the movie, we won't pay for it. And we won't release the rights."

"Then it will behoove us to be most persuasive. When can we meet her?"

"Soon as we get to Denver. Let's say lunch tomorrow at the Brown Palace, if we can round up Miss Cook and your stage manager."

"Henry Young is not a principal."

"My wife will have questions of a technical nature best addressed to the stage manager."

42

The Cutthroat dreamed he was a boy in London.

The boy found a broken sword. He polished the rust with sand and honed both edges like a Roman *gladius*. He stole a file and shaped the broken end to a needle point.

He dreamed they chased him through narrow streets.

He fled to a seaport that reeked of salt and grease and smoke.

He sprawled, seasick, retching his guts out on a splintered deck. The ship finally stopped moving in a hot Southern city where the girls spoke French.

He killed them and fled up the Mississippi River on a steamboat. No—the dream went backwards and started over. The steamboat was behind him. He was on an immense raft, a floating theater, *pushed* by a steamboat. Up the wide, wide river from New Orleans, day and night, day and night, day and night, Memphis, past Cairo, up the Ohio River. Off the raft at Louisville, on again, and up the river, and off at Cincinnati. Safe at last.

Suddenly he was an animal sleeping in his den.

He was a wolf. Something paced at the mouth of the cave.

———

He opened his eyes.

He lay still, adrenaline overflowing his arteries, heart thundering, every sense aware.

His dream wolf had felt a presence.

He steadied his breath and stilled his heart. What did it mean?

Eighty men and women were sleeping on the train. This late at night, the only sounds he heard were mechanical—the huff of switch engines, wheels grinding on rails, the muffled clash of couplers, the hoot-hoot of engine signals, the clank of bells, the urgent hiss of locomotives bleeding steam, and the long, long whistle of a train leaving for the West—this train, this special bound for Denver—rumbling out of the yards, thumping through switches, then smooth on the main line, swaying as it picked up speed, whistle howling, drive wheels thundering.

What had his instincts latched onto? What had he noticed? It was there, almost beside him, something close, which he could not quite touch yet. He had to let his mind drift . . . The broken sword had started his dream. He remembered it well. He had found it when the tide exposed the muddy Thames bank. It took an edge beautifully. A razor's edge. It was eventually too light, for he had taken on size and developed hard muscle as he grew older. The double-edged Roman short sword was a better fit, and he had used a variety of them—*gladius*, the longer *spatha*, the short *puglio* dagger—choosing one over the other on whim, enjoying one or the other, before moving on to thinner, whippier blades he could hide in a cane.

———————

He sat up in bed, his mind clamoring.

Change plagued touring companies. Every imaginable mishap felled actors. They got sick. They got drunk. They got pregnant. They couldn't remember lines anymore. They were arrested for debt, locked up for bigamy. They married. They divorced. They even got homesick. Or they simply vanished. But whatever the mishap, the company had to replace them, and backstage people, too—carpenters, riggers, electricians, wardrobe. So regular turnover was typical of a road show. But he could not recall as many new faces as he saw in the *Jekyll and Hyde* company—all at once, back in Cincinnati.

Two actors: the new Mr. Pool, Archibald Abbott; the new maid, Helen Mills; a replacement stagehand named Quinn, just hired away from *Jimmy Valentine*. Then there was the newspaper reporter who had talked his way into the publicist's good graces, Scudder Smith; and the Hartford angel, Isaac Bell; and now Bell's wife, Marion Morgan Bell, who had looked familiar, though they had never met before the movie meeting the day before.

The wolf of my dream knows that his den has been invaded.

I am no longer safe when I sleep.

ACT FOUR

HOLLYWOOD

The Cutthroat saw Isaac Bell fall from the trestle

43

Rumor ricocheted the length of the Jekyll & Hyde Special.

They were steaming on the High Plains, and from the loco-motive to Isaac Bell's private car and back again. Scrambled in the crowded Pullman dormitory cars, and simultaneously denied and amplified in the dining car, guesses, gossip and speculation, confused players, stagehands, carpenters, electricians, clerks, publicists, advance men, and musicians, and set all on edge.

Mr. Barrett and Mr. Buchanan had had a huge blowup.

Bigger, much bigger, than their usual rows.

The *Jekyll and Hyde* tour was canceled.

Because the crazy writer killed himself? Cox. They found him in the suburbs.

The tour would be speeded up.

They would skip Denver . . . But what a great theater town.

The tour was extended to include Los Angeles.

The tour was canceled.

Barrett and Buchanan had had a terrible fistfight.

Mr. Young had tried to stop it. The poor stage manager had to throw himself between them. The reward for his pains? He had been beaten bloody. The sight of Mr. Young drinking coffee in the dining car without a mark on him only added to the confusion.

Harry Warren thought the stage manager looked almost happy, not his usual appearance. He offered a smoke from a pack of Young's favorite Turkish tobacco, Murads.

"Bless you, Quinn."

The twitch in Young's cheek that the regular stagehands said always jumped like a frog on closing days and opening days—when every stick of scenery and every stitch of costume had to be loaded onto the train the second the curtain came down—was barely pulsing.

They lit up. Warren said, "I overheard the boys saying you stand in for Barrett and Buchanan."

"Who said that?"

"Couple of sceneshifters . . . Do you?"

"On occasion."

"You must be one slick fencer to survive that Dream Duel."

"So far, at least."

"And a heck of an actor to make Mr. Hyde as evil as they do."

Young smiled at the compliment. "Thank you, Quinn. It's harder than dueling, I'll tell you that."

"Do folks in the audience ever complain?"

"No, bless them. They've been kind. I actually receive ovations. Often more sustained than Barrett's or Buchanan's."

"Do the stars mind?"

"Green-eyed with jealousy?" asked Young, with another smile.

"For all your extra applause."

"They're too grateful for the chance to pull a disappearing act. And of course they're not in the theater when I receive my applause. At least not the one I'm standing in for that night."

"Where do they go on their disappearing acts?"

Henry Young shrugged. "Who knows. Mr. Barrett is probably off writing. He constantly tinkers with scripts."

"Buchanan a writer, too?"

"Not that I'm aware of— What's the time? I must go. Thanks for the smoke."

"Anytime, Mr. Young. Say, what's the news? Are we closing?"

"I honestly don't know."

———

Harry Warren reported to Isaac Bell in the privacy of a wind-blown platform between two cars. They were into Colorado now, and Bell could feel the engine begin to strain on the light but constant grade that presaged the Rocky Mountains.

"My gut said don't push him any further. What do you think?"

"You nailed his leverage. Barrett and Buchanan are willing to overlook Young's past because they can count on him to stand in for their 'disappearing acts.' How long do they disappear?"

"The news backstage is, Mr. Young fills in for one or two nights in a row."

"How often?"

"Not often. Couple of times a month."

"Mr. Buchanan probably disappears with his rich girlfriends. Where do you suppose Barrett goes to write?"

"I'll ask around. Somebody'll know."

"What do you think about Mr. Young?" Bell asked.

"I don't see how the stage manager would ever find the time to kill anybody."

"Archie says the same. So does Helen."

"How about you, Isaac?"

"I'm not so sure."

———

The rumor that the Jekyll & Hyde Special would not stop for their scheduled performances in Denver was about to meet its test. The stage manager announced a full company meeting. Actors, musicians, sceneshifters, riggers, carpenters, wardrobe ladies, ticket sellers, and callboys crowded into the dining car and waited anxiously while stopped outside the city center in the 36th Street yard. Their locomotive took on water and their tender's coal, and they waited some more when grocery trucks and butchers' wagons parked beside the dining car. When the train was replenished, would it be shunted toward Union Station or onto the main line west across the Rockies?

John Buchanan looked relaxed and in charge.

Jackson Barrett, too, looked like he hadn't a worry in the world.

Maybe the worst rumors weren't true?

Are you kidding? Mr. Barrett and Mr. Buchanan are *actors*. Who knows what they're thinking or how they feel?

"O.K.," said Buchanan. "Is everyone here? We have our cast. We have our backstage people and our out-front people. We have our train crew. We have our stewards and cooks. We have our guests—the angelic Mr. Bell, the journalistic Mr. Smith, and the 'filmalistic' Mrs. Marion Morgan Bell—more about her in a moment. We even have the pilot of our *Jekyll and Hyde* billboard in the sky, and if Mrs. Bradford looks too young to fly a biplane, look again, for she is a married woman and the mother of two little girls almost as pretty as she is."

"Get on with it," Jackson Barrett muttered through an opaque smile.

"Hazel Bradford," Bell whispered to Marion, "set speed and altitude records last year."

Buchanan stepped back, and said, "Your turn."

Jackson Barrett said, "The rumors you've heard are NOT true. Our tour is NOT over."

Eighty people smiled.

"So don't worry. Our play lives on. And will continue to live on as no Broadway play ever has before."

Everyone leaned forward to hear what the devil that was supposed to mean.

"After Denver and San Francisco, we will immediately steam down to Hollywood, which is just outside Los Angeles, where

Marion Morgan Bell will transform our play into a movie. Yes, you heard right. A movie."

Buchanan said, "Our final performances will play to Marion Morgan Bell's cameras rather than on the stage. We will continue salaries at their current rate. Anyone who absolutely must get back to New York, we understand, and will replace you."

"But," said Barrett, "we hope that everyone will make the time to be watched by movie audiences forever."

Bell whispered to Marion, "Congratulations. You've got your four-reeler."

"Your investment syndicate doesn't exist. How am I going to pay for it?"

"I've already spoken with Uncle Andy that you're coming straight from San Francisco to Los Angeles to set up a four-reeler of *Dr. Jekyll and Mr. Hyde*."

The formidable Andrew Rubenoff, a onetime banking colleague of Bell's father and a friend of Bell's, had shifted his assets from steel, coal, and railroads to autos, airplanes, and movies and moved to California.

Bell grinned. "He's deeply impressed that you snagged Isabella. You have your syndicate, Rubenoff and Bell."

With that, the tall detective strolled casually from the dining car, accepting congratulations from well-wishers. He kept smiling until he was alone in his private car at the back of the train, where he laid his long fingers on his telegraph key and pondered what to send.

He was running out of time. The show would be in and out of San Francisco and on the way to Los Angeles before he knew it. If he didn't arrest the Cutthroat before Marion finished the movie, the murderer would have his "immortality" and nothing would stop him from murdering another girl the next day.

Closing night in Denver, while Marion roamed the Princess Theatre backstage scouting angles for her cameras, Isaac Bell watched *Dr. Jekyll and Mr. Hyde* from an eighth-row house seat on the aisle. The fans and critics who raved about the famous Dream Duel when Jekyll's potion triggered hallucinations had not been exaggerated. Bell was impressed.

He had fenced for Yale and still practiced religiously. At the Fencers Club on 45th Street, his best opponent was U.S. Navy saber champion Lieutenant Kenneth Ash, whenever both men found themselves in New York. Together, the detective and the naval attaché were developing a new attack—the "back shot"—which had judges scratching their heads and opponents bewildered.

In *Jekyll and Hyde*, the actors' swordsmanship was miles above swordplay taught in drama schools. They were saber fighters of the first rank, Buchanan quick and powerful, Barrett possibly his superior, but not by much.

Where did I see you, Mrs. Bell?

The Cutthroat watched Marion Morgan Bell while she was deep in conversation with the head carpenter and the head rigger. The tall blonde was as beautiful as any actress yet seemed oblivious to the effect she had on the seasoned backstage hands. The men were following her around like a pair of puppies and vying with each other to capture her attention with the intricacies of moving the subway car and biplane out of the Princess Theatre and back on the train.

Where did I see you?

44

SAN FRANCISCO

The Jekyll & Hyde Special was racing on the Nevada flats, whipping past telegraph poles at seventy miles per hour. But thanks to improvements in Thomas Edison's electrostatic induction, Isaac Bell did not have to climb them to tap the lines. Edison's "grasshopper telegraphy" did the job for him, jumping Bell's orders from his private car to the wires beside the railroad tracks the instant he touched the key.

He sent three last-ditch messages in a swift hand.

Dashwood—whom Bell had ordered back to St. Louis to sit in on the postmortem examination of Rick Cox—received

CLEVELAND

BANKER'S WIFE

DISAPPEARING ACT GIRLFRIEND?

Joseph Van Dorn was glad-handing Justice Department prosecutors in the agency's Washington, D.C., field office in the New Willard Hotel on Pennsylvania Avenue when he received

LEND A HAND NEW YORK

FIRE ESCAPE

YACHT

Van Dorn sent blistering wires to his men, who had turned up nothing but goose eggs in either of those investigations. Then he caught the B&O's Royal Blue to New York, read the goose-egg reports word for word, and headed into the theater districts.

Joe Wallace's message from Isaac Bell read

SPELVIN

FULL SPEED

———— •—•—— ————

The Cutthroat was still on the train to San Francisco when he finally remembered where he had seen the woman.

Columbus, Ohio.

Last month, before Chicago, Cleveland, Toledo, and Detroit.

An evening performance.

The house manager was delaying the curtain, and he had peeked out at the audience to see why it was being held.

Typically, a couple were taking their own sweet time strolling to their seats on the aisle—local luminaries, the usual richest man in town who had married the prettiest girl—an ordinary occurrence of which he had thought nothing at the time as he ducked back from the curtain to take his place. In fact, he had barely noticed them, for what had caught his eye was a woman directly behind them. She was walking alone, as poised as a duchess escorted by cavalry, into the theater to see him again onstage. Blond and perfect. His heart had soared. Emily.

No, not Emily, Mrs. Isaac Bell. Why were you in Columbus?

And who are you, *Mr.* Bell?

Are you the leader of the new faces?

I think you are. I think you command them. I think you are hunting me.

I don't know why. I doubt you're a copper. But I don't care who you are, Mr. Bell. No dead man can lock me up.

You first. Then your lovely wife. Back-to-back.

A vital murder.

A joyous slaughter.

———

"May I join you?" Isaac Bell asked Henry Young, who was sitting with a cup of coffee in the dining car. The train was crawling up the Sierra Nevada pushed by two extra engines. The mountains, deep in spring snow, looked as remote as the far side of the moon, but soon the special would crest at Donner Pass—only five short hours from San Francisco.

"Of course, Mr. Bell."

"It occurs to me, I don't think I've ever seen you sitting down before."

Young smiled. He looked ten years younger, and the twitch in his cheek had vanished.

"And you look very happy."

"I am," said the stage manager. "I had my best night's sleep in a year."

"You're not troubled that the tour is almost over?"

"I am thrilled. I let The Boys talk me into this one against my better judgment. Touring is a young man's game. Give me a Broadway play I load once instead of fifty times. Mind you, every stage manager should learn his trade on the road. Earn the right to stay home and then *stay home*."

"I've heard you're quite the fencer."

Young replied with a modest shrug. "I'm a student fencer."

"Who's your teacher?"

"Mr. Barrett."

"They say you can handle yourself."

"Mr. Barrett is a gifted teacher. I had the advantage of being a dancer when I was a kid, which makes one fluid, shall we say. But I still give ninety per cent of the credit to Mr. Barrett's instruction. Basics, like relaxing the grip for point control. Fluidity—as in dance."

"Did he teach Mr. Buchanan, too?"

"I believe he 'polished' him. I gather Mr. Buchanan was adept to begin with."

"You said you danced?"

"My aunts and uncles were hoofers. The Dancing Bookers."

"Of course. Booker's your middle name. Did you dance in England?"

"Canada."

"Do you know what a 'panto' is?"

"Panto? Panto . . . Oh, the English pantomime. Christmas shows for children."

"Do you have pantos in Canada?"

"No. Perhaps in some of the other British colonies, but not in Canada. You're full of questions today, Mr. Bell."

"Every day," Isaac Bell shot back. "Every day with all of you on this train is a chance to learn a lot at once about the stage."

———

Joseph Van Dorn stepped out of a Tenderloin District saloon that catered to actors and found the sidewalk blocked by a broad-shouldered hard case wearing a blue suit and a derby.

"Care to tell me why the founder of a private detective agency, with field offices in every city worth its name and foreign outposts in London, Paris, and Berlin, has spent two full days personally sleuthing around my precinct, asking about an actor manager who fell off a lady's fire escape last October?"

"Keeping my hand in. How are you, Captain?"

The old friends shook hands warmly.

"How are you making out?"

"Better than your boys did in October."

Honest Mike Coligney bristled. "What's that supposed to mean?"

"The husband everybody said was chasing Mr. Medick claims he wasn't."

"What do you expect him to say? A man died. He didn't want to get charged with manslaughter."

"He also says he wasn't cuckolded."

"That's not what he said last October."

"He *thought* he'd been cuckolded at the time, but now he says he was set up. Some 'friend' sent him a letter: 'Dear sir, I thought you should know that your wife is running around on you.'"

"Do you believe him?"

"His wife swore she never cheated on him."

"Do you believe *her*?"

"She swore it on her deathbed."

"What deathbed? She couldn't be older than thirty-five."

"TB. Gone in March."

Mike Coligney crossed himself. "Mother Mary . . . So what was Medick doing on her fire escape?"

"He got a letter, too. Supposedly from the lady."

"I remember the letter. Along the line of 'Come up the fire escape, I'll let you in my back window.'"

"She swore she never wrote it," said Van Dorn. "Same deathbed."

"Who did?"

"Whoever threw Mr. Medick off the fire escape."

"Except for one thing," said Coligney. "Detective Division matched that letter to a typewriter in the lady's office where she worked."

"There are two ways of looking at the typewriter," said Joseph Van Dorn. "Either she lied on her deathbed . . . or the person who threw Mr. Medick off the fire escape typed the letter on that typewriter."

Coligney knew that and changed the subject. "Medick was supposed to be afraid of heights. Where'd he get the nerve to climb four stories of fire escapes?"

Joseph Van Dorn rubbed his red whiskers, took off his hat, and ran a big hand over his bald scalp. He blinked, and his deep-set Celtic eyes grew dark with melancholy. "According to the lady's poor devil of a husband, she was a woman worth taking chances for."

"So Medick knew her."

"Hoped to know her better," said Van Dorn, "encouraged by a letter written by someone who knew his weakness for other men's wives."

"How come no witness ever saw that 'someone'?"

"But they did see him," said Van Dorn. "He just didn't look like someone who could throw a fit young actor off a fire escape."

"What are you talking about, Joe?"

"I spoke with three people who remember an old man hanging around her building. One thought he was a tramp, another a rag-picker, another just a drunk. They all believed he was harmless."

Isaac Bell read Van Dorn's wire the night that *Dr. Jekyll and Mr. Hyde* closed in San Francisco.

FIRE ESCAPE

OLD MAN

ACTOR

45

"In all my years on the stage," groaned Isabella Cook, "I cannot recall a closing-night cast party the equal of last night's. Nor a hangover more vicious. Oh, Isaac, what were we thinking?"

"Yours is not the only hangover on the train, if that's any consolation."

"How is yours?"

"About what I deserve," Bell answered. In fact, with an awful sense he was running out of time, he had sipped dark cider in Manhattan cocktail glasses while he kept a clear, but ultimately fruitless, eye on Jackson Barrett, John Buchanan, and Henry Young.

"It's your wife's fault. The prospect of her movie obliterated

closing-night blues. Everyone's excited. I saw love affairs spring-
ing up all around me, and couples who had ceased to speak making cow eyes . . . Would someone tell the engineer to stop
clattering the wheels?"

"We're almost there."

"I never thought I would be so happy to get off a train in Los
Angeles . . ." She cast a dubious eye out the window. "Sunny Los
Angeles? I see nothing but storm-swept orange groves and sod-
den cattle. Do you suppose this rain will follow us all the way to
Hollywood?"

"Marion has rented a studio, just in case."

When Bell spoke long-distance with her last night, she had
ended her report with a grim, "But it's still raining."

———— ·— ——

No one had to light a fire under Joel Wallace.

Fourteen retired chorus girls—since Isaac Bell left London—
fourteen strikeouts. Then all of a sudden, his new friend, Dolly,
who he had met on this wild-goose chase, said that when her
mother was in the chorus in *Tra-la-la Tosca* way back in 1891,
she had known a girl who went with a boy named Spelvin.

Wallace waited for them in a tearoom on Piccadilly, around
the corner from the Van Dorn field office. In they came, all
spiffed-up for Central London. One look at her mother told
Wallace that her daughter would age very nicely. Mother paused
to reminisce with the tearoom manager, and Dolly forged ahead
to Wallace's table.

"I brought me mum, like you asked. She thinks you're going to marry me."

"Dolly, you know I'm not the marrying kind. I never lied, did I? Told you the night we met."

"Well, you better not tell Mum that or she won't talk to you."

Joel Wallace's cable found Isaac Bell in the rain-swept Los Angeles Arcade Depot rail yards, when Bell's car rolled in on the back of the Jekyll & Hyde Special. It was a potent reminder that Joseph Van Dorn had tapped the right man to ramrod the London field office.

```
SPELVIN CON 1891
IMPERSONATING ITALIAN FENCING TEACHER
GIRLFRIEND DISAPPEARED
SPELVIN LAST SEEN LIVERPOOL STATION
ON MY WAY TO LIVERPOOL
```

It was one thing to impersonate an Italian, thought Bell, the Whitechapel barber Davy Collins being a prime example. But quite another to teach fencing, as Mr. Barrett trained Mr. Young. Double that to teach the exquisite skill of Italian fencing.

Detective Eddie Tobin waited at the Chelsea Piers in a fast launch. Joseph Van Dorn clambered aboard. Tobin started up a pair of eight-cylinder Wolseley-Siddeley gasoline engines that Isaac Bell had had shipped over from England and thundered across the crowded, smoke-shrouded harbor toward Staten Island.

Tobin, whose misshapen face reflected a terrible Gopher Gang beating when he was a Van Dorn apprentice, lounged at the helm like a man who had been born in a cockpit, nonchalantly dodging tugs, coal barges, railcar floats, victualing lighters, sail and steam freighters, and liners, at thirty knots. Ordered by Chief Inspector Bell to look afresh at the Oppenheim yacht explosion, the young detective had found a witness.

"How come the cops never talked to him?" Mr. Van Dorn wanted to know.

"He doesn't talk to cops. And he won't talk to us either, at least not directly."

Van Dorn assumed the witness was one of his cousins as the tight-lipped Tobin-Darbee-Richards-Gordon-and-Scott clan of Staten Island scowmen included oysters tongers, tugboat men, coal pirates, and smugglers.

"The problem is, Mr. Van Dorn, it's going to be hearsay."

"I'm not building a court case," Van Dorn growled. "All Isaac needs is ammunition."

Into the harbor at St. George, Tobin slowed just enough for two muscle-bound oyster tongers to jump on from a pier head. Van Dorn nodded coolly but shook hands. Jimmy Richards and Marvyn Gordon were in and out of jail regularly, but they were by and large larcenous, not vicious, for which he would cut them some slack. Tobin raced out into the Kill Van Kull, slowing a mile in and cutting the engines when Richards and Gordon pointed at an oyster scow anchored beside a derelict schooner. A pretty, dark-haired girl stepped out of the low cabin. Van Dorn figured she was about fourteen.

"Molly, this is Mr. Van Dorn, who I told you about."

Molly extended her hand to shake Van Dorn's solemnly but invited no one aboard her boat.

Tobin said, "Molly's father told her what he saw. She's going to tell you."

Molly said, "An old Italian greengrocer with a big hooked nose hired Father to take him to the yacht."

"The Oppenheim yacht?"

"The one that blew up. He delivered crates of lettuce. The water was rough, and he got sick on the way back. Seasick. Sweating and throwing up. When Father helped him up to the dock, his nose fell off."

"His *nose*—"

"And his big black mustache. The Italian kind."

———————

Van Dorn wired Isaac Bell in Los Angeles.

YACHT

OLD MAN

ACTOR AGAIN

"Now we know that he doesn't kill only for twisted pleasure," Bell confided in Marion, whom he had been consoling with a late supper after another day of rain had forced her to take her cameras indoors. "He kills for profit, too."

"He killed to get control of the show."

———

The Cleveland field office was not thrilled to have an investigation reviewed by a detective as young as James Dashwood. That Dashwood reported directly to Chief Investigator Isaac Bell did not make the Cleveland boys love him more.

"Interesting," Dashwood commented politely after a painstaking examination of photographs from the morgue.

"Yeah, what's interesting?"

"Well, that you could conclude that the murderer did not carve crescent shapes on the victim's arms."

"Which we did."

"On the other hand, these marks on her legs could be interpreted as crescent-shaped."

"They could also be interpreted as stab wounds inflicted during their struggle."

"What struggle? The coroner concluded that death was rapid, if not instantaneous, due to this wound in her throat, or this separation of vertebrae C3 and C4 . . ."

The Cleveland chief concealed a longing to march Dashwood off a Lake Erie pier. "Is there anything else?"

"There is something odd about this theater program that Mr. Buchanan inscribed to the lady."

"My pleasure," John Buchanan had written over his name in the *Dr. Jekyll and Mr. Hyde* cast list. And under it, his signature.

Both flowed in a clear, bold English round hand, decorated with beautiful hooks and dramatic flourishes.

"What about it?"

"You did a remarkable job of documenting their 'visits' with each other."

"Rich folk don't go to a lot of trouble to hide it. If the lady's husband didn't notice, or didn't want to notice, who's going to call them on it?"

"And it was genius discovering the husband's girlfriend."

"Thank you, sonny."

"But what is it about this program? It's driving me nuts— May I keep it, please?"

"You'll have to sign a receipt."

"My pleasure," said Dashwood.

———————

The Cutthroat had waited too long.

The rain had slowed everything to a maddening crawl.

It was time—long past time—to attack.

A vital murder.

A joyous slaughter.

46

Joel Wallace outdid himself with his second cable to Isaac Bell:

```
EMPTY COTTON SHIPS
LIVERPOOL TO NEW ORLEANS
NO PAPERS
```

With little hope for more than a list culled from old newspapers, and even less for a quick answer as to where the murderer had gone next twenty years ago, Bell wired the New Orleans field office:

```
GIRLS MURDERED AUGUST—DECEMBER 1891
```

A letter arrived at the railcar. The envelope was addressed to

Isaac Bell, c/o the Arcade Depot, where the Jekyll & Hyde Special was parked.

The letter inside read

Dear Boss,

Mile 342. SP. Midnight.
Come alone, old boy.
At the end of the day, isn't it just between us?
I couldn't blame you if you don't come alone.
Or don't come at all.
I ask too much of bravery.
One of us is immortal, and you know it isn't you.

"Twenty-to-one, it's a hoax," he told Archie Abbott.

"You going anyway?"

"Have to."

"Alone?"

"Like the man says."

Bell recognized the handwriting as similar to the "My funny little games" letter that Jack the Ripper wrote to the Central News Agency in 1888—which Scotland Yard had thought authentic and put up on posters in the fruitless hope someone who knew him would recognize the handwriting.

A crescent was inked under Jack the Ripper's signature, which anyone could have picked up reading the papers. But "Dear Boss" was more intriguing, as that first letter to the Yard had also been directed to "Dear Boss."

"What the heck is 'Mile 342. SP'?" asked Archie Abbott.

Bell showed him a map.

"The Southern Pacific Railroad counts track miles from San Francisco. That puts Milepost 342 a hundred and twenty miles up the coast from Los Angeles, between Gaviota and El Capitan."

The tracks hugged the Santa Barbara Channel shore.

"Middle of nowhere," said Archie.

"Nothing but a water tank."

"What if he pulls something?"

"If he doesn't, I'll be mighty disappointed."

"Why don't I just tag along a ways back?" Abbott asked.

"He'll be looking for you."

Abbott knew his friend too well. Because he blamed himself for Anna's death, Isaac Bell would go alone—rather than risk frightening him off—fight alone, and come back alone with a captive or a body—or alone in a coffin—and no force on earth could stop him.

"Twenty-to-one, it's a hoax," Bell repeated.

"By whom?"

"My old friend Abbington-Westlake is 'having me on,' as the Britons say. His forgers could imitate the Ripper's handwriting. But they made a mistake with this word."

"'Immortal'?"

"The Ripper wrote slang: 'Fix me' and 'buckled' for 'arrest'; 'codding' for 'playing jokes'; 'work' and 'job' for 'murder.' Calling me Boss, they got right. But not 'immortal.' More to the point, he's never sent a letter since he left London. Scotland Yard did him a huge favor claiming he was dead, and he's kept it that way."

"He can't resist playing his games—like the crescent code—now he's playing games with you."

"I hope you're right," said Isaac Bell.

"Isaac, let me come with you."

"I want you here with Marion."

"O.K. Of course. I'll watch her. Listen, it's still raining. I lifted a cowboy slicker from Wardrobe. You take it."

Bell went to the Southern Pacific freight yards. The rain that had plagued Marion since they arrived in Los Angeles was falling steadier than ever, and he was glad of Archie's full-length waterproof oilskin. He bribed a yard bull with a ten-dollar gold piece to put him into an empty freight car headed up the California coast. Six hours later, he jumped down when the slow-moving train shunted onto the Mile 342 water siding.

Dusk was gathering and the rain had thickened. Fair-size waves were breaking on the sandy shore, and the cold fog drifting off the water bore the icy breath of the Pacific Ocean, which the channel joined a few miles to the west. He lost sight of the red caboose lantern when the freight train trundled back onto the main line and crossed the trestle bridge that spanned the canyon.

He had four hours before midnight to ferret out surprises.

The water tank, which had a huge pivot spout to replenish steam engines' boilers, was raised high above the tracks on legs. The single main line track paralleled the channel. The water siding ran just inland of it. Inland of the siding was a sandy path for maintenance carts. Just beyond the switch where the water siding rejoined the main line, the land dropped into a canyon. The rain-swollen arroyo that had scoured the canyon with eons of floodwater rushed thirty feet under a trestle bridge. Bell climbed down and confirmed that no one was hiding in the under-supports.

Thunder began rumbling. The rain fell harder.

The open area under the water tank offered shelter. But after inspecting it and climbing a side ladder to the roof of the tank to make sure he was alone, Bell chose to button up his slicker and conceal himself within girders of the trestle. From that forest of steel, he watched the tank and the tracks in both directions. If the letter was not fake, the Cutthroat would arrive as Bell had, on a train that stopped for water, or in a wagon or auto or on horseback on the cart path.

Several trains did pull in, watered, and steamed away. Others steamed past without stopping, and passenger Limiteds with lo-comotives and tenders designed to go longer distances roared by at seventy miles an hour, their golden windows glowing warm through the rain and fog.

Five hours later, at one in the morning, the Cutthroat had not shown up. The rain poured, lightning bolts split the black sky, and Bell surmised he had indeed been set up by Abbington-Westlake. A southbound freight pulled onto the siding. No one but the brakeman got off, and as it huffed slowly from the tank, Bell considered running after it to hop a ride back to Los Ange-les. He decided to stick it out until dawn.

It was still pitch-dark when the rain stopped abruptly. The wind shifted north—crisp and chill. The fresh weather swept the clouds from the sky, and Bell saw his first stars since they crossed the Rocky Mountains. A million of them shone so brightly that they lighted whitecaps on the Santa Barbara

Channel, a quarter-mile stretch of the railroad in both directions, and penetrated the dark within the trestle.

Bell sprinted to the black shadow under the water tank.

The starlight revealed something moving on the siding, about a hundred yards away at the switch where it linked to the main line. It was coming toward Bell very slowly. Long minutes passed before it hardened into a bent figure plodding on the rails. It drew within twenty yards, close enough for Bell to see that he was an elderly tramp, hobbling on a crooked staff.

Bell unbuttoned his slicker and loosened the Colt in his shoulder holster.

The tramp began to sing. He had a weak, reedy voice.

At first, Bell heard only faint snatches of a lyric:

"*. . . mirth and beauty . . .*
. . . frail forms fainting . . ."

At twenty yards, he recognized the Stephen Foster lament.

"*Many days you have lingered around my cabin door,*
Oh! Hard times come again no more . . ."

At ten yards, Bell could smell him.

The tramp reeked like death, the homeless man's unwashed stench of months of filth accumulated deep in the fibers of his rain-drenched shirt and overalls. He had the long white beard of a Civil War veteran, which would make him a very old man in his seventies or eighties—as old as Bell's father, whose Old Soldier beard was as white. Bell stepped out from under the tank, out of the shadows, and let the starlight fall on his face. The tramp did not acknowledge him but veered warily to avoid him, staggering across the siding and onto the main line. Starlight gleamed on steel; he had a hook for a left hand. One eye was covered by a patch. His slouch hat drooped, as soaked through as his clothes, and he had strapped his possessions around his shoulders in a ragged rucksack. Bell thought of his father, sleeping warm and dry in his Greek Revival town house on Louisburg Square.

Safe on the main line, the tramp resumed his song:

"Let us pause in life's pleasures and count its many tears,
While we all sup sorrow with the poor . . ."

Just before he reached the trestle, he stopped and faced the sea and stared as if mesmerized by the stars glistening on the wild water. He turned and gazed at the trestle. He looked back at the sea and down in the canyon. The wind carried another whiff of his deathly smell, and Bell suddenly realized this was no masquerade. It was the end of the line. The old man was staring at the sea as if to say good-bye to beauty before he jumped from the trestle.

"There's a song that will linger forever in our ears;
Oh! Hard times come again no more."

Suddenly Bell heard a train. It was coming from the west, and in the starlight he saw a locomotive rounding the curve with a string of low-slung flatcars, another slow-moving freight. The old man saw it, too, and plodded onto the trestle.

Many would have let him seek the respite he would never find in life. Godspeed! But there was something stern and hopeful in Isaac Bell that would not give up hope on the most hopeless. A hot bath, clean clothes, and a square meal could change everything, and if the Ripper letter was a hoax, at least it had put him here on the railroad tracks at a moment that called for action.

"Hold on, old-timer!"

The veteran heard him. His head turned slightly, but instead of stopping, he pushed along with his staff to go faster. The locomotive's dull headlight angled in from the curve, which made the beam bounce among the girders. No whistle. The engineer saw nothing amiss in the crazy leaping shadows. The old man opened his arms wide, embracing the end.

Bell ran full tilt after him, shouting over the rumble of the locomotive, "Hold on, sir! Let me help."

He halved the distance between them, and halved it again. He thought he might make it—the engineer still didn't see them, but the train had slowed for the curve. He put on a burst of speed and was reaching for the old man's shoulder when he heard the sizzle of steel unsheathed.

47

Blade high, the Cutthroat whirled in a lightning pivot.

Isaac Bell's right arm stretched forward and whipped the loose tail of his slicker at it. The Cutthroat's blade sliced the oilcloth like tissue paper, and for one precious instant he had startled the Cutthroat, throwing the murderer off balance. His first blow missed Bell's arm. The Cutthroat slashed again, slicing the slicker to shreds.

Bell pulled his gun and was yanking the slide to cock his first shot when the Cutthroat lunged. His blade leaped in a sudden rapier thrust. Bell parried it with his gun barrel, deflecting all but the lightest touch. It barely pierced his upper arm, but the needle point seemed to strike a nerve, and he felt his hand convulse as if jolted by an electric shock. It popped his fingers open. The pistol fell.

The Cutthroat whipped his blade high.

Bell, in a lightning move, caught the falling gun out of the air with his left hand, forced his right to close around the slide, and cocked it. The locomotive passed them in the instant he fired. Its main rod, which connected the piston to the drive wheels, brushed Bell's shoulder like a steel fist. It banged him against a trestle girder. The girder kept him from falling into the canyon. But his shot went wild, his gun flew under the flatcars trundling past, and the Cutthroat slashed downward.

The killing blow plunged squarely into the crown of Isaac Bell's hat.

———————

The Cutthroat delivered his *coup de grâce*—a skin-flaying slash.

The tall detective was toppling backwards between two girders. He raised the shredded remains of his slicker as if it were a shield.

This time, the Cutthroat was ready. Nothing could distract him.

But to his astonishment, even as Isaac Bell fell backwards, even locked in the remorseless grip of gravity, he evaded the blade with a twist of fluid grace, took cool, deliberate aim, and flicked his left arm violently. The strip of oilcloth cracked into the Cutthroat's face like a bullwhip.

A metal button seared the tender flesh beneath his eye.

Roaring in rage that Bell had marked him, he wheeled beside

the moving train, vaulted onto a flatcar, and caught hold before it rolled him off. His last glimpse of Isaac Bell had been of the man falling backwards. Now he was rewarded by the sight of an empty trestle.

His spirits soared.

We'll never know, Mr. Bell: Did my singing fool you? Or the stench?

By a miracle, his rucksack had stayed on his back. It reeked of its contents, a rotting length of a human leg. Thank you, Beatrice.

By now, Isaac Bell's corpse was tumbling down the flooded arroyo.

The worst the Cutthroat suffered was a black eye.

48

Archie, thought Isaac Bell, I owe you a drink.

The alloy-steel derringer rack inside the crown of his hat had saved his skull, but the oilskin cowboy slicker that Archie had lifted from Wardrobe had served him three times—distracting the Cutthroat while he drew his gun, parrying a sword thrust with a counterpunch to the Cutthroat's eye, and now acting as a lifeline.

The shreds of it had caught in the thicket of beams under the trestle. Dangling above the rushing arroyo, he swung in among the supports and hauled himself up onto the tracks.

The freight train's red lights were fading toward Los Angeles.

Bell started after them at a dead run. He would never catch it, but dawn was graying fresh rain clouds, and morning trains would soon crowd the line to the city.

———————

Isaac Bell jumped off an express from Santa Barbara and telephoned the Van Dorn railcar from a coin telephone. Harry Warren answered, sounding jubilant.

"We nailed him, Isaac. John Buchanan."

"Buchanan? How?"

"Dashwood did it. He found a *Jekyll and Hyde* program that Buchanan inscribed to one of his rich ladies—the banker's wife he killed in Cleveland."

"But he must inscribe programs to all of his rich ladies."

"This one was for the Cincinnati show."

"She was killed before Cincinnati."

"That's what Dashwood tumbled to! It was printed ahead of time. Only Buchanan could have given it to her. Here's the best part: Buchanan's got no alibi. He did one of his 'disappearing acts' that night. Young stood in for him. Buchanan claims he was sick and slept on the train. Train crew says no. They saw him leave. Buchanan refuses to say where he went."

"Does he have a black eye?"

"What?"

"Does he have a black eye?"

"Who knows? He's slathered with makeup. We got him in Glendale on his way to Marion's movie."

"Where'd you put him?"

"We got him right here in the car."

"Scrub him off!"

"What?"

"Remove his makeup! On the jump!"

Bell waited, drumming his fingers, depositing more nickels when the operator asked for them. Harry Warren came back on the telephone. "No black eye. What's the big idea?"

"Where are Jackson Barrett and Henry Young?"

"Taking pictures."

"With Marion?"

Harry Warren laughed. "Nothing stops that wife of yours. The minute we grabbed Buchanan, she telephoned Young to stand in for him."

"Who's with her?"

"Barrett, Young, couple of camera guys, and that lights lady—Rennegal."

"That's all?"

"It's raining. She gave the rest of the company the day off."

"Hang on to Buchanan. Don't give him to the cops 'til you hear from me."

"Where are you going?"

"Glendale."

49

Making up as fast as he could in a tiny hotel room on the outskirts of Glendale, eight miles from Los Angeles, Henry Young dabbed spirit gum on his nose. While it dried, he lighted a candle, kneaded some toupee paste into a soft lump, and melted the surface in the flame. He worked the thick paste onto his nose, altering the shape to make it appear broad and flat. A bushy wig already heightened his brow and had the grotesque effect of making his head look extremely wide.

Just as he was finishing his new nose with a bluish grease-paint that would turn his face a ghastly pale white for the camera, the door swung open so hard, it banged against the wall. Through it strode Isaac Bell.

"That's a sensational effect, Mr. Young. I doubt your own mother would recognize you face-to-face."

"What? What are you doing here?"

"Catching up. What are you doing?"

"Your wife asked me to stand in for Mr. Buchanan. He seems to have gotten arrested."

"I have a question for you: How's your eye feel?"

"My eye? Fine."

"Show me."

Henry Young wet his lips and looked around nervously. "I don't understand, Mr. Bell."

Bell snapped up a small bottle of olive oil.

"Wipe off that makeup and we both will."

———

The rain was driving Marion Morgan Bell to extreme measures. It would not stop. She had yet to film a scene out of doors, and her leading lady, who was even more compelling on the screen than on the stage, was threatening to jump on the Golden State Limited to Chicago and the 20th Century home to "civilization."

She had already lost John Buchanan—but that to a great cause, the end of Jack the Ripper's rampage, which she couldn't wait to hear about when Isaac returned from wherever that chase had taken him. She still had a star, in Jackson Barrett, and a stand-in, in Mr. Young. But no female "Mr. Young" existed who could replace the Isabella Cook, the "Great and Beloved."

Her only chance was to show Isabella a compelling scene to

recapture her interest in the movie and keep her engaged. And so with the rough-and-ready ingenuity she had learned making topical films on the fly, Marion moved her Dream Duel scene indoors—deep indoors—inside a collapsed tunnel abandoned by an interurban streetcar company.

It was tailor-made for filming a sword fight—the rubble an illusion of an ancient castle. It was a hundred feet long from the mouth to the rocks that partially blocked the back end, ten feet high and twelve feet wide, and so far away from town that they'd never be found by gawking tourists. Like a castle, the long, narrow, high-ceilinged hall had nooks and crannies indented in the rough walls—where she could hide her cameras.

Marilyn Rennegal—Marion's equally rough-and-ready Cooper Hewitt operator on *The Iron Horse* film—had festooned the rocky ceiling with mercury-vapor lamps and dangled them with hundreds of white silk ribbons for visual effect. A dynamo outside the tunnel generated electricity for the lights. It was powered by an ingenious system of drive belts turned by the same eight-cylinder airplane motor that spun Marion's wind machine. From inside, that contraption looked like an airplane about to fly into the tunnel at the expense of its wings.

The ninety-horsepower V-8 Curtiss Pusher airplane engine drove an enormous pusher propeller at fourteen hundred revolutions per minute. The wooden propeller's blade faces were carved with a reverse twist to push air in front of it. It stood taller than a man, and when spinning at top speed, the varnished blades disappeared in a lethal blur.

Marion had plastered warnings inside the tunnel and out:

STAND CLEAR

Isaac Bell had neither returned to Los Angeles alive nor had his body been found. Perhaps another "perfect crime"?

That Van Dorn detectives had arrested John Buchanan seemed to shout, "Yes! Perfect!" But to be on the safe side, the Cutthroat had cleared a path through the rubble at the back of the tunnel in order to escape, with a hostage, if he had to.

He could not have known that Bell was a detective, too. Their boss, no less. But it didn't matter. Framing Buchanan for the Cleveland murder had worked as planned. Buchanan had no alibi. Not without naming the woman he sneaked off with that night. The philanderer had lost his heart to a pretty little airplane pilot who loved the children she would surely lose in a divorce. Love had made him honorable. Rather than betray her, the poor fool would rot in prison until they executed him.

Plan. Anticipate. Hope.

The *Jekyll and Hyde* movie had vaulted his usual optimism to stratospheric levels.

Marion Morgan Bell showed them pictures she had taken of the Dream Duel rehearsal.

"Immortal" was hardly the word. Seeing his face and his body in motion had a thousand times the impact of a photograph—ten thousand times—and it was easier than ever to believe that he would never die. And would sure as hell never be captured.

———————

"Please take your places before we start the machines . . . Mr. Davidson? Mr. Blitzer?"

"Right here, Mrs. Bell," said Davidson. He was standing beside her in the first cranny, twenty feet from the wind machine.

"Here," Blitzer called from his nook on the other side of the tunnel, fifteen feet deeper in.

"Mrs. Rennegal, please get off that ladder and tend the dynamo."

Rennegal adjusted one more Cooper Hewitt, descended the ladder reluctantly, and carried it out of the tunnel.

Kellan, Davidson's assistant, hurried outside to run the wind machine.

"Mr. Barrett?"

Barrett saluted her with his saber. He was the image of a hallucinogenic swordsman, in a plumed musketeer's hat, thigh-high black boots, and white shirt with puffed sleeves. Above his head, Rennegal's ribbons stirred in the draft of air drifting from the back of the tunnel.

"Where's Mr. Young? . . . Is Mr. Young making up at the hotel?"

"Hyde here! Sorry I'm late."

Mr. Hyde squeezed past the wind machine, observed the various fencing weapons laid out on the prop table, noted that

Barrett was holding a weapon with a flat blade and knuckle guard, perfect for thrusting and cutting actions, a dueling saber. He selected a weapon that felt as if it was born in his hand and took his place facing Dr. Jekyll.

Head to toe, his costume was black, his shirt and trousers as tight-fitting as a dancer's, his hat, helmet-like and unadorned, a stark frame for his grotesquely bloated face mask. He wore a cape that came below his knees.

Marion picked up the megaphone she would need when the wind machine crackled and whirled into action.

"Ready, Mrs. Bell!"

"Lights!"

"Dynamo ready!" Rennegal called.

"Kellan, start the motor!"

"Contact!"

Mrs. Rennegal threw an electrical switch placed well out of range of the propeller. Its violent whirlwind yet to come.

Young Kellan gave the propeller a couple of turns, and when he reached a compression-resistance point, tugged up hard. Two more pulls and the Curtiss clattered to life, pistons popping, valves rattling, propeller building a stiff breeze. Even at idling speed, the silk strips danced and Jekyll's and Hyde's capes fluttered.

"Lights!"

Mrs. Rennegal engaged the belt drive powering the dynamo. The Cooper Hewitts flooded a harsh blue-green glare on Jekyll and Hyde.

"Cameras!"

Davidson and Blitzer began to crank slowly.

Marion shouted, "Mr. Barrett, Mr. Young: Good and evil battle to the death. Be ferocious—just please don't accidentally kill each other, because we have a lot more film to make—if it ever stops raining."

Jekyll and Hyde poised for engagement.

"Speed!"

Davidson and Blitzer cranked their cameras to take twenty frames per second.

Jekyll and Hyde saluted each other as a gesture of respect by raising the blades in front of their faces. The scenario, adapted loosely from the play, called for their first exchange to be aggressive. No hallucinogenic flouncing about, but good and evil tested severely. The hard beats of saber on saber rang loudly.

Jackson Barrett was still getting used to the idea that the audience in a movie would not hear the actual steely battle clang of the sabers, but the orchestra's sound effects. On the other hand, the fact that they would not hear any words the actors spoke made for a rather fun game.

"Are you up for a fencing lesson, Mr. Young?"

In answer, the stage manager attacked without engaging in any feint, and Barrett was stunned to see Young use a counter-beat that swept under Barrett's blade.

"The cameras are making you bold. Slow down."

Hyde's next lightning thrust actually forced Barrett to retreat.

His anger mounting, he snarled, "I'm putting a halt to this before I hurt you, and hurt you badly."

He advanced to attack.

The stage manager surprised him with a sharp parry, then disengaged and executed his own attack with a sudden leap.

"Your moves are inventive," said Barrett, with a quick parry. "You must have been practicing since the last time we were on-stage."

The stage manager had yet to speak. It was as if he were devoting himself to every move far in advance. Seeing Young display his sudden skills stunned Marion and the crew. They knew this was unlike any previous movie duel, as he handled a saber with unbelievable agility that was never there before.

"Mr. Young, if you try that again, I shall make you very sorry. Now, follow my lead. I will attack and you will retreat."

Barrett tested him with a couple of hard beats, striking steel to steel, feinted with a hard beat, and lunged into a calculated move to show the audience the evil Mr. Hyde as if he were a rat scurrying down a dark alley.

It was becoming clear that Young was more adept than Buchanan with a saber. Barrett soon realized he was against one as good, if not better, with a sword than himself.

The stage manager made a direct riposte that ended in a thrust with no feints but with a total circle around Barrett's blade. Barrett was half a second too quick to disengage and avoid Young's offensive action.

Everyone on the set stood mesmerized, not certain if the fight had really become a vicious battle or only staged action for the movie.

Hyde waited to parry until Jekyll's sword arm was fully extended and the point of his saber was only one inch from piercing his shoulder. His riposte pierced the sleeve on Barrett's out-thrust and carved a deep cut in his forearm.

"A late parry, Mr. Hyde? You have neither the sense of

distance nor the point control with your tight grip to put one over. How did you do that?"

Hyde gave no answer, and Barrett began to use tactics he hadn't used in years. He deflected Hyde's next attack with a straight, smooth line without wavering to attract a reaction—a swift, strong, clean parry without him seemingly noticing the blood flowing from his forearm.

Hyde did not immediately reengage Barrett but stepped back, gave his opponent a grotesque grin through his makeup, and spoke loudly so his voice carried to the crew over the wind machine.

"Jack Spelvin, my name is Isaac Bell, I am an investigator with the Van Dorn Detective Agency. I arrest you for the murder of Anna Waterbury and only God knows how many other women."

50

Barrett shouted, "Are you crazy? Your fellow detectives arrested Buchanan. He's the Ripper."

Blitzer the cameraman yelled over the exhaust roar of the wind machine. "Keep fighting, keep fighting. We're still running the cameras."

Bell, keeping a surly eye on Barrett, ignored the crew, their voices mixing with the wind machine and echoing in chorus throughout the cavern.

"Don't bother attempting to escape, Barrett, or Spelvin," said Bell. "Or whatever your name is. We found your little escape passage in the rear of the tunnel and it's guarded by two heavily armed agents."

"Playing the role of a shrewd detective?" warned Barrett. "It's still your wife's movie. I wonder which one of us will see the ending."

"It won't be you," said Bell, with ice in his tone. "Now, wipe the makeup off your left eye. Buchanan did it. So did Henry Young."

"What did that prove?"

"Neither is Jack the Ripper."

"Why are you mucking about with a saber? If you really intend to arrest me, where's your gun?"

"I lost it in a canyon." Bell spread his arms. There was no room in his skintight costume for a gun. "If you resist arrest, I will slice you worse than you sliced women in your maniacal murder spree."

To add to the horror of the moment, Jack the Ripper, alias Barrett, removed his makeup with his cape, revealing a bruised eye, and uttered a loud, nauseating laugh that echoed throughout the tunnel above the exhaust from the wind machine.

There were no niceties, no respectful salutes. Like a bolt of lightning, the Ripper attacked like an ancient predator. Bell was prepared. He knew Barrett's intent by a slight shift in his footwork. It came as an advance lunge. Bell parried and deflected the encounter with a sharp feint.

"Thank you," said Isaac Bell. "I was hoping you'd resist."

The production crew watched the engagement in awe. As the fight progressed, it gained momentum. The contact between blades seemed to come in microseconds, as the speed of the sabers flashed under the Cooper Hewitt lights. It became obvious to the crew that the two duelists were in a brutal fight to kill one or the other.

Bell drove the Ripper back into the tunnel, past the second camera and beyond the weird gleam of the lights. Visually, it was stunning, because the wind machine had kicked up a small cloud of dust that swirled under the lights.

Concerned when Bell was out of sight, Marion used her megaphone to amplify her voice over the roar of the wind machine. "Isaac!" she shouted. "Come back! You're out of the light."

The Ripper recovered the initiative and fought back hard, using speed, strength, and extraordinary point control to put the tall detective on the defensive.

Bell used his retreat to discover the Ripper's methods, his skills and tricks. They both fought as though they were fighting for their souls.

Jack the Ripper had developed the precision of hand that Italy's masters were famous for. But, in actual fact, he was more predictable than any Italian. The monster enjoyed butchering his victims, favoring to shed blood than land internal wounds. To lose to him would be to suffer a slow death. But the open blows that he delivered in his desire to cut were also an invitation for an opponent to run him through.

Jack the Ripper fell back, but the tall, blond detective had to battle for every foot gained. The Ripper left no opening untested. In a parry-thrust, he wounded Bell by a cut in the bicep. Luckily, it barely broke the skin, but blood trickled down his arm, threatening to wet his weapon's grip and make it slippery. Bell squeezed his shirtsleeve to absorb it.

Now Bell realized how Jack the Ripper could overwhelm the women he killed and startle them into defending themselves in ways he could predict.

The way to beat him was to be unpredictable. And no attack was more unpredictable than the back attack Bell devised with his naval friend.

Isaac Bell struck the Ripper's thrust aside and lunged past. Inside the arc of his saber, Bell suddenly switched it to his opposite hand and plunged the tip all the way across his stomach and around the back of his waist toward the Ripper's left lung. He felt it scrape a rib that kept the saber from going deep.

Now ten feet from the whirling propeller, warned by the increased strength of the wind against his costume, Jack the Ripper exploded in a counterattack. He started with a feint rather than a thrust. Then a fake thrust, and a fake feint.

Bell parried and retreated past Marion, who was on the right side of the cave, where rocks had been piled. In the split second he saw her, the Ripper feinted left, spun around and grabbed Marion with his free hand, using her as a shield by wrapping his arm around her body and pulling her close to his chest. Bell's eyes went wild.

"You sewer scum, don't even think of hurting her," he roared like a lion that took a bullet to save his mate.

"I'm leaving," said the Ripper. "And your talented wife is coming with me."

"Take your bloody hands off her."

"Maybe I will and maybe I won't," the Ripper said with hideous malignity.

The Ripper again felt the force of the wind on his back and began to advance. Bell could do nothing but retreat, knowing he could not put Marion in any worse danger. But while the two men were distracted with each other, Marion lifted her foot off the ground and stomped with all her strength on the Ripper's toes. In almost the same instant, she rammed both her elbows into his ribs and twisted free of his grasp. Bell dropped his sword and took hold of Marion, as they watched Barrett struggle. The cameraman, Davidson, who had long since stopped filming, had followed Marion as she had closed the gap with the duelists.

Stunned and thrown off balance, the Ripper stumbled. His balance and sense of direction lost for a brief instant, he backed away from Bell and closer to the wind machine. The propeller caught the Ripper's cape, his hand was thrown up and his sword swallowed by the blade as it pulled him into the wind machine. His cape and shirt ripped from him as he was thrown forward. Multiple crescents carved deeply in his back. His saber lost, the Ripper, wild-eyed, in pain and fear, turned and ran toward the tunnel opening past the wind machine.

Davidson took Marion by the hand. Bell leapt forward, following the Ripper out of the tunnel. Just as Bell rounded the outside of the propeller, he tackled the Ripper and took him down. The Ripper twisted out from under Bell and, as Bell recovered, the Ripper kicked out at him. Bell grabbed his boot and twisted the Ripper. Bell was able to stand quickly and square off with Barrett. The force of the air being pulled into the blades made it difficult to keep their balance, but Bell got off three jabs to Barrett's wounded chest and then an upper cut that sent the Ripper reeling backwards. The wind machine's turbulent slipstream that sucked into the tunnel was too much. Generated by the tremendous torque of the huge propeller, it seized Jack the Ripper. He grabbed on to the engine and screamed in agony when the red-hot aluminum exhaust manifold seared his hands.

With nothing to hold on to, he shrieked in despair.

In less than two seconds, Jack the Ripper disappeared before Isaac Bell's eyes. Chunks of flesh and bone flew into the rear of the tunnel as a fine mist of blood sprayed the walls.

Marion, unable to see who had been cut to pieces, in panic started to run to the tunnel opening. Davidson reached her and restrained her. Desperate, she lamented in a pitched wail, "Isaac!"

Alone, with the roar of the engine and the horror of the moment, Bell threw the switch. As the propeller blades started to slow, Isaac made his way around the wind machine and saw Marion running toward him, tears flooding her cheeks. He reached out and held her tight in his arms. She was trembling, shivering, as if frozen in a wintry wind.

"I thought you'd died!"

Bell kissed her lightly on the forehead, and said softly, "Not yet. Not for another fifty years."

EPILOGUE

NEW YORK, 1955

———————

"'That's Grandpa!'—'The one and only,' said Grandma."

DR. JEYKLL AND MR. HYDE

DIRECTED BY

MARION MORGAN BELL

SPECIAL THANKS TO

ISAAC BELL

"Grandma!" came a howl from the next room of a sprawling apartment on Central Park West. "Your name's on TV."

"Just a minute, dear. Grandpa is holding me."

"That's putting it mildly," said Isaac Bell, tightening his grip when Marion attempted, halfheartedly, to slip off his lap.

"Grandma!"

They were visiting the New York branch of what had become a large family of private detectives. This bunch descended from dark-eyed offspring of Harry Warren, with dollops of Millses, Dashwoods, and Abbotts.

"I better see what's happening."

"I'll back you up," said Bell.

In a book-lined room filled with toys and children, the TV was tuned to Channel 9, a local New York station that showed old movies. Film credits were flickering oddly, frozen on the screen.

"Look, Grandma."

It looked to Bell like the projectionist was on his coffee break. Marion said the film-chain's pull-down claw had ripped through adjacent sprocket holes. A transparent "fire door" was keeping the hot projector lamp from melting the stuck film, and wasn't it wonderful they had transferred flammable nitrate film to safety stock.

"Grandma!"

"Marion, what time did you say the Abbotts were coming to pick up all these little urchins?" Bell asked. "They're taking all of them ice skating in the park, aren't they?"

"They'll be here by three."

"Look, Grandma," called a persistent voice.

Marion found her glasses and looked at the end credits still shivering in place.

"Oh, it's *Jekyll and Hyde*. Did you like it, children?"

"Yeah, it was neat."

"*Yes*, it was fun to watch?"

"It wasn't fun to make," said Bell.

"Isaac!"

"See, Grandma? It says 'Marion Morgan Bell.' That's you."

"Why's your name on the movie, Grandma?"

"Because I made it."

"You did? It was really scary, Grandma."

"Really spooky," added a little boy, who had climbed the back of the chair and was now seated on Bell's shoulder. Another started climbing the tall detective's leg.

"Grandma, did you know Grandpa when you made the movie?"

"Look down in that corner. Can you read that?"

The frame was jumping and reading it was difficult.

"'Special' is the first word," she prompted.

"'Special . . . thanks—to Isaac Bell.' That's Grandpa!"

"The one and only," said Marion Morgan Bell.

"With the scars to prove it."

"Isaac, what a terrible thing to say."

"Well, it's true."

"Isaac, really," Marion replied, with a shake of her head.

The little boy clinging to the back of the chair interrupted, "Was there really a Jack the Ripper?"

"Yes, he truly existed," Isaac said. "A very evil man who was far more nasty than Grandma could show in the movie."

"But you socked him good, didn't you, Grandpa?"

"He certainly did, and then some."

"Marion, it's just . . ." Isaac paused as he rose from the chair. "It's what I said all those years ago."

Marion gave him a quizzical look.

"'A renewal.' Let's open a bottle of Billecart-Salmon Brut Rosé. Just you and me, after Archie and Lillian pick up the children."

Marion smiled at her silver-haired hero.

"I promised you another fifty years. Let's celebrate to many more."

Then swept her into his arms and kissed her.